NOTHING IS NEGOTIABLE

MARK BENTSEN

Copyright 2013 Mark Bentsen
Print Edition Published by Mark Bentsen, 2013
Cover design by Phillips Covers
Photography by Glenn Frels of Connie's Studio by Glenn
Formatting by A Thirsty Mind Book Design

ISBN: 978-1494432850

All rights reserved. No part of this book, except in the case of brief quotations embodied in critical articles or reviews, may be reproduced in any form by any means, including information storage and retrieval systems, without prior written permission from the author.

This book is a work of fiction. Names, characters, places, and incidents are either products of the author's imagination or are used fictitiously. Any resemblance to actual events, locales, business establishments, or persons, living or dead, is entirely coincidental.

The scanning, uploading, and distributing of this book via the Internet or via any other means without the permission of the copyright owner is illegal and punishable by law. Please purchase only authorized print and electronic editions, and do not participate in or encourage piracy of copyrighted materials. Your support of the author's rights is appreciated.

Special thanks to:

My wife, Sharyn: Your patience and encouragement were much more important than you will know. Your honest feedback helped me stay on course and get this project finished.

Karen MacInerney, founder of Austin Mystery Writers. You blazed the trail ahead of us and gave us hope and guidance.

Other members of Austin Mystery Writers over the years: Kay George, Laney Henelley, Dave Ciambrone, Mary Jo Powell, Kimberly Sandman, Sylvia Dickey Smith, Janet Christian, Gale Albright, Manfred Reimann, and Kathy Waller.

Consultants along the way: Paul Jeffers with the RCMP, Dr. Steve Bentsen, Dr. William Gorman and Dr. Anna Bell – for helping me with all my medical questions. Also, Nolan Card for answering many questions about Cardston and Canada.

Editors: Mindy Reed, Jim Thomsen, and Pam Headrick.

Proofreaders – Friends and family who helped include: Doug and Marinel Hayes, Jackie Kayser, Lori Singleton, Tim Bentsen and Stacy Eleuterius.

Cover design – Karen Phillips – I wish everyone in the world was as easy to work with as you.

Photographer – Glenn Frels of Connie's Studio by Glenn.

Sharyn's mom and dad, Betty and Verbon Anthony for their support (And I want to apologize to them in advance for the profanity in this book. Overall, the language isn't really too bad, but I had trouble with a few characters...I had no control over their foul mouth. It's just the way they were).

And a special thanks to my Dad's cousin, Kenneth Bentsen. At a family reunion in 1988, he insisted I read Larry McMurtry's novel *Lonesome Dove*. I hadn't read many novels at the time but I promised him I would. That novel hooked me on fiction and cannot imagine living without it today.

Dedication:

To my Mom and Dad, Marion and Vivian Bentsen – they sacrificed so much for my three brothers and me. Our only regret is that we lost them much too early.

Chapter 1

The golden leaves of autumn reflected in the smooth water where a grizzly stood knee-deep looking at her twin cubs. They perched on an egg-shaped rock in the middle of the river where they watched their mother as if she were telling them the story of Winnie the Pooh.

"My boss took that picture up on Lee Creek last fall," the teenage girl cheerfully said as she slowed her pace to admire the framed photograph for the umpteenth time. She carried a bronzed sculpture of a buffalo to a wooden table and set it down. She turned around and said, "Aren't those cubs the cutest?"

Luke Wakefield studied the details of the framed photograph. He recognized the qualities of a good picture because his wife, Bonnie, an outdoor photographer with two coffee table books to her credit, had shared her love of photography over their twenty years of marriage. Though she focused on Texas ranches, wildlife and sunsets, the characteristics of a good photo knew no boundaries.

"It's a great shot," he said as he stepped back and panned the walls of the studio. "Did he take all of these pictures?"

"Yes, sir. All of the photos are his. The other stuff, like those paintings and these bronzes, were done by other people. But they're all from here in Montana."

Bonnie and Luke had stopped at Glacier Gallery and Camera Supply to pick up a battery for one of her cameras. While she bought the battery, Luke wandered into the gallery to browse. The double doors that connected the camera store to the gallery were open and as Luke moved closer to them he could hear an animated discussion. He looked around the corner and saw his wife across the counter from a tall man with shoulder-length blond hair.

"Excuse me, Miss Wakefield, but that was no poor lady," argued the man. "She's from Orange County in California and will spend more money on her vacation than I'll make in a year."

Luke wondered how he knew her name.

Bonnie listened sympathetically but said, "I'm sorry, but even if she is rich, that's no reason to take advantage of her."

"I was not taking advantage of her," he said, stabbing his finger on the glass case. "That camera is worth every nickel of the price I quoted her."

"That's not what I mean," she retorted. "I know it's a good camera. I shoot Nikon. I love Nikon. My dog's name is Nikon. But that camera was too much for that lady."

"She wanted that camera. You had no business telling her not to buy it."

Bonnie's face hardened. "When she asked me for my opinion, it became my business. She's a soccer mom, for God's sake. This is the camera she needs," she said, pointing to a simple point and shoot in the adjacent display case.

"I know you mean good, lady, but let me explain something to you." The man glanced at Luke who had stepped into the store and slowly moved toward them. The man lowered his voice a notch. "You're in northern Montana right now, not Texas. I'm only open eight months a year because it gets so frigging cold up here. The rest of the year we're snowed in, windblown and all alone. Roads are closed and outside it's colder than a witch's tit. There are no tourists, no camera shoppers, and no one buying art in the gallery. And that means no income."

Bonnie tried to speak. "But if—"

He cut her off. "That means if I want to keep my doors open, I have to make as much in eight months as you people down in Texas make in twelve." He thrust an open hand toward the blue sky out the window and said, "And besides that, the rains we had in June just about killed this year's tourist season."

Luke knew Bonnie could take care of herself and wouldn't want his help in a simple argument, but he didn't like the hostility in the man's tone. He stepped in a little closer and said, "Hey, Babe, you about ready?"

"I'm sorry you lost your sale," Bonnie said, grabbing Luke's arm who had ambled up next to her. "This is my husband Luke."

Reluctantly, the tall man extended his hand. "Sonny Diamond."

"Those are some incredible photos in the gallery," Luke said, trying to interject a positive comment. "Are they all yours?"

Sonny's tone was sour. "Yeah, but that's another problem. Maybe you can explain this to your wife. I'm a good photographer, but there's a shitload of *great photographers* up here. I sell a few prints now and then, but I'm nobody. Everyone wants a picture by the next Ansel Adams. It's hard to make a living up here." He looked from Bonnie to Luke. "Do you know how many three thousand dollar sales I get in a year? Two, maybe three." He looked at Bonnie and thrust an open hand toward her. "I had one today, but Miss Guilty Conscience couldn't stand it."

Luke had been in enough arguments with Bonnie to know that when she folded her arms he knew she'd had enough. "I'm sorry, Sonny, but I'd do it all again if it came down to it. She asked me for my opinion, and I gave it to her."

"I wasn't doing one thing unethical," Sonny insisted.

After a few uncomfortable seconds of silence, Luke said, "Did you get what you need?"

"Not yet," Bonnie said. She dug around in her purse and pulled out a small gray battery. "Do you have one of these?"

Without speaking, Sonny turned to the shelves behind him and pulled one off the display. Bonnie paid him, and within seconds she and Luke were out the door with no *Thank you* or *Have a nice day.*

As they headed back toward their car Luke glanced up at

the window and saw Sonny watching them. There was no doubt he was still upset.

"What was that all about?" Luke asked trying to keep up with Bonnie's pace.

"He's a jerk," she said coldly.

"I picked up on that. What happened?"

"A lady in the store was looking at a camera and she told me she was really confused. She saw my name tag and asked me if I was a photographer."

Luke glanced at Bonnie's blouse and saw she was still wearing her name tag. Across the top in small letters it said, *American Society of Outdoor Photographers.* Under that in bigger letters it said *Bonnie Wakefield, Lampasas, Texas – Speaker.*

"I told her I was. She said she wanted to buy a camera, and Sonny told her she needed a Nikon camera with three lenses, a tripod, filters, extra batteries, and three flash cards with sixteen gigs of memory each. She asked what I thought. I asked her a couple of questions to figure out how camera-savvy she was and what she was going to use it for, and knew immediately it was way too much for her. I told her she'd probably like the little Canon Elph. I told her how versatile and easy it was to use. She said that was exactly what she wanted. So, she spent three hundred dollars rather than three thousand."

"I can understand why Sonny might be pissed, especially if she was ready to spend three grand."

Bonnie stopped on the sidewalk and glared at him. "Luke, that lady had no business buying a camera like that. She told me the only camera she'd ever used before was an Instamatic. And one that used film, for God's sake. And he was trying to convince her that she was going to be the next Kristen Westlake." Kristen was a talented outdoor photographer who mentored Bonnie while she was getting started as a photographer.

"Yeah, well, the guy has a point. If she's got the money, let her spend it."

"That's *not* the point," Bonnie said sharply. "You should have seen her. She was dripping with diamonds and I think he saw an easy mark. She didn't have a clue what she was doing and he was taking advantage of her."

"Yeah, I reckon you're right," Luke said, knowing when to quit. He put his arm across her shoulder and pulled her closer. "But next time you pick a fight, pick on someone a little smaller."

Her expression didn't change.

"Please?"

She glanced up and slowly a smile crept across her face. "Oh, come on. He wouldn't have had a chance against this redhead. And even if I did need your help, you could have kicked his butt."

Luke scoffed. "Did you see him? I'm six foot and weigh two hundred pounds, and he was as big as me, three inches taller and ten years younger."

"Come on. I've seen you throw bigger, meaner steers than that."

"Yeah, but that was fifteen years ago. See this gray hair." Luke lifted his cap to reveal his dark hair which showed signs of gray at the temple. "Those cowboy days are long gone. I'm way past forty and I can barely get a bale of hay in the back of the pickup without throwing my back out. I don't need to be fighting someone like that."

Luke pulled a key chain from the pocket of his cargo shorts and punched the button to unlock the doors. Bonnie looked over the top of their rented Chrysler Sebring and said, "But you'd do it for me, wouldn't you?"

As they slid into their seats, Luke buckled his seat belt and said, "Of course I would, Buttercup. I'd take on Rambo, a pack of rabid pit bulls, Rosie O'Donnell and the Vienna Boys Choir, all at the same time. Anything to protect your cute little ass."

Bonnie grinned and rolled her eyes. "You're so full of shit."

That was one thing he loved about her. After twenty years of marriage, she still laughed at his corny jokes. Smiling, he pulled the car onto U.S. 89 and headed north.

The day before, Luke and Bonnie had flown from Austin, Texas to Calgary, Alberta, then driven three hours south to St. Mary, Montana for the regional workshop of the American Society of Outdoor Photographers. This year, the three-day conference took place at Glacier National Park on the Canadian border and Bonnie had been invited to be one of the speakers. It was her first speaking engagement outside of Texas and she was excited about it. She'd been a member of the organization for a few years but had never attended any of their functions. Then four weeks ago she got a call asking her to be a speaker at their summer workshop, talking about two of her favorite subjects: Sunsets and Silhouettes.

Luke changed the subject. "Did you find out how they picked you to be one of the speakers?"

"Yeah, I spoke to the program coordinator. He said one of the members was at the talk I gave at the Wildlife Expo in Austin last fall. A lady named Rita."

"You must have impressed her. Did you talk to her?"

"Just briefly. They had some problems with the computer equipment and my talk got bumped to twelve o'clock. So, while they ate, I talked. She saved me some lunch which I ate about one thirty. She's a nurse in Cardston."

"Cardston? That name sounds familiar."

"It's the last town we went through before we crossed the border into Montana. About fifty miles north, I think. She had to get back to work right after I gave my program."

"What's a nurse doing at the workshop?"

"Lots of the members have real jobs to pay the bills. She said photography's just a hobby for her."

"Why'd they wait until the last minute to contact you? Someone get sick or something?"

"Worse than that. One of the speakers was killed in a freak accident. His daughter had just picked him up at the airport and when they got back to his house, he walked inside with a lit cigarette, and it blew up. Killed both him and his twenty-five-year-old daughter. Really sad."

Luke turned off the highway onto a gravel road that led to the Red Eagle Lodge. The rustic old motel sat in the shadow of Gun Sight Mountain on the outskirts of Glacier National Park.

As they made their way to their second-floor room they passed several guests sitting outside enjoying the beautiful day. In front of each room were two plastic chairs, perfect for watching the sun as it dipped behind the mountains to the west.

Luke unlocked the door and Bonnie pushed past him. "You know, the more I think about that jerk at the camera store, the more pissed off I am. If it's okay with you, I think I'll go run off some of this steam."

"Fine with me. How far do you want to run?"

Bonnie was training to run in the New York Marathon in the fall. It would be her first marathon and it was only three months away. She looked out the window toward the mountains and said, "Not too far. If I ran eight miles I could do that in about an hour and fifteen minutes. Would that be okay?"

"Sure. Where will you run?"

"You know that road we were on this morning over by the KOA Campground? It was pretty flat."

"Perfect. While you do that I'll go to the store and pick up that stuff on your shopping list. On my way back I'll stop at the river that crosses that road and do some fishing. It's about a mile from here. When you go by, you'll see me there. Just yell when you come by, and I'll come back then, too. After we get cleaned up, it'll be about time for dinner."

Bonnie opened her suitcase and pulled out her jogging shoes, shorts and a white t-shirt with a picture of the state of Texas on it. Under it, it said *Don't Mess with Texas*. Meanwhile, Luke grabbed a cold beer, kicked off his hiking boots, and stretched out on the queen-sized bed to watch Bonnie change clothes.

When she pulled off her blouse he admired her lean

physique. He'd always thought Bonnie had the perfect body. She was five-eight, and running helped keep her firm and her weight under one twenty-five. She always said her breasts were too small, but he didn't agree. Not too big, not too little. Just about perfect.

After she tied her shoes, she stepped outside onto the walkway and threw one leg up on the railing and leaned over it to stretch. Luke followed her outside, glancing across the horizon at the blue sky.

"I can't believe it's seventy-five degrees in July. I could get used to this weather," Luke said. In Texas, they lived about seventy miles northwest of Austin where Luke ranched with his father. This was their first trip to Montana, and the beauty of the Rocky Mountains blew him away.

"Until winter, then you'd freeze your ass off." Bonnie kissed him on the cheek, then looked at her watch. "It's three forty-five now. I'll see you at the river about five."

"Sounds good."

When she hit the parking lot, she broke into a trot.

He cupped a hand around his mouth and shouted, "Watch out for bears, I hear they have an appetite for redheads."

She turned around and grinned while jogging backwards. "I'll outrun 'em."

"Hell, you're probably too tough for them anyway…at least, too tough to chew."

She answered him by thrusting the middle finger of her right hand high in the air as she headed down the hill.

Luke loved that about Bonnie. If someone told her she couldn't do something that was just another reason why she'd try. She was independent and confident. He knew he was lucky to have her. He watched her auburn ponytail bounce from side to side until she made the turn at the highway and disappeared from sight.

He went back into their room and tossed his empty beer can in the trashcan. From his suitcase he pulled out his old jogging shoes, he'd wear them in case this type of fishing required wading in the river.

The street was crowded with minivans, SUVs and travel trailers as he made his way back into town. Only one store in St. Mary sold groceries and every aisle and checkout line was packed with tourists. Luke blew off Bonnie's list and headed for Old Mill Road. A mile down the road he came to the river and pulled onto the dirt shoulder by the bridge. Grabbing his fly rod and a box full of flies, he went around the bend where the stream widened. It looked like an ideal spot so he put down his gear and rigged his rod.

He'd never done any fly fishing before and after ten minutes he was thankful no one was around to watch him. From watching several programs about it on The Outdoor Channel and didn't think it looked all that hard. But it took only a minute to find out he didn't have a clue what he was doing. Half the time he spent getting the line out of the bushes along the bank and the rest of his time he spent trying to learn how to cast a fly that weighed less than a gnat.

The more he tried, the more frustrated he became. This was nothing like bass fishing, he decided. Without a doubt he'd have to take some lessons if he wanted to learn how to do it right.

Time passed quickly and when he checked his watch he realized Bonnie was half an hour late. This wasn't like her. He glanced back at the bridge and saw a steady stream of cars and campers moving in both directions. The traffic was much heavier than it had been earlier and he began to worry about Bonnie jogging on this narrow two-lane road.

Luke hurried back to the car, tossed his gear in the trunk and headed up the road, tracing the route Bonnie told him she was going to take. The road followed the river and a couple of miles down he saw her sitting on a rock, knee deep in the middle of the river. Something was wrong.

With a rocky cliff on one side and a drop off on the other, he couldn't stop. He pounded his fist on the steering wheel in frustration. A hundred yards ahead he came to a turnout and pulled over on the shoulder of the road. He ran back but couldn't find an easy way down to the river and finally pushed aside some branches and vines, sat on his butt, and slid down the rocky wash to the riverbank. He ran the rest of the way through the shallow water to get to her.

"Bonnie! Are you okay?" he said as he got closer.

She was bent over with one hand in the water. "No, I'm sick as a dog and I think I broke my thumb. Look." she said, pulling her hand out of the water to show him. Her thumb was swollen and red. "I can't believe it, but this icy water is numbing the pain."

Luke saw leaves, dirt, and twigs in her hair. Her arms and legs were streaked with red scratches and mud covered one shoulder of her t-shirt. One of her cheeks was red and puffy, as if someone had hit her.

"What happened?"

She propped an elbow on her knee and rested her head in her hand. "About half an hour into the run, my stomach started churning and I felt like I was going to throw up. I stopped and started walking. I was right up there." She pointed to the stretch of road with the steep drop-off on the near side and a bluff on the other.

"Then it hit me and I started puking my guts out. I heard something and when I looked behind me, a huge camper was coming, hauling ass, right for me. There's no shoulder and it was muddy. When I tried to get off the road, I slipped and fell down the side of the hill—tumbling, head over heels."

Luke pulled dried grass and twigs out of her hair. He could tell she was in pain. "Those assholes. Did the camper stop?"

"No. I don't know if they even saw me."

"How bad are you hurt?"

She sighed heavily. "I feel like I've been trampled by a herd of wild horses and could puke again any minute. Let's go back to our room."

Ten minutes later, Luke helped Bonnie upstairs. They saw

an older man and a young woman, who looked about college age, sitting outside the room next to theirs. On a small table between them was a bottle of white wine with some cheese and crackers. When the couple saw Bonnie their relaxed appearance turned to concern. Bonnie's pain was apparent and as they pushed their chairs out of her way, the guy said, "Oh my, are you okay?"

"She took a fall and hurt her thumb pretty bad," Luke said.

The young lady asked, "What happened?"

Bonnie gave them a weak smile and said, "I was jogging and got forced off the road by a camper, and I slipped down the riverbank. But I think I'm okay, just kind of banged up." She held up her hand, and turned it from side to side, and added, "I either broke my thumb or sprained it really bad."

They retreated to their room where Bonnie dropped down onto the edge of the bed, her head in her hands. Luke came over with aspirin and a zip lock bag full of ice.

Bonnie held her thumb up and tried to move it. "I don't think it's broken but it hurts like a son of a gun. I can't believe this. I don't even know if I can hold my camera with this hand."

There was a knock on their door. It was the young lady from next door. Luke couldn't help but notice her striking looks: long blonde hair and sparkling blue eyes. In her hand she held a white box with a red cross on it.

She glanced from Luke to Bonnie. "I don't want to bother you, but we had this in the Hummer and thought something in here might help."

Luke stepped aside and she walked over beside Bonnie. She set the first aid kit on the bed and opened it. Luke could smell her perfume. She hadn't been hiking all day that was for sure.

"Thanks, but I'm not sure what I need at this point," Bonnie said.

"There's all kinds of stuff in here, even an elastic bandage for your hand."

"I'm going to take a shower and get cleaned up. Then I'll be able to see the damage a little better."

"I'm Christina," she said, backing toward the door. "If there's anything we can do, let us know. And if you feel up to it, come out and have some wine and cheese with us. It might help kill some of the pain."

"We might do that. Thanks," said Luke.

Christina stepped outside and Luke closed the door behind her. As he turned around, he saw Bonnie rush into the bathroom and slam the door.

Seconds later, he heard her being sick again.

He waited a minute and heard it again.

"You okay?" was all he could say.

"I think so," she said weakly.

A few minutes later, Bonnie staggered out and sat on the side of the bed.

"Want me to go get something for your stomach?"

"No, I've got some Pepto in my suitcase. It was probably something I ate for lunch. But let's not let this ruin our trip." She kicked off her running shoes. "I'm already feeling better. I'm going to take a shower, why don't you have a drink with our neighbors? They seem nice."

As she disappeared into the bathroom, Luke realized there was nothing he could do, so he stepped outside, and closed the door behind him. The man rose and extended his hand. "I'm Jack, and you've met Christina."

Jack's grip was firm, but his hand was soft and Luke couldn't help but notice the gold Rolex on his wrist. He stood about five-ten with curly dark hair and looked to be about fifty, considerably older than Christina.

"How is your wife?" Jack asked.

"Not so good right now," Luke said. "In addition to her fall, something she ate didn't agree with her. She's pretty sick, too."

"She's just having a bad day all around, isn't she?" Jack seemed sincere. "Sit down, Luke. May I pour you a glass of wine?"

"Sure, thanks," he said, settling into the chair beside Christina.

Jack picked up a leather case beside his chair and opened it. Inside Luke saw two more wine glasses and a silver corkscrew encased in red velvet. Jack pulled out one of the glasses and filled it for Luke.

Jack was a lawyer in Kalispell, a small town on the west side of Glacier National Park. He and Christina came for a few days to do some hiking and just "hang out." For the next ten minutes they made casual conversation. Jack told some of his favorite lawyer jokes, which led to what Luke did for a living, and then to what brought he and Bonnie to Montana.

A few minutes later the sun had dipped behind the mountain and Bonnie stepped out of their room. She had a bottle of water in one hand and a small digital camera in the hand that now was wrapped in the elastic bandage. Her auburn hair looked freshly brushed and hung beautifully down past her shoulders.

When she sat down, Luke took the camera and motioned toward the mountain to the west. "Glad you brought that. I was about to miss a beautiful shot."

"That's a tough shot with the sun setting behind it," she said.

"She never quits," Luke said admiringly. He stood up and pointed the camera westward where the huge mountain was silhouetted with golden rays of sunlight reaching skyward on all sides. He took several pictures before setting the camera on the table.

Jack picked it up and examined it closer. "A Canon Elph. I've got one just like it. This is a great little camera." He turned it on them and said, "Move over a little closer and I'll get a picture of you guys to document your first traumatic day in Montana."

Jack snapped a couple of shots and handed the camera back to Luke.

"Let me get one too," Luke said as turned the camera on

them and snapped a shot.

After the picture, Jack gave Christina a quick kiss on the lips, and then reached over and picked up the bottle of wine and held it toward Bonnie. "We've got a great Chardonnay that will help numb your pain."

"Thanks, but my stomach is still pretty queasy. I'd better stick with water, but I'll take a few of these crackers, if you don't mind."

He pushed the tray of crackers and cheese toward her. "Luke tells us you're up here as a speaker at that Photography Workshop over in Glacier."

"That's right. I gave my presentation at noon."

"How'd it go?"

"I think it went pretty good. I got a lot of positive feedback from the audience and quite a few orders for my new book, too."

"That's fantastic. Luke told us about your book. We'd like to order one, too," he said. "Now that you're done with the workshop, what are you going to do?"

Bonnie looked at Luke and shrugged. "Just some things we found in the guide books. We've got another week—a few more days here and then up to Canada for the rest of the trip. We were hoping to get some tips from the locals up here."

"I can give you some ideas. If I wasn't a lawyer I'd be a tour guide." Jack squeezed Christina's thigh and said, "Sweetie, go grab that box in the back of the Hummer."

Christina downed the remaining third of her glass of wine and strutted toward the stairs. Her short shorts distracted Jack's attention momentarily, and then he returned his gaze to Luke and Bonnie. "Over the years, I've collected a variety of maps and trail guides. I have a few that will really be helpful to you."

When Christina returned she carried two boxes. One was a small plastic file box and the other was about half the size of a briefcase and made of beautiful dark wood.

"I thought you'd want to bring this one inside tonight."

"Oh yeah. I forgot to bring it in earlier," Jack said. He took the wooden box and set it on the table in front of Luke. "Let me show you something. Being from Texas, I bet you like guns."

He unlocked the gold latches and opened it. Inside they saw a pistol which, like the corkscrew, lay on red velvet.

"What a beauty," Luke said. "Is it a Colt?"

"That it is," Jack said. "I don't know a darn thing about guns, but what I've learned it isn't just any Colt. It's a limited edition, factory-engraved .38. The model is a 'Super Match'. It was made in 1935 and was the first pistol Colt made for National Pistol Matches. And this one's never been fired."

"It's beautiful."

"I got it when a client was short on cash. I don't have much interest in guns, so I'd like to sell it."

"How much?"

"Twenty-five thousand," Jack said.

Luke chuckled and leaned back. "That's a little out of my price range."

"Another reason we came over here was to show it to a rancher who thought he might like to buy it. He thought I'd come down to twenty, but I have several others who are interested. So I'm going to hold out for twenty-five." Jack latched the case and set it on the floor beside the table then opened the other box and pulled out a handful of maps.

During the next forty-five minutes, they pored over the maps and Jack opened two more bottles of wine. It was obvious he knew the area well and Luke took copious notes. When Jack mentioned some great spots to photograph wildlife, Luke looked at Bonnie, expecting a comment. Instead, he saw her holding her hand on her head.

"You don't look too good, Babe. Are you feeling bad again?"

She nodded with her eyes closed. "I think it's best I go in now." She stood up. "Thanks for everything," she said to Christina and Jack. "Maybe we'll see you tomorrow."

"I'm right behind you," Luke said. He saw Christina

whisper something in Jack's ear and Jack smiled mischievously.

Jack finished his wine and said, "I think it's time for us to go in too."

Inside, Bonnie was on the side of the bed, talking on the telephone. "That was Mrs. Johnson, the owner of the lodge," she said when she hung up. "I asked her if there's a doctor in town and she said there isn't. The closest one is at the clinic in Cardston. I guess that's the one where Rita works." Bonnie dug through her purse and pulled out a business card. "Rita gave me a card with her phone number on it. I'm going to call her and see what she says."

Luke went to the bathroom and when he came out, Bonnie was just finishing her call. "Rita told me to come in around ten in the morning and she'll get me in as soon as she can."

"That sounds good. But right now, I'd bet you need to eat something. Anything sound good?"

"A bowl of soup would be good. That café down the hill might have some."

"The Park Café," Luke said, opening the phone book. After he called, he said, "I ordered you a bowl of vegetable soup and a pizza for me.

"Be careful. You've had plenty of wine."

"I'm fine, and it's not even a mile from here."

Twenty minutes later, Luke returned to find Bonnie was wrapped in a blanket, sitting in the middle of the bed, with a big grin on her face. She held a finger up to her lips and pointed at the wall behind her. Luke looked at the wall and saw nothing but a cheap painting of a snow-capped mountain.

"What's so funny?" he asked. Then he heard a rhythmic banging on the wall. "What's that?"

"I think it's the headboard on Jack and Christina's bed. It started about five minutes after you left."

Luke listened as the pounding continued, at times accompanied by a series of grunts or an occasional high-pitched squeal.

"Jack and Christina?"

Bonnie nodded with a grin on her face.

"I noticed Jack could hardly keep his hands off of her." He grinned and stood closer to the wall.

"He didn't appear to be in the best physical condition. I hope she doesn't kill him."

"If she does, he'll be a happy man when he goes."

Then, like a locomotive gaining speed, the pounding got faster and louder, until, as if on cue, the picture above their bed slipped sideways and fell off the wall. And the pounding stopped.

Chapter 2

When the bed moved, Luke's eyelids fluttered, and he woke. That was when he realized the pain. It felt like his head was in a vice. Suddenly, the pillow covering his face was pulled away. He squinted as his arm flew across his forehead to shield his eyes.

Bonnie rubbed him on the belly and said, "Come on, time to get up."

"That wasn't nice," he whined.

"It's almost seven-thirty. I've been trying to wake you up for twenty minutes."

"I feel like shit," he moaned. He moved his arm just enough to expose one blue, bloodshot eye, and said, "How about you? Do you feel any better?"

"A little. My stomach is still pretty queasy and I've gone to the bathroom twice."

"How's your thumb?"

"Sore and swollen, but not as bad as I thought it was going to be. It hurts to move it," she said, holding it up and rotating it slowly. "I doubt it's broken. Probably just sprained."

Luke pulled his arm away from his eyes and squinted at her bandage-wrapped hand.

"But some painkillers would be nice," she added.

"I'll second the motion for painkillers," Luke rolled over and slowly sat up on the side of the bed. "I only had three glasses of wine and I feel like hammered shit."

"I think you had more than three glasses. And you had a few beers before the wine and several more with that pizza. You always have a hangover when you mix beer and wine. It's your own fault."

"No it's not. It's Robert's." He slowly stood up and staggered toward the bathroom.

"Who's Robert?"

"Robert Mondavi. He's the one that made that wine," he said as he stepped into the bathroom and closed the door.

He cranked up the hot water and within a minute steam filled the room. The hot water felt good pounding on his shoulders. Years ago someone told him that sweating would cure a hangover, so he always tried it. But, it never worked. Ten minutes later he walked out of the bathroom and saw Bonnie trying to button her shorts with one hand. Luke stepped over and buttoned them for her.

About that time, her cell phone rang. She answered, talked a minute, then folded it shut.

"Who was that?"

"Rita. She was just checking on me. She also told me how to get to the clinic."

"Can she get you in?"

"It shouldn't be a problem, but I'll just have to wait a while. When I told her I was starving, she said to try dry toast and juice."

"Okay, let's get something down at the café and then head out?"

Luke opened the suitcase and rummaged around for something to wear. "I guess we won't be taking that hike we planned for today."

"Yes, we will," Bonnie said firmly. "There's an easy hike up by Many Glacier. I'm not going to let this stop me from having a good time."

"That's my girl," he said, pulling out a white polo shirt and a pair of brown shorts.

They left the mountainous terrain driving north out of St. Mary toward the rolling grasslands of southern Alberta. Half an hour later, they came to a lone brick building at the Canadian border—the Chief Mountain Border Crossing. The two story building had a flat roof with big square windows on the bottom floor and tall windows all around the second floor.

As they got closer, the road widened into three lanes, two of the lanes led to detached booths with glass windows on all sides.

The road approaching the building was deserted with no other vehicles in front or behind them. Orange cones blocked the two right lanes so Luke eased the Sebring up to the window of the booth connected to the building. He lowered his window and rolled to a stop as the sliding glass window opened. An agent in a dark brown uniform peered down at them.

"Good morning," Luke said, trying to smile through his hangover.

The agent didn't smile or return Luke's greeting. Instead he reached out and said, "Passport and driver's license please."

He appeared to be in his mid-thirties, pointed chin with a dark brown moustache that hung over his lip. A black nametag above his pocket said his name was Sharp.

Luke handed him both passports and driver's licenses. Sharp took them without making eye contact. Twice he looked up, comparing them to their photos. After a silent minute, he asked, "What is your destination?"

Luke answered, "Cardston."

"Purpose of your trip?"

"We're going to the doctor."

"Are you sick?"

"My wife is."

The agent looked through the car at Bonnie, then back at their passports. "Where did you get this car?"

"We rented it in Calgary."

"Could I see the rental contract please?"

Luke pulled it from the glove compartment and handed the papers to the man. Again he compared names on all documents, and returned them to Luke.

"Are you going to Calgary from Cardston?"

"No, just to the doctor, then back to Glacier National Park."

Sharp's gaze moved to the backseat. "Are you in possession

of any fire arms?"

"No."

Luke checked the rearview mirror and saw no one on the long straight highway behind them. The agent didn't seem to be in any hurry and to Luke it seemed like the guy was bored and killing time.

"Do you have any pepper or bear spray?"

"No, why? Is that against the law?" Luke chuckled, thinking that was a crazy question to ask two people on their way to the doctor.

The agent ignored Luke's question. "How much cash do you have in your possession?"

"I don't know, about four or five hundred, I guess." Luke was growing curious about all these random questions, but the agent seemed to be trying to think of more questions to ask.

"Is the purpose of your trip to buy drugs?"

"No. Like I said, we're going to the doctor."

"Are you in possession of any illegal drugs?"

"No, sir, we are not," Luke said defensively.

Without looking at them he said, "One moment, please." The agent slid the window closed and went into the building where Luke saw him walk to the adjacent office and start speaking to another agent. He showed his colleague the passports and licenses, occasionally looking at Bonnie and Luke as he talked. Finally the agent came back, returning their passports and licenses.

"Please pull into the parking lot next to the building," he said pointing ahead. "Park in space number three. Go up the stairs and into the first door on the left, room 202. An agent will meet you there."

"Could I ask—" was all Luke could get out before the window was closed and the agent walked away.

"I wonder what in the hell this is all about?"

Bonnie shrugged, equally as puzzled.

They did as they were told and found a long counter dividing room 202. The door behind the counter opened and a hefty female agent, whose nametag read Driver, came in. She looked like a professional wrestler, as tall as Luke, but heavier. Her hair was frizzy blonde with black roots. "I need to see your passports and driver's licenses," she said.

"Is there a problem?" Luke asked.

The agent held out her hand and said, "I need to see these documents, please."

Luke was tired of being treated so rudely. "Did we do something wrong, or do you treat everyone like this?"

Glaring at him, she tilted her head and stuck out her hand. "Sir, do you have the documents I requested?"

Luke held her gaze briefly, then looked at Bonnie, whose expression told him not to mess with her.

Luke handed her their passports and driver's licenses. She took them and as she turned to leave, said, "Take a seat."

Luke was in no mood to take a seat. He remained standing, watching the door she left through. After a minute of waiting, he began to pace.

Bonnie tried to soothe him. "Luke, this is probably routine."

"Oh, bullshit! We haven't done a damn thing wrong. I told that guy outside you were sick and needed to get to the doctor, for God's sake."

After a long five minutes, she returned. "Can you tell me you destination today?"

"I already told the guy out there," Luke said, pointing toward the booth where the first agent questioned them.

"Well, now you can tell me," she sneered.

"My-wife-is-sick," he said, slowly enunciating each syllable. "We are going to the doctor in Cardston."

"Which doctor are you going to see?"

"We don't have an appointment. We're just going to the Cardston Clinic."

"So, you have no appointment?"

Luke rolled his eyes, and spoke as if he was talking to a child, "That's what I just said. We don't have an appointment.

My wife didn't plan on getting sick. It just happened."

Her eyes narrowed and she continued. "Do you intend to buy prescription drugs to resell in the United States?"

"What in the hell are you talking about? I have no intentions of doing anything like that."

Driver, obviously annoyed, stiffened her lip, and continued, "How much cash do you have?"

"Like I told that guy out there, about five hundred dollars."

"American or Canadian?"

"American."

"If you need more than that, do you have any backup money?"

"What the hell is backup money?"

She sighed. "Sir, just answer the question. Do you have a way to obtain more money?"

"You mean, like credit cards, ATM cards?"

"Yes."

"Yes, we have credit cards and ATM cards."

"How many credit cards do you have?"

"Two."

"Have you ever been charged with a crime?"

"What? Have I...NO! I have *never* been charged with a crime."

"Do either of you have any outstanding warrants?"

Luke rolled his eyes. "No, we do not have any outstanding warrants."

"Have you ever gone to court?"

"Years ago, I did."

"When was the last time?"

Luke rolled his eyes and said, "The last time was the only time. Probably around 1983."

"And what were you charged with?"

"Speeding."

She ignored his answer. "Do you plan to buy any drugs while you are in Canada?"

"I already told you. Why can't you understand?" Luke had

never been known for his patience, and he had finally reached his limit. Speaking one word at a time, he repeated, "We-are-going-to-the-doctor. My wife is sick. Is it a fucking crime to do that?"

The agent's face turned beet red. She rocked back on her heels and took a deep breath and stepped away from the counter, drilling him with her eyes. "Sir, you are not in the United States. You are in Canada and you are required by Canadian law to answer every question we ask you. Do-you-understand?"

"I am answering your questions. But what I don't understand is why you are treating us like this. We're tourists, not terrorists, for God's sake."

Luke held her stare until she finally said, "I'll be right back."

The door slammed as she left the room. Luke turned toward Bonnie and said, "I've just about had all the bullshit I can take."

"Luke, it looks as though they are just about finished. After all, what else can we do? I'm sure they'll let us leave in a minute."

He leaned against the windowsill with both arms outstretched and closed his eyes. His head was killing him. Nothing made him feel worse than a wine hangover, and this confrontation had his blood pumping so hard he could feel every heartbeat in his temples.

Bonnie quietly walked up behind him about the time he lost it.

"This is bullshit," he screamed as he pushed away from the window and spun around.

Not knowing Bonnie was behind him, his arm caught her under the chin and his forearm whacked her across the face. It knocked her back into the row of folding chairs. The chairs overturned and scooted across the floor as Bonnie lost her balance and fell. Trying to break her fall, she put out her hand, her weight fell on her injured thumb, and she screamed out as she met the floor, face first.

Just before they collided, the door behind the counter opened and Driver and Sharp stepped in just in time to see Luke knock Bonnie to the floor.

"Get away from her," she shouted.

Luke ignored her and knelt down by Bonnie, who had rolled onto her side. Blood oozed from her lip and she held her injured thumb with her other hand. Her face contorted from the pain. Sharp ran up behind Luke, grabbed the back of his shirt, and jerked him away from her.

Luke fell onto his back and rolled over. To Sharp he said, "What the hell are you doing? Let me help her."

"Stay where you are," Driver said, positioning herself between Luke and Bonnie with her hand on the handle of her pistol, as if she might draw it if Luke didn't follow her instructions. To Sharp, she said, "Cuff him."

Luke stood up as Sharp pulled out his handcuffs and grabbed Luke by the forearm.

"I'm just helping my wife," Luke said, jerking his arm free. "It was an accident."

"Coley! Get in here," the female agent screamed toward the open door behind the counter. Standing between Bonnie and Luke, she held her arm out with her palm toward Luke, indicating he'd better stay where he was.

Luke looked around her to see Bonnie grimacing, tears welling in her eyes.

Another agent in a brown uniform busted into the room. He looked from side to side to assess the situation. He was Luke's height with bulging biceps and broad shoulders. His dark hair was clipped Marine-short and he had a tightly cropped moustache.

"Help Sharp get cuffs on him," Driver said, not taking her eyes off Luke.

Coley and Sharp came from opposite sides, grabbed Luke's arms and pulled them behind him.

"It was just an accident," Luke said as he felt the handcuffs snap closed on one of his wrists.

He yanked his hand away from Sharp, whose head spun around, hitting Coley hard on the chin.

"Son of a bitch," Coley said touching his chin where Sharp's head hit him. Blood oozed from a spot where the skin was now crimson red. Sharp pounced on Luke, pinning him face first against the back wall. Coley moved over to help Sharp get Luke's hands cuffed behind him.

After they settled down, Driver helped Bonnie into one of the folding chairs.

"Listen to me," Bonnie said, her voice quivering. She held her throbbing thumb and tried to explain, "He didn't do anything. We accidently ran into each other, and then I stumbled back and lost my balance. When I fell down I couldn't catch myself because my thumb was already injured."

Sharp said, "We could hear you arguing down the hall."

"We were not arguing," Luke said adamantly. "We were discussing all the stupid questions you were asking us." He glared at Driver, and then exchanged looks with Bonnie.

The agent's attention was on Bonnie. She saw her bleeding lip, her cheek was red where Luke had hit her, and her arms and legs were covered with scratches from her fall the day before. "Coley, take him across the hall," Driver said.

Blood dripped from Coley's chin onto his shirt as he dragged Luke across the hallway and into a smaller room. Luke stood across the room watching as Coley pulled a handkerchief out of his pocket and dabbed at his chin. When he took the handkerchief away Luke could see a bloody patch of skin the size of a dime where Sharp's head had scraped the skin off his chin.

Sharp and Driver were left in the room with Bonnie. Sharp stood over her as Driver pulled a tissue from a box on the counter and sat down beside her. She started to dab at the blood on Bonnie's lip.

Her mood became compassionate. "You don't have to cover for him. We can get you the help you need."

Bonnie gave her a puzzled look and said, "What are you talking about?"

"We saw him hit you."

"That's not what happened," Bonnie said. "He didn't do this on purpose. It was a simple accident. Then I lost my balance and fell."

The agents exchanged a disbelieving glance. Driver said, "Mrs. Wakefield, he hit you. We saw him do it."

"Not on purpose he didn't," Bonnie said, adamantly. "It was my fault. I walked up behind my husband and he didn't know I was there. When he turned, we collided and I lost my balance. It was an accident."

"Look at you," the woman said looking at her bruised cheek and scratched arms and legs. "Are you going to sit there and tell me he didn't do this to you? I could see the hostility in that man before I left the room. No woman has to put up with an abusive husband."

Bonnie knew they weren't going to believe her regardless of what she said. She was ready to go, "I don't care what you think you saw, that's not what happened. Can we go now?"

Driver sighed, and said, "If that's what you want to do."

They walked across the hall and opened the door. To Luke she said, "You're free to go."

Sharp turned Luke around and unlocked the handcuffs and without a word Luke followed Bonnie and they walked briskly down the hall and out of the building. They got in the car and didn't speak until they were accelerating away from the building.

"Bonnie, I'm sorry," Luke said. "I didn't know you were behind me. Are you okay?"

"I'm okay," she said dabbing her puffy lip with a tissue. "I know it was an accident. I think they were looking for trouble from the time we drove up."

"I wonder what their problem was," Luke said as they crested a hill and the building disappeared behind them.

Chapter 3

They discussed the episode for a few minutes and finally Bonnie said it was time to forget it. It wasn't going to ruin their trip, much less their day. Luke agreed and as they talked about the hike they planned to take that afternoon, their attitudes gradually improved.

As pastures gave way to doublewides and used car lots, they passed a sign welcoming them to Cardston, home to thirty-five hundred "Friendly Canadians." In the middle of town they turned left on Second Street and saw the Cardston Clinic in the middle of the block. Luke parked diagonally in the last remaining space across the street from the clinic.

They crossed the street and opened the door to find a waiting room with about thirty chairs, almost all occupied. Bonnie noticed that many of those waiting appeared to be Native Americans and she remembered seeing a big sign in a pasture before they got to town that said, "Welcome to the Blackfeet Nation." It made her curious about the local culture.

Bonnie turned to Luke and said, "Looks like it might be a long wait. Would you go back to the car and get the guidebook for Alberta, and that paperback I'm reading? And it's kind of cool in here so would you also bring my UT windbreaker?"

While Luke went back to the car, Bonnie went to the window with a sign above it that read: *Check in Here.*

The receptionist, a dishwater blonde with a gold tongue piercing, handed her a clipboard. "Please fill out this new patient form and bring it back when you're done."

"Sure. Do you have any idea how long it'll take before I can see a doctor?"

"We're real busy this morning," she said. "Probably an hour, maybe more."

Bonnie remembered Rita had said to let her know when

they arrived and hoped she could get her in quicker. "I understand," she said politely, "but Rita told me to let her know when I got here. Can you do that?"

"Yes, ma'am, I will."

Bonnie took the clipboard and turned to find a seat. The only one available was between a man in a business suit and a huge Native American man. When she sat between the two men, the Native American looked down at the elastic bandage on her wrist.

"Looks like you hurt your arm?"

Without a doubt, he was easily the biggest man she had ever seen. He appeared to be in his mid-forties with straight black hair tied in a ponytail that hung a foot past his collar. His arms crossed his chest and his sleeveless shirt exposed a tattoo on each bicep. One was of an Indian chief and the other had barbed wire encircling his arm. In his left ear a small diamond earring sparkled and from his belt she saw a long hunting knife in a scabbard.

"Yes, I did." She put her purse down beside her chair.

He seemed friendly, though he didn't smile. "If you need anything, I will get it for you. I'm Willy Standalone." Then he pointed to a handsome young man sitting across from him. "And that's my boy, Little John." The boy was in a daze, holding an iPod in one hand and an earplug in each ear. He appeared to be about eighteen and clean-cut. Like his father, he was muscular, but not nearly as big.

"Okay, thanks."

Pointing to a coffee machine against the wall, he said, "Do you want some coffee? It's free."

"No, thank you. I'm fine."

"Want a magazine?"

"No, thank you," she said as the front door opened and Luke stepped in and scanned the room for her. They made eye contact and he started walking her way.

Willy saw him approaching and stood, pointing to his chair. "Take my chair."

Luke seemed in awe by the man's size and stepped back. "No thanks, please, keep your seat."

Unsmiling, Willy pointed. "Sit."

Luke sat.

A minute later, a nurse stepped into the waiting room and called out some names; an elderly couple across the room and the man in the suit beside Bonnie got up and followed the nurse back through the open door. Willy stepped over and plopped down next to Bonnie.

"Little John's going to college on a football scholarship," Willy said. "He has to get him a physical."

Bonnie, distracted from filling out the form, looked at the boy and smiled. "That's great. He looks very strong."

"He's the quarterback."

"I bet he's good." She smiled and looked over at Little John who appeared to be in his own world listening to his iPod.

Luke nudged Bonnie and whispered, "Let's move over there." He pointed at the empty chairs where the elderly couple had been sitting. The chairs were off in a corner, where they'd be out of the way. She nodded and reached down for her purse.

As they started walking away, Willy spoke, loud enough for the entire room to hear, "What's the matter, don't like sitting next to Indians?"

Startled, Luke said warily, "No, it's just a little crowded in here. I just wanted to get out of the way. That's all."

Luke and Bonnie hesitantly moved over to the corner and sat down. For the next five minutes, every time she looked at Willy, he was staring at Luke, his massive arms across his chest. A few minutes later the nurse returned and called Willy and Little John. When they went back, Luke and Bonnie finally relaxed.

Half an hour passed, and Luke became fidgety. Bonnie noticed and reached into the outside pocket of her purse and pulled a folded piece of chartreuse paper and handed it to him. "We still need to get the stuff on this list. Why don't you go get it? I don't know how much longer it's going to be before I see the doctor."

He looked at the list, handed it back to her and said, "The grocery store's a ways from here so I'll just go to the drugstore we saw on Main. You keep the list. I can remember aspirin, Kleenex, and sunscreen. They aren't going to have lettuce, tomatoes, bread, or mayo. We'll stop at the grocery store on the way out of town."

"Just hang on to the list."

"I'll lose it," he said.

She rolled her eyes.

He carefully tore the paper in half and held the top half out to her. "You take this part and I'll get the rest."

She didn't take it, just stared at him, and said, "Luke…"

With a smirk on his face, he bent over and stuffed the top half of the paper into the outside pocket of her purse, and then put the other half into his pocket. "How's that?"

She shook her head and smiled. "Always have to have it your way, don't you?"

Smiling back, he said, "It's usually the best way, isn't it?"

With a slight tilt of her head, she grinned and said, "Of course not."

He leaned over, kissed her, and stood to leave.

"Keep your cell phone turned on and I'll call you when I'm finished."

Luke pulled his phone out and flipped it open. "I forgot to charge it last night and it's almost dead."

"Mine is too. Let's not forget to charge them tonight."

"I won't."

When Luke stepped outside he considered taking the car, but the weather was sunny with the temperature in the mid-seventies. Since the drugstore was only a couple of blocks away, he decided to walk.

It only took a few minutes to get there and when he stepped inside, a nostalgic feeling swept over him. He hadn't seen a store like this in thirty years. On one side was a grill where teenagers sat on metal stools with fountain drinks in short glasses. In the back was the pharmacy where two gray-haired ladies stood laughing and talking to the druggist behind the counter. It reminded him of the way drugstores used to be before the national chains started putting identical stores on opposing corners across America. Maybe that trend hadn't yet hit Canada, he thought.

A few minutes later he was on his way back to the clinic when he saw a shop on the other side of the street called The Sportsman's Outfitter. In the windows he saw several posters with people fly-fishing in rivers and streams. After his disastrous attempt at fly fishing, he thought he'd check and see how much it would cost to go with a guide.

It was quiet inside, except for Jimmy Buffett's "Margaritaville" coming from a small speaker on top of a filing cabinet. Posters, photographs, and maps covered the walls around the store and in the front of the store were several long tables filled with brochures and photo albums.

Luke could faintly hear a woman's voice coming through an open door on the back wall. The voice got louder and a woman stepped through the door.

"Those days are available. How many will there be?"

She wore khaki shorts, hiking boots, and a purple polo shirt. She stepped over to a desk and opened an appointment book and as she bent forward to write, her long black hair fell forward, blocking her face.

"Did you say four? Is everyone over eighteen? Has everyone been fly fishing before?" she said, glancing at Luke and making eye contact.

"Yes, sir. All I'll need to hold the reservation is a credit card number."

She held up one finger and mouthed the words, "I'll be with you in a second."

Luke smiled and nodded, then shifted his position to see her more easily. She was about Bonnie's height, looked to be in her mid-thirties, but definitely heavier because she filled out her polo shirt much more than Bonnie. When she quit writing and looked back at him, he realized he was staring at her and looked back at the brochure and started reading about fly fishing.

For the next few minutes she answered the caller's questions, glancing at Luke every half-minute or so with an apologetic smile.

Luke walked around the store looking at posters and maps, glancing at her occasionally. She was a very attractive woman. After a few minutes she put the caller on hold and turned to Luke, "I'm sorry, but this is going to take longer than I thought. Some folks from Arizona are booking a fishing trip and they have a jillion questions. Can you wait a few more minutes?"

Luke looked at his watch. "Maybe I should come back later. I just wanted to see what kind of fly-fishing trips you have."

"Don't go, I'll be done in a few minutes," she said, moving towards him. "I know all the best places and you won't find anyone around here that can catch more trout than I can."

Luke was surprised. "Really? Are you a guide?"

"I am!" She spoke with a playful arrogance. "If you go fishing with me you won't be disappointed. We'll have a great time and catch a lot of fish, too. I promise."

"That's what I'm looking for…" he glanced at his watch again, "but I'd better be going."

"Okay then. I'm Lauren," she said and reached out to shake his hand. "I'm the owner."

He accepted her firm grip. "I'm Luke. I'll try to catch you a little later."

She released his hand and said, "Where are you from, Luke?"

"Texas."

"I pegged you as a Texan as soon as you opened your mouth."

"Well, I guess I do talk a little different from y'all."

In a mock Texas accent she said, "Y'all shore do talk different than we do up here." Then she giggled. "But I like it."

Luke felt his cheeks redden. "I guess I'd better quit talking and let you get back to your phone call."

She wanted a commitment. "Now, you are going to come back later, right?"

"Yes, ma'am, I'll try."

"Don't call me ma'am, okay." She was firm, but smiling. "Just call me Lauren. And what do you mean you'll try? You said you'd come back, right?"

Now embarrassed, he got a little flustered. "I'm sorry. I won't, but I will."

Puzzled, she said, "You won't, but you will? You're going to have to explain that one to me."

"I guess that doesn't make much sense." Luke said shyly. "What I mean is I *won't* call you ma'am. But I *will* come back."

"Okay, that's better," she chuckled. "I was getting confused."

Grinning sheepishly, Luke said, "Yep, me too…but I'll come back later."

"Good." She leaned forward, poked him in the chest, and with an old West accent, said, "Now don't make me come lookin' for ya."

He grinned and said, "Okay," then turned and walked out the front door. As he started down the sidewalk he looked back through the window at her. She gave him a little wave, and then tilted her head, letting her hair fall away before putting the phone back to her ear.

Luke was lost in thought as he walked back to the clinic. Ordinarily he was pretty quick and witty, but Lauren had totally destroyed his concentration. She seemed to be flirting with him, which he enjoyed. At least he thought she was flirting. It had been a long time since anything like that had happened.

Luke was already inside the clinic when he realized he forgot to put the bag with his purchases in the car. He looked around and noticed the waiting room was now almost empty. Since he didn't see Bonnie, he assumed she was back with the doctor. He sat back in the corner where they had sat earlier and pulled out the paperback he bought at the drug store.

After reading for less than five minutes, he looked up and saw that he was the only one left in the waiting room. He checked his watch. It was noon. Assuming they closed for lunch, he went to the receptionist to check on Bonnie.

"Do you have any idea how much longer it will be before my wife is finished?"

"What is her name?"

"Bonnie Wakefield."

After flipping a page in her book she looked back at Luke. "She's already checked out."

"You're kidding," Luke said in disbelief.

She shook her head and gave him an *I'm sorry*, kind of shrug.

He thanked her and headed for the door.

Bonnie was probably waiting for him at the car, he thought. He felt like an idiot for not even noticing the car when he came back. His mind had been elsewhere, thinking about Lauren and how she was flirting with him.

As soon as he stepped out the front door he saw their green rental car sitting across the street. All of the cars that filled the parking spaces earlier were now gone. He hustled across the street and though he wasn't expecting to see Bonnie inside, he felt compelled to look.

"Of course she's not in there, you idiot. You've got the only key," he murmured.

He scanned the sidewalks in both directions, and on both sides of the street. They were deserted as far as he could see. He stood on the curb and made a complete three-sixty degree turn.

Where in the hell did she go?

Chapter 4

Luke pulled out his cell phone and pressed Bonnie's speed dial number. It rang once and went directly to her voice mail.

"Hey, Babe, I'm at the car. Waiting. Call me."

For a few minutes he waited, unsure what to do. It wasn't like Bonnie to wander off, but, knowing her, she probably had a good reason. He scratched his chin trying to remember their last conversation. It was likely he wasn't thinking clearly since he was suffering from a world class hangover, but he couldn't remember her mentioning anything she needed to do. Only that she wanted him to keep the shopping list.

He'd said she needed to get the rest of it from the grocery store. Maybe that's where she went. But, the one they saw coming into town was at least half a mile from where he stood, maybe more. *She wouldn't go that far without leaving a note, would she?*

He sat in the driver's seat and looked at his watch. Five past twelve. *It would probably be best if I just wait. She should be back in a few minutes.*

He rolled down the window and pulled out the brochures from the Sportsman's Outfitter and started to leaf through them. After about five minutes he got restless.

Luke tried to think of where else she could have gone. Maybe she went to look for him. Or, even better, she probably went to the drug store to fill a prescription. And he didn't see her because he was at Lauren's store. He hoped she didn't see him in there because she'd accuse him of flirting. *Maybe I'd better find a guide who's a guy.*

He waited, watched the sidewalks and checked his watch every minute or two.

Ten minutes later his patience was gone. He couldn't believe she'd wander off like this without telling him first. If he did something like this, she'd be all over him for being inconsiderate. And he'd get the silent treatment at least an hour, for sure.

Now it was twelve-twenty. It had been thirty minutes since he had returned to the clinic. It was time to go find her. The town was small. Downtown couldn't be more than four blocks long. He'd leave her a note.

He tore a piece of paper out of a notebook and wrote: *Bonnie- Looking for you. Stay here. I'll be back at 12:30, Luke.* He stuck it under the windshield wiper, locked the doors, and started to walk.

On Main Street, there were about a dozen people on the sidewalks, but none with red hair. Luke headed toward the drugstore, glancing inside every storefront he passed.

Inside the drugstore he checked every aisle as he hurried to the pharmacy in the back. There a bald, rotund man in a white lab coat glanced up and asked if he could help.

"I'm looking for my wife and thought she might have dropped off a prescription to be filled? Could you check to see if you have anything for Bonnie Wakefield."

"That name doesn't sound familiar, but let me look." The pharmacist turned to a counter behind him where little white paper bags were arranged in a series of rows. "When did she bring it?"

"I don't know that she did. We got separated and I thought maybe she came over here to fill a prescription. It would have been in the last hour."

"Nothing here, but let me check those I haven't filled yet." He turned and looked through a short stack of paper. "Nope, nothing for Wakefield," he said. "Go ask Irene if she's seen her." He pointed to the front of the store where a little white-haired lady stood behind a cash register. "She sees everyone who comes and goes. Has for the last thirty-three years."

"No, I've not seen anyone like that today," Irene said, shaking her head. "And I would know, because I get here every day at eight-thirty, except on Sunday. I don't think we should even be open on Sunday but when Mr. Wilcox died, Arthur started opening on Sunday and I told him I wasn't going to work on Sunday because I—"

"Thank you ma'am," Luke said, cutting her off and backing away.

Luke started back to the clinic, this time on the opposite side of the street. He slowed for a closer look inside the gift shop and ladies' boutique, but no sign of Bonnie.

At Second Street he turned and saw the rental car. As he got closer he saw the note on the windshield, exactly where he left it. Bonnie had not been back.

He checked his watch. Seven minutes left. He had been told the grocery store was only six blocks away.

He walked briskly in that direction, catching sight of a redhead across the street with her back to him. But she had on a bright green blouse with yellow slacks. Even though Bonnie had green eyes, she never wore green.

But that made him think: *what was she wearing?* He couldn't remember.

When he got to the grocery store, it was 12:28. The store was so small that it didn't take but a few minutes to check every aisle. In the back corner of the store he saw the restrooms. A lady wearing a blue apron was walking out. He stopped her.

"I'm looking for my wife. Is there anyone else in there?"

She shook her head.

As he started back to the car he pulled out his cell phone, but the screen was dark. He pressed a button and nothing happened. The battery was dead.

When he got back to the car it was twelve thirty-five, and nothing had changed. His note was still exactly where he left it.

Flustered, he unlocked the car and sat down. Looking at his phone he recalled a recent conversation where Bonnie had said they needed to get smartphones. All of her friends said sending texts was easier than making phone calls all day long. Luke thought it was a waste of time. His friends had told him how it works. They said you'll be working, moving cattle from one pasture to another and your phone will buzz. You'll have to stop your horse, pull out your reading glasses, clean the dust off them and read a message on the phone that says, "How's your day going honey?" That kind of bull shit he didn't need. He tossed his dead cell phone on the passenger seat, and thought, *and another thing. I can't even remember to keep* this *little piece of shit charged up.*

Luke turned on the radio and tried to think of something else. But, two minutes later he turned it off. It was impossible to sit still, so he got out and stood in the open door looking over the roof of the car toward Main.

Where else could she have gone?

Luke closed his eyes and massaged his temples. His headache was almost gone. Food, he thought, might help, but he'd wait until Bonnie came back. He vowed to drink no more wine on this trip. Maybe no more wine in this lifetime.

A few minutes later he sat back down in the car. He glanced over the seat and saw the paperback he bought at the drugstore. Then it hit him. On the flight to Calgary Bonnie said she was almost finished with the book she was reading and needed to get another one before they left civilization. This small, nothing of a town was about the last chance. She probably went to find a bookstore, if they had one. And when Bonnie was in one, she lost all track of time. *I'll give her a few more minutes, then I'll find out if there is a bookstore in town.*

With that logic, Luke relaxed; he knew she'd walk around the corner any minute with a new mystery or romance paperback in her hand. His anger seemed to settle down a notch, but they'd still have to talk about wandering off without leaving a note.

But five minutes later he couldn't stand it so he walked up to the corner and watched, scanning the faces of the pedestrians as they came and went. For the next fifteen minutes, he walked half a block one way then the other. Just before one, he looked back at the car and noticed most of the parking spaces in front of the clinic were filled again. He might as well check with the receptionist one more time. He hurried inside and when he got to the open window the receptionist smiled with a look of recognition.

"I was in here before lunch looking for my wife. You haven't seen her, have you?"

Her expression changed to confusion. "No, sir. Was she going to come back?"

"I don't think so, but I can't find her. If she comes back, would you tell her I'm looking for her?"

She nodded. "Yes sir, I will."

He started to leave, and then turned back to her, "Is there a bookstore in town?"

"There's only one and it sells mostly used books."

"Can you tell me how to get there?"

"Just go to Main and turn left. It's down on the left about five blocks."

Luke thanked her and as he started walking he felt as if he was on a wild goose chase. She wouldn't go that far without telling him. But he was out of ideas.

The Great Exchange Bookstore was bigger than he expected for a town this small. The bookshelves were tall and the aisles were narrow. As he walked through the store he felt like he was in a maze as he rushed from one aisle to the next, looking hopefully around every corner.

After passing an old man wearing a dirty gray Stetson for the third time, the man stopped him. "You look lost, son. Can I help you find something?"

"You work here?" Luke said, eyeing the old cowboy curiously.

"Not really, this is my wife's store, but I kind of know my way around."

"I'm looking for my wife," Luke said. "She's about five-eight with long reddish blonde hair. She might have a cast on her forearm."

"You don't know if she has a cast on her arm," the man

said. He gave Luke a wary look.

"It's a long story, but bottom line is that we got separated down at the clinic."

He nodded as if he understood, and said, "I haven't seen her, but let's go ask Ruthie." He started toward the front of the store, talking as he walked. "I just got here a few minutes ago. Brought Ruthie some lunch."

At the checkout counter he relayed the question to his wife. She said, "I can't remember seeing anyone like that, but I could have missed her. Lots of people come and go."

Disappointed, Luke thanked them and started back to the car.

On the way he came to the fire station and saw two fire trucks and an ambulance backed into the stalls. Two EMTs in black uniforms were standing near the open doors, one smoking a cigarette. *What if something happened to her,* Luke thought. *If she got hit by a car or fell on the sidewalk and got knocked out, no one in the clinic would know about it. The EMTs would take her to the hospital, if there was a hospital in town.*

"Excuse me," Luke said as he stepped over and spoke to the EMTs. "I wonder if you could help me."

"We'll try," the smoker said. "What's up?"

"I'm looking for my wife. We got separated a couple of hours ago and I've looked all over town and can't find her. She was at the clinic waiting to see the doctor and I left for about an hour. When I came back, they said she was gone. Have you guys gotten any calls to pick up a woman this morning?"

"No, we came on at seven this morning and haven't had a call at all. You might go down to the hospital and see if they know anything. It's down there in the next block," he said, pointing down the street. "Go in the emergency entrance and talk to the lady at the desk. If she was taken in for any reason, she'll be able to tell you."

"Okay, thanks."

At the hospital Luke explained the situation and was told

no one had been admitted all morning.

Back at the clinic he found the car exactly as it was when he left. He dropped into the driver's seat and with his thumb and forefinger rubbed his eyes while he tried to make sense of it.

He knew that something was not right. This was a little town, the downtown area not more than four blocks long and he'd searched it over and over for the past two hours with no luck and now his concern turned to fear.

As he looked out the window, a couple of kids on bicycles rode past on the sidewalk, and his imagination began to wander.

Maybe someone grabbed her when she came out the front door? No way, he thought. *Not at eleven thirty in the morning in broad daylight in this little Podunk town.*

Maybe the police arrested her for something, like J-walking.

Or maybe those jerks from the border crossing came and got her and now are trying to convince her to file charges against him as a wife-beater. She'd never do it, because it wasn't true.

Luke shut his eyes and unconsciously shook his head. None of those options seemed possible. Nothing made sense and he knew he had to do something about it now.

He locked the car and trotted back to the clinic. As soon as the receptionist saw him, she stopped typing and gave him a stunned look.

"You still haven't found your wife?"

"No, I haven't. Rita's a friend of hers, and I was wondering if I could talk to her."

"She's busy with a patient right now, but let me tell my boss."

The receptionist disappeared around the corner and a minute later returned. She took Luke back to an office where an attractive blonde sat behind a desk.

As soon as she saw him, she stood and walked around the

desk toward him.

"I'm Mitzi Lindsey, the office manager. Monica told me you can't find your wife. That's bizarre. I've never heard of such a thing. Let's go talk to Rita."

He followed her down a hallway to the nurses' station where a brunette in a green smock stood making notes in a file. She appeared to be about forty with a trim body and dark hair in a ponytail. As they got closer, she gave them a sidelong glance and said, "What's up, Mitz?"

"Rita, this is Luke Wakefield. He said his wife was in here this morning and is a friend of yours?"

"That's right," she said, looking at Luke.

"He's got a few questions. Can you help him?"

"Sure," she said. She closed the file and looked at Luke. "Your wife is a fantastic photographer. Everyone loved her presentation and I can't wait to get her book. I ordered one for me and one for my mom."

"Thanks, I know she enjoyed coming up here to talk," Luke said, shifting his weight. "Did you see her this morning?"

"I did, but just for a few minutes," Rita said, pulling another file. "Is she feeling better?"

"I don't know. I left her here at the clinic about ten-thirty to run some errands and when I came back they said she was gone. I've been looking for her since noon and can't find her. Did she say anything about going anywhere else?"

"No, she didn't say anything. We barely had a chance to talk." Rita leaned against the wall and studied Luke's face. "When I saw her it was all routine. I got her information and found out what was going on. She told me about getting sick and falling down the side of the cliff, which sounded really scary. I'm glad she didn't get hurt any worse than she did. Anyway, we took an X-ray and gave it to Dr. Duncan. The clinic was busy, I doubt if I talked to her for more than five minutes. Maybe Dr. Duncan can tell you something. Let me see if he has time to talk to you."

Luke followed her down to the end of the hallway where

she stopped at a brown paneled door and knocked softly. When there was no answer, she pushed it open and they walked into a spacious office. In the middle of the room was a massive mahogany desk. Across from it were two arm chairs.

"Have a seat and I'll go get him." Luke sat down and she walked out, closing the door behind her.

Behind the desk numerous plaques and diplomas decorated the wall. Below them on a credenza were a number of framed photos. In one, a tall, gray haired hunter knelt beside a fallen elk. In another, the same man knelt beside a dead bear.

About ten minutes later, the hunter in the photos walked in, wearing a white lab coat with R. C. Duncan, M.D. monogrammed above the chest pocket.

"Rita told me you can't seem to find your wife," the man said as he walked over and perched on the corner of his desk.

"Yes, sir and I don't know exactly what to do. I thought maybe you might give me some help, or at least an idea where to start looking for her."

"I'm sure there's a logical explanation. I've never heard of anyone disappearing around here before. I'm sure everything will be okay." Under normal circumstances, the doctor's voice and demeanor would have been comforting.

The doctor laced his fingers in front of him as he recounted his visit with Bonnie. "Rita gave me the X-ray of her thumb. It wasn't broken, but it is sprained pretty badly. That's a common injury when people fall forward like that. So, I put a splint on it and told her to wear it as long as she feels she needs it. Then she said she'd been sick, vomiting. But it didn't sound too bad to me. I think she'll be over it by tomorrow, but I gave her some antibiotics to take. The drug companies send us lots of free samples, so I gave her some of those. I told her to drink lots of liquids. And just in case she's not better by tomorrow, I wrote her a prescription for something a little stronger. And for her thumb, I told her to just take some Tylenol or Advil."

"How long were you with her?"

"Oh, about five minutes."

"When you finished, where'd she go?"

"After we finished, we walked out of the exam room and I remember watching her walk back toward the front desk. People who haven't been here before get turned around in the hallways, so I usually watch them to make sure they go the right way. Which she did."

Nothing sounded the least bit unusual. Now it seemed clear to Luke that whatever happened to her, happened after she left the clinic.

"I guess I just have to keep looking," Luke said as he stood up. He walked over and pulled the door open. "Thanks for your time."

"I wish there was more I could tell you."

"There is one thing. Can you tell me how to get to the police station?"

Chapter 5

Luke was a bit confused. "RCMP?" he asked.

"I forgot you're from the states," Dr. Duncan said. "Here in Canada, we have the RCMP. The Royal Canadian Mounted Police. It's our federal police force. You can find their office out past the grocery store about half a mile."

Something about taking the car made him feel like he was abandoning Bonnie, so again, he walked. He found their office with no problem and when he entered the small lobby it was empty and quiet. Through an open door on the back wall he saw a long deserted hallway. He heard faint laughter and the sound of footsteps and a few seconds later, a very pregnant Native American woman in orange pants and a paisley blouse rounded the corner with her head down as she rummaged through her purse. As she got closer she stopped at one of the doors in the hallway.

"Chief, remember, I won't be in until noon tomorrow since I'm going to the doctor in Lethbridge."

When she started toward the waiting room she saw Luke and turned back down the hallway, and to no one in particular, said, "There's someone at the counter." As she walked toward Luke, she smiled and said, "Someone will be right with you," then walked past him and out the front door.

A few seconds later, a man with a gun on his hip stepped into the hallway. He was short, robust, with gray hair and a bushy mustache. He was wearing khakis and a white short-sleeved shirt and looked to be in his late sixties or early seventies.

"Can I help you?"

Luke took a deep breath and said, "I hope so. My wife is missing."

The man hooked his thumbs in his front belt loops and let

his arms rest. He furrowed his brow and said, "What do you mean, missing?"

Luke wasn't sure where to start, so he started talking. "We were at the clinic, and while she waited to see a doctor I ran a couple of errands. Came back about an hour later and she was gone." He looked at his watch and said, "That was about noon and I've been looking all over town since then and I can't find her. I don't know what to do. We're from Texas and here on vacation, it's been over four hours and—"

"Hold on, son," the lawman said, holding up his hands. "Come back to my office."

Luke followed him into his office and sat across the desk from him.

"Where in Texas?"

"Lampasas. A little town northwest of Austin."

"What are you doing here in Cardston?"

"We were over at Glacier and my wife got sick, so we came over here to the clinic. Being from Texas, I'm a little confused on what to do here in Canada."

"I see." The man reached into the pocket of his shirt and pulled out a cigar. As he unwrapped the cellophane wrapper, he spoke. "It's a little different here but not that much. I'm Ernest Oliveras, the commanding officer of this detachment, kind of like the chief of police where you're from. You can call me Ernest." He stuck the cigar in his mouth briefly, then pulled it out and examined it a few seconds before wrapping his index finger around it.

"Now, start from the beginning and tell me what happened since you got to Cardston."

As Luke talked, Ernest nodded, and interrupted a few times asking for more details. After a minute Luke stopped and Ernest asked a few more questions.

"You didn't have a big fight, did you?"

Luke shook his head, "No, sir."

"And before you came up here, things were good at home?"

"Yes sir, everything's perfect."

"Um hum," he said. "You folks got a bunch of oil wells back in Texas? Lots of money?"

"No oil wells. Not much money."

"Got any enemies back home? Anyone who'd like to get even with you for something you did to them?"

"I don't think so."

"Made any enemies here?"

Luke thought about that guy at the camera store, but was sure that wasn't anything to worry about. "I don't think so?"

Ernest leaned back and stuck the cigar in his mouth again but didn't make any move to light it. He looked out the window and appeared deep in thought then said, "What did she have with her the last time you saw her?"

"All she had was her purse, with the normal stuff in it. You know, billfold, make up, a little cash, a cell phone. But nothing else I know of."

"Is she on any medication?"

"Nothing much, maybe some allergy medicine, but nothing I know of. She's real healthy."

"Is she bipolar? Suffer from depression or anything like that?"

"No sir, about as normal as any woman can be, I guess."

Ernest smiled and gave a silent chuckle. "I hear you. Does she have problems with her health? You know memory, fainting spells, does she get confused easy?"

"No sir. Like I said, she's as healthy as a horse. Even training to run the New York Marathon in November," Luke leaned forward. "That's what I'm saying. She's perfectly normal. I just can't understand—"

"She ever do anything like this before?"

"No. Never."

The chief asked, "Do you have any friends in Cardston or anywhere else in the area?"

Luke explained about Rita, the talk Bonnie gave at the workshop, and also about his conversation with Dr. Duncan.

"Did they see her talking to anyone else at the clinic?"

Luke shook his head. "I don't know. I didn't ask that question."

"But they did say they saw her leave alone?"

"No, they didn't say that." Luke looked down at the floor and shook his head. "I'm not sure how well the receptionist or anyone else can see the door from where they sit. There's a little window between them and the waiting room. When you're in there, you can't see the receptionist until you walk up to that window."

"Yeah, I know how it is," Ernest said. "I've been in there a hundred times myself." He turned his wrist to see his watch. He stood up and said, "It's been about four and a half hours. Ordinarily, we usually don't get started on a missing person this quick, but I think we should. Let me get you a form to fill out with all the information and I'll need a picture of her. Do you have one that's recent?"

Luke nodded, "No, not with me." Then he remembered he took some pictures of her the day they arrived. "Wait a minute. I took some pictures of her yesterday. If I bring in that memory card from my camera, can you print some pictures?"

"Not really. The printer we use for pictures is on the blink, so it would be best if you go to the camera shop on Main Street. They can do them while you wait."

For the next half hour, Luke filled out forms and answered more questions.

"I'll get those pictures made and get back here as soon as I can."

Ernest followed Luke as he made his way to the front door. "Luke, I'm sure she's okay. I don't think we've ever had anyone kidnapped or abducted in Cardston. I'm sure there's a perfectly good explanation for this."

"That's the same thing Dr. Duncan said. I hope you're right."

***

Luke hurried back to the car, hoping to find Bonnie there waiting. But she wasn't. He grabbed the camera, ejected the memory card, and headed for the camera shop. Rocky Mountain Photography was a few blocks away and as soon as he stepped inside the teenage girl behind the counter pointed to a clock that said 5:35. "I'm sorry sir, but we close at five-thirty."

"I understand, but this is an emergency," Luke said. He held out the memory card to the girl and said, "The police have asked me to get some pictures made for them as soon as possible."

"All of our equipment has been turned off for the day. I don't know…"

"This is very important. My wife is missing and the police need some pictures printed now. I'll pay whatever it takes."

She backed away and said, "I'll have to talk to the manager." She walked around the corner and disappeared in the back.

While Luke waited, he looked out the big window across the front of the store and watched people walking by, hoping to see a redhead.

"Can I help you?" came a voice behind him.

When Luke turned around he recognized the tall man with long blond hair. Sonny Diamond, the man Bonnie had argued with in St. Mary. Sonny recognized Luke and his expression hardened.

Luke sighed and regained his composure. "I'm Luke Wakefield from Austin, Texas. I…we met yesterday at—"

Without emotion Sonny said, "At my camera store in St. Mary. I remember you. What can I do for you?"

"You own both stores?"

"I don't own them, but I manage both of them. How can I help you?" he asked impatiently.

"My wife has disappeared and I need to have some pictures of her printed to give the police."

"What do you mean, she disappeared?" he asked. "Was she

hiking or something?"

Luke explained.

"That's the strangest thing I've ever heard," Sonny said. "Who'd you talk to at the RCMP?"

"An older man named Ernest. I think he's in charge over there."

"Yeah, Ernest's the one to talk to. He's been the commanding officer here in Cardston as long as I can remember. He'll find her." Sonny reached for the memory card Luke was holding. "Give me that and I'll make some prints for you."

Sonny told the teenage girl she could go, then stuck the card into the machine, and the photos Luke and Bonnie had taken the day before came up on the monitor. Luke pointed to the photo that showed Bonnie's face the best.

A moment later, Sonny slipped a stack of 4 x 5s, and some 8 x 10s into an envelope and slid them across the counter to Luke.

"There are plenty of prints in there. Give some to the police and you might post some around town."

"Thanks. How much do I owe you?" Luke asked as he pushed a fifty-dollar bill across the counter, but Sonny slid it back.

"Don't worry about it."

"I appreciate that," Luke said, and the two men headed to the door.

"What are you going to do now?" Sonny asked.

Luke looked back down the street in the direction of the police station, "I'll take these back to the police and then, I don't know. Just wait at the car, I guess."

"Where's your car?"

"I left it parked in front of the clinic. When Bonnie comes back, I want it to be there."

Sonny nodded and said, "C'mon. Let me drop you at the RCMP office."

They got into a dark blue BMW that smelled of new

leather and as they started down the road, Sonny asked, "Where are you staying?"

"At the Red Eagle Lodge in St. Mary, but I'm not going back without Bonnie. She's here somewhere and I'm not leaving without her."

"I don't blame you. I'm going to see some friends tonight," he said. "Give me a couple of those pictures and I'll pass them around."

Luke handed him three of the photos.

"It's a small town. You never know who might have seen something, and the more people looking for her the better."

A few minutes later Sonny rolled to a stop in front of the police station.

"If you haven't eaten, the diner next to my store has excellent home cooking."

"I haven't eaten since breakfast. I'll try it." Then he extended his hand to Sonny. "Hey Sonny, thanks for everything," Then awkwardly added, "and…I'm sorry about what happened in St. Mary. Bonnie didn't mean to—"

"Hey, don't worry about it. I kind of lost my cool. I can be a real asshole sometimes," Sonny said with a chuckle. "Let's forget it."

Luke smiled and nodded as he pushed the door closed. Sonny made a U-turn and headed back toward town.

When Luke walked into the lobby, an officer he hadn't seen before took him back to Ernest's office.

"Give me about six of those pictures," Ernest said. "I'll scan one and get it on the wire as soon as I can. Within an hour, every detachment in Alberta will have a copy of it. I'll also get these others out to the officers on patrol."

"What should I do now?"

"We'll contact you as soon as we know anything. Where are you staying?"

"Our room is at the Red Eagle Lodge in St. Mary, but I'm not leaving without Bonnie. I'll be in my car across from the clinic."

"Okay. If she doesn't show up, check back with me in the morning."

Luke walked back to town; the sidewalks were deserted and the lights were turned off inside most of the storefront businesses. Just past Sonny's store, he came to the diner. His omelet from early that morning had worn off hours ago. Just thinking about eating without knowing where Bonnie was seemed wrong, but he needed food. He ordered two burgers and two Cokes, to go. He couldn't see getting something for himself without something for Bonnie. Just in case.

Fifteen minutes later, with a brown paper bag in his hand, he rounded the corner to the clinic. The Sebring was the only car left, and from half a block away, he could tell there was something different. The passenger window in the front seat was down. Bonnie must have come back…and somehow, gotten in. But, he didn't see her anywhere.

He picked up his pace, breaking into a trot, a tinge of excitement lifting his spirits. But when he got closer, his stomach sank. Broken glass sparkled like diamonds beside the car. The window wasn't down. It was broken out.

His pace slowed to a stop while he looked from side to side, as if whoever did this was still nearby or watching him from behind the bushes. But, there was no one in sight. He edged closer and peered inside. Everything appeared to be as it was when he was there an hour ago, except now there was a brick sitting on the console between the seats and small pieces of safety glass decorated the interior.

He checked the backseat. The ice chest, picnic supplies, and even the binoculars were still there. But when he looked back in the front seat, he realized what was missing. It was the camera he had carelessly tossed on the passenger seat, and his cell phone.

"Damn it," Luke said, scolding himself for being careless. A camera and a cell phone sitting in plain sight were like Twinkies at a Weight Watchers meeting. The temptation was obviously too much for someone to resist.

Then he remembered that most of Bonnie's expensive camera gear was in the trunk. To get it, all a thief had to do was use the trunk release beside the steering wheel. He went to the back of the car, held his breath and opened the trunk. Everything was all still there. He let out a sigh of relief.

Whoever did this was an amateur, an opportunist. Replacing the equipment Bonnie brought on this trip would have cost at least ten grand, probably more. The camera and the cell phone were not a tenth of that. He felt lucky.

But then he wondered if it might be more than a coincidence. Could it be related to Bonnie's disappearance? Doubtful, but how did he know? He opened the glove compartment where Bonnie had put their passports and insurance papers. All still there.

But the more he thought about it, the more he felt like he needed to let the RCMP know about this.

Leaving the car behind earlier turned out to be a mistake, so this time he'd drive to their office. But, if Bonnie came back and found the car gone she'd panic. He looked in the backseat and saw a cardboard box with their picnic supplies. He unloaded all of the paper plates, napkins and other things onto the backseat, then with a black marker, he wrote on the side of the box: *Bonnie—I'm looking for you—I'll be back about 7:00 PM—Stay Here!!! Luke.*

When he got back to the police station, Ernest's cruiser was about to pull out. Luke screeched to a stop in front of him and rushed over to his window. He thrust his arm back toward the broken window. "Now someone broke into my car."

"What'd they take?" Ernest said.

"As far as I can tell, they only took a camera and my cell phone," he said, shrugging his shoulders. "Do you think it would have something to do with Bonnie?"

Without answering, Ernest got out of his vehicle and ambled over to check out the damage. Before looking inside he walked around the car, looking it over the way a prospective buyer might. When he got to the broken window, he leaned close and looked inside. The brick sat on the console and broken glass was scattered everywhere.

"Where was the camera and the phone?"

"Right there on that seat," he said.

"Hell, you were just inviting trouble leaving a camera out in plain view like that."

"I know, I wasn't thinking." Luke bent over and looked closer at the door handle. "Would it do any good to get the fingerprints?"

"No. I doubt they even touched the door handle. I'll make a note in your file, and if the rental company needs a police report, let me know and I'll get you one."

It was what he expected but he felt better at least reporting it. When he got back to the clinic, the box with his note was still there. No sign of Bonnie.

Luke quickly downed one of the now-cold burgers and when he was finished he was in no mood to sit and wait. He changed the note on the box to say he'd be back at nine, and started driving.

First he went down all of the streets north and south, then he did the same thing on the streets east and west. The town was small and in less than an hour he'd seen the entire town. He went back to his parking space across from the clinic. The street was deserted and after a few minutes he got out and paced up and down the street until finally stopping to peer across the roof of the car back toward Main Street.

He saw two, maybe three cars a minute drive past on Main, and none on the side streets. Just like any other small town, even back home in Lampasas, after the workday was over you might as well roll up the streets. Everyone's gone home for the night.

But, he wasn't home. And neither was Bonnie. Something was wrong. And for the first time in his life, Luke didn't know what to do.

Chapter 6

As the starlit sky gave way to dawn, Luke leaned across the roof of the car, his thoughtless stare transfixed on the glowing horizon to the east.

He rubbed his eyes and stretched. His night had been restless. It took a while to fall asleep and he dozed for only a few hours before a barking dog woke him. That was about two in the morning. After that, he never was able to get back to sleep. His mind constantly worked through all the different things that could have happened to Bonnie. None made sense, and he came to the same conclusion each time; something was horribly wrong. He wouldn't allow himself to consider anything beyond that.

After a long drink from a bottle of water he realized that he really needed to take a leak. Though the streets were still deserted, he wouldn't piss right there; it would be best to find an alley. He locked the car and crossed the street to the sidewalk in front of the clinic where he walked toward the end of the block. Next to the clinic he came to an empty storefront with a *For Lease* sign that hung on the dirty plate glass doors. Inside the store, brown paper covered all of the windows from the ground to about six feet high, hiding whatever was inside.

He slowed when he came to an area where the tape had lost its hold and one corner of the paper had partially fallen. When he peeked inside he could barely make anything out since the windows were dirty and a large cabinet blocked most of his view. So, with pressing business at hand, he walked on. At the end of the building, he turned and went down half a block to the alley. The cool morning breeze hit him in the face and old yellowed newspapers cart wheeled toward him like tumbleweeds. Half a dozen brown dumpsters dotted the alley intermittently and weeds grew in the cracks of the pavement against the building.

While he looked for an appropriate corner, he noticed graffiti on the back door of the vacant building. It wasn't the common gang script as he'd seen in big cities, like Austin, but written more in the style of a sixth-grader with a can of spray paint. *LNR loves CB* was legible across the top and below it was a pretty good drawing of two dogs having sex, missionary style. If Luke weren't so tired, he would have laughed.

Then something weird caught his eye. The back door of the vacant store appeared to have been opened recently because some weeds growing next to the building were closed inside the door. This was interesting since the front door looked like it had not been opened for a year or more. For the hell of it, he tried the handle. And as expected, it was locked.

He walked a little further and ducked behind a dumpster and unzipped his pants. While he peed, he heard a faint, muffled cry. He twisted his head around and stood motionless, and focused on the noise. After he finished he stayed still and listened. Ten silent seconds later, he heard it again. It was coming from the dumpster.

He stepped on the side and lifted the lid. A small orange cat lay curled up on a pile of bulging black garbage bags about three feet below the lid. The cat meowed at Luke, stood up and meowed again.

"Come on Kitty," Luke said as he opened the lid fully.

The cat wasted no time. He sprang and landed on the edge of the dumpster about three feet away, then jumped to the ground. It casually trotted down the alley a dozen steps then stopped and looked back, as if to thank him, and then slowly sauntered away.

Luke started to close the lid when he noticed one of the plastic bags had a tear in it, and a patch of burnt orange caught his eye. He grabbed the bag and tore at the plastic. The single item in the bag spilled out onto the dumpster lid sending a shiver down his spine.

It was an all-too-familiar windbreaker with The University

of Texas Longhorns embroidered across the back. Bonnie's windbreaker. The one she never left home without.

His heart began to pound as he held it up and examined it. Near the collar, a dark red stain about four inches long stained the fabric.

Luke dropped it onto the pavement, frantically pulled out another bag, and tore it open. Junk mail, copy paper, large brown envelopes torn in half and magazines slid out. He grabbed the next one. Soda cans, an empty box that earlier had been filled with donuts, chicken bones, and a box that said Lean Cuisine Glazed Chicken across the front. He ripped into the next one; damp paper towels and tissues spilled out and then his fingers felt something slimy. He almost gagged as he jerked his hands back. He was about to reach back for another bag when he felt something hard poked him in the leg.

Startled, he jerked his leg away and looked down to see a man looking up at him. He was a bum with a scraggly gray beard, wearing a dirty blue trench coat and black fedora. In one hand he held a crutch, the end of it pointed up at Luke.

"What 'cha doing up there?" the bum said, not smiling.

"Just looking," Luke said as he cautiously watched the bum. Then, looking back in the dumpster, he thought quickly, and added, "Just looking for something I lost."

The bum looked away from Luke, down the alley. Luke followed his gaze and saw two more people halfway down the block looking in other dumpsters. He shifted his focus back to Luke and stepped closer, "Come on, man. What ya looking for?"

Luke jumped down, away from the bum, and stumbled backwards a few steps. When he gained his balance he looked toward the other bums and noticed they were running in his direction. One was a stout guy with a beard that covered most his face and could have easily hidden a bird's nest. He was about thirty yards away, and closing fast. Under one arm he carried a bedroll. The other was a squatty little woman no more than four feet tall, running as fast as her short legs would carry her.

Luke stepped over and looked to where he had dropped the windbreaker and noticed it was gone. He saw it in the bum's other hand.

"Give me that," he said, jerking it out of the grasp of the bum, who cowered as if Luke was going to hit him.

Luke saw the others closing in.

"You don't look like the type to be hanging around in alleys," the bum with the crutch said. He apprised Luke's silver watch, clean shorts and Columbia shirt. "Especially before six in the morning."

As the bearded one approached he slowed to a trot then walked around behind Luke, as if to surround him.

Slowly Luke took a few steps backwards, trying to position himself where he could see them both. They watched him the same way a dog watches someone eat a barbecued rib.

The little woman finally got there, huffing and out of breath. She made her way between her partners and stopped directly in front of Luke.

The bearded one glanced at her, and then to Luke. "Come on, Bud. What were you looking for? People like you don't just look in dumpsters unless you're looking for something really good."

Luke didn't answer because the woman stepped closer. He could tell she had an attitude. In a nasally voice, she turned to her bearded friend and said, "Shut up, Griz, I'll handle this." Her head spun around toward Luke and she pointed a finger at him. "Listen, cocksucker, this is my fucking alley and I don't remember you asking me if you can come looking in these here dumpsters."

"Wait a second, Queenie," the bearded one interrupted. "I bet he'll cut us in on it. Won't you, Bud?"

Shooting an annoyed look at her bearded friend, Queenie scolded him. "Griz, when I want your opinion, I'll tell ya. Now shut the fuck up." She looked back at Luke and stepped a little closer. "So what's the deal, prettyboy? Why are you in my alley at six in the morning?"

This unlikely trio didn't appear to be dangerous, but Luke had never been confronted by homeless people, and he was obviously on their turf.

"I'm sorry. I didn't know I was supposed to ask anyone. I was looking for this," he said, hold out the windbreaker for Queenie to see. "It belongs to my wife."

He started walking briskly for the street and they followed. The faster he walked, the faster they walked. When he was directly behind the vacant building, Luke spotted a piece of bright green paper on the ground. He stopped and reached down to pick it up.

The bums stopped too.

The paper was folded in half and Luke unfolded it and read: lettuce, tomatoes, bread, mayo. It was Bonnie's half of the grocery list that he had put in the outside pocket of her purse.

The threat of the bums instantly evaporated as he tried to make sense of this. *Why would this note from Bonnie's purse be in this alley?*

His eyes scanned the ground. A few feet away he saw a pair of smashed sunglasses. He picked them up. Little silver hearts adorned each arm and were still intact and shiny. The lenses were shattered and the arms were splintered. He turned them over and saw the name Brighton inscribed on the inside of one arm. Lots of Bonnie's jewelry was made by Brighton. She loved everything they made.

Suddenly he felt the presence of the bums. They gathered around him, trying to see what he had in his hand. When he looked at them, they stared back, a curious look on their faces.

Finally, the bearded one smiled and said, "So…what's up, bud? Did you find what you were looking for?"

Luke hesitated and then said, "I don't know. Maybe."

Queenie said, "What do you fucking mean, 'you don't know'? Either you fucking did or you didn't. Which is it, prettyboy?"

"I'm looking for my wife. She disappeared yesterday." Luke

held out the glasses. "These were hers."

"What do you mean, she disappeared?" asked Queenie. "This ain't New York City. People don't just fucking disappear in Cardston."

"While she was waiting to see the doctor in the clinic, I left for an hour and when I came back, she was gone."

They watched him as he studied the green piece of paper and the mangled sunglasses.

"The last time I saw her, she had this piece of paper with her. And this is her windbreaker and these are her sunglasses."

This puzzled Queenie. "People don't just fucking disappear from the doctor's office."

"I know. But she did. The police are looking, but they haven't found anything. These are the first clues we've found."

"Do you think she's in that dumpster? Is that why you were up there?" asked the guy with the crutch.

"Shut up, Doc, you fucking dumbass," Queenie snapped at her friend. Then she looked back at Luke and said, "So, what 'cha gonna do now?"

"I guess I'm going to go to the police and show them what I found," he said as he started walking toward the street.

The trio hurried along with him as they exited the alley and made their way back to Second Street. Doc walked along side Luke and he couldn't help but notice that he wasn't using his crutch.

Doc noticed his attention and said, "My neurotetronitus isn't bothering me much today. That's why I'm not using my crutch."

Luke glanced toward Queenie with a confused look. She shook her head in disgust. "He's a fucking idiot."

"It is, Queenie," the man said pleadingly.

"Whenever someone asks him what's wrong he always makes up some fucking disease. He thinks he's a fucking doctor. There ain't nothing wrong with him. He just uses that fucking crutch so people will feel sorry for him and give him some money."

Luke gave her a knowing nod and kept walking.

Her short legs made it hard to keep up with Luke's pace. She broke into a trot and said, "We can help you look for her if you want us to," The other two nodded in agreement as they crossed the street. "You know, we don't got nothing else to do."

"Thanks, I can use all the help I can get." Luke approached the car and punched the button of his keychain and the door locks popped up. Luke noticed the stack of pictures lying on the backseat and considered it. *It couldn't hurt,* he thought. He opened the back door and grabbed one of the pictures of Bonnie and handed it to the little woman.

"Her name's Bonnie…and my name's Luke. If you see or hear anything, could you let the police know about it?"

As she started to look at it, the other two looked over her shoulder at the photo. "She pretty," Queenie said softly, the other two nodding in agreement.

Luke watched them as they studied the picture and couldn't help but notice their meager possessions. Ragged clothes and bedrolls appeared to be all they owned in life.

As he turned to close the back door of the car he saw a paper sack full of groceries. Bonnie had packed it for their lunch the day before. There wasn't much, just peanut butter, jelly, and crackers, which is why Bonnie had wanted him to go to the grocery store. He pulled it out and handed it to Griz.

"Take this food? I'm not going to eat it."

They glanced at each other, and Griz said, "Sure, bud."

On the floor in the backseat, he saw the small Styrofoam ice chest. He pulled it out and set it on the curb in front of Doc. He opened the lid and said, "There's some orange juice, fruit and other stuff in there, too."

Luke got in his car and pulled out onto the street. Griz held up two fingers in a piece sign and said, "Right on, brother."

Luke tried to smile, but his heart wouldn't let him. As he drove away, he glanced at the broken sunglasses and blood on the windbreaker. He knew he had to find Bonnie before it was too late.

Chapter 7

She was in a dimly lit hallway. The ceiling was low, just a few inches above her head. There was a closed door at each end. There was an eerie silence as she looked from one door to the other, unsure what to do. The door on one end opened and an old man stepped out. He had scraggly white hair and a long hooked nose. With an evil eye, he scowled at her and pulled a stethoscope out of his ragged coat. She backed up a step then turned to the door behind her. It opened and the same man stepped out into the hallway, holding the same stethoscope.

Bonnie blinked hard and woke up gasping. It was just a dream. Wild, vivid dreams had been part of her life since she was a kid. She exhaled loudly and immediately forgot about the dream when she became aware of the severe pain in her temples. It felt like her head was in a vice. Her natural reaction was to squeeze her eyes shut, but that made it hurt more. She rolled her head to the side and opened her eyes a little. Bright lights from a window across the room made her close them again.

She flung her arm across her eyes and the brightness disappeared.

Never in her life had a headache hurt this bad. She took a deep breath and slowly rolled away from the window wondering why her head hurt so much. She buried her face in the soft pillow and slid her hand underneath it causing her thumb to bend back. Instantly she recoiled from the pain, pulling it back and putting it in full view of her squinting eyes.

What the hell? There was some kind of plastic contraption on her wrist and hand. Where did that come from and why did her hand hurt so much. Again, she closed her eyes and let her head drop back onto the pillow.

For a bit she tried to think, concentrate on what happened,

but her mind was too foggy. Then she realized she had her shoes on. And her shorts. *All* of her clothes. What was going on? What time was it, morning? And where's Luke?

She groaned and with her other hand reached over to the other side of the bed and felt for Luke. But, he wasn't there. Slowly, she propped herself up on one elbow and glanced around the room through the narrow slits in her eyes. There was nothing that looked familiar about this room. Her thoughts were coming more clearly now. She knew they were on vacation in Montana but the last motel room she remembered had white walls. This one had beams of wood, like a log cabin.

There was an old wooden dresser and mirror next to a door, which was probably the closet. On the adjacent wall was a small table beside a leather chair. Next to it bright sunlight came through a window covered by cream colored curtains. On the wall closest to the bed was a door.

"Luke?" she said weakly toward it.

There was no response.

Bonnie swung her legs over the edge of the bed and sat up. When she tried to stand she felt the blood drain from her head and she thought she might pass out. She dropped back onto the mattress, winded. For a minute she took deep breaths and regained her strength.

"Luke?" she said a little louder.

Still nothing.

After a minute she slowly rose and shuffled to the door. The handle was old and brass, a dark tarnished copper color. She twisted on it but it didn't turn. *Is it locked? Why?*

"Hello?" she said to the door.

There was no noise of any kind. No clocks ticking, no electrical appliances running, no TV off in another part of the house…nothing. She was alone, and locked in a strange bedroom.

While she waited, she eyed the handle closer. Under it was an old-fashioned keyhole. The kind that used a skeleton key.

Why would the door be locked?

Maybe the handle's just stuck. She grasped the handle with both hands and twisted it. Then she pushed and pulled. It wouldn't budge.

This small amount of activity exhausted her so she propped herself against the door and this time, a little louder said, "Hello?"

Still nothing.

She knocked a few times. "Luke?"

She knocked louder. "Luke? Are you there?"

Nothing.

It didn't make sense. She rubbed her pounding temples and tried to think, but nothing was clear. Looking at the contraption on her wrist she knew it was some kind of brace and when she moved her thumb pain shot up her arm. The memory of falling down the hillside returned. And she remembered the neighbors drinking wine on the patio. And Luke joined them.

But it hurt to think.

She started toward the other side of the room but felt light headed, so she dropped down into the leather chair to catch her breath. Across the room she saw a digital alarm clock on a nightstand that said 6:23. She pulled open the curtains to behold an amazing sight. Beautiful mountains covered with pristine forest as far as she could see. Between the mountains, a rocky canyon snaked between jagged cliffs. There was not a sign of civilization. No roads, no houses, no telephone poles; nothing but forest and mountains. It was beautiful, but where was she?

Looking down she noticed the ground was far below, maybe a hundred feet. *The house must be on a cliff.*

She let the curtains fall closed and she noticed a cardboard box in the corner beside the window. Inside it she saw bottled water, granola bars, bread, grape jelly, peanut butter, and a plastic spoon.

She started back to the door and caught a glimpse of

herself in the mirror above the dresser. From the way she felt, she thought she'd look worse. Her nose was red and in the corner of her mouth she saw something crusty. With her fingernail, she scraped at it and small flecks came free. *Blood?* When she pressed her lip together they felt tender and swollen, but she didn't remember hurting them in the fall.

On the dresser she noticed a dish with two different kinds of pills. Beside them was a short typed note:

– The light blue pills are for your upset stomach. Take one morning, noon and night.
– The white capsules will relieve the pain in your sprained thumb. Take one every four hours with food.

Unconsciously, she rotated her thumb, and it sparked the memory of her visit to the clinic in Cardston. A few other memories came back too but weren't clear. Like the guards at the border crossing and the big Indian man at the clinic. But those memories faded as quickly as they came.

She took one of each pill and pulled a bottle of water out of the box on the floor. After she took them, she went back and stretched out on the bed.

Her eyelids grew heavy and as she started to drift off, she wondered, *Where is Luke?*

Chapter 8

"Ernest isn't in right now. What can I do for you?" asked the skinny officer who stood at the coffeemaker with the carafe in mid-pour.

"I really need to talk to him. I'm Luke Wakefield."

"Oh, you're the guy whose wife is missing. Did you find her?"

"No, but I found some stuff behind the clinic and I need to talk to Ernest about it."

"Ernest had to go over to Medicine Hat for a meeting. He didn't say when he'd be back." The cop finished filling his cup and dropped in two cubes of sugar. He pulled a pen out of his shirt pocket and started to stir. "Anything I can do for you?"

Luke laid the windbreaker, the broken sunglasses, and the piece of chartreuse paper on the counter in front of the Mountie. Holding up the windbreaker and pointing to the red stain, Luke said, "This was my wife's. Look here. Blood. I found this in the dumpster behind the clinic in a plastic bag. Someone had thrown it away."

"Was there any blood on this before?"

"No."

"Did anyone say anything about this to you at the clinic?"

Luke shook his head. "No."

Luke pointed to the other items. "And look at this. These sunglasses and this grocery list were in her purse when I left her. I found both of them in the alley."

The cop put down his coffee and looked at the glasses without touching them. Then, by using his pen, he rotated the piece of small piece of paper around and read aloud, "Lettuce, tomatoes, bread, mayo. Do you think she was she going to go to the grocery store after she left the clinic?"

"No, the receptionist said she checked her out in the front

of the clinic. There would be no reason for my wife to have been in the alley. It's obvious someone was trying to hide this windbreaker. And it didn't have blood on it when we got to the clinic. Don't you think it's proof that they're hiding something over at the clinic?"

The cop raised one eyebrow. "Leave the detective work to us, Mr. Wakefield."

"Don't you think you should send some cops over there to question the people at the clinic?"

"Ernest will make that decision."

"What are we going to do?"

"*We* aren't going to do anything. Like I said, when Ernest gets back, I'll give this to him and he'll make that decision." He rummaged around under the counter and came up with a plastic bag. He picked up the windbreaker, shopping list and sunglasses and put them inside.

"My wife has been missing for over eighteen hours. Somebody needs to do something pretty quick."

The cop took a deep breath and in a consoling tone said, "We have done something. The information about your wife has been sent to all RCMP outposts and all other law enforcement agencies. At this time, there's not a lot more than that we can do. Okay?"

"I'm positive that if she was in the alley, it wasn't of her own free will."

"Mr. Wakefield, I understand you are worried, But, there's nothing else we can do at this time. Do you understand what I'm saying?"

It seemed clear that until Ernest came back, there was nothing he could do. He took a deep breath and said, "I guess so."

Chapter 9

Luke left the building mad and frustrated. As he slid into the car he was suddenly aware of how much his body ached. Sleeping in the car hadn't worked out too well. He decided there was nothing he could do here so he might as well go back to St. Mary for a while.

It took about forty-five minutes to get back to the Red Eagle Lodge. His first stop was to talk to the owner, Mrs. Johnson. The day before he had called and told her about Bonnie's disappearance. In the process of planning their trip, Bonnie had talked to her on the phone numerous times and said she felt a connection to her. She told Luke she was like the grandmother she never had.

"I've been worried sick ever since you called yesterday," she told Luke. "We've been renting to tourists for over thirty years and we've never had anything like this happen."

"The people at the RCMP said the same thing, but they don't seem to be doing much," Luke said. "I'm going to shower and rest a while. It might be best to get a room over there."

"I understand how you feel, but let me warn you—tourist season is at its peak right now and there aren't many rooms available to rent."

"I don't care if I have to sleep in the car. I just need to be there."

On the way to his room he saw Jack and Christina putting their suitcases in the Hummer. Luke told them what had happened and asked Jack if he had any contacts in Cardston.

"Man, I'm no help at all. I've done very little business in Canada. I don't know anyone with the RCMP, no private investigators or even any lawyers in Cardston or the area. But, I have a friend in Calgary I can call," Jack said. He reached in his wallet and pulled out a business card. On the back he scribbled a number. "That's my cell phone number. We're on our way home so give me a call tomorrow and I'll let you know what I find out."

Luke said he would and went to his room. After a hot shower he collapsed on the bed and within minutes he was asleep.

Five hours later there was a knock on the door. He bolted upright and saw at the clock. It was after two. He hadn't intended to sleep that long. Dressed only in his boxers, he cracked the door to see a young girl in blue jeans with a vacuum cleaner at her side.

"Give me ten minutes and I'll be out of here, okay?"

He dressed quickly and grabbed a quick lunch at the café before heading back to Cardston. As he approached the border he dreaded a repeat of the day before. But, none of the agents looked familiar and after he showed his passport and driver's license they passed him through without incident.

As soon as he got to Cardston he stopped at the police station. Ernest was back in his office and Luke asked him if he'd been given the items he found in the alley earlier that morning.

"When I called in, they told me you left them here and I told them to turn everything over to Paul Simpson. He's one of our officers here. We don't have a full time investigator but he's real good. I just got back a few minutes ago so I haven't talked to him yet."

"I'd really like to see what he's found out. He needs to go over to the clinic and see if he can get some answers. I found all that stuff in the alley behind it. And her windbreaker was in a garbage bag in the dumpster, like someone was trying to hide it. It needs to be checked for DNA and—"

"Luke, settle down. I know you want to help, but I think it's best if you just let us handle it, okay? Paul will get to it when he has time."

Luke screamed, "When he has time? What in the hell is more important than this? Writing parking tickets?" His blood was on the verge of boiling. "My God, Ernest, Bonnie's been missing for over twenty-four hours and you only have one person who's going to work on it *when he has time?*"

"No, there's a lot more happening than that," he said, trying to settle Luke down. "Trust me Luke; we're taking this very seriously. Every law enforcement agency in Alberta has been notified as well as personnel at all border crossing. Here in Cardston, every patrolman has her picture and we are looking all over the county. The sheriffs and highway patrolmen also have been briefed."

"I crossed the border about seven this morning and no one even noticed my name," he exclaimed. "I would think they'd notice my name if they were paying attention to this crap. It doesn't sound to me like they're taking it serious."

"They are looking for a woman, not a man. That's one reason they didn't pay attention to you."

Luke turned and stepped over to the window. He pulled off his cap and ran his hand through his dark hair while he thought. It seemed obvious that they weren't equipped to handle an investigation like this. "Is there a private detective around here I can hire?"

"No. The closest one you can find is probably in Calgary."

"So, what do I do now? Go to the motel and watch soap operas?"

"I know it's hard, but give us some time. There's not much to work with here. Paul's good and he's checking out that stuff you brought in. Let's just give him some time."

"I can help, Ernest."

Ernest shook his head. "Luke, give us a little time."

Chapter 10

The next time Bonnie woke it was almost eleven. The door was still locked and Luke was still not there. After knocking on the door and calling his name a few times she fell back onto the bed, still lethargic.

She had slept hard, this time not dreaming and hardly moving. Her mind went back to her last memories. It was being in the doctor's office. She got the drugs for her thumb and her stomach. And they gave her a tetanus shot. Maybe she had an allergic reaction or there were too many drugs or something, because she had never felt so wiped out in her life. It was still hard to wake up.

The pain in her thumb was not as bad as it had been, so the pills she took earlier were working. And even her stomach felt better. It had been about four hours and now it was time to take pills again.

She went to the dresser and picked up one of each of the pills. As she took them she grew curious and pulled open the top drawer. Inside she saw handkerchiefs, t-shirts, boxer shorts, and an old cigar box. This was definitely not a motel room. This was someone's private home. But how did she get here?

Inside the cigar box she saw pens, pencils, paper clips, and a key chain with several keys. A glimmer of hope crossed her mind, so she grabbed it. But the keyhole was too big. These keys were for small, modern locks.

Disappointed, she threw the keys back in the drawer and rambled through the rest of the contents. A handful of change, safety pins, a compass, an old belt buckle, and some shoelaces. The second drawer was less revealing: more clothes. In the bottom drawer was an insulated jump suit.

She opened the closet door. It was small and almost empty. On a hanging rod were about six hangers with a few jackets and flannel shirts. On the closet floor was a cardboard box full of old books and magazines. In the corner she saw an empty plastic bucket and a roll of toilet paper.

Surely not. Did someone expect her to stay in this room with only a bucket for her relief? The mere thought just about gagged her. Did this mean she was going to be here a while?

She unconsciously shook her head and continued to look. Above the hanging rod was a shelf, empty except for a blanket and an extra set of sheets.

Before she closed the door, Bonnie caught sight of the bucket again and it made her realize she needed to go. But, she was going to hold out as long as she could.

Her mind seemed to be functioning more clearly now. *It's very clear that I am in a strange house with the door locked and no memory of how I got here. There's enough food in that box to last for days, I have a bucket to use for a bathroom, and there's no sign of Luke. If I was safe someone would have left me a note explaining the situation. Considering those facts, all I know is that I need to get out of here as soon as I can.*

Her mind began to look for answers. How do I get out of here? The window was not an option because the ground was too far down, so that left the door. In the closet she saw several old wire hangers. In old movies, she'd seen them use hangers to jimmy locks on old doors.

She straightened one out, put a little bend in the end of it, and inserted it into the keyhole. She pushed it, pulled it, turned it, jabbed it, yanked it, and shoved it. Nothing. She tried bending it differently, but that didn't help either. After half an hour, she grew frustrated and she pushed the wire harder and wilder. Finally, the wire snagged something and wouldn't give. She jammed on it and pulled back but it was still stuck. Wrapping both hands around it, she put all of her weight into it and yanked. Her grip failed and the jagged wire slipped through her clinched hands, tearing flesh as she fell back.

Bonnie stumbled and screamed in agony. Looking down at her hands she saw several long pink lines of exposed flesh where wire ripped away her skin. Blood began to ooze, and the pink slashes turned red.

Her chest heaved as tears filled her eyes. She clenched her burning hands tightly and stepped back and kicked the door. Then kicked it again. "Let me out of here." she yelled.

Furious now, she knew she needed more force. She looked in the closet and saw the box of books. She grabbed the top two and flung them at the door. They hit the door where the hanger was and it fell out and bounced on the floor beside the books.

Maybe it sprung the lock. She rushed over and twisted the door handle and pulled.

Still locked.

Hysterical now, she grasped the next book out of the box. It was Ken Follett's 973 page epic, *Pillars of the Earth*. Using both hands she poised to throw it at the door, but stopped. It would do no good. The door was too sturdy; there was no way she was going to break it down with a book. She lowered it and turned away. Across the room, she saw bright light flooding through what was probably the only other exit. She took three quick steps, and, like an Olympic shot putter, let the book fly.

The lower two windowpanes exploded and the book disappeared out of sight. Her heart pounded as she ran over and looked out the window to get a full view of her surroundings.

She leaned out and looked down. As she feared, the cabin appeared to be perched on the edge of a cliff. The ground was far below. She grabbed another book and dropped it. It took at least three seconds to reach the rocky canyon below.

"Help," she screamed, her voice echoing through the mountains. Five seconds later she cupped her hands around her mouth and yelled again. "Can anyone hear me? Help me!"

Nothing. No one yelled back. No cars engines started. Not one sound from the civilized world.

Bonnie's heart sank. Slowly she backed away and dropped on the bed. Blankly her eyes fell to the floor that was now littered with pieces of the broken window.

Her heart sank and she sat in silence. Nothing made any sense. Why was she here and where was Luke. He wouldn't allow this to happen.

After a few minutes she got a t-shirt from the dresser and used it to wipe the broken glass under the bed.

It was then she realized how hungry she was, so she grabbed an apple out of the box and just before she took a bite, a distant rumble pierced the silence. Quickly she moved to the window and listened. It was a faint, low whine that sounded like the engine of a vehicle. It moaned, the pitch changing as it accelerated and slowed, probably for curves or inclines on the mountain roads. This was the first sound, other than her own voice, she had heard since she woke just after dawn.

She tensed with anticipation. Finally, someone was coming for her. *It has to be Luke.*

But, as the sound grew louder, it became painfully clear that it wasn't their rented Chrysler Sebring. It was probably a truck, she thought. The noise grew louder and louder, until finally there was no doubt it was coming to her.

The sound came closer and closer, until it was so close, it was just outside. She could hear gravel crunch under the tires as it came to a stop. The engine idled a second, then everything went quiet.

She prayed that the next thing she heard was Luke's voice.

A door opened, then slammed.

Footsteps crunched on gravel, but there was no hurry in them. The cadence was nothing like Luke's.

She began to tremble.

Bonnie turned from the window to the door. She inched a step closer.

In the distance, a latch mechanism tumbled as a door was unlocked. Hinges squeaked like a door opening.

Bonnie was an optimist and wanted to believe someone was there to help her. She wanted to call out to whoever was there. Tell them to unlock the door. Instead, every terrifying novel she had ever read came to mind. All the fictional characters created by Dean Koontz, Steven King and James Patterson suddenly became real. She thought about all the sadistic murderers that dismembered their victims, the serial killers who tortured and killed random strangers, the kidnappers who lock their prey in old farm houses where rats nibbled on their fingers and toes when they became too weak to fight back.

But, no, she told herself, nothing like that could happen to her. They were on vacation. There's a simple explanation for this. It would all be okay.

Then, at once, the door was slammed with the force of a freight train. The entire cabin rattled.

Bonnie gasped. And stepped back.

The same door squeaked again, and now she heard a loud growl as the door was slammed again. Two more times it was opened and slammed with the force of a rabid gorilla.

Bonnie couldn't move. Her heart began to hammer as she backed away from her door.

Footsteps now on the wooden floor came closer. Heavy steps, like hiking boots. *Definitely a man's walk, but definitely not Luke's.*

Now, just on the other side of the door, they stopped. His breathing was loud and guttural, almost a low growl. She saw the door handle turn, just a little. And then the other way. She heard him push and pull the door as if checking to see if it was securely closed.

Then she heard something, it was like a hoarse whisper. Words, but they were inaudible. She inched closer to hear. He whispered something again, but not quite loud enough.

She slowly stepped closer, trying to understand.

Then, as if a bomb went off, he attacked the door while growling viciously.

Bonnie screamed and jumped back. For ten seconds it sounded as if the door would fly off its hinges. Like the mad man was beating both open hands against the door. Two large pictures, one on each side of the door, crashed to the floor and the glass in the frames exploded into a million pieces.

The entire cabin shook. Without even realizing it, Bonnie ran to the other side of the bed, and wedged herself into the corner, fearful the door would fly off and the beast would have her.

Then it quit.

Now all Bonnie heard was his breathing.

A few seconds later, footsteps moved away from the door.

She waited. She looked out the window again and wondered if he came after her, would falling to her death be less painful than being tortured by this madman.

A moment later, in the distance, a chair scooted on the wooden floor. Silence followed. But, after a minute, footsteps came back and a sheet of lined yellow paper slid under the door. On it was only one handwritten line. In large capital letters, it read:

DO YOU WANT TO LIVE?

For a few seconds she couldn't comprehend what it meant.

She had no idea what to do or say. She wanted to ask a million questions. *Who are you? Why am I being held? What did I do to deserve this? What do you want with me?*

Words wouldn't come. Five seconds passed and as her mouth opened to speak, her lip quivered uncontrollably.

She had to say something. She licked her lips and stepped closer to the door to answer.

It was too late. Violent pounding erupted, accompanied by the same growl.

Bonnie screamed while trying to back away from the door, lost her balance and fell back. Her natural reaction was to break her fall by using her hands and when she did, it felt like an electrical jolt hit her in the injured thumb. Another picture by the dresser fell off the wall and the frame shattered, spraying glass all around her.

The growling stopped but the pounding got louder and harder. The door bounced in the frame. It was going to splinter.

Terrified, she scooted back further and with a burst of air, screamed, "Yes!"

The pounding stopped at once.

As she pulled her throbbing thumb against her body, another note slid under the door:

YOU WILL LIVE IF YOU DO WHAT I TELL YOU.
DO YOU UNDERSTAND?

Meekly she answered. "Yes."
Another note was slid into view:

YOU HAVE FOOD AND DRINK.
DO NOT TRY TO ESCAPE.
WE WILL GIVE YOU MORE INSTRUCTIONS LATER.

Bonnie read the note but was still struggling to understand what was happening. "Can you tell me why I'm here?"

NO QUESTIONS.

But, she asked one anyway. "Can I go to the bathroom?"

NO.

Through her tears she whined, "I won't try to escape."

IF YOU TRY TO ESCAPE I WILL KILL YOU.

"I promise I won't."

NOTHING IS NEGOTIABLE.

DO YOU UNDERSTAND?

Fighting back tears, she said, "Yes."
There were no more notes.
While she sat on the floor trembling, she heard him walk out the front door.

Chapter 11

Give them time. Luke was afraid Bonnie didn't have time.

He parked across from the clinic as he had the day before. He went down Main Street, showing Bonnie's picture in every store he passed and asking if they'd seen her.

After half a dozen stores he came to the camera store. Through the window he saw Sonny at the counter, and went inside.

"Last night I told a group of friends about your wife and passed out the pictures," Sonny said. "They said they'd pass her picture around. So, the word is out. We'll have the whole town looking for her before long."

"You don't know how much I appreciate it."

"Luke, I was raised in this town and know everyone here. Later today, I'm going to the St. Mary store. I'll post a picture in the window there, too. Having a business on both sides of the border I've got contacts everywhere, in all walks of life. I can probably find out stuff the cops can't. Keep me posted on what's going on, okay?"

"I will. Thanks."

As Luke started down the street, he thought about his first impression of Sonny. After Bonnie's run-in with him, he was convinced Sonny was a jerk. But looking at it from Sonny's point of view, he had reason to be upset. And now, he was going out of his way to help. Obviously they had misjudged him.

Luke went back to the street and after a while came to the Sportsman's Outfitter. Inside he spied Lauren sitting at her desk. As he opened the door, she looked up and smiled. "I was about to give up on you."

"I'm sorry, but a lot has happened since I was here," he said walking over to her desk. "Yesterday, while I was here, my wife was at the clinic waiting to see a doctor. She had taken a fall and we came over here to get her thumb X-rayed. While she waited to see a doctor, I ran a few errands. That's when I found your store."

"How's her thumb?"

"I don't know. When I went back to the clinic, they said she had already checked out and left. I went out to our rental car and waited but she never showed up. I looked for her all afternoon and never did find her. I even slept in the car last night hoping she'd show up. But she didn't. She just disappeared."

"Oh, my God. Did you go to the RCMP?"

"I did. I talked to the guy in charge over there and he put out a missing-person report. He said nothing like this has ever happened in Cardston."

"I've lived in this town most of my life and he's right, I can't remember anything like that ever happening here. It's a safe place...so safe it's boring."

Luke said, "I just left the camera store and the manager is doing some stuff to help me. He seems like a pretty nice guy."

Lauren averted her eyes and looked out the window. "Yeah, he can be nice."

"I guess you know him? Sonny?"

"Oh, yeah," she scoffed. "We dated in high school and college."

"Then I guess he's someone I can trust?"

She considered it briefly. "I guess so…"

"You don't sound so sure."

"Our relationship didn't end too well and we haven't spoken in almost fifteen years."

That shocked Luke. How could you avoid someone for fifteen years in a town this small? There was obviously some bad blood between them, but it didn't have anything to do with his problem. Thinking about the way Sonny lost his temper talking to Bonnie, he could see how the he might be hard to get along with. Just the mention of his name seemed to strike a nerve, and she looked like there was something she wanted to say.

"That's interesting. The reason I ask is because Bonnie had a little run-in with him over at his store in St. Mary and he seemed like a real jerk. But, when I went to his store over here, he seemed like a nice guy. He even went out of his way to stay open late and make some pictures for me. And said he was going to pass them around to some of his friends. From the way he talked, I thought he'd be a good contact here in Cardston. Am I wrong in thinking that?"

Lauren quickly backed off. "No, not at all. Sonny does know a lot of people around here. He's a good contact. He can probably get information the police can't."

"Yeah, that's what he said, and I can use all the help I can get."

"But, when talking to him, don't mention my name. We do everything we can to avoid each other."

"I'll remember that." Luke remembered the photos and held one out to Lauren. "Would you mind putting this in your window or on your counter so people could see it?"

Lauren took it and looked at Bonnie's picture. "She beautiful."

"Yes, she is."

As Luke stood and walked back to the door to leave, Lauren said, "If there's anything I can do, please let me know."

Luke nodded and stepped outside. On the sidewalk a young couple approached, both wearing matching t-shirts, obviously brand new, that said Glacier National Park on them. He held out the picture of Bonnie.

"This is a picture of my wife. She disappeared yesterday." They took the photo and glanced at it. "If you see anyone that looks like her please give the police a call. The number's there on the bottom."

They gave him a sympathetic look as he turned and walked away.

An hour later, out of pictures, he went back to his car. He

got in and leaned his head back against the headrest. *What else can I do?* He'd been in every business in town. Driving, he'd crisscrossed every street from east to west and north to south to the point that the residents probably wondered why he kept driving by their houses. The RCMP said they put the word out all over the province and told him now he'd just have to wait.

But wait for what? Bonnie had been gone for more than thirty hours. *Did someone abduct her? Was she dead now?* He pressed his fingers against his eyes holding his eyelids tight. He would not cry. Bonnie was OK. He had to believe.

At about seven, he got a burger at the diner and ate it in the car back in front of the clinic. At eleven he drove back to St. Mary.

Chapter 12

Bonnie dropped into the corner and pulled her knees up to her chest. Trails from her tears streaked her face. Across the room light reflected off tiny pieces of glass scattered across the floor from the broken picture frames. The man's violent performance left her more terrified than she had ever been in her life.

From where she sat, she saw the notes on the floor. If she didn't do what he said, he'd kill her. But what would she have to do? She could only imagine the worst. Why else would he lock her away and terrorize her?

Regardless of what he said, somehow, some way, she had to escape.

From the violent attack she just witnessed, she knew there was no way she could break down the door, so her only escape was through the window. She went over and looked out. The ground seemed too far but in old movies she had seen people escaping through windows by tying bed sheets together. On the shelf in the closet, she pulled out the extra set of sheets, there were two. Including the ones on the bed, that made four. If she tied them all together, she'd have about twenty feet of rope. But that would leave her dangling at least fifty feet above the ground. There were some rocky ledges on the way down and if she swung she might be able to land on one. But if she missed, she'd fall to her death. No way would that work.

Bonnie threw the sheets back in the closet and went back to the window. Maybe she could go up. If she stood in the window, she could reach the top of the outside wall, but there was nothing to hold onto to pull herself up on the roof. So, that wouldn't work. And moving along the side of the building was not an option either because there was nowhere to stand and nothing to hold on to.

That meant there was only one way out—the door. She had to pick the lock.

Off and on for the rest of the afternoon she worked with the clothes hanger, but had no luck. As darkness fell, she stood at the window and listened to the mournful howl of the wind. When the cool air started to flow into the room Bonnie regretted breaking the window. She curled up under the blanket on the bed and tried to sleep, but the wind made the darkness come alive. Desperate to feel safe, she grabbed the blankets, sheets and pillows and retreated into the closet where she shut the door on the cold and wind and the mountain sounds.

In the morning she woke and stepped into the cool bedroom, bright from the morning sun. She felt better, much closer to normal that she did the day before. The alarm clock said it was almost nine. The curtains swayed in the gentle breeze and she parted them to see the blue, clear sky.

After a long night her bladder was full. She glanced over at the bucket and thought about her experience using the bucket the day before. It wasn't all that bad, but she decided she'd hold out as long as she could.

Her thoughts were interrupted by a sound of a truck engine in the distance.

Oh, no, she thought. He's coming back. A chill ran down her back when she thought about what was about to happen. Quickly, she put on her hiking boots, and when she bent to tie the laces, she noticed the broken glass from the day before.

Bonnie noticed a long pointed piece. It was at least eight inches long and looked sharp enough to pierce a hole in a tire. She pulled an old t-shirt out of the dresser and wrapped it around the wider part for a handle. Now she had a formidable weapon.

Creeping back to the window, she heard the truck getting closer. A minute later it was so close she could hear music.

There hadn't been music the day before. And this had the recurring beat of rap music. Not at all what she expected.

The sound got louder until she heard gravel crunched under the tires on the other side of the cabin as it came to a stop. Then the engine and the music fell silent. At once the truck door opened and closed, but it sounded different than the day before. Footsteps came quickly to the front door where she heard the mechanism in the door lock tumble. The door opened, and this time, closed gently.

Bonnie wiped her sweaty hand and gripped the crudely made knife. She turned it from side to side, wondering if she had the courage to use it at all. Her thoughts went to the last time she used a weapon. It was the first and last time she went deer hunting with Luke. She shot at a deer, but the animal moved just when she pulled the trigger and she hit it in the throat, only wounding it. The suffering animal thrashed about, making a god awful bleating sound, and blood spurted everywhere. The animal was suffering and its obvious pain was too much. She couldn't handle it. Luke sent her to the truck while he finished the job.

But this was different. It was her life and she had no choice. She would thrust the crudely crafted knife into the human being who said he'd kill her if she didn't do as he said.

Focusing her attention on her visitor, she positioned herself behind the door, ready to attack, and tried to calm her shaking hands.

Beyond the door, she heard shoes squeak as they moved about in the room beyond her prison. A chair some distance away scooted across the floor. A few seconds later, squeaky shoes came to her door and a piece of yellow lined paper slid into view. Leaning closer she read:

– Are you okay?

This note was written neatly with nice penmanship, all on one line. Yesterday it was scribbled in huge, crudely printed letters that filled the entire page.

She spoke to the door. "Yes."

On the other side of the door, it was silent. No movement, nothing. She took a chance. "I really need to go the bathroom."

On the other side of the door, she could hear scribbling, and a few seconds later the next note slid under the door:

– There is a bucket in the closet you have to use.

"I've done that once. Please don't make me do that again."
No answer.

She waited about half a minute before asking again. "Please, I just need to go to the bathroom. I won't try to run away."

No answer.

"How long am I going to be in here?"
No answer.

Begging, she asked, "Can you tell me why I'm here?"
No answer.

As the weight of her situation came crashing down on her, she began to whimper. She glanced at her glass knife and knew she couldn't use it. Quietly she put it in a dresser drawer. "Please, I don't want to die?"

From the light that shined under the door she could tell he was still standing just outside. Another note:

– Nobody's going to kill you.

Still crying, "Why am I here?" There was no answer and Bonnie could hear him shuffling around outside the door.

She waited, and again begged. "Could I please go to the bathroom? Please. I won't try anything. I promise. I just want to go to the bathroom. That's all."

No answer. She heard him walk away, which made her cry more.

He came back to the door. In a soft voice, he said, "Okay,

here's the deal: I'll let you go to the bathroom, but you have to do what I say. Take a pillowcase off of one of the pillows and put it over your head and I'll take you to the bathroom."

"Okay."

His voice was quiet, but firm. He sounded younger than she expected.

"But, if you try anything, I'll beat the crap out of you, gag you, and tie you up with duct tape. Do you want me to do that?"

"No. I promise I'll do exactly what you tell me to do."

She got one of pillowcases and put it over her head. After a quick prayer she stood in the middle of the room with her hands to her side, and said, "Okay, I'm ready."

Bonnie heard the key unlock the door and a faint squeak when it opened. Cool air rushed past her from the broken window.

She held her breath while she waited for him to come to her. Suddenly, he loudly blurted out, "Holy shit, lady. You busted out the window."

She cowed as he yelled at her. "I'm sorry. I'm sorry." Expecting to be slapped or hit, she pulled her arms up in front of her face.

"Man, when he sees this he's going to blow a gasket."

It was obvious he was referring to the animal who had been there the day before. "I was scared and I didn't know what to do," she explained. "And besides that, I couldn't put up with that nasty bucket in here so I dumped it out the window."

"He's gonna be pissed, I'll tell you that." He grabbed her by the wrist. "Come on."

As they left the room, she put her other hand out in front of her the way one does when moving in the dark.

It felt like they stepped outside the bedroom and turned right a few steps when suddenly there was a loud noise behind her, almost like an explosion.

She gasped and pulled her hand away.

The guy grabbed her hand and said, "It's okay. The wind

just made the door slam."

They continued another dozen steps and stopped. He moved behind her and gently grabbed her shoulders and pushed her forward a few more steps.

"Ma'am, do your business and do it fast. Keep your head covered and don't lock the door. If you do, I'll break the door down. You got it?"

She said okay and heard the bathroom door close behind her. Immediately, she pushed up the pillowcase and panned the room. In front of her was the toilet; to the left a prefab lavatory with cabinets on each side. The bathtub was on the right wall with a shower curtain. There was one small window above the toilet covered with thin white curtains.

Bonnie parted the curtains and saw a big red pickup with huge tires in the driveway. A long driveway went through an open meadow and disappeared into the forest about a hundred yards from the house. She tried to see the license plate but the truck was at the wrong angle. A large bush blocked her view in the other direction.

She checked the size of the window and estimated it was big enough for her to crawl through it if the glass was gone. But for now, she didn't consider trying to escape with him pacing on the other side of the door.

When she was finished she washed her hands and splashed some water on her face.

"C'mon," the guy said, pounding on the door.

"I'm almost done," she said, drying her hands. She pulled the pillowcase back down over her eyes and told him she was ready.

He grabbed her arm and led her back to her prison.

Bonnie tried to get more information as they walked. "What do you want from me?"

Irritated he said, "Damn lady. Quit asking me all these questions. I'm not even supposed to talk to you."

"But why me? Why—"

"Quit asking me questions, okay?" he demanded. "I can't

tell you anything because I don't know anything."

"But, how—"

"When that other guy comes back, don't tell him I let you go to the bathroom. Just keep your mouth shut. Whatever you do, don't try to break out of here and run away. Even if you get out, you'll never find your way back before the bears or wolves get you. The safest thing you can do is stay here. Okay?"

"What are you going to do to me?"

"No more questions." he said, pushing her back into the bedroom.

She knew he was put out with her but she couldn't help but ask one more question, "When are you coming back?"

The bedroom door slammed and locked. Seconds later, she heard him go out the front door. The truck started and roared away.

As the engine sounds faded in the distance, she stood at the window and thought about him. He sounded young, like a teenager. And called her "ma'am." He must have been there when they brought her to this cabin because he knew about the bucket.

With him, Bonnie felt safer. He gave her hope, but she was still a prisoner. And there was no doubt the worst was yet to come.

Chapter 13

"It doesn't seem to me like they're trying very hard and I can't sit over here doing nothing," Luke said to Mrs. Johnson. "I'm going to get a room in Cardston and camp out on the front door of the RCMP if I have to."

"I'm so worried about her. Please call me and tell me when you find her."

He nodded. She hugged him the way a mother would hug a son going off to college.

As he drove out of St. Mary, black clouds spilled over Gunsight Mountain and light rain peppered his windshield. The closer he got to the Canadian border, the harder it rained. Luke was glad he had taken the time to put a piece of cardboard over the broken window before he left. He breezed through the border checkpoint without a problem and drove on to the RCMP Detachment Office to see if they had any news.

"Hey Luke, I'm glad you're here," Ernest said. "Come with me. I want you to meet Paul. He's got some things he needs to talk to you about."

They entered a room that was empty except for a long wooden table with two chairs on each side. A manila folder was open with half a dozen pieces of paper scattered across the table. The man at the table rose as they entered. He was average height, barrel-chested with a round face and a full head of dark hair.

"Paul Simpson," he said, extending his hand to Luke.

His grip was firm and his smile was friendly.

Luke rounded the table and took a seat across from Paul. He noticed a long horizontal mirror on the opposite wall. Ernest closed the door and stood over by the wall.

"There are some things we need to go over," Paul said.

Among the papers in front of him, Luke saw copies of his and Bonnie's passports and driver's licenses. He didn't remember providing them.

As Paul picked through the papers, he casually asked, "Have you heard from your wife, Luke?"

Strange question, Luke thought. "No, I haven't."

Paul handed the missing persons report to Luke and asked him to verify all of the information. When he was finished he asked, "Is there anything else you can think of that might have happened or be important for us to know?"

"I don't think so."

Paul pulled out some other papers. "This is a report that says you assaulted your wife at the border crossing on Tuesday morning."

"I did not!" Luke exclaimed, realizing immediately where they got the copies of their passports and drivers licenses. "I explained it to the officers at the border station and so did Bonnie. We accidentally ran into each other and Bonnie fell over some chairs. I certainly did not assault her."

"This report says you were put in an interrogation room for a routine interview and you got into a fight while you were waiting. The report says you were arguing and then you hit her, knocking her down."

"That's not right."

Paul continued, "The agent's report says, 'We could hear them arguing down the hall. Upon entering the room I saw Mr. Wakefield strike Mrs. Wakefield, knocking her to the floor. We had to restrain Mr. Wakefield. During the altercation, Mrs. Wakefield injured her thumb and bloodied her lip.'"

"That's bullshit! Her thumb was already hurt."

Paul leaned back and looked at Ernest. "This is the report that was filed by the agents."

"I don't care what they filed. That's not what happened. She sprained her thumb the day before while she was jogging. And she scraped her hands and legs when she fell down the side of a hill. That's why we came over here—to go to the doctor."

"The report says you claim her thumb was already injured, but when you spoke to the first agent about entering Canada, you said your wife was sick. There was no mention of an injury to her hand."

"I didn't know I had to explain everything just to get across the border."

"The report states 'Mrs. Wakefield is a textbook example of a battered woman. She had scrapes and bruises on her arms and legs, including a busted lip and a bruise on her cheek. She would not file a complaint or call in the police, but it was obvious she feared her husband.'"

"Oh, come on." Luke turned his attention to Ernest who was leaning against a side wall, listening. "Ernest, that's total bullshit."

"It says you were separated from each other and the agent that interviewed Mrs. Wakefield said it was obvious she feared retaliation from you if she filed charges against you. There was nothing they could do but let you go."

Luke was on his feet. "None of it is true. Bonnie and I were talking about how those agents at the border crossing were treating us like criminals. That's why I was upset. Not upset with Bonnie, but upset with your people. And another thing: Bonnie would never say she was afraid of me."

"Have you ever hit your wife, Luke?" Ernest asked.

"Never."

"Luke, you've got a temper," Ernest said. "Is it common for you to lose it?"

"No." He knew he looked like a hothead, so he took a deep breath and calmly said, "Not unless I have a damn good reason and what you're saying is not right."

"Okay, sit down."

Luke eased back into his chair.

"It says that they heard Mrs. Wakefield tell you numerous times to settle down," Paul said as he lowered the report to the table.

"She may have said that because *your people* were treating us like criminals and they had no reason to."

"Ever been charged with assault, Luke?"

"Absolutely not!"

"How long have you been married?"

"About twenty years."

He leaned back in his chair and crossed his arms over his chest. "Has she been a good wife?"

Luke didn't like the way that sounded. "What do you mean?"

"Do you have to discipline her very much?"

Disgusted by his insinuations, Luke shook his head and rolled his eyes.

"So, how often do you hit her?"

"I've never hit her."

"Have you had any other problems over the past twenty years?"

"No."

"So, you say she's been a good wife…no problems?"

"We've never had any problems."

Paul leaned over the stack of papers in front of him and pulled out another one. "Not according to the deputies with the Lampasas County Sherriff's Department. They said you and your wife were separated recently."

Luke was shocked that they knew about this. "We were separated for a while, but we aren't anymore."

"Why were you separated?"

"I don't think it's any of your damn business."

Ernest intervened. "Luke, you have to tell us what's going on here."

He sighed and said, "It was something totally out of our control. It didn't have anything to do with our relationship. We're doing fine now."

"Now, why would you separate if everything was fine? Something's not right and what I see is a troubled marriage and a missing wife. Unless you can convince us you're telling the truth, we're going to have to hold you until we find her." Paul leaned back and tapped his pencil on the table. "We need you to explain this. And this time why don't you *start* with the truth."

Luke looked to Ernest for some help but noticed his eyes narrowed and locked on his, waiting. Luke knew it didn't sound too good, but all he had to do was explain things and they could get back to looking for Bonnie.

"When the drought hit Texas a few years ago it was really hard on us. We didn't have much grass in our pastures and had to sell most of our cattle. For a while we had some serious money problems. We were having trouble paying the bills and Bonnie wanted me to borrow some money from my parents. I didn't want to do that.

"I wanted her to get a real job because her photography wasn't bringing in enough money. She was working on her second book and said if she didn't get it finished, her publisher would probably drop her. This was her dream and she didn't want to quit. We had some tough decisions to make and didn't agree on what to do. Things got bad for a while and we just needed some time away from each other. But we finally worked it out and there haven't been any problems beyond that. We got along great the whole time we were separated and now we are back together."

"How long were you separated?"

"About a year."

"Did she want a divorce?"

"No, neither of us did. We never had any other problems."

"No problems?"

"No."

Paul pulled another piece of paper out of the folder and slapped it on the table in front of Luke. "C'mon Luke, I don't have time to play all these games. You're trying to make it sound like you were Ozzie and Harriet when you were far from it."

Luke picked up the paper and scanned it. His heart sank.

"This is a copy of the restraining order she filed against you back in December. Don't you think this means there were some serious problems?"

"This isn't what it sounds like." Luke glanced at Ernest. "It was a big misunderstanding."

"People don't file restraining orders for misunderstandings."

"When we separated she continued to live in our house. It's on my family's ranch," he said. "The barn and stables are beside the house, and that's where I do lots of my work. A rancher's job is not nine to five and Bonnie knew that. She didn't have a problem with me being around. We didn't hate each other, we were just taking a break…we thought it might help."

"Why a restraining order, Luke?" Ernest tone was to the point, demanding. His arms remained crossed across his chest.

"Look, here's what happened." Luke leaned forward, laced his fingers and rested his forearms on the table. "One night while we were separated, Bonnie had some friends over to the house for a little Christmas party—about ten people I guess. I told her earlier in the week that I'd stay clear, but the weather changed and it started to sleet. I went over to put the horses in the barn."

"So you invited yourself to her party."

"Nothing like that. I didn't have any choice. When I got there, some cars were parked blocking the barn doors so I went to the house and asked her to have them move them. As you can imagine, she wasn't too happy about me showing up at ten-thirty during her party, but I really didn't have any choice. These two guys came out to move their cars. One was a local banker and the other was a lawyer and they were both drunk. They started talking loud so I would hear them, saying all this bullshit that wasn't true. About how we were behind on our loan payments and we were on the verge of losing the ranch. The lawyer said he was going to represent Bonnie in her divorce and she'd end up owning the ranch."

"Was that true?"

Luke lowered his head and nodded. "Yeah, we were behind on our note, but my dad had talked to the president of the bank and they had worked out some new terms. We weren't going to lose the ranch."

"Did you know these men?"

"The banker is the son of the president of the bank. He's a local rich prick named Tyler McAllister. I've known him all my life and we've never gotten along. His father actually owns the bank. I didn't know the lawyer, but I know they're both arrogant assholes and they just wanted to see how far they could push me. I ignored them as long as I could, but finally Tyler told the other guy that Bonnie was the best piece of ass he'd ever had and I lost it. I nailed him right between the eyes. He flew backwards, landing on the hood of his Mercedes. You'd have done the same thing if you were in my shoes."

Luke leaned back and continued. "As soon as he regained his balance he got up and ran back into the house holding his bloody nose. Later I found out they told Bonnie I picked the fight. She was really pissed and the lawyer convinced her to file a restraining order, which she did the next day."

"I don't show that there were any other charges filed against you."

"No, just the restraining order."

"Was your wife involved with these men?"

"She said she and Tyler went to dinner once, but that's it."

"If you and Bonnie were getting along as good as you say, why do you think she went out with him, especially if she knew you two didn't get along?"

"Because he bought a bunch of her pictures to hang on the wall in the bank. She said she thought he was a nice guy."

"Did you and Tyler have any other confrontations?"

"No, I never saw him again."

"When did you and Bonnie get back together?"

"First of February."

"Anything else you can tell us about this restraining

order?"

"It was only in force for about a month. Finally, when Bonnie realized what a jerk Tyler was, she called and we talked. I told her what actually happened that night and she dropped it the next day."

"Do you think Tyler is holding any hard feelings?"

"I don't really give a damn if he does. It's all small-town bullshit."

Paul closed his file, leaned back and looked at Ernest who gave a small nod.

"Is there anything else you want to tell us at this time?" Paul asked.

Luke thought a second, "No, but how about that stuff I brought in here yesterday?"

Paul pulled out a different piece of paper and ran his finger down it. "Her windbreaker with blood on it, a shopping list, and sunglasses she had in her purse."

"Right. It was all at the clinic. Don't you think something's going on over there?"

"We're not sure what to think of it."

"Why not?"

Paul stood and stared at the floor a few seconds, then glanced at Ernest before he spoke. "Think about it, Luke."

"What do you mean?" Luke asked.

"How do we know you found this stuff there? You told us she was wearing the windbreaker, but no one in the clinic seems to remember it. How do we know this list was in her purse? And the sunglasses? You didn't mention it when you filled out the missing persons report. But, now, it's your story, but you don't have one bit of proof to back it up."

"Why would I make it up, for God's sake?"

"So far, everything you've told us has been a lie. Why should we believe this story is true?"

Luke couldn't believe they had turned everything against him. Never in his life had he been called a liar. He had nothing but his word, and now it looked as if that wasn't worth anything. He gritted his teeth and said, "Because it is."

Ernest tilted his head down and glared at Luke over his glasses. "Luke, what we've found shows that you and your wife have a history of marital problems. The agents at the border crossing said you hit her, and from what I can tell, it probably wasn't the first time."

"Ernest, that's not right," Luke pleaded.

Ernest straightened up and said, "Stay here. We'll be back in a few minutes."

When they left the room Luke's mind was in a tailspin. He couldn't believe Ernest believed he hit Bonnie. But he knew he had to convince them they were wrong and wasting valuable time.

A few minutes later, Paul opened the door and said, "That's all we have for now, so you can go."

Luke followed Paul down the hallway, through the reception area and out the front door. Paul lit a cigarette and flicked the match into the grass before turning to face Luke.

"Let me fill you in on something. About ten years ago, against Ernest's wishes, his daughter married a guy she'd only known for a few months. He was about ten years older than her but seemed like a great guy. After a few months, Ernest noticed she was changing. She wasn't the happy-go-lucky girl she'd been. She seemed nervous all the time and quit spending time with the family. He started to notice bruises on her arms. Once she had a black eye and when he asked her about it, she said she fell down, and everything was fine.

"But, one Sunday after they'd been married about a year, she didn't show up for church, so he went to check on her. The son of a bitch had beaten her up. Broke her jaw, ruptured her spleen and did some other stuff to her I won't even mention. Turned out he'd been beating her and sexually abusing her since they got married. They filed charges against him and when he got out on bail, he skipped and hasn't been seen since."

"I'm sorry to hear that, but what does it have to do with

me?"

"Anytime anything like this comes up, Ernest takes it very personal."

Luke raised both hands, palms toward Paul. "I understand, but you need to believe me. This is not what's going on."

Paul nodded. "Luke, before I was a cop, I worked in the security business for thirteen ass-sucking years. I can read people pretty good and I can tell you're a good man. I believe everything you said in there, but Ernest is the one calling the shots on this, and there's nothing I can do."

Chapter 14

Luke was unlocking his car when he saw Ernest get into a black and white GMC Denali parked beside the building. He had to talk to him and make him understand.

"Ernest, can I talk to you a minute?" Luke said, running up to his vehicle.

Ernest fixed his gaze on him but didn't take the car out of gear. Hopeful, Luke said, "You have to believe me, I wouldn't do a thing to harm Bonnie."

He glared at Luke. "I'd like to believe you, son, but I don't like the way things look right now."

"All that stuff that happened back at home doesn't mean anything," Luke said as he dropped down on one knee at the open window. "It's all in the past and doesn't have a thing to do with our relationship now."

"I'd be more inclined to believe you if you had told me about it. Right now I can't do anything for you." Ernest turned his head away from Luke and looked out the windshield, staring at nothing in particular. After a silent moment, he looked back at Luke over his bifocals, and said, "In fact, I'm pretty darned pissed at you."

He jabbed his finger towards the building. "You embarrassed me in there. I've been standing up for you all along and now, to have all of that come out like that makes me angry. Those inspectors at the border say they're sure you hit her."

"They're wrong! I've never hit her in my life and never will. You have to believe me."

"This is a small town. I've known most of those inspectors since they were kids and I've only known you for one day, Luke. They don't have any reason to lie."

"Ernest, I'm telling you the truth. Let me tell you—"

"Luke I've got work to do right now."

"Do you think I'd be hanging around the police station if I had something to do with my wife's disappearance? What can I do to make you believe me?"

"I don't know, but every trail we have ends with you." Ernest looked back toward the highway and sighed. "If you want me to believe you, you've got to give me something to work with. Can you think of anyone else you talked to in Cardston?"

Luke pondered a few seconds. "There was one guy in the waiting room at the clinic. He was huge, must have been six-eight and weighed at least two hundred and fifty pounds. Looked Native American. When I came in he was talking to Bonnie and I wanted to move over to the corner out of the way. He got pissed off and made a scene. Everyone in the waiting room looked at him like he was about to start a fight."

"Sounds like Willy Standalone. Did he have a tattoo of an Indian chief on his arm?"

"Yep, that's him."

"That's Willy, and he's one mean son of a gun. Everyone in town's got a story about Willy. You don't want to get on his bad side. Over the years he's always been in some kind of trouble. Usually getting drunk or fighting." Ernest took off his straw hat and wiped the sweat from his forehead. "One night about six or seven years ago, he was drinking down at The Sunny Side Inn, and some guy picked a fight with him. Willy hit him one time, crushing his skull. Killed him instantly. Judge sent him to prison for manslaughter."

"I thought he looked like someone I didn't want to mess with."

"He is and most folks around here were glad he was gone because everyone's scared of him."

Ernest reached in his shirt pocket and pulled out a cigar, removed the cellophane wrapper, and looped a finger around it. "He got out of prison about a year ago and came back to town. Hasn't been in trouble since. But, he's a powder keg that might blow any minute."

"He wasn't too happy with me, that's for sure. He glared at us until he went back to see the doctor. Bonnie said that his son was with him."

"Probably was. Got one they call Little John. Just graduated from high school this year and he's going to college in the states on a football scholarship. He's got potential but I don't see how he's going to make it unless he gets his head on straight. When Willy went to prison, Little John started running with the wrong crowd. It's such as shame, because deep down he's a good kid. And pretty smart, too."

"Do you think they could have anything to do with it?"

Ernest shook his head, "I doubt it. This isn't Willy's style and no way I can see Little John involved in something like this. But I'll look into it."

Chapter 15

Ernest looked at his watch. His wife wasn't expecting him for lunch for about an hour, so he might as well get this over with. Willy worked at the Cardston Auction Barn east of town. It took about ten minutes to get there and when he stepped inside the building he could hear the chatter coming from the office. He walked back and poked his head around the corner and saw the owner, Butch Purdy, drinking coffee with some local ranchers.

"I could smell the bullshit a mile before I got here. But I didn't know it was coming from your office, Butch."

One of the ranchers said, "Come on in, Ernest, you know that's the smell of money."

"I know bullshit when I smell it, Grady, and you're usually in the middle of it."

They laughed as Ernest shook hands all around.

Butch offered him a chair and said, "How are you doing, Ernest? Been a while since you've come to the poor side of town."

"Well hell, Butch, some of us have to work for a living."

"What brings you out here today? I haven't known you to make many social calls during daylight hours."

"I wish it was social, but I need to talk to Willy."

"Oh, shit, I think it's time for us to be going," one of the ranchers said, reaching for his hat. The others followed suit and scrambled for the door.

"I was hoping that wasn't the reason you were here. Willy's been a good hand since he got out," Butch said as he stood up. He pulled a dusty black Stetson off the hat rack and put it on. "He's unloading some heifers from Scott's Ranch. Come on, let's go find him."

They piled into his old Yamaha Mule and headed down a

muddy pathway between crowded pens of noisy cattle. It reeked of cow crap and flies pestered them as they made their way through an open-sided barn.

Butch pulled to a stop at some loading docks and they made their way around the cow patties to a large corral full of bawling calves. There, three men were trying to herd the calves into a chute that led to a series of pens.

Butch climbed on the bottom rung of the wooden fence and cupped his hands around his mouth and yelled. "Willy."

"Yo," came a shout from the other side of the herd.

"C'mere."

Ernest bent over and peeked between the top two slats and saw Willy at the back of the herd. Now and then, a calf would try to run around him and he'd step in front of it or grab it and push it back with the others. He looked like a tackle protecting the quarterback.

Finally when the herd was corralled and Willy headed their way. His sleeveless shirt was soaked with sweat and he pulled off his straw-colored cowboy hat and wiped his brow with his bare arm.

"Ernest needs to talk to you."

Willy's eyes went from Butch to Ernest, who was looking between the boards of the corral. His expression turned sour with a "what now?" look on his face.

He strode up, leaned on the fence and pulled a pack of cigarettes out of his shirt pocket and shook it. A few cigarettes popped up and his lips curled around one and he pulled it out. He strummed a lighter and a yellow flame danced at the tip of the cigarette. Willy took a long draw and blew a stream of blue smoke skyward.

Any time Ernest was close to Willy he was in awe. He had the muscular body of a lumberjack and stood more than a foot taller than him. His hair and eyes were black as coal and his skin, in spite hard living, was smooth as a morning lake.

"What's up, Chief?" he asked, not looking at Ernest.

"Willy, I hope you can help me out here." Ernest tilted his

head down and kicked a dirt clod. "We're trying to find a woman missing in town, and we thought you might remember seeing her."

Willy turned his head slowly and gave Ernest a look that would back down a mountain lion. "Why you asking me?"

"Because you talked to her at the clinic on Tuesday. Her husband said you got mad at him because he didn't want to sit by you."

He rolled his eyes, a memory seeming to come to mind. "Oh? That asshole? I talked to his woman, but I didn't do nothin' to her."

"Nobody's saying you did anything Willy, we're just…"

"Then why're you here? I just talked to her and her fuckin' old man told her to move away from me. Like I stunk. Like I'm not good enough to talk to her. Like he don't like Indians."

"You're the only person we know who talked to her. I'm just trying to—"

"Fuck that fuckin' fucker cuz I didn't do nothing to her." Willy moved closer to Ernest and spittle flew from his mouth as he spit out the words. "I did my time and now you're pulling this shit. I didn't do nothing, so why don't you just fuck off."

Ernest narrowed his eyes and said, "Don't use that language with me, Willy."

"You guys are always trying to blame me for shit I didn't do."

"Willy, listen to me. You're on parole and all it takes is one phone call and they will haul your butt back to the pen. Is that what you want?"

Willy backed up a little and said, "No, but…it just seems everyone wants to blame me for everything…"

Ernest said, "I'm not blaming you for anything. I'm just asking you a few questions."

Willy flicked the cigarette into the air, then turned and watched the calves across the fence. Ernest waited, and finally Willy huffed and said, "What?"

"This lady who disappeared is a tourist and nobody's seen her since she was at the clinic."

"So, I didn't do nothing to her."

"Dadburnit, Willy. Just listen to me. Her husband said you were the only one he remembers seeing talk to her." Ernest pulled out the picture of Bonnie and held it out for him. "Here's a picture of her. Her husband said you and Little John were there."

He glanced at the picture and nodded his head. "I remember her. She sat down beside me and—"

"I know what he did Willy. He told me and so did you. But, listen to me. You're the only one we know who talked to her. How about Little John? Did he talk to her?"

"Shit, no. Little John didn't talk to nobody."

"Did you see anyone else talk to her?"

"I didn't see nothing."

"After you saw the doctor, did you and Little John leave together?"

"Not together. I had my truck and he had his. I went to work and I don't know where he went."

"When you were leaving the clinic, did you see her in the waiting room or at the counter paying or did you see her come outside?"

"Like I said, I didn't see her nowhere. I didn't see nobody nowhere. I just walked outside, got in my truck and left."

"When you left the clinic, where did you go?"

"I went and picked up Joey. Sometimes he rides to work with me."

"You were supposed to come to work at noon? Did you get here on time?"

"No, we were late."

"Why's that?"

"I don't know. Joey had some stuff he needed to do."

"Like what?"

"I took him over to see his cousin and we kind of lost track of time."

"What time did you and Joey get to work?"

"Joey didn't come in."

"Why not?"

Willy shook his head and shrugged. "I don't know. He said he was going to stay and help his cousin fix his car."

Ernest asked, "When did you get to work?"

"About one-thirty, I think."

"Are you sure about that?"

"I don't have a fucking watch."

"Did you punch a time clock when you got here?"

"No. Now we do it on a computer." Then Willy's anger got him sidetracked. "Did her old man say I did something to her?"

"Willy, just answer my questions. We're just trying to find this lady and we don't have a lot of time, okay?"

"You can tell that asshole—"

Ernest interrupted, "Have you seen Joey since then?"

Willy shook his head and turned back to watch the calves.

Ernest knew he wasn't going to get anything else. "Okay, Willy. Thanks."

As they drove back to the office, Ernest asked Butch to verify what time Willy got to work and found that he had not clocked in at all.

Ernest asked. "Does he forget to clock in very much?"

"It used to be a problem, but now I dock 'em an hour when they forget. I can't remember the last time Willy forgot. He's been working on Jesse's crew lately. Let me check with him, he'll know what time he got here."

Butch called Jesse on his two-way radio. Jesse said, "Willy didn't get here until about two-thirty. I know because we had a load of heifers come in about two-twenty. We needed some help and I was looking for him when I saw his truck pulling in the parking lot."

Ernest thanked Butch and headed back to town, thinking things over. Willy had been working hard since he got out and hoped his time in prison would settle him down. But he knew he had a temper and the smallest things could set him off.

And what scared him was something he'd heard him say many times before: I don't get mad, I get even.

He hoped this wasn't one of those occasions.

Chapter 16

Luke was stopped at a red light in town when he couldn't help noticing a woman admiring a turquoise necklace in the window of the jewelry store. She had platinum blonde hair past her shoulders, hot pink stiletto heels and a short skirt. Before the traffic light turned green, she turned and hurried across the street. As he watched her, he realized it was Mitzi, the manager of the clinic. Halfway down the block she entered the office supply store.

When he talked to her at the clinic she had made it clear that she was the one in charge. It gave him an idea.

He pulled into the parking lot on the side of the store and hustled inside. Down about three aisles he found her standing in front of a display of pens, pencils and markers checking the selection. Hesitating briefly he concocted a plan.

She was deep in thought when he thrust his arm in front of her.

"Excuse me," he said as he snatched a package of pens.

Startled, she jerked to the side, almost knocking over a kiosk of note pads. She gave a little giggle and put her hand to her chest. Breathlessly she said, "You scared me."

"I'm sorry," Luke said, acting embarrassed. "That was rude of me. I was in a hurry, you know, and just, well, I just wasn't thinking…are you okay?"

"I'm fine, really. You just caught me off guard, that's all," she said, smiling, stifling a laugh.

"I'm really sorry," he said taking a couple of steps backwards.

Still a little flustered, she laughed again and said, "It's okay, really." Her eyes met his. She pointed her finger toward him, and with a flirtatious grin, said, "I know you, don't I?"

He narrowed his eyes and pointed a finger back at her.

"You're Mitzi, right?"

"Why, yes."

"I'm Luke Wakefield," he said more casually. "I met you Tuesday afternoon at the clinic."

"Oh, yeah. I knew I recognized those blue eyes," she said with a smile. She ran a finger over her brow and parted her blonde bangs. "You and your wife got separated and you were trying to find her."

"That's right, and I still haven't."

"Oh, my," she said and covered her mouth with her hand. "She's still missing?"

"Yeah. I've got the police looking for her, but they don't seem to be having any luck either."

"You know, a cop came to the clinic yesterday and asked some questions, but I didn't know she was still missing."

"She is and I can't seem to find out what happened to her after she left the clinic." Luke slapped the package of pens against his other hand and shook his head. "I'm not from Canada and I don't know how the police operate here. But it doesn't seem like they are trying very hard."

"Who are you working with at the RCMP?"

"A guy named Paul Simpson. You know him?"

"God, yes. He's the cop that came by." Mitzi rolled her eyes and scoffed, "What a dickhead. I went out with him a couple of times. He's not bad-looking but he thinks he's God's gift to women."

Luke chuckled. "Well, I don't know him *that* well."

Mitzi laughed and tossed her hair to one side. She rolled her eyes again and said, "You know, it was funny when he came to the office to ask about your wife. He came in and showed everyone his badge, then came to up to me." Mitzi used a deep masculine voice to imitate him and put her hands on her hips. "'Excuse me, Ms. Lindsey, have you seen this lady?' And I said, 'Paul, for heaven's sake, just call me Mitzi.' He thinks he's such a big shot."

Luke faked a half laugh and Mitzi snorted at her own

story.

"Anyway, he didn't really ask many questions, maybe three or four. Then he was gone. When you came by, you asked more questions than he did. You talked to the nurse *and* the doctor. He didn't talk to anyone else."

"You're kidding." Luke couldn't believe it. They told him they'd checked out all leads and interviewed everyone at the clinic, but obviously they did a half-assed job. It seemed they spent all their time investigating him rather than looking for Bonnie? This made no sense.

"No, really," she said, as she stepped closer. "I don't like that guy, and if you ask me, I don't think he's a very good cop."

"Well, I'll be damned." He paused as he digested this new information. Slowly he leaned closer and touched her on the elbow, "Mitzi, I'm glad I ran into you. You're just the person who can help me."

"I am?" Her eyes widened in anticipation.

"You remember when we talked the other day? You told me no one really saw my wife leave. You said the receptionist checked her out but no one actually saw her go out the door."

"Right…"

"I need to find someone who saw her leave. I want to talk to the other people who were in the waiting room when she was there. You know what I mean?"

"I do, that's a good idea. I bet Paul didn't think of that."

"Could you get me a list of those people who were in the clinic at the same time we were there?"

"Oh, I'm sorry. I can't do that." Mitzi said as she stepped back, moving her arm out of Luke's reach. She looked around them to make sure no one was listening. Whispering, she said, "We can't give anyone's information unless the patient says it's okay."

"Mitzi, you are my only hope." Luke stepped around in front of her. "I've got to talk to those people. One of them might have seen something. You're the only one who can help me."

"Dr. Duncan would fire me if he found out," she said, just above a whisper. She sounded firm, but sympathetic.

"Mitzi, please," he begged. "My wife disappeared. I don't even know if she's alive. She's running out of time. You *have* to help me."

She eased backwards and hugged herself around her waist. "I'm sorry, but I just can't do it."

Luke couldn't let her get away until he had those names. Again she reached up and flipped her hair and he noticed three gold rings on her fingers, all bearing large colored stones. As he looked closer he noticed her gold necklace and diamond earrings, which he thought were probably fake.

He reached in his back pocket and pulled out his billfold and took out a bill. Making sure no one was watching, he grabbed her hand, put the bill in it and closed her fingers around it. "I need that list. I'll do whatever it takes to get it."

Slowly she opened her hand and saw a folded hundred-dollar bill. It didn't take her long, maybe half a second, to make her decision.

"But you can't tell anybody," she whispered.

"I won't."

"I can lose my job," she said sternly as she took another peek at the bill.

"I can lose my wife."

She nodded at him, affirming his dilemma. "Okay, I get off at four-thirty. Come to my apartment about five?"

"Tell me where you live and I'll be there."

Luke was barely back to his car when he saw Mitzi come out the front door with her bag of purchases. He'd never seen anyone run in high heels, especially any as tall as hers. There was a little red Miata convertible parked in front of the jewelry store with the top down. When she got to it, she chunked the plastic bag into the passenger seat and hurried into the store, the hundred-dollar bill clutched in her hand.

Chapter 17

Luke thought about the comment Mrs. Johnson, the owner of the lodge in St. Mary's, had made, as he drove back toward the edge of town. She said tourist season was in full swing and it would be hard to find a room. But, there were four motels at this intersection. Surely one would have a room.

The Best Western looked newest so he pulled into the parking lot. Inside he found a young lady filing her nails and glued to *The View* on a small TV behind the check-in desk.

"Do you have a non-smoking single room available? Upstairs if you have it."

"Sorry, sir, we're all booked up," she said, her eyes never leaving the TV.

"Are you sure?" Luke asked, glancing at her computer. "Could you check?"

"Don't have to. Hot air balloon festival over by Waterton Lakes, same time every year. We get booked up at least six months in advance. We have a no-cancellation policy within two weeks of check-in, so we won't have anything available until about this time next week."

"Next week? You're kidding me."

"No sir, I'm not," she said as if she'd already answered that question twenty times today.

"Is there another motel you'd recommend?"

"Not really. You can check the Moutain-Aire across the highway, but they won't have anything either," she said without expression. "Same with the others in town. You'll be lucky to find a room within seventy-five miles of here."

Luke thanked her and drove across the highway. They told him the same thing: there was nothing available and no hope of cancellations. He tried the other two and their story was the same. Discouraged, he headed into town hoping to find a bed and breakfast, a boarding house, or something. He remembered there was a newspaper machine outside the drugstore. *There might be something in the want ads*, he thought.

He slipped into a parking space and checked the machine but it was empty. Down the street he found another machine in front of Sonny's camera shop, but there were no papers in it either. Sonny saw him through the window and stepped outside.

"The paper comes out once a week—every Friday. They're usually gone by the next day," Sonny explained. He tilted his head toward the diner. "They usually hang onto a couple for the customers to read. Why do you need a paper?"

"I'm trying to find a room. All the motels are booked up. Any ideas where I might look?"

"Try the real estate office two blocks down. They usually have a list of apartments and houses for rent. You might find someone who'll rent you one by the week."

"Good idea. Thanks."

"Cops found anything yet?"

Luke's first thoughts were Ernest's accusation, that he was the only suspect at this time. Disgusted, he bit his lip and said, "No."

Sonny nodded and said, "You know, I saw a show on TV one time about a guy who had a reaction to a drug that caused him to have amnesia. He wandered off for a few days and no one knew where he was. They said most amnesia cases last only twenty-four to forty-eight hours, and can be brought on by all kinds of things, even a concussion. Maybe they gave your wife some drugs at the clinic that affected her. She walked out of the clinic and being confused, she wandered off."

"Interesting," Luke said. "It's a possibility, I guess."

"You said she took a pretty good spill when she was jogging. Maybe that could have something to do with it."

"Yeah, but that was the afternoon before, at least twelve hours earlier."

"What else could it be? No one's going to grab her in broad daylight, not at the clinic or on the street. Not in this town. She'll show up before long. I'm sure she will."

Luke shook his head and glanced down the street. "Yeah, I hope you're right."

When Luke stepped inside the diner the smell of home cooking made him realize how hungry he was. He had skipped breakfast and now his stomach was reminding him. He asked a waitress for a copy of the newspaper.

"Let me check in the back," she said. "Sit wherever you want to. Meatloaf's the special today. And it's better than your momma makes."

He sat down and a minute later she came back and dropped a paper on the table. "The sports section is missing. Hope that's not what you wanted."

It didn't take long to discover there were no listings for rooms or houses for rent. Half an hour later he finished the meatloaf, which *was* better than his mother's, and headed for the realtor's office.

There he found a young lady with a pierced eyebrow engrossed in a Sudoku puzzle. She smiled and asked if she could help him. He explained his predicament and she pulled a piece of paper off the credenza behind her.

"This is the most current list. I don't know if any of them will rent by the week; but it wouldn't hurt to call and ask."

He started down the sidewalk looking for a payphone. Halfway down the block he came to The Sportsman's Outfitter and saw Lauren inside. She waved him in and Luke gave her an update on what had happened since he last saw her. When he mentioned his quest for a room to rent, she snapped her fingers and said, "You know, I've got an idea. Let me make a phone call." She dialed and a few seconds later put the phone down. "Line's busy. I'll try again in a minute."

He glanced at his watch and realized it was almost time to meet Mitzi. "I've got to meet someone in a few minutes and it shouldn't take more than twenty minutes. Would that be okay?"

"Sure. Come back when you are done."

Chapter 18

The Tudor-style apartment complex was small, about a dozen units. Mitzi's red Miata was parked in front of the unit on the corner and Luke pulled into the parking space beside it. He hurried up the walk to #12 and rang the doorbell. Inside he heard a couple of dogs start yapping. The barking continued until Mitzi opened the door, a wiggling Yorkie under each arm.

She had changed into jeans and a white blouse with a plunging neckline. Around her neck he saw a turquoise necklace that looked just like the one he saw in the window of the jewelry store.

"How do you like my twins? Aren't they cute?"

Luke assumed she was referring to the dogs.

"Very cute. Smaller than I expected by the barking." Luke stepped inside and with her foot Mitzi pushed the door closed. He noticed the pink stilettos had been replaced with taller, black spikes.

"Come in," she said as she put down the dogs. As he followed her, he realized why it took her so long to get to the door. Obviously it takes a while to put on half a bottle of perfume. She reeked of gardenias.

Her apartment was a small studio, nicely furnished in glass and chrome. Luke followed her into the dining room where he noticed framed photos everywhere—all of her.

"Have a seat," she said, pointing to a glass-topped table. The dining room was separated from the kitchen by a breakfast bar, over which she held a clear plastic pitcher, half filled with a slushy white concoction. "I just made a pitcher of margaritas. You'll help me drink it, won't you?"

"I'd better not. I'm going to try to talk to a few people on that list before it gets too late."

"Oh, come on," she whined. "With all you've been through, I think you need it." She walked around the corner with two drinks and set one in front of him. She leaned over the bar and picked up a couple of pieces of typed paper. She slid them in front of him and said, "Here's the list of patients we saw Tuesday morning."

As he scanned the list, she sucked down her drink. There were about a dozen names on it with addresses and phone numbers.

"This shows everyone who came in that morning," she said between slurps. She stepped around to the side of the table and stood while she swirled what was left of her drink. "These names are listed according to when they checked in. It includes everyone from about nine o'clock until we closed for lunch. Everyone on the first page saw Dr. Duncan. Those on the second page saw Dr. Birdwell."

"Did they check out in the same order they saw the doctor?"

"I doubt it, but let me see," she said as she bent over the table, proudly displaying so much cleavage that Luke felt obligated to check it out. She took her time as she looked down the list. "I think most of them did…except for Ed Couch, who was really sick, and Elsie George, who we had to send to the hospital. Marinel Hayes was in and out pretty quick, but I think she was about the last person to leave the office. I can't remember much about the others."

"This will help a lot. I can't tell you how much I appreciate this."

She picked up a pen from the table and looked down the list and put check marks beside three names. "These would be the ones I'd talk to first." Then she circled one name. "But if I were you, I'd start with Marinel."

"Why's that?"

"She's Miss Know-it-All."

"What do you mean?"

"If anyone ever needs to know something about anyone or

anything going on in town, she'll know about it. I don't know how she does it, but she keeps up with everything."

Mitzi stood up, grabbed her empty glass and headed to the kitchen. Luke saw her get a refill over the breakfast bar.

"You need some more?" She held out the pitcher, swirling the margaritas.

"No, I'm fine," he said as he picked up his glass and took his first drink.

"Anyway, she got there at least an hour before her appointment. She's always early everywhere she goes. We talked a little bit, but I had lots of work to do. Let me warn you, she can talk your ears off."

"You think she'll talk to me, even though she doesn't know me?"

"God yes, honey," she laughed. "She'll take one look at your gorgeous face and drag you in the front door."

"If that's the case, I'll keep my distance."

"Oh, I was just kidding. But, poor Marinel, she's not bad, but she's never been married. Just can't get a man."

Luke nodded as if he understood.

Then she raised her eyebrows and smiled when she said, "And from what she told me on Tuesday, she's *really* in the mood for a man...if you know what I mean."

"Then I'll *definitely* keep my distance."

She took the list from Luke's hand, jotted something on the bottom of the page and handed it back to him. "That's my cell phone number. Call me if you need anything else."

"Thanks." Luke stood and looked at the list.

"Tonight I'll be at The Stampede. It's a bar and dance hall on the north side of town. Stop in and let me know what you find." She patted Luke on the hand and wiggled her eyebrows. "And I want to hear how it goes with you and Marinel."

He grinned and said, "I might do that."

They started to the front door, Mitzi swirled what was left of her margarita and said, "Since you're going to see Marinel first, you don't need to worry about having a margarita on your breath. Knowing her, she'll probably have had a few by the time you get there."

Before Luke could get out the door, she hugged him and gave him a kiss him on the cheek. "Good luck…and remember I'll be at the Stampede until about midnight."

"Okay," he said as he closed the door behind him.

After Luke got in his car he checked himself in the mirror. He pulled a bandana out of his back pocket and wiped the lipstick off his cheek, then rolled down the windows, hoping the smell of her perfume would dissipate.

When he got back to Lauren's store she was on the phone so he took a seat across from her and waited.

"Yes, sir. I'll send a confirmation of your reservation to your e-mail address." Her eyes came up to Luke with a furrowed brow, then said goodbye to the caller and hung up. With a sour look, she asked, "Do I smell gardenias?"

"Yeah, but that's another story. Did you have any luck?"

"Yes, but not exactly what I was expecting."

"So…what does that mean?"

"I called my dad. He has some rental property and I thought he might have something, but he said he doesn't at this time. But, he suggested something else."

"What's that?"

"My place. Why don't you stay at my place?"

Chapter 19

"Stay with you?" Luke said hesitantly to Lauren. "I don't know…"

"Not really with me. I live on my daddy's ranch. We have a bunkhouse out back and no one lives there right now. Back when I was a kid we always had a bunch of ranch hands living there, but over the years they've all decided they'd rather own their own place. Our foreman lived there until he got married a few months ago and moved to town. Now it just sits there empty."

"That sounds good to me, but I don't want to be too far from town."

"It's only four miles west of here. It's a great little house. Got everything you need: dishes, linens, towels. But it doesn't have a TV or telephone."

"Fine with me. Let me pay you for a week right now."

"No, you're not going to pay rent. It's just sitting there empty."

"But—"

She shook her head. "No buts." Luke opened his mouth to argue, but before he could speak she said, "And that's final."

"That's awful nice of you."

Lauren glanced at the clock on the back wall. "If you want to run out there, I've got time right now."

"Okay, but I need to take my car to the local rental agency. The window is broken and with this rain, I need to get it fixed or trade cars."

"I've got a better idea. See that sign?" She pointed to a chart on the back wall that listed the services she offered. In addition to guide service, it also said she rented Jeeps. "I have six Jeeps. Four are rented now, but the other two are at the ranch. Why don't you use one of them?"

"Sounds great," he said as he pulled a credit card from his billfold. "But I'm paying for this."

"Okay, but let's take care of that later," she said pulling a long white form out of a drawer and handing it to him. "Here's the rental agreement. Fill it out and bring it back to me later."

Light rain was falling as they returned the Sebring with the broken window to the rental agency located in the Chevy dealership. They transferred all of Luke's gear into Lauren's white Suburban and headed out of town on a two-lane ranch road.

"Do your parents live out here, too?"

"No, a couple of years ago, my mother had a stroke. She's doing okay, but she can't climb stairs anymore, and their house has two stories. They couldn't really sell it since it's on the ranch, so they came to me with a deal. They wanted to trade houses."

"That sounds interesting."

"I had a home here in town and it was only one-story, just right for them. It was a perfect deal for me because I kept a lot of my equipment for my business at the ranch anyway. So, they moved into my house and I moved out to the ranch."

A couple of miles down the road Luke saw a two story Victorian style house with a wraparound porch that sat about a hundred yards off the highway. It was on what appeared to be about five acres, with pastures on the east, west and north sides. The house wasn't huge, but it was stately and well-kept. There were several other structures scattered around the property.

"That's my house over there," she said, pointing. The truck slowed and turned down a dirt driveway on the edge of the property.

"Very nice. You live here alone?"

"No, Elvis and Buddy live here, too."

"Elvis and Buddy?" Luke raised an eyebrow.

"Um hum."

The rain had stopped and they rolled down their windows

as they drove down the drive that snaked between tall pine and spruce trees that dotted the property. They passed an equipment barn that was open on one side and a red barn that appeared to have a fresh paint job. Luke saw a black Labrador Retriever, followed by a much slower, brown Dachshund, running their way as they approached a small white clapboard house in the back corner of the property.

"This is it," Lauren said as the SUV rolled to a stop. "It doesn't look like much but I think it'll work just fine."

Lauren climbed the three steps to an unpainted porch that wrapped around the cottage and pushed open the front door.

"You don't keep it locked?" he asked.

"No, as long as Elvis and Buddy are here, no one's about to come on this property. That's Elvis," she said pointing at the brown wiener dog that was almost to the porch. The black lab was already standing next to Luke, nuzzling his hand to be petted. "And that's Buddy. They're dangerous, believe me," she said in a no-nonsense tone.

Elvis climbed the stairs onto the porch and ambled over to Luke. As soon he bent down to pet her, she rolled over to have her belly scratched. Luke obliged her and Buddy moved in, vigorously licking Luke on the face.

Luke pushed Buddy away. "I can see how dangerous they are. Elvis trips them by rolling over in front of them, and then Buddy drowns them with slobber."

"I think you've got it figured out," Lauren said.

Luke wiped his shoes on the doormat and followed Lauren inside. The air was musky and stale, and he saw she was already opening windows. A stone's throw beyond the bunkhouse was a barbed wire fence that separated the pasture where hundreds of black cattle grazed in belly-deep grass.

They left the bunkhouse and went over to the barn where Lauren opened a side door and disappeared in the darkness. Luke waited and a few seconds later a row of florescent lights began to flicker on one side of the building. As the lights came on, he made his way over to where she was waiting.

"Daddy's office is in here," she said, pointing to a closed door back in the corner. There's a phone in there you can use. Make all the calls you want. I'll put all of your charges on your credit card when I bill you for the Jeep."

He followed her around a tractor and together they slid open a wide door on the front of the barn. As sunlight flooded in, Luke noticed among the assortment of farm equipment, bales of hay, saddles and bridles, and welding equipment. Along one wall were two Jeeps, both Wrangler Unlimited models.

"Take your pick," she said. "These two are practically brand new."

One was black with four doors and a removable hardtop. The other was red with two doors and a cloth top. He eyed the black one and said, "I'll take this one."

"That's great. These new ones have a GPS tracking device on it. If you get lost, I can find you." Lauren opened the door and sat down in the driver's seat.

"Does that happen?"

"Oh, yeah," she said as she opened the center console and pulled out a key. "It's easy to get lost in the mountains."

Luke's eyes scanned the dashboard. "I don't see it. Can I use it like a map?"

"No. It's not a navigation system. It's a small device attached onto the undercarriage that I can use to see where the vehicle is. You won't even know it's there."

She started the engine and pulled outside beside the Suburban. "Have you driven a Jeep before?"

"Yeah, I've got an old one back home."

"Good. I've got to go back to the shop for a while. Let me know if you need anything else."

Chapter 20

As Luke headed to town he pulled a folded piece of paper from his pocket. Mitzi had circled Marinel Hayes. She was the first person he'd visit. Earlier he had picked up a city map when he returned his rental car.

Her address was easy to find and less than five minutes later he pulled up to a small bungalow on the north side of town. There was a light blue Honda parked in a one-car garage beside the house. Luke parked the Jeep in front and walked up the sidewalk. As he passed the large picture window he saw a TV on inside where *Wheel of Fortune* was blaring.

When he rang the doorbell, the sound was muted, and a thin, attractive, fiftyish woman with beautiful green eyes opened the door. He remembered her from the clinic. She smiled widely, showing perfect teeth, and said, "Hi," as if she was expecting him.

This is not the woman Mitzi had described. She wasn't supposed to be attractive and perky. "I'm looking for Marinel Hayes."

"I'm Marinel." She was short, maybe five feet on a good day and wore her brunette hair frosted, in a spiky kind of hairdo.

"Miss Hayes, I'm Luke Wakefield from Texas and here on vacation. I have a big problem and I was hoping you could help me out."

The smile disappeared in a flash. "Well if you're here for money you can forget it because I don't give money to beggars. So you can just go." The door slammed.

Through the front door he said, "No, ma'am, it's nothing like that. I'm trying to find my wife. She disappeared from the clinic on Tuesday. I believe you were there at the same time she was. I was hoping you might remember something that will help me find her."

It was silent for a few seconds then the door opened a few inches. Marinel, peeked out, and said, "I was there on Tuesday. What do you mean she disappeared?"

Luke started to explain what happened and Marinel's face lit up. She interrupted him, "I remember you. You asked Monica where you wife was, and she said she had already gone."

"Right, I asked the recep—"

"And you still haven't found her?"

"No ma'am, I haven't and I—"

"Well, isn't that strange. " Marinel pulled the door open wide. "Come in. I don't know how I can help but I'll try. And call me Marinel, everybody does. What was your name?"

"Luke Wakefield, ma'am. I—"

"Luke, have a seat over there," she pointed to the sofa as she walked toward the kitchen, "I just got in from working in the yard a few minutes ago and I'm having me a little cocktail, can I get you one? It sure helps me relax."

"No ma'am, I'm fine. What I really need is—"

"Now, let's go back to the beginning," she said as she came back and sat on the edge of the sofa facing him, an amber-colored drink in hand. "I remember seeing you and your wife come in. Her hair is beautiful. Is that her natural color?"

"Yes it is, but—"

"I thought so. But, you know, the clinic was really busy that day. It's been a mess since Mrs. Milligan died. She ran that place for almost thirty years and Lord, did she do a good job. She died last winter—heart attack. She was seventy-nine years old but she wouldn't retire.

"Marinel, did you see—"

"She worked for Dr. Duncan for twenty-eight years…or was it twenty-nine? Anyway, that doesn't matter. It was a long time. But, now Mitzi runs it. She's really doing a good job. She used to work for a doctor in Calgary. That's how she got the job. Have you met her?"

"Yes, ma'am I did, but—"

"I thought you would," she said, a knowing grin on her face. "She's a looker, that's for sure. Men notice her right away," Marinel said raising her eyebrows.

Luke tried to get her back on track. "Marinel, you said you remember seeing my wife, right?"

"Oh, uh, well, yes I do. What was your wife's name?"

Luke did not like the past tense reference. He said, "My wife's name is Bonnie."

"Wasn't she kind of tall?"

Maybe tall to you, he thought. "Yes ma'am, about five-eight. We were sitting against the wall over near the water fountain."

"I always sit right next to the check-in counter. That way I can say hello to my friends when they are checking in or out, you know. I've lived in this town all my life, I know just about everyone here."

Mitzi said she seemed to know everything that went on in town. *Maybe that's why she knows so much—she listens in on everyone's conversations.*

"Do you remember them calling my wife in to see the doctor?"

"No, I don't remember that. I probably went in to see the doctor before she did."

"So after you saw the doctor, did you leave?"

"No, my car was down at Merle's Service Station getting the oil changed and the tires rotated. I do it every three thousand miles. They said it wouldn't be ready 'til noon, so I didn't see any reason to leave. I just stayed there in the air conditioning. We've had such a hot summer. I think it's the humidity 'cause when the rain started—"

"Do you remember my wife coming out to the reception area after she saw the doctor?"

"I think so. When she came out she had some kind of brace on her arm. Did she break her arm? How'd that happen?"

"No, she sprained her thumb." He ignored the other

question. "So then what happened?"

"She gave Monica her credit card, some kind of gold card I think, maybe a MasterCard. And just before she left, Rita, that's Dr. Duncan's nurse, said the doctor had something else to tell her, so she went back to the doctor's office."

"Then what? Did you see her come back out?"

Her eyes drifted to the side as she thought about it. "No, I don't think so, but I can't remember for sure. My friend Joyce Pratt was there. Joyce's husband was mayor for two terms…got beat last time. Joyce may be my friend but, glory be, her husband was a horrible mayor. They say he sold out to big business…you know, that mobile home factory. But anyway, we started talking about cars. Joyce is going to buy a new car and she was asking me about my Honda. Those Hondas are really good cars. Have you ever had one?"

Luke could see why this lady wasn't married—she never shut up long enough for someone to ask her. "Marinel, could we stay on the subject please? When did you leave the doctor's office?"

"Right at twelve, a few minutes after you did."

"So you saw me leave?"

"Oh, yeah. You were the only one in the clinic I didn't know that day…so I remember you."

"How long before I got there did Bonnie go back with Rita?"

"I don't know, five minutes, maybe ten."

"I see. And after I left, did you see my wife again?"

"No, but I could have been talking to Joyce when she came out."

"But you noticed me and you weren't watching for me, right?"

"But you're a man, and I notice men." Coyly, she looked down at the floor, "Especially the nice-looking ones…you know, just like you noticed Mitzi. Know what I mean?"

Luke forced a grin and said, "Yeah, I think so. But don't you think you would have noticed her if she had come out?"

"I'm pretty sure I would have, but I couldn't swear to it." She got up and walked toward the kitchen rattling the ice cubes in her empty glass and said, "Are you ready for one yet?"

Luke needed one now. "Sure, I'll have whatever you're having." When she came back she was carrying a couple of translucent gold drinks in short cocktail glasses. She put his on a paper napkin on the coffee table in front of him.

"So tell me, Marinel, if Bonnie went back in to see the doctor, and didn't come back out into the waiting room, is there a back door or another way to get out?"

"Oh sure, there're two other doors. There's a door at the end of the hallway that opens out into the alley."

"Do patients ever leave that way?" Luke picked up his drink and sipped it. Something sweet. Too sweet for him.

"I never have. I think it's mostly employees that use it because they park in the alley parking lot. The other door is from Dr. Duncan's apartment and opens into the alley, too."

"What do you mean, his apartment?"

"Oh. I guess you wouldn't know about that. He has an apartment, it's kind of behind that vacant building next door.

"You mean that closed-up store next door?"

"Yeah, Computer Solutions. They closed last year, but the building is kind of deceiving. The computer store only occupied the front part of the building. The back half is Dr. Duncan's apartment."

"How do you know this?"

"I used to be manager of a Commercial Cleaning Service here in Cardston. We cleaned lots of the businesses around town, including the clinic and the computer store."

"So there's an apartment connected to his office?"

"That's right. See, Dr. Duncan owns the whole block. Twenty years ago he lived up in the mountains and during the winter the roads are dangerous. They're covered with ice and snow, so he remodeled that building and put an apartment back there so he didn't have to make that dangerous drive home every night during the winter."

"But, he doesn't live there now?"

"After his wife died he moved to town, so he hasn't used it for at least ten years."

"What do they use it for now?"

"I don't know, but they use it for something because I think I saw the carpet cleaners there a couple of days ago."

"When was that?"

She tapped on her nose and thought. "I guess it was the day I went to the doctor. Because I had just picked up my car at Merle's and when I drove past the clinic I saw a white van in the alley. Two people were putting one of those long rolled-up carpets in the back of it."

Luke scooted onto the edge of the sofa and turned directly to face her. "You're sure it was a carpet?"

"I guess so. It took two people to carry it."

"What carpet cleaners? Did you see the name?"

"Well, I said carpet cleaners, but I don't know for sure. All I know is that it was a silver van."

"I thought you said white." Luke felt like his star witness was falling apart on the stand. The more he wanted her to be sure the less she wanted to commit.

"Well, either silver or white. A light color. I can't remember for sure. It might have been gold."

Luke made a mental note to check out the carpet cleaners in town. "From what I've heard," he said, "Dr. Duncan is a pillar of the community. Everyone loves him."

"That's true, he's wonderful. He's been the 'Citizen of the Year' at least five times. Maybe more."

"Let's go back to the clinic for a minute. Did you see Willy Standalone leave?"

"Oh yeah. Willy and Little John left together, a few minutes before you came back. I know that because I remember thinking that you were lucky he didn't start a fight. He's a troublemaker. Did you know he went to prison for killing a man?"

"I heard that, but—"

"That's not the only one, either. They say he killed someone else too but they don't have any proof."

"Is there any—"

"He was messing with another man's wife and—"

"Marinel, we're getting off track here." Luke knew she would ramble all night if he didn't keep her focused. "Is there anything else you remember about that morning? About Willy or Bonnie or anything that might be unusual?"

"I'm sure there's something I'm forgetting." Marinel got up and walked back toward the kitchen. "Let me think about it, how's your drink?"

"I really need to talk to some other people tonight," he said as he stood up and moved toward the door.

Marinel stepped out of the kitchen with a bottle of Southern Comfort, "Why don't you have another drink. I'm sure I can think of something else you need to know."

"I think I've got enough for now, Marinel."

"Don't you want to know about the other man Willy killed?"

"Not right now," he assured her as he opened the door. "But if I do, I'll call. Okay?"

"Okay," she said, seemingly disappointed. "Anytime."

Chapter 21

Luke left Marinel determined to find the carpet cleaning company and ask them some questions. Inside the grocery store he found a pay phone and telephone book. In the yellow pages, there were half a dozen carpet cleaners were listed, but none in Cardston. All were in Lethbridge. He ripped out the page and stuffed it in his pocket so he could make some calls when he got back to the bunkhouse.

Luke called the next two people on the list. At the first one a kid answered and said no one was home but him and he got an answering machine at the other.

He checked his watch and saw it was getting close to eight. He was starving. For dinner, he'd buy the biggest T-bone he could find. He'd throw it on the pit and sit on the porch and watch the sun go down. It would give him time to think this through.

At the grocery store, it took only a few minutes to find a steak, a premade salad and a twelve pack of beer. Luke left the store and walked to the parking lot on the side of the building. As he walked down the sidewalk he could hear someone coming up behind him. They sounded like they were in a hurry so he stepped over closer to the building for them to pass. Then suddenly he was hit in the back by what felt like the front line of the Dallas Cowboys.

He flew into the brick wall. First his shoulder hit, then his face. His body ricocheted off and he tripped and landed face first, on the pavement. The groceries and beer scattered all around him.

Luke turned to see what hit him. There were two men coming at him; the closest one was Willy Standalone and he had fire in his eyes. The other one was someone Luke had never seen before. He hung back, a cigarette dangling between his lips. He was tall and lanky with long, oily dark hair.

Luke tried to scramble to his feet, but before he could, Willy grabbed him by the neck of the shirt and waistband of his jeans and slung him down the sidewalk. Luke broke the fall with his hands, but skidded along the concrete, the skin scraping off his palms.

Willy kept coming.

"Wait a minute," Luke said, as he rolled over, gasping for air.

Willy didn't stop. Luke had been in his share of fights in his life and knew he had to get out in the open. He rolled off the sidewalk and crawled between two cars. Quickly he got to his feet and started backing up.

"What the hell are you doing?"

Willy didn't speak and Luke kept backing away from him. But the other guy had come around and blocked his escape, so Luke circled one of the cars until he was back on the sidewalk. Now he was trapped. Luke backed up against the wall so he could see both of them. As they closed in on him, Luke bolted. He jumped on the hood of the car in front of him, and scrambled toward the roof. Willy's hand grabbed his leg and yanked him back onto the hood, off the car, and slammed him against the wall, as easy as if he were a bag of charcoal.

With one hand pressed hard against Luke's throat, Willy lowered himself to Luke's height and put his face in Luke's. "I don't like you."

Luke was gagging. He coughed out, "I don't even *know* you."

"You told the cops I did something to your wife."

"No, I didn't."

Willy stabbed a finger repeatedly into Luke's forehead. "Don't you fucking lie to me, you little piece of shit. I didn't do nothing to that bitch of yours and now the cops are on my ass. You want to know how much it pisses me off?" Willy tightened his grip, and pushed Luke's head harder and higher against the wall. His toes barely touched the ground.

Luke's throat was squeezed shut and he couldn't breathe. Luke pushed and pulled at Willy's hands and fingers, trying to break his grip, but it was no use. Willy was too strong.

With his free hand, Willy pointed his finger at Luke's nose and said, "I don't know who you are or where you came from, and I don't really care. All I know is you're fucking with the wrong Indian."

Luke sucked hard for a breath. With just enough air he choked out, "I didn't do anything."

Suddenly Willy's grip tightened even more. His fingers dug into Luke's neck and the pain was unbearable. Luke was afraid he was going to rip out his windpipe.

Luke couldn't take much more. He couldn't breathe and though he tried to pry Willy's hand from his throat he knew it was futile. His arms dropped to his side, things were going dark. Slowly his eyes closed.

Whack! Out of nowhere, something crashed into Willy's head. His grip loosened and he fell to the ground. Luke sucked in a lungful of air.

"Let him go, you big fucking douche bag."

Luke knew that nasally voice. It was Queenie, the homeless woman he had seen the day before in the alley. He hoped she had her friends with her.

Whack! The attack on Willy continued. This time Luke recognized Doc's aluminum crutch as it crashed onto Willy's head.

"Goddamn it," Willy screamed as he backed up and kicked. "Get off me, you fucking runt." Queenie was on him like a bulldog on a buffalo. Her legs and arms wrapped around his huge leg and she bit him while he spun around, kicking, like he was trying to shake off a mad Chihuahua. The harder he kicked the harder she bit. Doc drew back the crutch to swing again.

"Joey, get this bitch off of me," Willy yelled, then noticed his friend had his own problems. The twelve-pack that Luke had bought was strewn across the sidewalk and Griz picked the cans up and threw them at Joey, one after another, with deadly accuracy.

Doc's crutch came down on Willy's head again, but this time Willy grabbed it, ripped it from his grasp, and slung it in the opposite direction. Doc quickly retreated like a cowardly dog, out of Willy's reach. But Willy was more interested in Queenie.

"Damn it, Queenie. Quit biting me."

She didn't. He reached down, pulled her off and held her in the air by one arm like a rag doll.

"Put me down, you fucking asshole," she screamed while kicking her legs and swinging her other arm at Willy. Finally he dropped her. She confronted him, ready to fight. "He's my friend. You'd better leave him alone."

They both turned to look at Luke, who had moved to safer territory by putting a car between him and Willy. Blood oozed from the scrapes on his face and nose where he'd hit the brick wall. He had finally caught his breath and stood massaging his throat. They locked eyes and Luke tried to make him understand. "Listen to me, I didn't tell the cops you did anything. I told them you talked to my wife at the clinic. That's all."

"I didn't do nothing to your wife." Willy pulled a wadded-up handkerchief out of his pocket and dabbed blood from the top of his head where Doc had nailed him with his crutch. As Willy backed up, Joey got in his pickup and backed out of his parking space. Willy started toward it. When he turned away, Luke noticed he no longer wore the diamond stud earring he had on in the clinic. Now a small gold cross filled the pierce in his left ear. It was a unique design. Ricky Wilson, a friend and jewelry designer in Austin, had made it for Bonnie as a wedding gift. It was one of a kind and she always wore it.

"Hey, wait. Where'd you get that earring?"

"Fuck you!"

Luke was right behind him, following just out of reach, as Joey's truck pulled up. Willy slid into the passenger seat.

"That's my wife's earring," Luke shouted.

As Willy slammed the door, he turned to Luke and gave him a defiant glare. "Screw you," he said as the tires spun and the truck raced out of the parking lot.

Chapter 22

While Queenie and Doc helped Luke gather his groceries from the sidewalk she asked, "You think that earring Willy was wearing was your wife's?"

"It looked just like it," he said as she handed him the steak and the bag with the salad in it. "And Bonnie never takes them off."

Griz walked up, holding two leaking beer cans in one hand and the rest of the twelve-pack in his other. "Sorry about the brewskis, bud, but I had to do something to keep Joey from helping Willy. These are wasted, but the others are okay—just a little shook up."

Luke waved him off, "Keep them if you want them."

"Thanks bud, but we don't drink."

"You don't?" Luke said with a look of disbelief. He had always heard that most of the homeless were alcoholics or drug addicts. "None of you?"

"Hell no," Queenie said peering up at him from her diminutive height. "No booze and no drugs. Being homeless and unemployed is hard enough without being a drunk, too."

Luke raised his eyebrows and smiled. "That's interesting. You guys surprise me." He tossed his supplies into the Jeep and climbed into the front seat. "Thanks for helping me out back there. I think Willy would have killed me if you hadn't been here."

"He was pissed, that's for sure. I've known Willy for a while now. He likes to make people scared of him, but I don't think he woulda killed you."

"How do you know Willy?"

"I met him at AA."

"Wait a second," Luke said, as he held up a hand. "AA? Like Alcoholics Anonymous?"

"Sure, down at the community center on Mondays and Thursdays. Part of his parole was that he had to go to AA meetings. We go too because they got good food and we can clean up in their bathrooms. We never miss it."

This homeless trio continued to surprise him.

"He looked mad enough to kill me."

"He's not a killer, I don't care what nobody says. That first guy he killed was an accident. Willy didn't even start the fight. They say he killed another guy, but who knows. There are all kinds of stories about Willy. You know, like the time he killed a full-grown grizzly with that knife he carries." Queenie shook her head slowly and looked from Doc to Griz. "But, he's not a killer, is he?"

"I don't think so," said Doc. Griz shook his head.

"But what about the earring?" Luke asked as he cranked up the engine.

"Willy's not stupid," Queenie said confidently. "If he had something to do with your wife's disappearance, he's not going to run around town wearing her earring unless he wants to get caught."

"Maybe so. But, I've never seen another one like it. I've got to get the cops on this right now," Luke said as the black Jeep started to roll forward. "Thanks again for helping me out."

When Luke walked in the reception area of the RCMP office it was deserted. He yelled down the hall and half a minute later an officer came out wiping his mouth with a paper napkin.

"Sorry, I was eating dinner back in the break room and didn't hear you come in."

"I'm Luke Wakefield and I have some important information for Paul."

"I've got a call into him already. When he checks in, I can give him a message if you want me to."

"How about Ernest?"

"I think they're together because I tried him, too."

Luke left a message and then headed back to the ranch.

Back at the bunkhouse he dropped the groceries on the table then stepped in the bathroom to look at his face. Where Willy had smashed him into the wall his cheek, nose, and forehead were skinned and his neck was still red where the huge hands tried to strangle him. In the medicine cabinet behind the mirror he found some hydrogen peroxide and dabbed it on the wounds to clean them.

Back in the kitchen he grabbed a beer then went out back where the Elvis and Buddy were waiting for him. After he cleaned up the old barbecue pit he started a fire. It would take at least twenty minutes before the coals were ready so he headed for the barn.

Lauren's father's small office was unlocked, and he stepped inside and flipped on the light. In the middle of the desk he saw a stack of unopened mail beside a dusty black telephone. From underneath it he retrieved a thin directory for Cardston. He thumbed through it looking for Dr. Duncan's name. He wasn't expecting to find it since most doctors don't list their home phone numbers, but there is was, *Duncan R.C.* After he dialed the number, he checked his watch. It was almost nine. The phone rang five times before he answered.

"Dr. Duncan, this is Luke Wakefield. I hate to bother you at home this late but I was wondering if I could ask you a few questions.

"Luke Wakefield?"

"Yes, sir. I'm the guy from Texas whose wife disappeared. You saw her Tuesday morning. She had a sprained thumb. I came in and told you she had disappeared."

"Oh, yes. She's still missing?"

"Yes, sir. Do you mind if I ask you a couple of questions?"

"No, not at all."

"I spoke to someone who was at the clinic at the same time my wife was there. She said that my wife came out and paid her bill just before noon, but before she left, a nurse told her you wanted to see her before she left, so she took her back again. You didn't mention that earlier when I talked to you."

"No, she didn't bring her back to see me, because I wasn't there. I left right after I saw her—men's bible study every Tuesday at noon. Rita knows that. I'll bet she had a question or needed some more information."

"That's interesting, because they said the nurse said *you* wanted to see her."

"Not me. I imagine someone got things mixed up."

Luke knew he wasn't mixed up, but he continued. "Okay, one other thing: I understand you have an apartment connected to your office."

"Yes, I do. How'd you find that out?"

"It came up when I was asking questions around town."

"I see. I haven't used it in years. Lately it's become somewhat of a junk room. Why? Do you think I hid you wife in there?" Luke noted a defensive tone in the doctor's voice.

"No, sir," Luke said with a light chuckle. "The person I talked to said she thought she saw some people carry a rolled-up carpet out the back door and put it in a white van. Maybe a carpet cleaner's van."

"Who's the person that told you this?"

"Marinel Hayes. Do you know her?"

"Marinel? Sure, known her all her life."

"Can I believe what she tells me?"

"I guess so, but, in this case, I'm sure she's mistaken. If she was driving past the alley, she probably didn't get a good look at the truck. I bet it was the linen service we use. They bring us sheets, lab coats, gowns, and towels several times a week. That's probably what she saw." There was a pause and he continued, "And none of my employees would have been in my apartment without my permission."

"And no one else would have been in there?"

"No, I've got the only key." He cleared his throat and said, "Son, I'm sure you're doing everything you can to find your wife, but I don't think anything happened to her at the clinic, or in my old apartment."

"But Marinel said she saw a rolled-up rug being carried out of your apartment."

"No one's been in there for months. Lately it's become a bit of a storeroom, a junk room. But, I'll tell you what I'll do. First thing tomorrow, I'll check with my staff and see what I can find out. Call me about ten and I'll let you know what they say."

Luke thanked the doctor and hung up.

When he got back to the pit, the coals were perfect so he put the steak on the grill. He brought the salad out and munched on it while the steak cooked. When he finished he nursed his beer as he watched the cattle graze beyond the fence.

When the steak was ready the dogs watched closely as Luke used his pocketknife to cut his first bite. He savored the beef and for the first time all day, he relaxed.

But his enjoyment was short-lived. He had barely taken his second bite when he heard a car door slam on the other side of the bunkhouse. *Probably Lauren coming over for the rental papers on the Jeep*, he thought. But then another door slammed. He stood and walked over to the side of the building and saw a black-and-white police cruiser in front of the bunkhouse. Paul was standing on the driver's side and Ernest was on the passenger side.

"Did you get my message?" Luke said as he chewed on his steak.

As they walked closer, Ernest focused on Luke's face. "What in the world happened to you?"

"I ran into Willy at the grocery store," Luke said, gently touching his forehead, "and he wasn't too happy that I talked to you."

Ernest examined the raw skin a little closer. "Are you okay?"

"I'm fine. Did you get my message?"

"Yeah, we did. Tell me about this earring."

"When we got married, a friend in Austin made some

earrings especially for Bonnie and said he wouldn't use that design again. They are simple gold crosses but the workmanship is unique. I can't describe it, but his initials are on the back: RW. If you want me to, I'll call Ricky and have him send you a picture of them. And you can compare it to the one Willy's wearing."

"I'll let you know if I need that," Ernest said as he glanced at his partner. "But Paul's got some information that has changed our investigation."

"You have? What is it?" Luke asked inquisitively.

Paul pulled a small spiral notebook out of his shirt pocket and flipped it open. "We've come up with some more information and we've concluded your wife left of her own free will."

Luke stepped back and with a confused expression. "What are you talking about?"

"When you filled out the missing persons report, we asked for all of your credit cards. You didn't mention a Discover card."

"A Discover card? Oh shit, I forgot about that one. Bonnie just got that one a couple of months ago so she could separate her business expenses from our personal stuff. I don't even carry one."

"We found that she bought a bus ticket to Calgary about noon on Tuesday. The bus left at twelve-fifty. The ticket agent said she remembers selling a ticket to a lady with red hair and a brace on her arm."

"Oh, bullshit," Luke spit out vehemently.

"There was also an airline ticket, Calgary to Dallas, bought with the same credit card. And the airline confirms that Bonnie Wakefield was on the plane that left at six forty-five Tuesday night," Paul said, glancing at Ernest.

Luke listened as Paul rattled off more information from his little notebook, "We've been in touch with the bus company and they contacted the driver of that run, Olin Carnell. He's been driving for Greyhound for twenty-six years. We faxed them a photo and he said he's pretty sure it was her. He said the bus had only about a dozen passengers on it from here to Fort Macleod and he remembers her sitting alone near the back of the bus."

Regardless of how much it sounded like her, Luke refused to believe it. He backed away and shook his head. "It wasn't her."

Paul continued. "I talked to the driver. He remembers her because she was in the back and keeping to herself. She never took off the big sunglasses she had on."

"She didn't have her sunglasses. I found them in the alley, remember?"

"Yeah, I know that's what you said," Paul said, glancing at Ernest.

"Anyway, the driver said that at Fort Macleod the bus filled up and he couldn't tell us much more about her, other than she did get off in Calgary, and she didn't have any luggage."

"It's not her! He's wrong, you're all wrong. There's no reason Bonnie would do that."

Ernest said, "Paul's going to Calgary tomorrow morning to meet Mr. Carnell and get his statement. We've already taken a statement from the girl at the bus station. We have no reason to doubt what she has told us."

"This is insane. Bonnie and I haven't had any problems since we got back together." He looked from Ernest to Paul for confirmation. Both watched him without expressions. "You've got to believe me."

"You said you have only been back together since February, that's only five months. Don't you think it's possible she changed her mind and just decided to go home?"

"Absolutely not. If there was a problem she would have talked to me about it." He ran his fingers through his hair and commanded them, "You can't quit looking for her."

"Luke you haven't been honest with us since this whole thing started," Ernest said. "Time after time, your version of the truth in reality has been lies. You need to be honest with yourself now."

"No. You're wrong. You don't have a clue what you're talking about."

Luke couldn't stand to hear any more bull shit about Bonnie. They didn't know her or him or anything about their relationship. All he wanted now was for them to be gone. The information he got from Marinel didn't matter anymore. Their minds were made up, and regardless of what he told them, it wasn't going to change anything.

Ernest took a step closer to Luke and pointed a finger at him. "We do know what we're talking about and the facts don't lie. Here's the truth as I see it: You hit her one too many times and she finally did the right thing and left you. I'd bet that by the time you get back to Texas you'll find that she's already moved out." Luke saw a vein in Ernest neck throbbing and his face was getting redder. "Women like her are used to being beat up. She covered for you because she knew if she didn't, she'd pay for it later."

"I've never hit her," Luke said through gritted teeth.

"I know your type, Luke. You are every woman's worse nightmare. I'll bet you can't wait to find her so you can beat the tar out of her again." Ernest inhaled deeply and stepped back. He held his chin high and said, "Now, we're done here. This case is closed."

Luke watched as Ernest turned and started walking away. Then he stopped and turned back to Luke. "And, one more thing: We'd appreciate it if you'd leave Cardston as soon as you can. We don't need your type here."

Paul hesitated as Ernest walked away, then said, "If you'd like I'll let you know what the bus driver says after I talk to him tomorrow."

It was over. It was no use. Luke gave him a cold stare and said, "Don't bother."

Paul gave a half shrug and said, "I'm sorry, Luke."

***

Luke looked Paul in the eyes and shook his head, then turned and walked away. He knew now it was up to him to find Bonnie.

Chapter 23

Luke walked around to the back of the bunkhouse trying to keep his temper in check. He was so mad he could eat nails. When he heard the Crown Victoria drive away he started to pace across the back porch. To think Bonnie had hopped on a bus to Calgary and flown back to Texas was beyond ridiculous.

For ten minutes he couldn't hold a thought, all he wanted to do was beat the crap out of that old man. Now Luke was considered a wife-beater, and probably every law enforcement agency in Canada would know about it before he could get out of the country.

He went to the refrigerator and grabbed another beer. When he got back to the porch he noticed Elvis and Buddy sitting beside the table where his T-bone sat cooling. It was scrumptious ten minutes ago, but now, his appetite was gone. He stepped over to the table, cut the meat in half and set the plate down in front of the dogs. Elvis grabbed the piece with the bone and ran off in one direction, and Buddy grabbed the rest and went the other way.

Luke took several long draws on the beer while he paced. It took at least ten minutes before his blood pressure settled down enough to actually think of something other than pistol-whipping the old man with his own gun.

But, he knew staying mad wasn't going to help anything. He had to do something. And now he had to follow his strongest lead.

He changed into blue jeans and boots and headed for town.

It was nearly dark when Luke found The Stampede on the north side of town. It looked like a Texas honky-tonk that passed its prime thirty years ago. The old wooden building was about half the size of a high school gymnasium and he could see where the tin roof had been patched at least a dozen times. The dirt parking lot was packed but he found a space between two pickups that looked like they'd been hauling hay all day. As he walked toward the front door he heard the whine of live country music reverberating off the wooden walls of the dancehall.

He stepped inside the front door and stopped to let a waitress with a tray of dirty plates and empty beer bottles cross in front of him.

Luke surveyed the crowded room through a haze of cigarette smoke. The front part of the building was a café where about twenty tables were covered with red-checkered tablecloths. Over on one side were half a dozen booths and on the other side of the room were four busy pool tables. Along the back wall was a long crowded bar. Just left of the bar was a swinging door with a faded sign that said *Cover Charge $5.00*.

He pushed through the crowd and wedged himself between two cowboys at the bar. He ordered a beer and took in the rowdy atmosphere. It was obvious that most of the drinkers at the bar had been here for some time. Loud laughter and an occasional whoop could be heard above the rumble of the crowd. It seemed like a typical small-town bar where everyone seemed to know each other.

The bartender set a beer down in front of Luke and as he reached back for his wallet, he caught the familiar scent of gardenias. He glanced over his shoulder and saw Mitzi walking toward the ladies room.

He dropped a five on the bar and kept an eye on the bathroom door. A few minutes later she emerged and strutted back through the crowd. As she walked past him he grabbed her by the arm. Turning, she recognized him immediately and said, "Hey baby, you made it," then swung her arms around his neck, once again smearing him with her latest splash of Jungle Gardenia. When she stepped away, she grabbed his hand and started dragging him with her. "I'm sitting down at the other end of the bar."

At the end of the bar Mitzi reclaimed her seat and Luke pulled up a stool beside hers. She summoned the bartender and said, "Johnny, give me a Crown and Seven?"

"I'm glad you came out," she said then leaned a little closer and tried to focus on the scrapes on his forehead. Luke could tell she'd already had too much to drink. "What happened to your head?"

"Oh, I ran into a wall," he said, not wanting to get into it.

She didn't seem to be concerned about it and swirled her new drink with her finger then licked it off. "So, how did it go with Marinel?"

He took a swig of his beer. "She remembered seeing Bonnie and me at the clinic."

"I thought she would," she said as she sipped on her drink.

"She told me Dr. Duncan has an apartment that's connected to the clinic. Did you know that?"

"Hell, yes." She said, slurring her words. "I could have told you that. I know everything about that place."

"I understand he keeps it locked and he's the only one with a key."

"That's bull shit," Mitzi gave him a crooked grin and shook her head. "One night Rita and I were working late and needed to get some old files that were stored in there. We looked around in his office until we found it."

"He keeps it hidden somewhere?"

"It's in his filing cabinet under K. It's got a big tag on it that says, 'Apartment'," she scoffed. "Like it took a brain surgeon to figure that one out."

"I'd really like to see that apartment."

"Why? Do you think Dr. Duncan's hiding your wife in there?"

"No, but Marinel told me she saw some guys carrying a rug out the back door. Dr. Duncan said she was wrong. I'd really like to check it out."

"I don't think anyone's been in there lately," Mitzi said.

"That's what Dr. Duncan said, but Bonnie was last seen at

the clinic and I found some stuff in the alley that was in her purse. And there was some grass closed in the door that goes to the apartment like the door had been opened recently. Seeing the inside of that apartment would help me put the pieces together. It won't take ten minutes."

"I can't do that. If Dr. Duncan knew I let you in there, he'd fire me."

He knew he could break through her resolve. "How would he ever know? Like you said, you're the office manager—you can come and go when you want to, right?"

"Yeah, but…" She looked at him and blinked, trying to focus. She slowly shook her head. "I don't know about going into his apartment."

Luke grabbed his billfold and took out a hundred-dollar bill. He held it below the bar where she could see it. "Luke, I can't."

She watched as he pulled out another crisp hundred and held it with the first one. She raised her stare from the bills to Luke. The corners of her intoxicated lips turned up. "I said no."

He took the last bill from his wallet and held it with the others. "It's all I have." His eyes moved from her bloodshot eyes to the bills, and counted them, one by one, then looked back at her. Her eyes went to the bills and stayed there. "I really want to see that apartment."

Mitzi closed her eyes and took a deep breath. Slowly her eyelids opened and she looked passed Luke and panned the crowd, which was oblivious to them.

She quickly pulled the bills from his hand and hid them in her purse. "You *cannot* tell anyone I let you in there," she said adamantly.

"Don't worry, I won't."

She tipped up her glass and guzzled the rest of her drink. "Let's go get this over with before I change my mind."

"I'm ready," he said, pushing back his beer bottle.

He walked behind her as they made their way to the door. She was inebriated, but he decided she could make the two-mile drive without a problem. He figured she was an experienced drunk and had probably made the drive a hundred times before, much drunker than she was now.

The streets of downtown were deserted and Luke followed her to the alley behind the clinic where they parked next to the building. It was dark except for a small sodium vapor light that illuminated the back door of the clinic. She unlocked the door and they slipped inside where Mitzi punched a series of numbers on a keypad on the wall and the flashing red light turned to a steady green.

"Okay, the alarms off," she said, "C'mon." She hit the light switch and the hallway lit up. They went down to the first door on the left. "This is Dr. Duncan's office." She twisted the handle, but it didn't open. She rattled it back and forth but it still didn't budge. "Well, crap. He locked his office."

She looked back at Luke and shrugged her shoulders.

Luke's heart sank. *Three hundred bucks down the drain.*

Then Mitzi burst out laughing and pulled a key chain out of her purse. She rattled it in front of him and said, "Don't worry, honey, I've got the key."

Luke sighed and shook his head while she opened the door, still giggling.

She turned on the light and walked over to a filing cabinet in the corner. A second later she pulled out a single gold key and walked over to the door on the adjacent wall and unlocked it. They stepped inside and she flipped a switch that turned on two lamps that sat on end tables on either side of a saddle-brown leather sofa.

They were in the living room. Adjacent to the sofa was a recliner; both were arranged around a coffee table in the middle of the room. There was an old television in a cabinet against the wall and a closed door just to the left of it. Visualizing the layout, Luke imagined the door opened onto the alley.

Behind him, against the wall, a dozen cardboard boxes were stacked neatly on the dark brown tiled floor. Next to them were a couple of old filing cabinets, an old desk, some office chairs, and some pieces of medical equipment he couldn't identify. He could see Dr. Duncan wasn't kidding when he said the apartment's primary function was that of a storeroom.

Just beyond the living room he saw a small kitchen on one side and adjacent to it was an open door where he could see the foot of a bed.

"Here it is," Mitzi said.

Luke walked ahead of her into the room. Mitzi followed him as he made his way to the bedroom. The room was small with only a queen-sized bed, a night table and a tall dresser. It was nice; no junk had been dumped in here. Beyond the bedroom was a small bathroom.

They went back to the living room where Mitzi went over and dropped into the recliner.

"What do you think?" she asked.

"I don't know. Give me a few minutes to look around," he said.

"Go ahead, but not too long," she said as she pushed back on the chair and a footrest popped up in front of her. "I don't want anyone to come by and see my car, okay?"

"Okay," he said.

Mitzi had already closed her eyes. Luke hoped she'd go to sleep; that would give him more time.

The first thing he noticed was a layer of dust on the framed photos and glass shelves by the TV which meant the apartment probably wasn't cleaned on a regular basis. But it was the rugs that he came to see and the best he could tell, there were only two. One was a runner, at least twelve feet long and a couple of feet wide. It was behind the sofa and stretched from the office door toward the bedroom. It was beige with a colorful pattern stitched into it.

The other one was under the coffee table and they matched. It was about eight feet square. Both looked new, the colors still bright. He squatted down and lifted one corner. The floor was shinier underneath it. He ran his finger along the floor and came up with a layer of dust. Gently, he lifted one side of the table a few inches and noticed the carpet was crushed flat where the table leg rested. There was no doubt this rug had been here for some time.

He stood and wiped the dust off his hands as he looked around for an area where a rug might be missing. But here in the living room there wasn't room for another one. He strolled through the other rooms but came to the same conclusion. There didn't seem to be an area where a rug was missing, especially one that would take two people to carry. He went back to the living room with the conclusion that Marinel did not see a rug carried out of this apartment.

But what she could have seen puzzled him. He glanced around one more time, but saw no reason to stay here any longer. As he leaned over to wake up Mitzi, something started pounding on the door in the clinic that opened onto the alley.

Bam, Bam, Bam!

Mitzi's eyes popped open like a Jack in the Box and she saw Luke's face in front of her. She was on the verge of panic so Luke quickly put his hand over her mouth. She started to fight, but quit when she recognized Luke, he pulled his hand away.

Bam, Bam, Bam!

"Shit," she whispered as she looked from side to side and struggled to get out of the recliner. She got up quietly and rushed to the office door, then turned to him. "Get back in the bedroom and stay there." She went to Dr. Duncan's office, closing the door behind her.

Bam, Bam, Bam!

Luke sneaked over to the closed door and listened.

He could hear Mitzi ask who was outside. A second later he heard her tell whoever it was to wait a minute and she'd open the door. He hurried back to the bedroom and waited.

A few seconds later he heard Mitzi laughing and a man's voice. It sounded like they knew each other. There were sounds of conversation and a minute later he heard the door close.

Luke sat on the side of the bed, relieved. The clatter of her high heels came his way and he remained still until she opened the bedroom door.

"We got lucky," she said as she crossed her arms and leaned on the door jam.

"What do you mean?"

"It was Kenneth, an old friend. I told him I was showing my new boyfriend where I worked. He was cool with that. Said he wouldn't mention it to anyone. Are you ready?"

"Yeah, I guess so."

As Luke stood, Mitzi leaned down and smoothed the bedspread where he had been sitting. "That's odd," she said.

"What's odd?" Luke followed her gaze back to the bed.

"Doctor Duncan has a handmade Indian blanket that is always on this bed. It was a gift from Mrs. Aponi, an old Indian lady here in town. It's beautiful. I tried to buy it from him but he wouldn't sell it because every time she comes to see him, she always wants to see it. And, it's always on the foot of the bed."

Luke looked back at the bed and all he saw was a cranberry bedspread with an intricate pattern. He considered this missing blanket. *Could Marinel have seen two men carrying a blanket?*

He ran his hand over the red bedspread and a thought hit him. He pulled back the top of the spread near the pillows.

"What are you doing?" Mitzi asked.

The underside of the spread was lined with white fabric. Without answering her, he pulled it back further. It looked normal so he pulled it back more, and more, until he got to the bottom, where he found what he was looking for. There were two red stains, each about the size of a quarter, soaked through to the cream-colored sheets. Cautiously, he touched it with the tip of his finger. It was mostly crusty, but a little sticky in the middle. He flipped it back over; the red stains disappeared on the red pattern. Red on red, they were impossible to see.

"Look," he said with the red stains in view.

She leaned over. "What is that?"

"It looks like dried blood to me." He knelt down to the floor, and with his face at ground level, he used the reflection of the light across the room to look for stains. "Here too," he said, pointing to two other droplets in front of the bed. Now knowing what to look for, he went back through the living room and into the doctor's office, pointing at more dark red spots. In front of the desk were two armchairs and in front of the one on the left he found a red smear the size of a credit card. It looked like someone had tried to wipe up a small puddle of blood.

"It looks like a trail of blood, from here all the way back to the bed," Luke said. He followed the dried red spots back into the apartment and to the bed. He checked the runner behind the sofa and added, "But there's none on the carpet. Either the person who was bleeding was avoiding the carpet runner. Or maybe being carried."

"What are you going to do now?"

"I've got to let the RCMP know about this."

In a panic she said, "You said you wouldn't tell anyone I let you in here."

"Don't worry, by law I'm not obligated to tell them how I got this information," Luke said. He had no idea what the law was, actually, but he didn't want Mitzi to panic. He wanted to keep her out of this, but he'd do anything he had to in order to find Bonnie.

She reset the alarm and they went out to the alley where she made Luke promise, one more time, that he wouldn't tell anyone. He did and watched her drive away, now much more sober than she'd been when they got there half an hour earlier.

He started the Jeep and at the corner tried to decide what to do next. It was close to midnight and from previous experience he knew no one would be at the RCMP office at this hour. Neither Paul nor Ernest would come out unless it was an emergency. He knew they wouldn't do anything tonight. He would get some sleep and contact Paul first thing in the morning and tell him about this new evidence. They'd have to keep the case open. It was obvious that something was going on at the clinic.

He turned right and headed for the bunkhouse.

Chapter 24

Luke held his hand under the faucet in the shower waiting for the water to heat up, but it didn't. Naked, he walked into the kitchen where he found the water heater. The pilot light was out. Using a book of matches lying beside it, he lit the unit, but at the same time decided there wasn't time to let the water heat up.

The first thing he learned was that tap water in Canada was nothing like it was in Texas. There was no doubt in his mind that the water he was standing under was being delivered directly from a glacier.

It was one of the fastest showers he'd ever taken, and when he was fully dressed he was still shivering.

He found his backpack with the rest of the hiking gear and threw in a travel guide for Alberta, binoculars, maps, a hunting knife, a notepad and pens. When he pulled open the front door to leave, the dogs greeted him, tails wagging.

"Sorry boy," he said as he walked past Buddy who followed him with a stick in his mouth. "No time today."

When he cranked up the Jeep, the bright lights on the dashboard came to life telling him it was six-thirty. Elvis watched from the porch as he pulled away from the bunkhouse and Buddy ran alongside until he reached the highway.

The streets in Cardston were deserted as he drove through town to the RCMP office. There he found the same officer he'd met a few days earlier.

"Paul's in Calgary this morning," he said, rocking back and forth in a squeaky desk chair while he stirred his coffee. "And Ernest won't get here until about eight."

Luke had forgotten that Paul was going to Calgary to interview the bus driver. Dealing with Ernest was not going to be pleasant. *Ernest will probably go ballistic when I refuse to tell him how I got into the apartment*, Luke thought.

"I'm going to the diner to eat, but I'll be back at eight," Luke said as he walked back toward the door. "If Ernest comes in, tell him where I am, okay?"

"Yes sir, I will."

The diner had just opened and a small group of men who looked like farmers sat at a long table in the middle of the dining room. When he entered, they glanced over and gave him that 'who are you?' look.

He ordered coffee and was going through a menu when Sonny stepped in the front door.

"Mind if I join you?"

"No, have a seat."

Sonny pulled out a cigarette. "You mind?"

Luke did, but said, "No."

"I didn't know you came to work this early," Luke stated.

"I don't, but I've got to get some stuff done because I'm leaving town today," Sonny said. He rubbed his eyes. "How are things going? Any news?"

Luke filled him in on his conversation last night with Ernest and Paul.

"So, what are you going to do?" Sonny asked.

"I've found something at the clinic that's pretty interesting."

"The clinic? What do you mean?"

"Next door to the clinic, Dr. Duncan has an apartment. There's a door from his office that goes into the apartment. I found what looks like blood on the bedspread and a trail of blood on the floor leading back to his office."

"How'd you get into his apartment?"

"It wasn't easy, but I did." For the next minute he spelled out his suspicions.

"Aw, come on." Sonny grinned and leaned closer. "You think someone had Bonnie rolled up in that blanket?"

"That was the last place anyone saw her," Luke said as he

pointed toward the clinic half a mile away. "If she walked out of that clinic voluntarily, she'd be here right now."

"Are you saying you think Dr. Duncan's involved in this?"

"No, not at all. I'm saying there are some things down there that don't add up."

"Does Ernest know about this blood you found?"

Breakfast arrived and as Luke spread jelly on a piece of toast, he looked at Sonny, "Not yet, but when he gets to work I'm going to go tell him about it."

"Good luck. It sounds like you've really made some progress," Sonny said. He pushed the coffee cup away, stood, and dropped a couple of bills on the table. "I need to get going. I'll talk to you later."

Luke nodded as he dug into the eggs.

Luke got back to the detachment at eight but Ernest still hadn't made it to work. The receptionist said they expected him soon. After waiting for almost an hour, the receptionist hung up the phone and said, "That was the chief and he's on his way."

"What's taking him so long?"

"His daughter teaches at Lethbridge High School. Someone called and said she was in an accident and on her way to the hospital."

"Is she okay?" Luke asked.

"Yeah, she's fine. There was no accident, it was some kind of prank," she said. "He couldn't even find out who called the police. He'll be here in about an hour."

Luke dropped heavily into a chair and pushed back his cap. He had no choice but to wait.

It was after ten by the time Ernest got there. The receptionist led Luke back to his office and it was obvious he wasn't in a sociable mood.

"Okay, what now?" Ernest said, looking over his glasses.

"I told you the last place Bonnie was seen was in the clinic and no one really remembers seeing her leave. I have a source who told me there is blood on the floor in Dr. Duncan's office and droplets of blood on the floor in his apartment that leads to his bed. There is blood on the bedspread and sheets. The big Indian blanket that is usually on the bed is missing. I spoke to Marinel Hayes, who said she saw some men carrying what looked like a large, rolled-up carpet out of the back door of the apartment on Tuesday just after noon. I think there's a good chance that the blood could be Bonnie's. And I think it's possible that what Marinel saw was someone carrying the Indian blanket with Bonnie rolled up inside it."

"That's the biggest bunch of baloney I've ever heard. Doc Duncan is at least seventy-five years old, for God's sake. What in the world would he want with your wife?"

"I'm not accusing him. All I'm saying is that the clinic was the last place Bonnie was seen and it needs to be checked out."

"How do you know this?"

"I've got a source at the clinic who told me in strict confidence. They said they'd get fired if I exposed them," Luke said. "But I really wish you'd check it out."

Ernest sighed deeply and shook his head. "Okay. Let me call Doc Duncan and see if he'll let us in. Wait for me out front."

Twenty minutes later, Luke followed Ernest and two officers to the clinic. They all entered through the front door and went back where Dr. Duncan was waiting for them in his office. Luke waited just outside the office while Ernest talked to him.

"You said this was about that woman who disappeared. What does this have to do with me, Ernest?"

"Doc, I know you've talked to Luke Wakefield. The last place anyone saw his wife was here in the clinic. Now someone said they saw blood on the floor here in your office and in your apartment. Do you mind if we check them out?"

"Blood in here? Who said that?"

"I don't know," he said, glancing at Luke. "But if we could

just check it out, I'm sure we can clear this whole thing up before it goes any further."

"That's fine. Just do what you have to."

"Okay." Turning to Luke, he said, "Come in here and show me where this blood is supposed to be."

Luke stepped into the office and stopped in front of the leather armchair where the red smear had been the night before. He couldn't see it so he leaned down to examine the floor more closely. But the floor was clean. Everything he'd seen the night before was gone.

He pointed at the floor, encircling an area as big as a basketball. "It was right around here." Not seeing anything, he walked over to the door on the opposite wall and pointed. "And over here."

Ernest and one of the officers pulled out their flashlights and bent over so they were a couple of feet above the floor. They moved along the path slowly following Luke until they got to the door.

"I don't see any blood."

"On TV I've seen them spray something on the floor that makes the blood more visible," said Luke.

"That's on TV, not here," Ernest said. "What about the other stuff you told me about?"

"The bedspread was in the apartment." Luke looked at the doctor who watched from behind his desk and said, "Can we take a look inside your apartment, Doc? It won't take but a minute."

The doctor went to the filing cabinet and got the key. He walked over and unlocked the door. As the door swung open, Luke stepped inside and walked slowly toward the bedroom, his eyes searched the floor for the drops of blood he had seen the night before, but saw none. His heart sank when he noticed a brown bedspread now covered the bed. And across the foot of the bed was a beautiful handmade Indian blanket.

"Is this the bedspread where the blood is?"

"No, the bedspread was red. It's been changed?"

"Doc, have you changed the bedspread lately?" Ernest asked the doctor.

"No. I don't think anyone's been in here for at least three months, maybe more."

"Do you have a red bedspread?"

"I might, but I don't pay attention to those kinds of things, Ernest. It's been years since I've slept in this bed."

Ernest walked over and picked up one corner of the blanket. "Is this the Indian blanket you've always had here?"

"Mrs. Aponi gave me that back in 1986. Been on this bed ever since."

"Ever send it out to be cleaned?"

"No reason to. It just lays on the foot of the bed."

Before he spoke Ernest gave the other cop and Luke a look that told them they were done. "Doc, I'm sorry about all this. Don't know where we got such mixed-up information. Thanks for letting us barge in on you like this."

After they got back outside, Ernest turned to Luke and said, "Are you satisfied now?"

"No, because that's not the way it was yesterday."

"How do you know it wasn't?"

"I just know," Luke said adamantly. He'd seen the blood with his own eyes but it was gone today. The bedspread was changed and the Indian blanket was back. Even if he gave up Mitzi, who could confirm his story and admit they were in the apartment less than eight hours earlier, it wouldn't help. They had no proof.

"Darnit, Luke. You've got to tell me how you know this if you want me to believe you."

Luke looked at the ground and shook his head. He came up with an outstretched hand. "Can you get that stuff and come back and check to see if blood had been on the floor?"

"Listen to me son," Ernest said as he stepped over and stood nose to nose with Luke. "Doc Duncan is a friend of mine. I've known him for over fifty years. He didn't have to let us in there because we didn't have a search warrant. There is no way

I'm going to humiliate myself by doing something that asinine when you won't even tell me how you got your information."

Luke stepped away and shook his head. "Something's not right here, because I know that blood was there yesterday."

"How do you know? If you can prove it, then prove it," Ernest seemed to have lost his patience. "Otherwise, you got nothing. Understand? Nothing."

As Ernest got in his cruiser his cell phone rang. He answered and listened for half a minute, then said, "That was Paul. The bus driver confirmed it was your wife. Said she was wearing sunglasses and remembers seeing a brace on her arm."

"There's something wrong here." *Someone is trying to make it look like she's not missing. Why?*

"Luke, go home," Ernest said as he started the car. "There's nothing else we can do for you. We have no evidence of foul play. Everything we have says she's left on her own."

"What about Willy? Have you asked him about the earring?"

"No, and I'm not going to."

Ernest backed out and pulled away, leaving Luke standing alone across from the clinic.

Luke open the door of the Jeep, but remained standing, trying to comprehend what had just happened. Again, what appeared to be solid evidence turned into a disaster. Someone had obviously cleaned up the scene. The question was, who?

It had to be Mitzi.

He closed the door of the Jeep and ran back into the clinic.

"I need to talk to Mitzi," he told the receptionist.

"She's running late today, but I expect her any minute now. Do you want to wait?"

Without answering, he left and ran to the Jeep. Her apartment was only blocks away. As he rounded the corner he saw her getting into her Miata. The Jeep skidded to a stop behind her car. When he jumped out of the Jeep he saw her look back over her shoulder.

He stomped up beside her. "Who did you tell about what we found last night?"

"No one," she said. "Why?" She appeared puzzled by his irate tone.

"I just left your office. The cops went down there to check out the blood we found, but guess what?"

"What?" she asked, confusion in her voice.

"The blood that was on the floor last night is gone. The bedspread's been changed, and even that Indian blanket you said was missing is back. Right where's it's supposed to be. Somebody found out about it. Who'd you tell?"

"No one," she said defensively. "You saw me go home and as soon as I got in bed, I passed out and didn't wake up until an hour ago. I over slept and the only one I've talked to is Monica, the receptionist, and all I told her is that I was going to be late."

"Then how'd they find out?"

"How would I know?" Her response was defensive but sincere. "Really, I don't. I've got to get to work right now. You didn't tell them I let you in, did you?"

"No, I didn't tell anyone anything."

"Good. Could you move your Jeep? I've got to get to work? I'm late…but check with me later and I'll let you know what I hear down at the office."

As Luke drove away, his mind was reeling. How did anyone find out they went down there? But there was no one else who knew.

Then it hit him.

Sonny. He told him everything at breakfast. *And Sonny drives a van, a silver van.*

His thoughts flashed back to the confrontation Bonnie and Sonny had in his camera store in St. Mary. Sonny had a good reason to be mad at Bonnie; she had cost him a three thousand dollar sale. But, surely not mad enough to go to this length.

He made a quick U-turn and headed for Rocky Mountain Photography.

The closer he got the more his fury grew. *All this time Sonny's been acting like a good friend, when in reality, he's been behind it all. He's been using me to follow the progress of the RCMP.*

When Luke pulled up to the stop sign at Main he could see the studio across the street. Through the windows he saw Sonny moving around inside.

While he waited for an opening in the traffic, he saw a silver van approach from the south and pull into a parking space in front of Sonny's store. A lady with long brown hair jumped out and scurried up the steps into the store.

She was quite animated while talking to Sonny. After a moment, Sonny grabbed her shoulders and pulled her close. She wrapped her arms around him and they kissed.

As she left the camera store Luke reached down to the floorboard on the passenger side and pulled the binoculars out of the backpack. Even without her green smock he recognized her. It was Rita, the nurse from the clinic. Quickly Luke's mind connected the dots between Sonny and the clinic. But it still didn't make sense. What would they want with Bonnie?

Rita got into Sonny's blue BMW parked next to the van and as she drove away Luke decided his confrontation with Sonny could wait. For now, he would follow Rita. He put on his left turn signal and pulled into traffic, about half a block behind her.

After Rita left, Sonny went back into his office where he had a view of the street. While he watched Rita back out, he noticed a black Jeep sitting at the stop sign across the street. In it the driver held a pair of binoculars pointed at Rita. When he lowered them Sonny recognized Luke at once.

When Rita pulled away, the Jeep fell in behind her.

Sonny pulled his cell phone out of his pocket and dialed.

Rita answered.

He said, "Looks like our plans just changed."

Chapter 25

"What do you mean?" Rita asked.

"Look in your rearview mirror. Black Jeep? That's Luke."

"Is he following me?"

"I think so. When you left the studio, I saw him watching you through binoculars. I'm afraid he's on to us."

"What do we do?"

"I've got to make some changes, but it will actually make the next step easier."

"So what do you want me to do?"

"He's probably going to follow you, so kill a few minutes then go to the Home Center. Park in the middle of the parking lot where there are a lot of other cars around you. Go inside and watch for him."

"Okay."

"He'll probably try to stay out of sight but watch what you are doing. I want him away from the front door so he can't see the parking lot. Go to the back of the store and mill around until I call you. At that point I want you to leave, and make sure he doesn't follow you. Go to your apartment and get what you need, then come to my place. We're leaving as soon as you get there."

While Luke followed Rita, he thought about his conversation with Sonny. Other than Mitzi, he was the only other person who knew about the blood. Luke ruled out Mitzi because she wouldn't have let him in the doctor's apartment if she were involved. That left only Sonny. And now knowing he was in a relationship with Rita, it all made sense.

Sonny was probably the one who called in the false alarm about Ernest's daughter being in an accident. This would delay him and give Rita time to clean up the blood and change the sheets and bedspread before the cops got there.

Luke clenched his jaw as he thought about how stupid he had been to trust Sonny. Sure, Bonnie had pissed off Sonny the day they arrived in Montana by costing him a huge sale, but was he the kind of guy who would do something like this for revenge? Or was it something else?

Luke focused on the BMW in front of him thinking she might lead him to Bonnie.

Halfway through town when Rita pulled into the Husky Food Store, he parked half a block away where he could watch her. Five minutes later she was back on the street but made it only a block before she pulled into the drive thru of Perk and Go Coffee Shop. Her next stop was at Alberta Discount Lumber and Home Center on the north side of town. It was a huge warehouse store and the parking lot was busy. From a distance he watched her park between a minivan and a motor home with Arizona plates.

After she was inside, he parked a few rows over and trotted over to check out the BMW. Other than a brown leather organizer in the passenger seat, the interior was spotless.

He went inside and spotted Rita as she browsed through an assortment of light fixtures near the back of the store. From there she stopped and talked to a sales person about mini-blinds and shutters until her cell phone rang. After a short conversation she flipped her phone closed and walked quickly out of the store.

Luke got to the parking lot about ten seconds behind her and ran to the Jeep. By the time he got the engine started he saw she was almost to the highway.

But when he started to back out, a metallic blue Cadillac had him blocked in. The Caddy was the size of Noah's Ark and the driver was a little blue-haired lady who could barely see over the steering wheel. He followed her gaze and saw she was waiting for a parking space where a couple of guys were loading some lumber into a pickup.

He checked for Rita and saw her pull onto the highway and accelerate into traffic. Luke laid on the horn for a full second, but evidently Miss Daisy wasn't wearing her hearing aid, because she never acknowledged the annoying blast of noise.

By the time Luke made it out of the parking lot, he was at least a minute behind Rita. He cruised through town, looking for the BMW in parking lots and on side streets. At Second Street he cruised past the clinic and checked the parking lot in front and in the alley, but it wasn't there.

After circling the block he pulled back onto Main and headed south. When he got to Rocky Mountain Photography he noticed Sonny's van was gone. The big windows across the front of the store made it easy to see that the only person inside was the teenaged employee he had met earlier in the week.

As he continued south he watched for the van or the BMW. He reached down to grab the bottled water in the console and noticed a large brown envelope on the passenger seat beside his backpack.

He didn't remember it being there before. He picked it up and noticed on the front, handwritten in block letters, *Luke Wakefield- Important.*

It was sealed. As he drove, he pushed a finger under the flap of the envelope and tore it open. He reached in and pulled out the contents.

A couple of pieces of white folded paper came out, followed by two glossy Polaroid pictures with white borders. Even at a distance, the auburn color of Bonnie's ponytail glowed brightly in the snapshots. His heart raced as he fumbled for them.

He focused on the first one. It was definitely her. She was on a bed, lying on her side with her head on a pillow. It looked like she was asleep but her hands were behind her. The quality and lighting in the snapshot were poor, but it looked like they were tied.

He flipped to the next picture, it showed her from a slightly different angle, but a closer shot of her face. Her eyes were closed and her lips were slightly parted. There was something under her nose. It looked like dirt or maybe dried blood. His first thought was that she was alive or else she wouldn't be tied.

An air horn blared and Luke eyes shot back to the highway. His Jeep had crossed the center stripe and a huge white semi was swerving to avoid hitting him.

"Shit," he screamed, as he jerked the Jeep back into his own lane. But he overcorrected and nearly sideswiped an old Chevy Camaro in the lane next to him.

The goateed driver dodged to avoid being smashed, then shot Luke the finger while yelling through his open window. "Watch where you're going, asshole!"

Luke backed off the gas and the Camaro flew past him. He pulled onto the shoulder of the road and skidded to a stop.

His heart pounded as he unfolded the pieces of paper. His eyes darted across the page. It was a map with some writing beneath it. Quickly he went to the second page.

His eyes narrowed as he read the computer-generated note:

YOUR WIFE IS ALIVE AND UNHARMED. IF YOU WANT TO SEE HER AGAIN, DO THE FOLLOWING:

-Make no more contact with the police. We will know if you do.

-Come to the location on the enclosed map. Be there PRECISELY AT 6PM.

-Come alone.

-Tell no one.

-Bring no guns or weapons.

-If we see any police or indication that you are not alone, you will never see your wife again.

-After you read this call the following number and leave a message.

On the next line was a ten-digit number.

He flipped back to the other piece of paper. It was a map showing much of Alberta and Montana. A circle was drawn around Whitefish, a town west of Glacier National Park. A yellow line outlined a route from Cardston to Whitefish.

On the bottom of the page it said: It will take about three hours to get there. He glanced at the digital clock in the Jeep. 1:22. Four hours and thirty-eight minutes from now.

He pulled out the snapshots and studied them again. Bonnie looked like she was asleep, but she was in an awkward position. Her head was on a pillow, but her body looked as if someone had put her there. It was obvious she was unconscious.

He turned the picture over and saw a single line written with a black marker that read *No cops or she dies*.

Luke stared out the window. His first thought was that he had no choice; he had to do what they said. But his logical mind told him he was crazy to go into this alone. It was obviously a trick, it was dangerous, and it might cost both of them their lives.

From the highway he heard a car honk twice. He looked over and saw a car stopped in the street and the driver of the car making hand signals at him. He looked around and realized he was blocking a driveway. He waved apologetically and backed the Jeep out of the other driver's way. Luke realized he was in front of the Cardston detachment of the RCMP.

His first thought was to go in and prove to Ernest that he was not an abusive husband and she had not gone back to Texas. Someone had abducted Bonnie and was holding her against her will.

He pulled into the parking lot and marched toward the front door. But as he got closer he imagined the confrontation playing out in his mind. They already suspected him of being an abusive husband. When he found the broken sunglasses, grocery list and windbreaker with blood on it, they did everything but accuse him of planting the evidence. He knew if he showed them the photos and letters, they wouldn't believe him. Instead, they'd probably arrest him and hold him until he told them where he was holding her.

Deep in thought, he slowed to a stop ten feet from the front door.

"You coming in?" the young officer asked as he held the door.

Luke thought about one of the lines in the note: Make no more contact with the police—because we will know if you do.

Could this be an inside job? Is someone with the RCMP connected in some way, or is this a bluff?

Luke looked through the open door and saw the friendly receptionist who had been concerned about Bonnie. She wasn't smiling now. He wondered if she knew they considered him an abusive husband. Luke looked down at the envelope in his hand and knew this was the wrong thing to do.

"No." He went back to the Jeep, and headed to the Husky pay phone. It took all the coins in his pocket to make the call. After half a dozen rings a generic greeting told him to leave a message.

"This is Luke. I'll be there at 6 p.m."

Chapter 26

Bonnie sat on the arm of the leather chair, looking out the window, watching the crows fly from pine tree to pine tree. This was the day she feared would bring pain or misery. Evil men, like the ones who were holding her hostage, seldom let their victims go unharmed. So far, no one had laid a finger on her, but she sensed that was about to change.

Yesterday morning was the last contact she had with anyone. That guy was less threatening than the first guy. He acted tough, but he was polite. Called her "ma'am," and sounded unsure of himself. She thought he was young, twenty or twenty-five at the most.

Bonnie slid down, laid her head back and closed her eyes. Today her mind was clear. Yesterday, as the hours passed, the gaps in her memory began to close and it became easier to concentrate. Now she remembered everything in detail, except how she got here. The last thing she remembered before waking up here was Rita giving her a tetanus shot. Almost immediately, she felt dizzy.

She looked down at the brace on her hand. After disconnecting the Velcro straps, she removed it and rotated her thumb. It was tender but didn't hurt the way it did the first day she was there. The doctor said it wasn't broken, just sprained. It felt much better already. And her stomach seemed to be back to normal. The pills had helped.

Bonnie's concentration was broken by a familiar whine. It was the sound of a truck negotiating the incline of the mountain road and the low, deep pulses of hip-hop music. Thank God it wasn't the other guy.

A few minutes later, the truck pulled up in the driveway. The music died and quick footsteps came in the front door.

She waited and watched the door that held her captive.

Squeaky shoes on wood floors. Then, "Hello, are you there? Do you want to go to the bathroom?"

"God yes," she said, a tremble in her voice. "Do I have to put on that pillowcase on my head?"

"Yes, that's the deal."

"Okay." She found it and put it over her head. "I'm ready."

Again, like the day before, the wind rushed past her when he opened the door.

She stood in the middle of the room facing him, the pillowcase covered her eyes. Her arms hung at her side, as if she was a teenager modeling a new dress for her mother.

She had long, well-toned legs, a tiny waist and a flat belly. The tight-fitting T-shirt showed the fullness of her breasts. The girls in his school were young and immature and lately he'd been fantasizing about older women, and she was exactly what he wanted. The afternoon they brought her out to the cabin he carried her sedated body in and laid her on the bed. The man left him alone with her while he retrieved some supplies from the van. He wanted to feel her breasts. She was drugged, out cold, she'd never know. But he wasn't a pervert. He didn't want it to be like that.

Now he watched them rise and fall with every breath, and he imagined how she looked naked.

"Are you there?" she said, bringing him back. She reached out in front of her like you do when you walk in the dark.

"I'm here," he said, adjusting his crotch that was suddenly too tight. He took her hand. It was shaking. "Relax," he said softly. "I'm not going to hurt you."

"I'm sorry, but I'm scared."

He led her out of the room, and again, like the day before, the wind caused the door to slam closed, and she jumped.

As he walked he reminded himself why he was there. They had promised him no one would be hurt and if he did everything right, he'd get a big payoff in the end. The problems his dad faced with the law would be over for good. But if he screwed things up, they had evidence that would send his dad back to prison for the rest of his life—and they said they would use it.

She held out her free hand and guided herself through the doorway and along the wall until they were at the bathroom. He guided her inside then closed the door behind her.

"Remember, don't lock the door," he said.

Through the door she asked, "Do you know how much longer I'm going to be here?"

"I don't know any more than I did yesterday. Please don't ask me a bunch of questions."

"I'm asking because it's been three days since I've had a shower. I really need one. I can be in and out in five minutes."

"No, I can't let you do that."

"Come on...you know how yucky you feel when you don't take a shower, don't you?"

"Lady..."

"I'll do it in four minutes, real fast, I promise."

He was silent while he thought. *Why not? She can't get away.*

"Please, please, please."

He knew he shouldn't but, what the hell? "Okay, but don't screw around, because if you pull anything on me I'll tie you up naked, blindfold you, and gag you. You hear me?"

"I won't. I promise." And before he knew it, he heard the water running in the shower.

While he waited he went to the kitchen and got a can of Coke. As he came back to the door, he began to worry about his decision. *But it's only a shower, and no one will know about it*, he thought.

He relaxed a bit and went out to his truck to get a bag of groceries he brought with him. After he grabbed the paper sack he started to push the door shut when he heard a sound that made his stomach cringe.

It was the knocking of a familiar engine not too far way in the forest. It could only be one person.

Holy shit!

He dropped the groceries back in the truck and ran inside. He knocked on the bathroom door and shouted, "You have to get back to your room! Quick!"

There was no response.

He pounded with his open hand. "Do you hear me? You have to get back to your room. He's coming."

Nothing.

Within a minute, two at the most, he'd be there.

There was no time to waste. He opened the bathroom door and reached for the shower curtain.

Steam boiled out of the shower as she turned around to rinse the shampoo out of her long hair. The hot water felt good as it ran down her neck and onto her back. The force of the water echoed in her ears as she rolled her head around, letting it massage the muscles in her neck. With her head under the pounding water, she heard some weird vibrations and it made her feel uneasy.

Just as she leaned out from under the shower head to listen the shower curtain flew to the side. Little John Standalone stood there, two feet away, his eyes wild.

Bonnie screamed and recoiled back into the corner. Not comprehending what he said, she begged, "Don't hurt me." Without concern about being naked, she extended her arms to hold him off.

"You have to get back to your room! He's coming!"

Though panic streaked his face, his eyes went immediately to her breast and locked there for an instant before coming back to her eyes. She could see the fear that controlled his actions and his words made no sense. Quickly she pulled back her arms and hands to cover herself.

"The other guy, he's almost here. I didn't know he was coming. Quick, you've got to get to your room." His eyes were wild going from her eyes to her body and back to her eyes and back to her breasts.

Bonnie grabbed the shower curtain and pulled it in front of her. As Little John leaned in and turned off the water, she watched him closely.

"He'll kill us both if he catches you in here."

Then she realized what he was saying. The other guy, the mean one, was coming back.

"The other guy—the one who was here yesterday. He's almost here."

A chill ran down her body. With the water off she could now hear the sound of the truck outside, not far away. They didn't have much time.

She looked around the shower curtain for a towel but the only one she saw was a hand towel by the sink. She had gotten in the shower so quickly she didn't even think about it. But, there was a cabinet across the room.

"I need a towel," she said.

He saw the hand towel and grabbed it for her.

"This is too little. Look in there."

He dropped the hand towel and looked inside the cabinet and found one. He flung it at her then stepped over and parted the curtains and wiped the steam off so he could see outside.

"Hurry."

Time was running out.

As Bonnie dried herself she noticed the mirror. It was steamed over, too. She knew that if that guy came in the bathroom, he would know someone had been in the shower. With Little John's hair dry, it would be obvious it wasn't him.

The truck was outside now. The engine rumbled as she heard it come to a stop. He was there, seconds from coming inside.

Her eyes darted around the room, looking for an idea. Immediately one came to mind, but she didn't like it. But it was their only chance.

"Take off your clothes and get in here." She dropped the towel on the floor then reached down and turned the water back on.

Little John's mouth hung open. "What?"

She pointed to the mirror. "He'll see the steamed up

mirror and window and know that since your hair is dry, it was probably me in here."

He seemed to understand and started to get into the tub.

Bonnie said, "No. Take off your clothes. You have to be taking a shower."

"But—"

"Just do it," she demanded.

He started peeling his clothes off like they were on fire.

Little John was about six-three, not nearly as big as his father, but when his shirt came off she remembered his father had said he was going to college on a football scholarship. His muscular arms and chiseled chest were that of an athlete sculpted by hours in the weight room. When he got to his boxers, he stopped and glanced at her to see if she was watching. She was, but quickly retreated behind the shower curtain just as he pushed down his underpants.

Outside, the sound of the engine died, and a few seconds later the door of the truck slammed.

Bonnie looked out at Little John. He stood naked, unsure what to do.

"Push the door until it's almost closed."

He did.

"Get in here."

He stepped into the front of the shower.

"Let me up front," she said. The shower was small and as they changed positions her breasts rubbed against him and she felt his penis brush against her.

Bonnie stood under the showerhead, facing him, making no attempt to cover herself. Little John couldn't control his eyes and kept glancing at her breasts while his hands were trying to cover his now semi-erect penis.

Bonnie realized Little John was waiting for her to tell him what to do.

"Get wet," she said pulling him into the stream of water. The bathtub was small and their bodies were now touching. He looked into her green eyes; his fear was now accompanied with confusion. Just above a whisper, she said, "Get your hair wet," and pulled him closer, under the stream of water.

Outside, they heard a cough. Their visitor was out of his truck, walking to the front door.

Little John looked at Bonnie and mouthed, "What now?"

"Just act normal—like you're taking a shower." She could tell he was scared. He needed to try to relax or he'd never fool this guy. "Settle down. Take deep breaths."

"Okay," he said, nodding vigorously. He took a few deep breaths then said, "What about you?"

"I'll get down here," she said.

"Oh, God," he said as she began to squat in front of him. "I'm sorry. I can't help it."

Bonnie wasn't sure what he was talking about, but when she lowered herself to her knees, she knew. Little John's penis was fully erect, right at eye level.

Although she tried to look the other way, she couldn't. It was only the second hard penis she had ever seen in her life.

"Our clothes!" Little John screamed in a whisper.

Bonnie was jolted back. Little John didn't have to explain. She pulled the shower curtain back just enough to see the floor. Clothes were scattered everywhere. Little John's covered hers completely, except for her bra.

She grabbed the bath towel off the floor and tossed it. Perfect shot. It landed on top of the bra.

But she saw two other problems: her scrunchie was on the back of the toilet, and her gold watch was over by the sink, at least six feet away. Too far to reach and too late to get out and get it.

She grabbed the hand towel and tossed it. Another perfect shot. It landed right on top of the watch and she ducked back inside. A few seconds later the door pushed open a few inches.

Little John pulled the shower curtain back a couple of inches to make eye contact with the visitor and said, "I'll be out in a minute."

Bonnie could hear the man step in further and push the

bathroom door closed behind him. Through the shower curtain, a quiet, raspy voice, said, "What the hell do you think you're doing?"

"Just taking a shower."

"Are you out of your mind? I never said you could take a shower out here. You know what you're supposed to be doing here and it sure as hell doesn't include taking a shower."

"I worked out before I came out here and just needed—"

"I don't give a flying fuck what you needed. When I send you out here, you do exactly what I tell you and nothing else. I don't want you to even take a piss in this room. You got it?"

"Yes sir, I'm sorry, but I thought—"

"I don't give a shit what you thought. Get out of here right now, got it?"

"Yes, sir."

Mumbling, the man stepped out of the room, pulling the door closed behind him. Little John looked down at Bonnie who was trembling below him. He gave her an *Oh, well* look and turned off the water.

They exchanged glances as he dried off. When he was done, he turned his back to her and dropped the towel. He bent over, picked up his boxers and pulled them on.

He was about to put on his jeans when Bonnie pointed to her clothes on the floor. She didn't have to explain. He threw them inside the cabinet.

After he pulled on his jeans, he sat on the toilet to put on his socks.

Bonnie whispered, "Hurry, you have to lock the bedroom door before he finds out it's unlocked."

Little John nodded and started moving faster.

"Get him outside and I'll go back to my room. Where's the key?"

"Table by the door."

The handle rattled and she drew back quickly. The door opened and in a hoarse whisper, she heard, "What's taking you so long? I want to talk to you outside. And when we're finished,

I want this room cleaned up. You got it?"

"Yes, sir."

When the man stepped out he left the bathroom door open. Little John quickly tied his cross-trainers and left the bathroom. For the next minute she could hear them walking through the cabin and finally, a door slammed. It wasn't the front door. *Another door?*

Bonnie got out of the shower and peeked out the open bathroom door. It was clear. She grabbed a towel and dried off just enough that she wasn't dripping, grabbed her clothes and ran naked back to the bedroom.

A small table along the wall held a kerosene lamp and the key. Quietly she unlocked it, returned the key, and stepped inside.

She was shaking all over. Never in her life had she been so scared. And it wasn't over. While she put on her clothes she thought about Little John and how scared he was. Something about his involvement didn't seem right. She sat in the chair by the window to put on her shoes. And then she remembered.

Her watch and scrunchie were still in the bathroom.

She had to get them. Immediately, she cracked the bedroom door and confirmed no one was inside. Remembering how the wind slammed the door, she pulled the door closed and padded quietly to the bathroom and just when she stepped inside, she heard the latch on the front door. There wasn't enough time to go back. She'd have to get back into the tub.

Quickly she climbed in and as she crouched to hide, she remembered—her watch and scrunchie.

The scrunchie was close enough and she reached out and grabbed it, but as she started to go for the watch, she heard the front door close and steps sounding like they were coming her way. All she could do now was stay where she was and hope the creep wouldn't come in the bathroom.

Chapter 27

"I'll go get the bathroom cleaned up right now," Little John said as they started back.

The man turned toward the kitchen, giving Little John time to lock the bedroom door and just before he dropped the key on the table, the man stepped into the hallway.

They locked eyes, and not meaning to, Little John nervously glanced back at the door lock.

The man gave him a *What are you doing?* look.

"Just making sure it was locked."

The man shook his head and muttered to himself as he walked back into the bathroom.

Little John came behind him as he stopped in the open door. The man noticed a puddle of water on the floor and the crooked bath mat. He said, "I want this room cleaner than it was when you took a shower. Look at this shit," and pointed to the towel lying crumpled next to the sink.

That's when Little John remembered Bonnie's watch was under it. His heart raced as he tried to cut in front of him to grab it.

"Not now," he scowled, pushing him away. Little John stumbled back against the shower curtain, dragging it slightly open. Inside, an unusual shape caught his eye. He glanced down and saw Bonnie crouching at the faucet.

He tried to stay calm as he pulled the curtain closed. Stuttering, he suggested, "Wh-why don't you go pee outside and I'll clean it up right now."

"Don't tell me what to do, dipshit. Now get the fuck out of here."

Little John backed out of the bathroom and went out onto the front porch. It was up to Bonnie now.

***

Bonnie wasn't expecting them to come into the bathroom, but when she heard steps coming her way she scooted close to the faucet and squatted down.

She heard the unmistakable sound of a zipper going down, and then he started to piss.

He was less than five feet from her, separated only by a thin plastic shower curtain. She was in an uncomfortable position, crouching and holding onto the faucet with her hands. Not a position she could hold for long.

His peeing into the commode sounded like a garden hose filling up a water trough. When he finished, he flushed the toilet and then she heard the water in the sink come on. She couldn't believe it. Out here in the middle of nowhere, he's washing his hands.

Then panic set in when she remembered, there was only one hand towel...and her watch was under it. Frozen in place, she held her breath.

The water went off and she waited.

Clunk.

It sounded like a meteorite hitting a barn.

"What the..." she heard him say under his breath.

She was sure she heard him bend down and pick it up.

But now, there was nothing she could do. He had to know she was there. She squeezed her eyes shut and waited.

When she heard him move, she expected the shower curtain to be ripped away. But instead, the footsteps left the bathroom and went out the front door.

Relieved, she took a deep breath and silently climbed out of the tub to peek through the curtains. It wasn't the best angle to see the front door because of big plants just outside the window. All she could see was the back half of Little John's red pickup that was parked in the driveway, about twenty feet away from the cabin. And next to it was another truck, a white one.

They were in the driveway talking, but the conversation was muffled, impossible to understand. It sounded like the guy was on Little John's ass about something. She grabbed the windowsill and maneuvered her body closer to the window just in time to hear Little John say, "I took it the other day when we brought her out. I was going to give it to my girlfriend."

Bonnie gave a sigh of relief. He was covering for the watch.

The rest of the conversation was inaudible except for Little John's 'yes sirs' and 'no sirs', until she heard their footfalls crunching in the gravel as they moved toward the trucks. Half a minute later she heard the engine of the creep's truck roar to life. Hopefully he was leaving.

That's when it dawned on her—this was probably her only opportunity to escape. But the second thing she thought of was Little John saying he'd kill her if she tried to escape. *But was staying here any safer?*

Bonnie had to make a decision, and she had to make it now.

She stepped over and peeked out the bathroom door. This was the first chance she had to see anything other than the bedroom, bathroom and hallway. Now, she could see an open living area with a sofa and several chairs. She took several steps in that direction. The entire back wall was windows, with a deck across the back. There was a door on the left side to the deck and another door on the right wall. Back to the right she could see part of the kitchen. The side door was her best way out.

She took a deep breath and closed her eyes while she tried to decide. But she knew she had no other choice.

Outside the engine revved again. It sounded like he was leaving. She had to hurry.

She ran through the living room to the side door and yanked on it. *Crap.* The door was locked. The one to the deck might be locked too, but she had to try. She ran between the chairs and sofa to the door and twisted the handle. It opened.

While she ran toward the other end of the deck she looked over the railing. It was like looking over the edge of the world.

There was a huge drop off, probably a hundred feet straight down, just like the bedroom. She held the railing tightly as she ran, wondering, w*hy would anyone want to live in a cabin in such a dangerous location?* At the end of the deck, about ten steps took her down to solid ground where a rising rock formation guided her away from the cliff. She turned and ran along the side of the cabin to the corner and slowly peeked around it. From there scattered native bushes and trees blocked her view back toward the front of the cabin. About fifty feet away she saw a dark brown building with no windows. It had to be the garage. Crouching, she ran from bush to bush until the front of the cabin came into view. Peeking between the branches she could see the pickups in the driveway. Little John was standing beside one and appeared to be listening to the man in the driver's seat. The glare on the windshield made it impossible to see the man inside. Bonnie slipped over behind the garage and paused to catch her breath.

Now she had to decide where to go from here. With canyons and cliffs on two sides of the house, her choices were limited. Behind the garage the forest was thick with dense underbrush and the rocky terrain made it look impenetrable. She eased over to the other side of the garage and surveyed the meadow and forest beyond. It would probably take her about thirty seconds on a dead run to get from the garage to the forest. As long as she had a fifteen second head start, she knew she'd be okay. She knew he was a quarterback, but that meant he could run fast for short distances. But, she was training for a marathon and knew she could outlast him. Once she got away, she could run for fifteen or twenty miles without stopping. Little John would come after her in his truck but she could hide in the forest.

This was her only real chance and she knew it.

Once the guy in the pickup left, she knew Little John would go back inside the house. By the time he discovered she was gone, she'd be halfway to the forest.

The white truck was idling, which meant the man was

probably about to leave. She went back to where she could watch when the pickup left. At the corner of the garage, she dropped down on all fours, crawled between the bushes over behind a stack of firewood, and waited.

A minute later she heard the transmission slip into gear. The white truck made a quick U-turn then hastily headed down the drive, leaving a trail of dust as it tore across the meadow. Little John watched until it entered the forest, and then went back to the house. As soon as he went inside, Bonnie slipped around the woodpile and with heart pounding, started running down the driveway. But when she passed Little John's Dodge pickup, she saw something she didn't expect. The keys were in the ignition.

New plan.

Bonnie opened the passenger-side door and slid across into the driver seat. She turned the key and with a vengeance, it roared to life.

The dashboard lit up with a constellation of flashing lights and was accompanied by an annoying alarm that chimed ping-ping-ping. She yanked down on the gearshift to put it in reverse.

It didn't move. She tried again. The son of a bitch wouldn't come out of park. It was stuck.

Hurry, she told herself as she shot a glance toward the front door. There was no doubt that Little John heard his truck start up. She had to get out of there before he came out.

She pulled on the gear shift again. And again, and again with such force she was afraid she'd break it. But, it still wouldn't budge.

Her hands shook while her eyes scanned the blinking lights on the dashboard, looking for something to tell her how to get the fricking gearshift out of park. But there was nothing.

Bonnie and Luke had a Ford truck at home. How could a Dodge be so damn different?

On the verge of hysterics, she pounded on the steering wheel then pulled herself closer to get more leverage. Out of the corner of her eye she caught movement. She looked up and saw the front door swing open and Little John fly through it.

Then for some weird reason, she remembered—you've got to push on the brake before it comes out of park.

Quickly she applied the necessary pressure to the brake and it slipped into reverse.

She mashed the gas pedal to the floor and the tires spun, throwing rocks forward, against the garage door. But, the big snow tires couldn't get a grip in the loose gravel and the truck only inched backwards.

Little John was almost to the truck when Bonnie saw his arm stretch for the door handle. She jabbed wildly at the electronic controls on the door, hoping to hit the power door locks.

Too late.

He pulled the door open and reached for Bonnie. She jerked her arm away and leaned out of his reach just as the big tires got the traction they needed. The truck catapulted backwards, slamming the open door into Little John's chest, knocking him backwards. But as he fell, he managed to grab hold of the steering wheel.

To stay out of his reach, Bonnie was laying almost flat on the seat of the truck, but she kept her foot on the gas pedal and the truck raced backwards. Little John was now half in and half out, and he pulled himself in more, holding onto the steering wheel. This caused the truck to veer off the driveway and careen through the grassy yard.

Panic washed over Bonnie when she realized the new course was taking them toward the cliff at rapidly increasing speed. For the last three days she'd had a view of that cliff out the bedroom window. She knew that if the truck went over, the fall would kill them both.

She tried to turn the wheel but Little John's grip was too tight, and he was now almost inside the truck. She spun her head around and saw the cliff approaching.

There wasn't time to consider her options. She closed her fist and smashed it into his nose as hard as she could. Cartilage crunched as his head flew back against the door. Obviously he hadn't expected that. He lost his grip and he fell away.

It was too late to turn the truck so she jammed both feet onto the brake and locked her knees. The truck went into a slide and Bonnie closed her eyes and braced herself for the fall.

The truck slid across the grass like it was on ice, but finally came to a stop. The driver's side door was still open and before she could breathe she looked out. Another three feet and the truck would have gone over the cliff.

She took a deep breath and pulled the door closed as Little John got to his feet. His nose was bloody and when he tried to come toward her, he bent down and grabbed his knee. It must have been injured when he fell from the truck. He limped toward the truck, but the pain was obviously too much and he dropped to the ground.

That was fine with Bonnie. She locked the doors and lowered the stick shift into drive. She could feel electricity firing through every synapse in her body as she stomped the pedal to the metal. The truck flew forward and as she went past Little John, he jumped up waving his arms. He screamed something as she blasted past him, but she didn't want to hear it. Undoubtedly he was yelling for her to stop, but she thought she understood one phrase. It sounded like "kill your husband."

It didn't matter what he said, it was probably a lie anyway. All she had to do now was get back to civilization and report him to the police. And end this nightmare.

As she hit the dirt driveway and sped toward the forest, his words echoed in her brain.

Bullshit. He's lying and I'm not buying it, she thought.

She looked back at Little John in the rearview mirror and thought about what she knew. Earlier he'd said he knew nothing about Luke. But, now, did he say they'd kill Luke?

What if he wasn't lying? She had to know.

As far as she could tell, he was unarmed and barely able to walk. If she went back and kept a distance between them, there was no way he could get to her. She turned the truck around and slowly went back, stopping about thirty yards from where he limped along in the open field.

With the push of a button the window went down. "What did you say about my husband?"

"I said they'll kill him," Little John said as he stopped and held his knee, undoubtedly in pain.

"Bullshit," she snapped. "You said you didn't know anything about my husband."

"I didn't until ten minutes ago."

"What do you know now?"

"I know they have him and I am supposed to take you to them. And if you don't show up, they'll probably kill him because they'll have no use for him."

Bonnie gnawed on her lip while she considered this. It didn't make sense. But, none of this made sense. "What do you mean no use?"

"I don't know. But the man said they have him now and I'm supposed to take you to them."

"I don't believe you."

"That's what they told me," he said with pleading eyes.

"You keep saying they. Who are they?"

"I can't tell you. And besides, it's best you don't know who anyone is."

"It's too late for that, because I know who you are. You're Little John Standalone."

His mouth fell open in shock. "How do you know who I am?"

"In the clinic I talked to your father and he told me your name. You were listening to your iPod and probably didn't hear him."

Little John closed his eyes and slowly shook his head. He sighed, and said, "I'm telling you the truth. They promised me from the beginning, no one would get hurt." He was silent a moment and watched her as she watched him. "If I don't show up with you, your husband's dead. I'm sure of that."

Bonnie glanced back at the road that disappeared into the forest. The dust had settled. She knew that all she had to do was drive away and she was free.

Her logical mind told her not to trust this guy. They'd been holding her captive for three days. Threatening to kill her if she didn't obey their every command.

However, for some reason she didn't understand, she felt as if Luke's life depended on the decision she made in the next ten seconds.

The palms of her hands were clammy and she rubbed them on her shorts while Little John wiped the blood that dripped from his nose. *Should I risk my life and take a chance?* Her brain said, no, but her heart said yes.

"I don't understand."

Calmly he said, "You will."

Chapter 28

Luke got back in the Jeep and checked the clock. 1:28. He had four hours and thirty-two minutes to be exactly where they wanted him to be. The map they provided said it would take two hours and forty-eight minutes if he went through Glacier National Park. But, it was the peak of the tourist season and roads would be crowded. It would be best to get on the road as soon as he could. But he needed his passport, and it was back at the bunkhouse.

When he got back to the ranch and as he started to gather what he wanted to take, he spotted a knife. It was a classic Buck with a four-inch folding blade. He pulled it out and immediately remembered the note. It said no weapons. *Screw 'em,* he thought. They'd have weapons.

As he started to leave an uncomfortable feeling in his gut told him something wasn't right. He shot a glance over by the foot of the bed and noticed Bonnie's suitcase was not where he had put it.

The bunkhouse was small and it took less than a minute to search every corner, behind every door, under every bed and inside both closets. It wasn't there. He scratched his head and wondered if his memory was failing him.

No, he distinctly remembered carrying the camera bag with the shoulder strap and a suitcase in each hand. His memory was fine.

But who took it? Lauren? No. She had no reason to take it.

A common thief would have taken the camera bag with well over ten thousand dollars worth of equipment. It had to be them, whoever had Bonnie.

Someone had been here while he was in town. They were watching his every move.

As he stared at the empty spot where the suitcase had been

he saw movement out of the corner of his eye. The front door was slowly opening. As he reached for his hunting knife, Buddy and Elvis came in, tails wagging. Buddy trotted over and dropped a long stick at Luke's feet with playful energy about him.

"Not now, boy," he said, giving Buddy a quick scratch between the ears.

A minute later Luke was back in the Jeep, but had yet to leave. A pang of guilt crossed his mind when he thought about all Lauren had done for him. In a short time, she had become a true friend and leaving without explanation didn't feel right.

He pulled the pictures of Bonnie out of the envelope and looked at them again. None of this made any sense. Odds were ten to one he was walking into a trap and no one knew anything about it. What if they didn't come back? No one would ever know that Bonnie was abducted.

Luke tapped the pictures on the steering wheel while he tried to decide what to do.

Someone has to know what was going on, and the only one he trusted was Lauren.

He pulled a pen out of the console, grabbed the envelope and ran back into the bunkhouse. Over at the table he laid the note and the photos. On the back of the envelope he wrote a brief message.

He went back out to the Jeep and strapped on his seatbelt. It was 2:15. He had three hours and forty-five minutes to get to Whitefish.

Chapter 29

In St. Mary, Luke saw a road sign pointing to the right for Glacier National Park via the Going-to-the-Sun Road. The 52 mile highway traversed the park. It had been one of the reasons they came to Montana. Bonnie heard it was one of the most beautiful drives in America. From the glacial lakes and cedar forest in the lowland valleys to the windswept tundra at the pass on the continental divide, the sights were supposed to be incredible to behold. They expected it to be the pinnacle of their trip. But now, he dreaded the drive.

At the entrance, he paid the ranger for a one-day pass and fell in formation behind the long line of tourists beginning their trek across the park.

As expected, the traffic was heavy. For the first seven miles the road traced the wooded shore of St. Mary's Lake where scenic turnouts held postcard-like lake views and short hikes to waterfalls. Steep mountains bordered the vivid blue waters of the narrow lake, but as the road began its ascent, the view began to change.

The road hugged the mountainside, and breathtaking scenery revealed itself around every curve. Rocky streams punctuated by cascading waterfalls gave way to the incomparable vistas of the Rocky Mountains that no photograph could ever totally capture. Luke's thoughts were of Bonnie five days earlier and her anticipation of driving this historic highway.

Traffic was slow but he got to the west entrance of the park in two hours and forty-five minutes. He went through the small towns of West Glacier, Hungry Horse, Columbia Falls, and finally into Whitefish.

On the other side of town he turned on High Meadow Road and followed it for six miles until he came to the defunct

Elk River Cabinet Shop. As instructed, he pulled into the parking lot and checked the time. 5:30. He'd wait there for the next half hour before going the final mile.

Time passed at a snail's pace but finally at five minutes before six, he stepped behind the Jeep to relieve himself. A breeze howled through the treetops, breaking the silence that hung over the forest. It was then he realized that only two cars had come down the road since he stopped. If they wanted to kill them both, this was a perfect place. But that didn't make sense. They had brought him and Bonnie over here for a reason. Now it was time to find out why.

He got in the Jeep and drove a couple hundred yards further to a road with no name, only a bullet-ridden sign that said *Dead End*. He took it.

Half a mile down the road he came to a dilapidated frame house with a free-standing garage. It looked as if it had been abandoned a decade ago. The sagging roof was missing shingles, and was littered with pine needles. On either side of the front door the windows were broken, and dingy green drapes hung mostly closed, hiding what waited inside.

In the front yard a sign for Dream Home Real Estate was propped against one of the trees near the road. Whoever put the bullet holes in the *Dead End* sign also found this sign a good target. The sign had a picture of a realtor on it with a big smile and short dark hair. Her eyes had been shot out, along with most of her teeth.

As instructed, he parked in the driveway and checked his watch. 6:00.

Just before he opened the car door he reached under the driver's seat and felt for the hunting knife. It was wedged between the fabric of the seat and the cushion. One last time he considered putting it in his sock, but again his gut feeling told him they'd find it.

He got out of the Jeep and stood in the shade of the towering pine trees. The air was humid and warm with an eerie silence that could almost be heard. Directly in front of the Jeep was the garage. It was old and dilapidated and looked like it might crumble to the ground any day now. He noticed the side door was open, so he slowly walked over to peek inside. It was dark but suddenly his eyes caught a flash of white and a loud screech came toward him. A huge owl left its perch in the rafters and swooped down toward the open door where Luke stood. He dodged and fell back, landing on his butt as the huge bird flew within inches of him as it escaped toward the dense forest behind the house.

Luke rolled over onto his hands and knees and tried to calm his jittered nerves as he stared into the thicket of trees where the bird had disappeared. He stood and brushed himself off, then turned his focus to the house. As he walked toward the front porch, his heart pounded with anticipation of something more sinister.

The front porch was a small rectangular slab of concrete, littered with yellowed newspapers and a doormat that might have once said Welcome. Sticking out of the front door were business cards from realtors, all tattered and curled by time.

This door hasn't been opened for years, he thought. *And no one has been in the driveway.* It didn't seem right.

Luke's mouth was dry; he licked his lips as he twisted the handle. The latch released and the door sprung inward. Like dead leaves in autumn, the business cards floated to the ground.

He held his breath, pushed the door open wider, and peeked cautiously around it.

The room was empty and dark. Dried leaves and animal droppings adorned the worn carpet that matched the lifeless curtains. He took two steps inside and stopped.

"Hello?"

No answer.

"Hello. Is anyone here?"

A muffled noise came from somewhere beyond.

On the back wall were two doors on the left side, both closed. Cautiously he went back and pushed on one. It opened, revealing a dark hallway where two rats skittered across the floor and through another open door further down. He pulled it closed and moved to the other door and pushed it open.

As the next room came into view he saw kitchen cabinets and a sink along the back wall. Hesitant, he spoke again.

"Hello?"

Again he heard it, but now closer and still muffled. He leaned in. Gagged and tied to a wooden chair in the middle of the room, he saw her.

Luke's breath caught in his throat.

"Bonnie!" he said, rushing to her.

She wore the same clothes she had on the day she disappeared and looked tired and pale. A black nylon cord bound her legs to the chair and her arms were behind her. There was something covering her mouth that looked like duct tape.

Bonnie's eyes locked on his and her head shook fast, from side to side. She moaned an urgent message but Luke didn't understand. Looking around he saw nothing to fear. The room was empty—no stove, no refrigerator, no furniture, no nothing. He dropped to a knee in front of her and reached to pull the tape from her mouth.

At that instance, her eyes went wide and the anxious moans turned to a muffled scream as she peered over his shoulder. His head spun around to see the pantry door on the back wall had opened and an arm extended toward him. A gun was pointed at his back.

His reaction felt like slow motion as he tried to move away, but it was too late. The gunman fired.

Chapter 30

Luke screamed and Bonnie saw his entire body go rigid. She watched as the gunman, whose head was covered by a Halloween mask that bore a resemblance to Albert Einstein, rushed toward Luke. Then behind her, she heard steps and something was pulled over her head, and the room went dark. Her breath caught in her chest as footsteps moved around her and the sounds of people struggling with Luke.

He groaned again and mumbled some words of protest. Someone said, "Hit him again."

Again, Luke groaned loudly.

Bonnie desperately squirmed and twisted, trying to break free of her bindings, but they were too tight.

"Don't fight us or we'll taser you again," a command came. "Next time it'll be longer and harder."

She could hear his breathing. It was heavy and labored, but now it didn't sound like he was fighting them.

Movement continued around her and a minute later they instructed him, "Sit still and don't move."

A few seconds later the bag covering Bonnie's head was jerked off.

Now Luke sat in a chair about six feet in front of her. His arms and legs were tied the same as hers. Strips of gray tape covered his eyes and another covered his mouth. His breathing was labored and his chest heaved with every intake.

It terrified Bonnie and she twisted from side to side, trying to signal their captors that he couldn't breathe.

She could hear them behind her, breathing hard, too. They were winded. Fighting with Luke and then getting him in his chair must have worn them out.

When she tried to look behind her, a vise-like grip clenched the back of her neck, forcing her head to face forward.

She winced as a raspy voice behind her said, "Don't turn around, understand?"

Bonnie nodded, cringing in pain.

"We don't want to hurt you, but we will if you don't cooperate," he said. "If you do as we say, both of you will be released soon. Do you understand?"

Bonnie and Luke nodded.

"This is very simple. Bonnie has an errand to run for us. If you do as we say and everything goes well, both of you will be released unharmed. But, if Bonnie doesn't do exactly as we say, Luke will be punished. Do you understand what I am saying?"

Bonnie watched Luke's chest heave as he heard their demands. His head moved slightly from side to side, as if he was trying to send her a message.

The masked man stepped over to Luke and slugged him hard in the face. Luke's head flew back, then snapped forward. She heard a defiant growl from deep in his chest.

"Are you going to cooperate?"

Luke lifted his chin higher, but said nothing.

Without a word, Einstein hit him again.

Blood began to flow from Luke's nose.

"I'll ask you again. Are you going to cooperate?"

Luke gave a slight nod.

Einstein looked at his partner behind Bonnie and said, "I don't think we've convinced him yet. Give him another hit."

From behind Bonnie, an arm extended forward and the taser gun was fired again. Wires flew into Luke's chest, causing his body to stiffen once more. He began to scream through the tape. She watched as a tremor ricocheted through his body. He jerked to the side, which caused the chair to topple over. Luke's head bounced as it hit the linoleum floor.

"No!" Bonnie wailed through the tape.

Einstein leaned close to Luke and said, "If you don't change your attitude, we'll start on your wife next. Got it?"

Luke lay still, inhaling deeply. He shook his head.

"And you listen, bitch, if you do not do as we say, your husband will pay. Is that clear?"

Bonnie clenched her teeth and nodded.

"Okay," the man with the gun said. "I'll ask you one more time—Are you going to do what we say or do we need to continue?"

Bonnie nodded vigorously and Luke gave two slow nods.

"That's better."

A piece of tape was put over Bonnie's eyes and pressed hard into place. Something, probably a pillowcase, was slipped back over her head and secured around her neck.

Einstein pulled off his mask and dropped it on the floor. It was Pete Coley, the agent from the border crossing just south of Cardston. Sonny Diamond, who had stayed out of sight, also pulled off his mask, and then gave Pete a nod.

They removed the tape that held Bonnie to the chair and walked her outside where a van was just pulling up in front of the house. The driver, Rita, got out and ran back to open the back door. They pulled out two long wooden boxes with **VIDEO EQUIPMENT** stenciled on all sides. They opened one and laid Bonnie down inside it, secured the latches on it, then put it back inside the back of the van.

Sonny and Pete went back inside and got Luke and brought him outside and put him into the other crate. They loaded his crate into the van beside Bonnie's.

Chapter 31

Lauren was exhausted when she pulled into her driveway. She had guided two retired couples from Sonoma Valley on the Crowsnest River. Fly fishing had not come easily to them and she had to watch them as closely as a mother watches a toddler around a swimming pool.

While she unloaded her equipment into the barn, she glanced over at the bunkhouse and noticed Luke's Jeep wasn't there. She had expected him to drop off the rental agreement, but when she stopped by the office, the employee who ran her office during the day said he never showed up. She'd check with him later.

On her walk back over to her house, her stomach growled. The only thing she'd had to eat since breakfast was a sandwich, and she was famished. It only took a few minutes to make a scrumptious salad and zap some leftover pasta in the microwave. With a beautiful setting sun on the horizon, she poured a glass of chardonnay, grabbed the latest Karen MacInerney paperback, and retreated to the patio to enjoy the remains of the day.

After two chapters she started inside when it dawned on her that Luke was still not back. She didn't worry about him but she wondered if there was any news about Bonnie.

As she climbed the stairs to her bedroom she decided to check her email. She logged on to her laptop computer and while her messages were downloading she looked out the window and found it interesting that Luke still wasn't home. Curiosity got the best of her and she double-clicked on the Car-Treker Unlimited icon. While she waited for the program to load, a pang of guilt swept over her. *Why am I spying on him?* But, Luke knew the Jeep had a GPS tracking program and she could find its location at any time.

She had not had a chance to use the tracking system since she bought the Jeep. The salesman promised she would be able to pinpoint the location of the vehicle within five meters anywhere in Canada or the States.

After she signed in she entered the number assigned to the black Jeep. A series of green lines ran along the bottom of the page and turned from green to blue as the computer calculated the data it retrieved from a satellite. Finally, a map of North America appeared on the screen and the computer pinged. She looked closer and saw a red arrow in the northwest corner of Montana.

With a furrowed brow, Lauren leaned closer to make sure she was seeing the map correctly. Each time she clicked her mouse on the plus sign in the corner of the screen, the map zoomed in until it highlighted the small town of Whitefish—a little town with a ski area on the west side of Glacier. She zoomed in again. It now pointed to a location out in the country, six miles from town.

Probably a glitch in the program, she thought. The system had been installed on her Suburban, too, and it was sitting right outside. That would be the easiest way to see if it was working. She entered the ID number for the Suburban and a second later, the map of Cardston came up, accurately pinpointing the location at the ranch, just west of town.

For a minute she stared at the location of Luke's Jeep. She couldn't believe he left town, or more accurately, the country, without telling her. He seemed more responsible than that.

Just to be sure, she reentered all of the information again. And again, Whitefish, Montana, came up.

Why would Luke be there? He'd said he was not leaving Cardston until Bonnie was found.

Lauren stared out the window and tried to make sense of it. *Could something have happened to Luke? Could someone have stolen the Jeep?* She ran downstairs and over to the bunkhouse.

She knocked on the door and waited a few seconds, but got

no response.

"Hello," she said as she pushed the door open. In front of her on the floor, she saw a box with their hiking and camping supplies, but no suitcases. In the bathroom she didn't see anything of Luke's. No razor, no toothbrush. Nothing.

Puzzled, she walked through the cabin and spotted something on the table. When she got closer she recognized them as Polaroid pictures. A closer look revealed a woman with her hands behind her lying on a bed. She tensed as she recognized the red hair. The other picture was the same person taken from a different angle. There was also a piece of paper with a typed message beside them. But her eyes were drawn to an envelope with a handwritten message scrawled in blue ink.

Lauren—I was right. Someone abducted Bonnie. I found this note in the Jeep today.

I have no choice but to do exactly what they say. I'm supposed to go to a location near Whitefish, Montana.

I'm 99% sure Sonny Diamond is behind this, but I don't know why.

I have no doubt I'm walking into a trap, but I have no choice.

Do not go to the RCMP unless you don't hear from me within 24 hours.

—Luke

Lauren shuddered as the message sunk in. The part about Sonny really surprised her. She knew he was a rotten human being but never would she have predicted anything like this. She cringed when she remembered the day Luke was in her shop asking for advice about Sonny and she told him to trust him.

After Sonny went to prison, Lauren learned how unscrupulous he actually was. He had cheated on her with numerous women and was heavily involved in drugs. However, she never thought he'd be involved in something like this.

She read the last line of his note:

P.S. Somehow, I'll get your Jeep back to you. Thanks for everything.

Lauren reread the note several times, trying to decide what to do. Her heart raced as she ran back to her house and checked her laptop. The Jeep was not where it had been earlier. It was on the move, now just north of Kalispell, a larger town about twenty kilometers south of where it had been earlier. For the next ten minutes she watched the icon move until it finally stopped.

She stayed glued to the monitor for the next thirty minutes. It didn't move again. Unable to sit still, she ran downstairs and made some hot tea. When she got back to the computer ten minutes later, it was still there.

Lauren went into the bathroom and washed her face with cold water and made her decision.

She went to the window and looked out at the bunkhouse, now silhouetted by the setting sun. She thought about her brief friendship with Luke and wondered why she felt so connected to him. He had walked into her store just four days ago, yet she opened her house to him and let him take one of her Jeeps without as much as showing an I.D. or signing any papers. There was just something that made her trust him and now she knew it was up to her to help him.

Fifteen minutes later she was packed and on her way to Kalispell.

Chapter 32

Rita and Sonny took Luke's Jeep and followed Pete Coley who drove the van south. Half an hour later they were through the town of Kalispell and turning onto an old country lane. It followed a meandering, rocky creek with old houses nestled back in the pines and spruces on large wooded lots.

"You're sure we don't have to worry about the landlord?" Sonny asked Rita as they crossed a narrow bridge.

"I'm sure. The realtor said the owner lives in San Diego and all they do is give a key to the renter, then send a cleaning service out after it's vacant again. It's used mostly by skiers who come up to Big Mountain in the winter. Since it's not real close to the mountains, it isn't rented much during the summer. I sent them a cashier's check for a month's rent and three days later Rosemary picked up a key at a realtor's office."

They drove another half mile, and after they crossed the creek again they turned down a dirt driveway. He drove past the old rock house and parked beside an old Winnebago motor home at the back of the lot. Pete pulled in and stopped it.

Sonny parked the Jeep behind the van and Rita unlocked the RV. Pete and Sonny carried one of the wooden crates inside and set it on the floor. Pete unlatched the top and they opened it to see Bonnie lying on her side, her arms still taped behind her back.

"Stand up," Pete said in a low, husky voice, as he grabbed her shoulders and helped her. He guided her over to a kitchen chair where he sat her down. He moved behind her and said, "Now sit here and don't move or we'll hurt you. Okay?"

Bonnie nodded and Pete untied the bag that covered her head. He slowly removed it making sure the tape over her eyes was still in place.

"Sit still. No one's going to hurt you. Understand?" Pete

said in a voice just above a whisper.

Again, Bonnie nodded.

Pete moved aside and Rita stepped in. She pulled the scrunchie off Bonnie's ponytail and her hair fell around her shoulders. A photograph was placed on the table beside Bonnie, and then Rita started to brush her hair. When it was ready, she pulled out a pair of scissors and made her first cut.

At first Bonnie jerked, but Pete forcefully held her head in place. Again he whispered. "No one's going to hurt you so sit still."

Over the next few minutes, six inches of red hair fell onto the newspaper that was spread out underneath the chair.

Rita still had the knack for cutting hair. It had been her profession for eight years after she flunked out of college. But she lost interest and left Cardston to pursue her dream of being a nurse.

Ten minutes later Rita held the picture and walked around and looked at Bonnie from all sides. Satisfied, she handed the photo to Sonny and stepped out of his way. He compared the photo to Bonnie and gave Rita the nod.

She stepped away and Pete put the bag back over Bonnie's head. As he removed most of the tape from Bonnie's arms Rita set the timer on the microwave Pete leaned closer and whispered in Bonnie's ear. "In three minutes you will hear a timer go off. When it does, you can remove the bag from your head and the rest of the tape from your arms, eyes and mouth. Beside the television you will find a piece of paper with your instructions. Follow them to the letter. Do you understand?"

"Mmmhmm," she said through her gag.

"There is a red cell phone beside the television. It will only work to call us. Don't even try to call anyone else. Is that clear?"

"Mmmhmm," she answered as she massaged her wrists where the tape had been.

"The door is locked from the outside and there is no way to escape. Just do what we say and you'll be released, unharmed, within twenty-four hours. Do you understand?"

"Mmmhmm."

They slipped out the front door and put a clip on the latch that locked Bonnie inside.

Chapter 33

When the timer buzzed, Bonnie pulled the sack off her head and the tape from her eyes and mouth. As she removed the duct tape from her legs, she took in her new surroundings.

In front of her was a small kitchen—a stove, sink and refrigerator. To the left she saw a narrow sofa against the wall and a couple of easy chairs. On the other side, a TV sat on top of a waist-high cabinet. Further up she saw the back of two captain's chairs and a big steering wheel on the left side. Beyond that was a huge windshield that was covered by something that looked like canvas. *Must be in a motor home*, she thought.

She looked the other way and saw an open door and beyond it, a bed. In front of her was a door with a small window in the top half. It appeared to be covered with newspaper from the outside. There were many more windows behind her, and they were all covered as well.

With the tape off her legs, she went and tried the door handle. It turned but wouldn't open. As they said, it must be bolted from the outside.

Back in the bedroom, Bonnie found a small dresser and nightstand next to a queen-sized bed. There were windows on three sides, all covered. In a corner she saw a canvas bag about three feet long. On the side it said *Pack N Play*. She'd seen one of those before at a friend's house who used it as a portable bed for her baby when she traveled.

Back in the hallway she opened a door and found the bathroom. It had been almost eight hours since she went and she felt like her bladder was going to burst. It was a tiny room with the smallest commode she had ever seen. But it satisfied her needs and when she finished she couldn't resist the urge to look at herself in the mirror. Her hair hadn't been that short since she was a teenager. As she ran her fingers through it she wondered why they cut it. She knew Luke was going to hate it.

Back in the living room, she found the piece of paper with her instructions. She read the typed message:

-Everything you will need is inside the blue box.
-Turn on the VCR and watch the tape marked #1.
-When it is finished, watch the tape marked #2.
-When you have seen both tapes, call us on the red cell phone by pressing speed dial #3.

The blue plastic box was beside the TV. Inside she saw three VCR tapes and several bulging manila folders. Beside them she noticed the red cell phone and picked it. It looked like one of those disposable models sold at convenience stores. She put it down and turned on the television, put the first tape in the VCR and pressed PLAY.

When the tape began to play, a small white church with a tall steeple came into focus. The red CNN logo was displayed in the lower corner. As a woman began to speak, the picture zoomed in on a tall slender woman in black slacks and a pink blouse standing on the front steps of the church.

"Last September, Kimberly Townsend and her daughter Olivia were in Kalispell, Montana, visiting her parents and as usual on Sunday morning they were here, at Cornerstone Bible Church. In the middle of the service, eighteen-month-old Olivia suffered a seizure. Fortunately, that morning Dr. Myron Sheppard, head of pediatrics at St. Luke's Memorial Hospital, was just two rows behind her in the congregation. Quick action on his part was crucial in stabilizing Olivia. She was immediately taken to the hospital where she was treated and underwent a series of tests."

The scene on the TV changed to a busy nurse's station inside the hospital where the doctor, a Colonel Sanders-looking man minus the bow tie, held a clipboard and made notes on a chart while speaking to a nurse. The story continued. "The tests Dr. Sheppard performed found that Olivia has a rare kidney disease that will require a kidney transplant."

The scene switched to show an attractive woman, who appeared to be in her late twenties, with a little blonde-haired girl sitting in her lap. They sat across from Dr. Sheppard in an exam room. "Today, Olivia comes to the hospital every other day for treatment, but otherwise she leads a relatively normal life."

As the camera slowly closed in on the woman's face, the commentator said, "If you think you recognized her, but don't know the name Kim Townsend, you might remember her by her maiden name, Kimberly Ann Kimber. Or as she was known in the sports world, Kim Kim.

"The day Kim Kim graduated from Kalispell High School she was ranked as the number-one high school tennis player in the United States. She accepted a scholarship to Stanford but in her third year of college suffered a crushed elbow in a car crash and that ended her tennis career.

"Kim stayed on at Stanford, graduated and met Wade Townsend in graduate school, whom she married a few years later. Wade's father, it turns out, was Alex Townsend, the hedge fund billionaire.

Still photos began to scroll as the reporter continued. "When Alex Townsend graduated from Harvard in 1962, his grandmother gave him ten thousand dollars and told him to invest it for his future. Over the next forty years he turned her gift into more than two billion dollars by investing in stocks and hedge funds."

In one picture Mr. Townsend, a tall, gray-haired man, was receiving a plaque from George W. Bush. Next was a shot of him shaking hands with Warren Buffett, followed by one of him playing golf with Donald Trump.

The next photo showed Alex standing behind an attractive, statuesque woman with short blonde hair who looked to be in her mid-sixties. She was presenting a check to Jerry Lewis, who was standing in front of three kids in wheelchairs.

"The Alex and Katherine Townsend Foundation is a charitable organization that supports many different charities, including the MS Society."

In the last photo, the Townsends were joined by a younger couple. The young man had one arm around Mr. Townsend and the other around Kim, and they were all laughing like they'd just heard a good joke.

"In September, Wade accompanied his parents on a trip to Boston, where they presented a twenty-five-million-dollar gift to the Harvard Business School. Shortly after the ceremony, the family boarded their private jet to fly home. They developed engine problems and an emergency landing was not successful. Their private jet crashed near White, South Dakota, killing all on board."

"Three months later, Kim gave birth to Wade's daughter, Olivia."

The picture changed to the diminutive Olivia in a huge hospital bed. "Kim and Olivia live in San Francisco, but when they are in Kalispell visiting her parents, Olivia needs her regular treatments. The hospital is small and has always been underfunded. They didn't have the equipment needed for Olivia's treatment, so to solve that problem Kim bought the hospital everything they needed. And as a way of saying thanks to Dr. Sheppard and St. Luke's Hospital, Kim has donated forty million dollars to improve services and build a new pediatrics center at the hospital."

The image on the television panned the room and Bonnie saw a nurse wearing hot pink scrubs adjusting the tubes that protruded from Olivia's tiny arm. As the nurse came into focus, Bonnie noticed her auburn hair. The camera zoomed in on the nurse and Bonnie's jaw dropped. As the nurse began to speak, she stroked Olivia's hair.

Bonnie fumbled for the remote and hit the pause button. She stared dumbfounded at the woman on the screen. She leaned closer for a better look, but the image was blurry. She pushed the rewind button and played the same scene again.

As she watched, a chill went down her back. "Oh my God," she said.

Bonnie stared for a few seconds, and then pushed the play button.

Now, the woman, identified as Dr. Tammy Owens, was speaking. "I was Olivia's pediatrician in San Francisco when her condition was diagnosed. I told Kim that Olivia would need constant medical attention and that she should consider getting a nanny who was a nurse. And since she could afford it, she might even consider hiring a doctor. Next thing I knew she made me an offer that I couldn't turn down. That was six months ago and things couldn't be better. Kim travels a lot, and most of the time Olivia and I go with her. About the only time we don't is when Kim travels overseas."

Again, she hit the pause button, and this time she saw a clear picture of Dr. Owens looking directly into the camera. Bonnie leaned closer and studied every feature of this woman's face. The lips, the nose, the eyebrows, the forehead. Everything looked just like hers—she could be her twin. But, Bonnie knew that was impossible. She was an only child. Her dad said her mom died of breast cancer shortly after she was born.

"What impact is Mrs. Townsend's donation going to have to the area?" the reporter asked.

"It's going to be huge. Because of Olivia's illness, Kim has become quite involved in the hospital and pediatric care. She is definitely committed to improving healthcare for all children in this area. Without a doubt, St. Luke's will become one of the leading pediatric hospitals this side of Spokane. We're all very excited."

"How is Olivia doing?"

"Olivia will be fine some day, but until she gets a kidney transplant, she needs her regular treatments and medication," Dr. Owens said, while using her fingers to brush the hair from Olivia's face. "Without them, she couldn't live more than three days."

The scene changed and the camera focused on several men and women standing around a large conference table covered with blueprints. The reporter said, "Construction of the Myron C. Sheppard Children's Center will begin next week and will be open for business in about eighteen months."

The recorded program ended and the screen went gray. Anxiously, she inserted the second tape. It was easily identified as a local news broadcast. The news anchor began: "Vice President Graham will arrive in Kalispell tomorrow to attend the groundbreaking ceremony for the Myron C. Sheppard Children's Center. Surgeon General Preston Howell, Governor and Mrs. Thompson will also attend the ceremony with the vice president. Guests of honor will be Mrs. Townsend and her daughter Olivia. Mrs. Townsend is a graduate of Kalispell High School and has donated forty million dollars for construction of the children's center. A black-tie dinner and fundraiser will be held at the Kalispell Community Center Sunday night at seven p.m. Tickets are still available for one hundred dollars each."

When the reporter began the next story, Bonnie stopped the tape and picked up the cell phone and pressed the speed dial button.

It rang once and the familiar voice said, "Have you watched the programs on the VCR?"

"Yes, I have."

"I'm sure you noticed the remarkable likeness you have to Dr. Owens."

"Yes, I did."

"Good. What you are going to do is very simple. This week, Kim and Olivia are in town for the dedication. Tomorrow Dr. Owens will take Olivia to the hospital for treatment. Dr. Owens always leaves for about two hours and goes to a health club across the street to work out. When she comes back, we are going to detain her and you will pose as Dr. Owens and pick up Olivia."

"What?" Bonnie exclaimed, tension in her voice.

"There is nothing to worry about. All you have to do is go up to the third floor, go down a hallway to the dialysis unit. DeWayne, your driver, will be there and as soon as he sees you he will leave to get the car. All you have to do is sign a form and they will turn Olivia over to you. You will bring her down the elevator to the garage where we will be waiting for you. After that is done, your husband will be released. Kim will pay a ransom and Olivia will be released unharmed."

"But I can't—"

"Yes, you can," There was brief pause, and he continued. "Everything has been planned down to the smallest detail. You can and will pull this off. And when it's done, you and your husband will be free to go. Is this clear?"

"Yes, but—"

"There are no buts. Kim is a billionaire. The ransom will be no problem for her. Neither you nor Olivia will be harmed in any way."

"But Dr. Owens—"

"Dr. Owens will not be hurt either. It's very simple. Either you do exactly as we say or we will kill Luke. Do you understand?"

She hesitated, but couldn't think of anything else to say. "I do," she said, weakly.

He continued, "On the dresser beside tape number three you will find a manila folder. Inside there is more information, including the floor plans for all three floors and the basement of the hospital. While you watch tape number three, pay close attention to the floor plan. The tape was made while walking the route you will take tomorrow. Okay?"

She looked over and saw the tape. "Okay."

"In the box is a folder with everything you need to know. There is detailed information about the hospital, plus information and photos of all of the employees you may see. You'll also find information about the Townsends, Kim and Olivia, and Dr. Owens. Study it all closely. You will have until midday tomorrow. At that time, we'll go over specific plans for picking up Olivia. And let me explain one very simple rule. If you were to escape, or if anything goes wrong, your husband will die." After a long silence, the man on the phone said, "Do you have any questions?"

After a pause, she said, "Just one."

"What?"

"Are you out of your fricking mind?"

Chapter 34

The line went dead.

Bonnie stared at the phone in disbelief.

Finally, she knew why she was abducted. She was supposed to impersonate a woman who looked just like her and kidnap the daughter of one of the richest women in America. This was the most bizarre thing she had ever heard in her life.

Question after question began to pop into her head. First, how in the world did the kidnappers find her? Next, would she actually have the courage to kidnap this child? If she did what they wanted would they really let her and Luke go? And if they did, would she be accused of kidnapping and spend the rest of her life in prison after she went to the police?

Unconsciously she shook her head. There was no way she could kidnap a child. Regardless of what they said, she knew she and Luke would most likely be murdered even if she pulled off the kidnapping successfully.

She collapsed on the couch and covered her face with her hands. *Maybe I should call 9-1-1 right now and get it over with.* The police could find her by tracking the cell phone signal. That might be their only real chance of either of them getting out of this alive.

She picked up the cell phone and when she flipped it open she noticed that something was not quite right with the keypad. She moved over to the kitchen where the light was better and noticed there was something very hard covering the buttons. Using her fingernail, she scratched at it, but it was no use. It was hard as plastic. She pressed on the numbers but they wouldn't move. Then she figured it out. The assholes had poured super-glue all over the buttons, except the one speed dial button she used to call them.

Disgusted, she dropped the phone back on the table and

reached for the bulging manila folder beside the television. Inside she saw photos, lists, drawing, pages from magazines and some large folded papers that looked like blueprints.

She pulled out the blueprints and unfolded them. Across the top it said *St. Luke's Hospital.* Flipping through the pages she saw a drawing for each floor, even a page for the basement and the parking garage.

Setting it aside, she pulled out a stack of photos. About ten were taken outside, showing the hospital from different angles. There were at least a dozen pictures taken from a variety of locations inside. On the bottom of each picture was a note written with a black marker identifying the location of each.

One picture showed an ambulance parked under a portico and behind it she could see a set of plate glass doors. Someone had drawn an arrow pointing to the side and scribbled: *This is the emergency entrance.*

She flipped through a few more and came to one that showed a long empty hallway where two men in white lab coats walking away from the photographer. At the bottom of this picture the caption said, *Room B1114 is halfway down on the left.*

She came to at least a dozen pictures of people and all of them had names and comments beside them. The first was a heavy black girl in scrubs: *Chondelle–nurse, always calls Olivia–Sugar Baby.*

Second, a white guy with a shaved head and earrings in both ears: *James–nurse, gay, very helpful, loves Olivia.*

Next, a white female with short blond hair, thin eyebrows: *Rosemary–in charge of Dialysis unit.*

Next, a trim, white female: *Leigh Ann–a fitness freak who always asks Dr. Owens about her workout.*

Also, *Angie—slow and lazy, but the patients love her.*

Next, an older Hispanic with oily hair: *Carlos–custodian, his English is hard to understand.*

Another one was a huge, muscular, black man: *DeWayne–bodyguard and driver for Dr. Owens.*

There were pictures of at least twenty people. It worried her when she realized she could run into any or all of these people and would need to know each one by name.

Under the photos she found an article torn out of a magazine. It was from the *Journal of American Pediatrics* with a profile of Dr. Owens. Included in the article was a studio portrait of her in a dress covered with a lab coat. An eerie feeling swept over Bonnie as she studied their incredible likeness. In this picture she noticed her beautiful blue eyes. Bonnie's were emerald green. Anyone who knew Tammy would know the difference in a heartbeat.

She grabbed the red phone and pressed the speed dial button.

"What?"

"Your doctor has blue eyes, light blue. And mine are very dark green. There's no way I can pull this off."

"Aw, shit. Hold on." The line was muted for a minute, and then he was back. "We'll get you some contacts that change the color of your eyes."

"But I already wear contacts and I'm blind as a bat without them. It won't work."

"You'll have to make it work."

"But it won't. I can't do this without my contacts."

She could hear some quiet discussion in the background and after a short pause, he said, "I don't give a shit if you can see or not. You do it, or you husband dies. Do you understand?"

"But that's not fair," she retorted.

"Goddamit! Listen to me!" he screamed. "Fair has nothing to do with it. Are you so fucking stupid I have to draw you a picture to make you understand? This is not a game. If anything goes wrong—if you don't get that kid to us because your eyes are the wrong color, your husband dies."

"But—"

"Nothing is negotiable. Do you understand?"

It was no use. She sighed heavily. "I understand." Knowing something as simple as the color of her eyes slipped past them made her wonder how much more of their plan was flawed.

"Good. Now I'd suggest you get busy learning everything, because tomorrow you only get one chance. If you fuck up and don't pull this off, you husband is dead. It's that simple."

"Okay," Bonnie said coldly.

"Good, one more thing. If you get hungry there's some food in the fridge."

Bonnie snapped the cell phone closed and slammed it against the desk.

She was hungry. Actually, she was starving. The only thing she had eaten in the past four days was granola bars and peanut butter. Inside the refrigerator she found a box with three pieces of cold fried chicken, cold French fries and a cold roll. Her first impulse was to throw it against the wall but she needed to eat. She pulled out the drumstick and took a bite.

While she ate she explored the trailer. In the bedroom closet, she found several sets of clothes on hangers. The first one was a business suit identical to the one Tammy was wearing in the interview. There were two more outfits and a dress. All size six. Her size.

There were also four sets of scrubs, all identical but in various colors. This probably meant they'd tell her what to wear after they saw what Dr. Owens was wearing tomorrow. All were embroidered *Dr. Tammy Owens.*

At the bottom of the closet was a dark gray suitcase that looked all too familiar. She pulled it out and saw the name on the leather I.D. tag—Bonnie Wakefield. *How in the world did they get my suitcase?*

Inside it was obvious someone had searched through her clothes because they were not neatly arranged as they had been when she packed it.

Just seeing her clean clothes reminded her how grungy she felt. She pulled out a pair of clean panties, a bra, and her makeup bag, and headed for the bathroom.

The water pressure in the shower was not much more than a trickle, but it was enough to rejuvenate her exhausted muscles. She pulled on an old T-shirt and pajamas and returned to the VCR. She pushed in the last tape and pressed the play button.

When it started, the hospital came into focus but the picture was jumpy like someone was walking while filming. Every time someone started to walk toward the camera, the screen went blank like the camera was hidden. Maybe a jacket or lab coat was pulled over it.

This segment of the tape lasted about four minutes. It showed the route she would take to pick up Olivia and get her back to the parking garage. The layout of the hospital was pretty straightforward—into the hospital, down a hallway, up the elevator, and down a hall to the dialysis unit. Then the same route getting out.

The part she worried about was fooling the staff when she tried to get Olivia. They had told her it was a foolproof plan but hadn't given her any details how it would be done. She didn't expect it to be as easy as they made it sound.

Bonnie turned off the tape and picked up the pile of pictures. One by one, she went through them, trying to learn everyone's name. Most of them were pretty easy to remember because the names seemed to go with the person. Half an hour later she needed a break so she set the photos aside and turned on the television. Only three channels came in clearly and she stopped on a local news program from Kalispell. Her mind wandered while they droned on about city council issues and budget cuts, but when they mentioned the name Kim Townsend, Bonnie sat upright.

They played a clip filmed earlier in the day with Kim and Dr. Sheppard posing for the cameras with four men. They all held shiny shovels full of dirt as they broke ground for the new children's center. Kim's happiness was apparent and in a short statement she said that Olivia was doing well thanks to the remarkable staff at the hospital.

Bonnie listened with interest, thinking how great it was that Kim was donating her money to help build a medical center where it was truly needed. But her heart sank when she remembered that she had to kidnap Olivia to keep Luke from being murdered. It was too much to bear. She bit her lip and fought back tears, telling herself she had no choice. She pressed a button on the remote and changed the channel, looking for anything to get her mind off the kidnapping. An old episode of *M*A*S*H* was just starting and it was exactly what she needed. Anything to get her mind off Olivia. It didn't take long before she started to drift off.

Hours later, a noise woke her from a deep sleep. Looking around all she saw was Suzanne Somers talking about the Thigh Master on TV. Was she dreaming or did she hear something? Grabbing the remote, she muted the TV and rubbed the sleep from her eyes.

It was dead silence. Maybe it was her imagination.

The luminescent glow of the clock on the microwave said 2:51. That meant she'd been asleep in the recliner for about four hours. Her back ached and she bent forward to stretch it for a few seconds. She needed to move into the bedroom so she pointed the remote control at the television. But, before she pressed the off button she heard a soft knock on the door.

She froze. That was the same noise she had heard earlier. *Who would be knocking at this hour?* It had to be those people who were holding her, checking on her. She waited and listened closely.

Again, she heard the soft knock, but this time someone spoke.

"Luke. Are you in there?"

Chapter 35

Bonnie jerked her head back. She could have sworn the person outside asked for Luke.

Again, the voice came. "Luke, it's Lauren. Are you in there?"

She forced herself to sit still, unsure what to do.

"I found your note and the pictures."

Who the hell is Lauren? And what note and pictures?

She heard the rattle of the latch on the outside of the door.

The door started to open. Just an inch at first, then two, finally enough for Bonnie to see a woman's face, her eyes searching, then locking on hers. The woman gasped and she raised a hand to her mouth.

"You're Bonnie?"

Bonnie was confused, surprised, and a little bit scared. She was expecting it to be the people who locked her in there, but this woman didn't appear to be one of them. She seemed to be equally as confused.

"Who are you?"

"Where's Luke?"

Bonnie had never seen this woman before. "Wait a minute...who are you?"

"I'm...Lauren Gray," she stammered. "You're Bonnie Wakefield."

A million questions flooded Bonnie's mind. "I know who I am, but *who* are you?"

"I'm a friend of Luke's. He left me a note and the pictures. I knew he would need help so I came to help. Is he here?"

"Just wait a second, okay?" Bonnie backed away and eyed her suspiciously. She was beautiful with long flowing brown hair; she looked like a model in an L. L. Bean catalogue. Cautiously, Bonnie folded her arms across her chest and demanded, "How do you know Luke?"

"He came into my store to get information about a fishing trip. I'm a fishing guide."

Nothing made sense. This beautiful woman is a fishing guide? The only fishing guides she'd ever known were men with five-day beards and the smell of yesterday's bait. "Yeah, right. And I'm a brain surgeon."

"No, I really am. I have an outdoor store in Cardston. I guide fishing trips and rent Jeeps. He came in my store earlier in the week and wanted some information about fly fishing." The brunette glanced nervously around the RV. "Then later he came by and said you had disappeared. He got the RCMP looking all over Alberta for you and he put flyers up all over town with your picture on them. There's one in the front window of my shop right now."

"How did you find me?"

"That black Jeep," she said, motioning toward the door, "it's one of mine. It's got a GPS tracking system on it. I can track its location on my computer twenty-four-seven."

"I have no idea what you are talking about, but get in here before you get us both killed," Bonnie grabbed Lauren by the wrist and pulled her inside. "Did you see anyone outside?"

"I don't think so. When I drove through the first time I saw the Jeep. And because of what Luke said in his note, I knew I'd better be careful. So, I parked down the street and came back through the woods so no one would see me."

"I'm totally confused. Start over and start with the Jeep."

"Okay, the Jeep sitting right outside. Luke rented it from me."

"Why would he do that? We rented a car in Calgary."

"I know, but someone broke a window out of it. So, I rented him the Jeep."

None of this made sense. They stood six feet apart and eyed each other. Should she trust this strange woman who showed up looking for Luke? She claimed she was a fishing guide and was there to help, But, she was also about as nervous as a woman who just got caught with another woman's husband.

"Okay, but I still don't know why you're here."

"When you disappeared, Luke left the motel in St. Mary and came to Cardston but couldn't find any place to stay so I let him stay in the bunkhouse at our ranch. I went over to check on him this evening and he was gone. But he left me these pictures and this note." She reached into the pocket of her sleeveless vest, pulled out a Polaroid picture and handed it to Bonnie.

With only the glow of the television, the picture was hard to see clearly, but it looked like her lying on a bed. It was starting to come together but Bonnie wanted to know more about this note she was talking about.

Lauren took shallow breaths while fidgeting with her keychain. "So, what's going on? I thought Luke would be here."

Bonnie held a finger in front of her lips. "Shh. They said they'd be watching me."

"Who?"

"I don't know. Whoever's been holding me prisoner for the past four days?" Bonnie wanted to get a better look at the picture so she went over and opened the refrigerator. Using the light on the inside, she examined the photo. It was her on the bed in the cabin with her arms tied behind her back and she appeared to be asleep.

"Luke left this, too." She handed Bonnie the piece of paper and she read down the list of instructions. "When I found it I checked the tracking program on my computer to see where the Jeep was and it showed it to be just outside of Whitefish."

"Whitefish?"

"A little town west of Glacier National Park. But by the time I got there, the Jeep had changed locations."

"How did you know that?"

"I can access the tracking program on my laptop which is in my car. I have an aircard so I have Internet service all the time," Lauren said. "The tracking program can pinpoint the location of the vehicle within a five meter area."

Bonnie was beginning to trust this strange woman. "Okay. I guess I understand how you found me, but I still don't understand why?"

"When you went missing, Luke came back to my store and told me. He asked me some questions about some people in Cardston. I told him he could trust someone I shouldn't have. I was wrong. It's my fault he's in trouble now."

Bonnie could tell Lauren was nervous, but her gut told her this woman was telling the truth. Lauren looked toward the bedroom at the end of the RV. "So, where's Luke?"

"Whoever was holding me prisoner is now holding him. And they've told me that if I don't do what they say, they'll kill him."

Lauren stared at her blankly. "What do they want you to do?"

It was then Bonnie decided this woman was their only hope. She had to trust her. "Let me tell you what this is all about."

For the next few minutes Bonnie spoke without interruption, telling her the entire story. Lauren listened, her face filled with confusion, disbelief, and anxiety. Bonnie pulled out a photo of Tammy Owens and showed it to Lauren. Her jaw dropped.

"That's unbelievable. You look just like her."

"I know. Scary isn't it?"

"So, are you going to do it?"

"I don't have much choice," Bonnie said. "If I don't pull it off, Luke dies."

"But, even if you do it, do you think they'll let you go."

"Not really, but what else can I do?"

"We have to think of something, because once you turn the little girl over to them, you'll be a liability to them. They'll have to get rid of you and Luke."

"I know. I've thought about that."

"Why don't we leave now and go to the police?"

"That would save me but then they'd kill Luke."

Lauren looked around the motor home as if a better idea was hidden on the wall or the shelf or on top of the refrigerator. Finally, she shrugged. "I'm sure we can figure something out."

"I hope so," Bonnie looked at the clock. It was 3:03 a.m. "Right now I'm brain dead. I'm so tired I can't even think straight."

"Me too. I've been up since five-thirty yesterday morning," Lauren said, yawning.

"I think right now, you need to get out of here. If they catch you here we're both dead. Literally."

"Ok, but how are we going to get back together?" She glanced around and saw the red phone on the table. "Is that a cell phone?"

Bonnie handed it to Lauren. "It is, but all the keys are covered with super glue, except for the one I use to call them."

"Interesting. This is one of those disposable phones, isn't it?" Lauren said, pushing on the keys that were frozen in place. "That gives me an idea." She reached in her back pocket and pulled out her cell phone. "I'll leave my phone with you and first thing in the morning, I'll go buy one of those disposable phones. I will call my cell phone and my new number will show up on the caller ID, then we'll be able to communicate."

For the first time in four days Bonnie felt she was not alone. She looked at Lauren and smiled as she took her phone. "Two can play their fricking game."

"In the morning after I get a phone, I'll run over to the hospital and check it out. Maybe it'll help us come up with an idea."

"Okay. They told me I had until midday before I have to do anything."

"That will give us some time. I'll call my phone as soon as I get a new one," Lauren said as she slipped out into the night.

For the first time, Bonnie felt there was hope.

Chapter 36

It was almost noon when the red cell phone rang.

"In the bedroom closet there are some clothes. Put on the blue jeans, brown leather belt, Clark loafers and the cream colored top."

"Okay."

"After you're dressed, go to the kitchen. Under the floor mat in front of the sink you'll find a brown envelope. Open it and take out the contents. Your instructions are on the piece of paper. Read them then call me back."

The clothes were a perfect fit and looked like something she would have bought for herself. She found the envelope and pulled out a piece of paper.

Follow these instructions:

-Within the next two or three hours we'll call and tell you to leave. The door will be unlocked at that time. You will drive the black Jeep that is parked beside the motor home. The key will be in the ignition.

-On the passenger seat there will be blue contact lenses and contact solution. There will also be a note with more information and another key.

-Leave immediately and drive to the hospital. There is a map on the back.

-Park in the basement.

-Enter the hospital at exactly the time we tell you.

-When you leave the Jeep put the key under the floor mat. DO NOT lock it.

-Go to room B1114 as shown on the VCR tape. The other key will unlock that door. It's a vacant office.

-Inside you will find jewelry. Put it on. If there are clothes there, put them on too.

-There will be a blue plastic bracelet like those worn by all hospital patients. You will need it to pick up Olivia. Put it on your right wrist.

-Wait in that room for a phone call for further instructions.

-When you pick up Olivia she will be in a stroller. Leave her in it and take the elevator to the basement and go into the parking lot through the same door you entered through. Do not stop for any reason.

-You will see a white Chevy van that says White Swan Paint Company on the side parked near the handicapped parking. Put the stroller by the side door. You get in the back door of the van. We will take you to another location where we will release you. The Jeep will be waiting for you there.

At this point, if you have done everything we asked you, we will release Luke. At that time you can turn yourself into the police or do whatever you want.

Bonnie flipped over the piece of paper and saw the map with the route highlighted in yellow. It appeared to be about three or four miles away. It sounded easy, but she still had a sinking feeling. Deep down, she didn't think there was any way she could pull this off.

She was a bad liar. The memory of trying to tell a planned lie reminded her of Luke's fortieth birthday, and the surprise party she planned. All she had to do was get him to The Draught House, a pub where he and his friends often met for a beer. That afternoon, she said she wanted to go along. He asked her why she wanted to go, because he knew she didn't even like beer. She knew he was going to ask, so she had a story prepared. But, when she started to talk, she started to stutter and got flustered. He knew she was lying and there was nothing she could do but tell him the truth. She was embarrassed and disappointed, but Luke felt so sorry for her that he acted surprised in front of his friends. She never lied to him again. Or anyone else, for that matter.

She punched the speed dial number. "Okay. I've read the instructions."

"We need to go over some important points," he said, and for the first time his demeanor was casual and friendly. "But first, do you have any questions?"

"Yes, how are you going to get Dr. Owens's jewelry and blouse? You said no one was going to be hurt."

"She won't be. When she comes back from the gym we're going to taser her and tie her up in a store room. The cleaning crews clean the basement between three and four, so someone will find her then. She won't be hurt."

"What do I do when someone knows me, but I don't know them? What's going to happen when I start talking? They'll know I'm not her." Bonnie stood and shouted at the phone. "For God's sake, I'm from Texas and she's from California or Montana or where ever she's from. We don't sound anything alike."

"Settle down," he said, soothingly. He gave her a few seconds, then asked, "You okay?"

"No! I think this is the stupidest fricking idea I've ever heard in my life."

"Listen to me. We've thought about this. Just hear me out, okay?"

"I'm listening," she said condescendingly as she rolled her eyes. "Tell me how I'm going to convince these people, who have seen this doctor every other day for the past three months, that I'm her? Tell me that."

"We've given you photos of everyone that she knows at the hospital. But it will be best to avoid talking to anyone. The best way will be to put the cell phone to your ear and act like you're on a very important phone call. Avoid eye contact and if anyone speaks to you, just smile and keep listening and turn away from them for privacy. They won't think anything about it."

She thought about it for a second. "Okay. That might work."

"When you get up there, the nurse who will help you will be Rosemary."

Bonnie remembered her picture—tall, slender, short blonde hair, and thin eyebrows. "She's the one who runs that department, right?"

"Right. Before she can give you Olivia, she will have to check your plastic bracelet and make sure they match. This is hospital policy to check it every time, even if they know you. To make sure that only the parents or guardians take children from the hospital. Even though they know Dr. Owens, they'll still look at it. But, it won't be a problem, okay?"

"Okay," Bonnie put her elbow on the table and rested her head on her hand while she tried to visualize how it would all come down. It sounded easy. Almost too easy. There had to be something they hadn't thought of.

"What if there are problems? What if you get caught trying to get Dr. Owens or what if they don't give me Olivia? Or something else?"

"There won't be any problems. We've made sure of that."

"But don't we need some kind of backup plan in case something happens."

"Don't worry, nothing's going to happen." He sounded like a dad talking to his daughter the first time she stayed at home by herself overnight.

"But, you never know what might happen in there. What if they realize I'm not the real doctor? Then what?"

"Think about it this way. There is a backup plan. If you don't convince them that you're the doctor and you don't make it out with the kid, then our deal is off. Luke's dead. That's it." He paused, and it was obvious he was agitated. "You got it? There's only one plan and that's it. You get that kid to us." He paused. "You know what? On second thought, why don't we raise the stakes a little bit? If you don't bring that kid to us, you're both dead. If you try to trick us, we'll kill Olivia, too. How's that?"

That sent a cold chill down her spine. "Okay, okay. I'm not

going to try anything. I'm just worried something might go wrong."

"Nothing's going to go wrong, okay? Now, any more questions?"

"No, but before I do this, you have to let me talk to Luke. I have to know he's okay."

Silence. Bonnie held her breath waiting for his answer. A few seconds later, he said, "Okay, we'll put him on when we call you just before you leave."

The line went dead.

Bonnie sighed. There was no backing out now. In a few hours she would kidnap a child.

She reached in her back pocket and pulled out Lauren's cell phone. Several hours earlier Lauren had called and now she had the number of her new cell phone. Bonnie called her and they talked about her new instructions.

"It sounds like a pretty simple plan. So, what are you going to do?" Lauren asked.

"I've spent the last four hours thinking about it and this is what I know. You could tip off the police right now. They could set up a trap and catch them before they even get out of the parking garage. But they told me if I try to pull something like this, before they're caught they'll kill Olivia. And one of them is with Luke, and he'll kill him."

Lauren said, "I have a strong feeling that if you get in that van with them, I'll never see you alive again."

Bonnie knew that was true. Regardless of what they said, she couldn't get in that van. "When you go to check out the hospital, see what our options are for getting out. I think if we escape with Olivia, we can negotiate Luke's freedom."

"And what about Olivia then?"

"I don't know. But at that point we'll have to involve the police to protect her. I think it's our only choice."

"Okay. I'll go check out the hospital and call you back."

Forty-five minutes later, Lauren called.

"I'm at the hospital now. I've seen one security guard

inside and none in the parking lot. I also saw a few surveillance cameras at the entrances but I didn't see any anywhere else," Lauren said. "And since Dr. Owens's driver always picks them up at the front entrance, our best chance is going to be the employee parking lot on the other side of the building. When you come out of the elevator in the basement, instead of going to the parking lot, you turn the other way and go through a door marked *Employees Only*. You'll go down a short hallway and the door at the end dumps you out into a smaller parking lot just outside the building. I'll be in a white Suburban."

"That sounds good. Just have the back door open and we'll jump in."

"I'll be there waiting."

"Thanks." Deep in her soul Bonnie wanted something better. Something to protect Luke. But, for now, this was all they had.

Chapter 37

As the minutes ticked by, Bonnie moved nervously around the small living area of the RV. The lighting was poor and with all the windows covered she felt like she was in a cave. When the red phone rang she jumped.

"Hello."

"I'm putting Luke on. You've got five seconds."

She heard what sounded like a chair being scooted across the floor. Then she could faintly hear, "Your wife wants to make sure you're still alive. Talk to her."

"Bonnie?" Luke's voice was hoarse.

"Luke?" Her heart raced. "Are you okay?"

"I'm...okay. Are you okay?"

"I'm fine," she said through strained emotions. "You don't sound good. Have they hurt you?"

"No, just a little sore and—"

"That's enough," the raspy voice interrupted. "He's okay and he'll stay that way if you do what you're supposed to. Got it?"

"Yeah, I got it."

"Good. The door is unlocked now. The Jeep's sitting right outside. Leave immediately. And one more thing: Someone will be watching you at all times." He clicked off.

Bonnie snapped the phone closed and stuck it in her back pocket beside Lauren's cell phone.

The moment she'd been dreading had finally come. She picked up the map and with great dread, pushed the door open.

The black Jeep was the first thing she saw. She went down the steps and opened the door. When she tossed the map in the passenger's seat she saw a plastic bag. Inside was a package of blue contact lenses. She studied them while she tried to remember the last time she went without her contacts. People had to be five feet away before she recognized them. What were the odds someone would notice her eyes were green, not blue?

It was an easy decision. Her real contacts were more important. With a flick of the wrist, the package of contacts flew into the backseat.

Also on the seat she saw a key and a piece of paper with the rest of her instructions:

When you get there, sit in the Jeep until exactly 2:10 by the clock on the dashboard. Then go to room B1114.

Once she was on the highway, Bonnie called Lauren and gave her the final details. Lauren said she'd be waiting for her in the employee parking lot at 2:11. From this point, she was on her own.

In less than ten minutes, the hospital came into view. Heavy machinery and a slew of pickups were working in the lot next door. A freshly painted sign on the street showed an architect's rendering of the Myron C. Sheppard Children's Center: *Opening in Spring of 2015.*

Bonnie parked in the lower level as directed. It was 2:06.

Across the parking lot beside the entrance, two women stood smoking cigarettes next to glass doors. From a sidewalk across the lot, another woman approached the entrance carrying a helium-filled balloon with *Get Well Soon* scrawled across it. When she got to the glass doors they opened automatically and she disappeared inside.

With the engine idling, Bonnie waited, getting more nervous with every passing second. Years ago she had taken yoga classes and they taught her how to calm herself with breathing exercises, but it didn't seem to be working today.

At 2:10 the smokers crushed their cigarette butts on the pavement and went inside. With a trembling hand, she turned off the ignition and put the key under the floor mat.

It was time.

After taking a deep breath Bonnie got out and stood beside the Jeep. Her legs felt weak, like they might buckle any minute. She started walking, but just before she got to the glass doors, a nurse pushing a woman in a wheelchair came around the corner.

When she got closer she recognized Chondelle, the chubby, black nurse she'd seen in the pictures. The woman was even bigger and overflowing the chair. Both women were laughing and trailing behind them was a skinny little man carrying a vase of flowers. The glass doors automatically opened.

Bonnie stopped just short of the door and waited while Chondelle pushed the wheelchair outside. She glanced at Bonnie. "Hi Dr. Owens. How are you today?"

Bonnie's stomach fluttered when she realized she forgot to hold the cell phone to her ear to avoid eye contact and conversation.

But, before she could reply to Chondelle, the large woman barked at the man who was obviously her husband. "Well, Leonard, are you gonna go get the truck or is Chondelle gonna have to push me all the way to Idaho?"

The small man said, "I'm goin', Hon," and scurried past them toward the parked cars. This caused the women to forget all about her and laugh even harder.

Bonnie slipped past the women, pulled out the cell phone, and pressed it against her ear as she hustled down the corridor. The hallway was empty and halfway down she came to room B1114. Quickly she unlocked it and stepped inside. She relocked the door, fell back against it, and released a long breath. Her first challenge was over.

She was amazed that Chondelle had only glanced at her and took her for Dr. Owens. It worked, but she still hadn't spoken to anyone.

In B1114 was an old metal desk and chair. On the desk she saw a white blouse, an assortment of jewelry, and a brown leather purse.

Bonnie pulled off the beige blouse she was wearing and replaced it with the white one. There were two gold rings—one with a cluster of small blue stones and the other one had a huge diamond in the middle with slightly smaller diamonds on each side. No one said which ring went on which hand, so she pushed the diamond ring onto her left hand. The other went on the right hand. A little tight, but they fit. There was also a gold chain with a locket. While she put it on she noticed the watch. It was a brand she'd heard of but never seen: Patek Phillippe. On the back it was engraved: *To Tammy from Kim: My Eternal Thanks.*

She quickly fastened it on her left wrist and picked up the hospital bracelet. It went on the right wrist and with a snap, it was securely in place.

Bonnie picked up the purse and unzipped the top and dug through the contents. In the billfold she found a California driver's license with a photo of Tammy Camille Owens that looked back at her. It was like looking into a mirror.

She returned to the contents and found several credit cards, a wad of bills, and other cards for insurance, AAA and Starbucks. She dug deeper and found lipstick, tissues, eyeliner, finger nail polish, and a pair of Brighton sunglasses. Bonnie had a pair just like them.

Several credit card receipts were in a side pocket. She checked one and saw the signature and thought it could be easily forged if it came down to it. She also found a key for a Lexus, birth control pills and a couple of pictures. In one she sat beside a Golden Retriever, and the other looked like it was taken in Hawaii. The doctor was with a good-looking man, sitting on a beautiful beach at sunset. Both were wearing leis.

She glanced at the diamond ring and decided it was definitely an engagement ring.

The cell phone rang and she answered with a whisper. "Yes."

"Have you changed your shirt and put on the jewelry?"

"I have. How about this purse?"

"It's hers. Carry it with you."

"Okay."

"It's time. Take the elevator to the third floor. Go to the Dialysis desk and make sure you deal with Rosemary. She'll check your bracelet, and then give Olivia to you. Okay?"

"Okay."

"And this time don't forget to hold the phone up like you're talking on it. You almost got caught in the basement."

A chill ran through her as she realized they *were* watching her, just as they said.

"I will."

Bonnie ended the connection but left the phone open in her hand. She put the leather strap of the purse over her shoulder, took a deep breath and stepped out into the hall. After closing the door behind her, she held the phone up to her ear and started toward the elevator.

She passed several people who appeared to be visitors on their way to the parking lot but made little eye contact. When she got to the elevator an elderly couple stood patiently waiting. She stood back, listening carefully to her imaginary phone call. Every now and then she'd say something, but not enough to create attention or disturb anyone.

"Okay…okay. That will work out fine."

An electronic bell chimed, and a second later the doors opened. The old folks got on first, Bonnie followed and pushed the button for the third floor before retreating to the back corner speaking in short sentences: "I'll have to check and let you know," then, "That's good."

On the first floor they stopped and the old couple got out and a young man wearing blue scrubs got in. He was pushing a stainless steel cart loaded with folded linens and didn't seem interested in anything but his iPod. She did not recognize him and stared at the floor while focusing her attention on her phone.

The elevator started its slow climb. This had to be the

slowest elevator ever made and now, as nervous as she was, her anxiety increased with every heartbeat. She watched the floor number change from one to two. And then finally, the elevator pinged on the third floor.

When the door opened, the orderly glanced toward her, a signal for her to go first. She took a deep breath then stepped off and marched down the hall with the phone held close to her ear.

She passed a nurses' station where a woman typed furiously at a computer. A male nurse with a shaved head—James, she thought—stood behind her, putting folders into a filing cabinet. No one seemed to notice her.

At the end of the hallway she came to the sign that said *Dialysis Unit*, with an arrow pointing toward two swinging doors, both closed. She pushed one open and stepped inside and saw DeWayne was standing over against the wall. As soon as they made eye contact, he gave a slight nod and left. There were two nurses standing there. Rosemary, who she recognized immediately, was typing on a keyboard, and the other was squatted down in front of a stroller cooing at its occupant. The stroller faced away from Bonnie so she wasn't sure if it held Olivia or not.

Rosemary glanced up and cast a quick smile at Bonnie, then returned to her computer screen. "You're just about ready," she said as she reached around and pulled a piece of paper off the printer.

The other nurse said, "If you don't want her, I'll take her home with me. She's so precious." It was Angie, the one whose description was *slow and lazy, but patients love her.*

Bonnie made no comment.

"Okay, Dr. Owens," Rosemary said, sliding a clipboard over to Bonnie. "I just need your initials on the bottom and you're good to go."

Bonnie grabbed the pen and scribbled "TO", making it like the signature on one of the receipts in the doctor's purse. She saw Rosemary turn around and say, "Angie, you need to get back and check on Mr. Webber. You know how he is."

"Okay," Angie whined. She stood up and looked at Bonnie, who lowered the cell phone from her ear. "Dr. Owens, you still going to be in town on Monday or will you be back in San Francisco?"

Bonnie's heart fluttered, reminding her of high school when the teacher called on her and she didn't know the answer. "We'll be here," she said.

"Good," she said. "See you then."

Bonnie smiled at her then looked away.

Rosemary stood, went to Olivia's stroller, and pushed it around her desk to Bonnie. "Okay, let me make sure you're who you say you are."

Bonnie's heart lurched. She held her breath as she held her wrist toward her. Rosemary checked the ID bracelet, and murmured, "Um hum."

Bonnie dropped her arm and took a deep breath. She looked down and saw the sleeping child. Instantly goose bumps rose on both of Bonnie's arms. Olivia's pretty blonde hair framed her angelic face. She was, as Angie had said, precious. Without thinking, Bonnie squatted down and reached out to smooth her soft hair.

A few seconds later Rosemary bent down beside her and in a quiet, but firm voice, said, "You need to get going." Bonnie looked at Rosemary, whose unsmiling eyes burned into hers. A second later her expression changed. She stood and smiled warmly. "Your driver will be wondering where you are."

Bonnie snapped back to reality. "Thank you."

Rosemary's eyes gave her a knowing glance. Bonnie knew—Rosemary was in on the kidnapping.

Rosemary watched as Bonnie turned and pushed the stroller through the doors and down the corridor at a deliberate pace. Along the way no one seemed to notice her until a nurse named Jackie barely looked up and said, "Have a good evening, Dr. Owens."

When she reached the elevators she punched the down

button and waited for what felt like an hour. When the chime sounded, the elevators on the left opened and two middle-aged ladies stepped out. Bonnie pushed the stroller through the open doors and pressed the button for the basement. Just as the doors started to close, she heard someone yell, "Wait!"

She froze.

Did someone already realize I'm not Dr. Owens? Have they called security and the cops?

No one appeared and the doors started to close, but at the last second an arm was thrust between them.

The doors opened and two teenage boys with their ball caps on backwards stepped into the elevator.

"Sorry, ma'am," one of them said. "I didn't mean to yell, but these elevators are so slow I didn't want to wait for another one."

"That's okay," Bonnie said, trying to calm her pounding heart.

Then she heard another chime. *It must to be the other elevator arriving,* she thought. Just as the doors of the elevator started to close, she saw a woman with red hair run in front of the elevator. When she looked back into the elevator Bonnie saw a look of panic on her face. As the doors closed, their eyes met.

It was Dr. Owens.

Something had gone wrong.

Chapter 38

As the elevator began to descend, Bonnie started to tremble. They said Dr. Owens would be out for at least an hour. But she was not out and from the looks of things she must have put up a fight, for she had a red bruise on one side of her face. If the elevator had gotten there ten seconds earlier, they would have met in the corridor, face to face.

Now it was a race against the clock. If she didn't get out of the hospital with Olivia, they'd kill Luke and come after her, too.

While Bonnie tried to stay calm the boys on the other side of the elevator started to argue. One wanted to eat at Taco Bell, the other at Pizza Hut. One reached over and pushed the button to stop on the first floor.

Bonnie rubbed her hands across her face and tried to settle her nerves. She checked the illuminated number above the door. It changed from three to two.

A falling feather would move faster than this elevator.

Finally it changed to one. When it stopped the boys got off. Bonnie jabbed the button to close the door three times. Two seconds later, it started down and slowed to a stop in the basement.

She cautiously peered out as the metal doors opened. Everything appeared normal so she pushed the stroller out and fell in behind two men who were walking toward the visitors' parking lot.

Ahead she saw several directional signs attached to the wall. One sign pointed to the parking lot, the other two signs pointed to the left—one for the employee parking lot and the other to the service elevator. Another sign pointed to the right to a small alcove where she saw a door with a small window and a sign above it that said, *Stairs.*

She turned left toward the employee parking lot and picked up her pace.

Behind her a door slammed, echoing down the empty corridor. Without thinking, she looked over her shoulder and saw a man entering the stairwell. He wore dark blue pants, a white shirt, and a black holster with a gun on his belt. It didn't take but half a second to know it was Rocky Giovino, the security guard.

She walked faster.

"Excuse me, Dr. Owens?" the guard called out.

"What is it, Rocky?" she said without turning or slowing down.

"Doc, could you hold on a minute? There's been some kind of problem upstairs and they told me to stop you."

Rocky was good-looking, about five-ten and built like a brick wall. She remembered the information on him. About a year ago he had gotten out of the army after a two-year tour in Iraq. He was married with a two-year-old son. At the hospital, he was the closest thing there was to a war hero.

He came up behind her and grabbed her by the bicep.

Jerking her arm free, she turned to face him. "Rocky, I'm really in a big hurry," she said tersely, averting her eyes. "Could you tell them to call me on my cell phone? I don't have time right now."

She glanced back at him and saw a look of confusion cross his face. "They said the person who took Olivia wasn't you, Dr. Owens."

"You can see it's me, okay?" she said curtly. "I really need to be going."

Bonnie turned to push the stroller, but Rocky grabbed it by the handle, preventing her from leaving. His jaw locked and all signs of friendliness were gone. "I'm sorry, ma'am, but they told me not to let Olivia out of the building."

"Rocky, please. I don't have time for this."

He grabbed the stroller by the handle and pulled it away from her. She looked from side to side, avoiding his eyes. His expression slowly changed from being confused to being perplexed. "You...aren't Dr. Owens, are you?"

"Of course I am," she snapped.

Rocky leaned a little closer and looked her up and down, even more confused. "I'm sorry, Dr. Owens, but I can't let you go."

She reached and grabbed the handle and pulled it, but he wouldn't let it go. Bonnie looked away, toward the door at the end of the hallway, then the other way. Finally, she looked back at him with pleading eyes. "Rocky, please."

He held his position and looked deep into her eyes.

This was exactly what she feared. She couldn't lie any more. She sighed loudly and said, "Okay, I'm not Dr. Owens. But I only did this because some men are holding my husband hostage and said if I didn't kidnap Olivia, they'd kill him."

Rocky's eyes narrowed and he leaned his head forward, as if he was trying to understand. "What did you say?"

Bonnie didn't know what else to do. Talking faster than before, she said, "I know it's hard to believe but this is what happened: these guys abducted me and my husband. Then they said that since I looked just like that doctor, I had to impersonate her, kidnap this little girl and then turn her over to them. If I didn't do what they said, they were going to kill me and my husband. And they'll even kill Olivia."

"Ma'am, I think you need to come upstairs with me," Rocky said as he took her arm.

She jerked away. "I know this sounds unbelievable but it's the truth. You have to believe me. There're about four or five of them. Even one of the nurses is in on it."

"Ma'am, please drop your purse and step back and face the wall," he said, now not so friendly. He reached down, pulled a small radio off his belt and toggled a switch on a microphone. "Base, this is Giovino, come in."

A garbled squelch came back over the radio.

"I have the child and the woman impersonating Dr. Owens. I'm on my way up."

Bonnie hesitated briefly but didn't turn away. "So I did what I had to do. You've got to believe me. Call the cops and send them to that parking lot." She pointed toward the basement. "That's where I was supposed to meet them and turn Olivia over to them. They're in a white van that says White Swan—"

"Shut up, you whore."

Bonnie and Rocky jerked their heads around to see a stocky man in a brown leather jacket. He had a trimmed mustache, aviator sunglasses, and a San Francisco 49ers cap pulled low on his head. As he raised his right arm Bonnie recognized the unmistakable form of a chrome pistol, but the end of the barrel had an extension that wasn't chrome. She'd seen enough cop shows on TV to know the gun had a silencer.

The gun leveled on Bonnie, she instinctively dove across the hall just before he fired.

Pfft. Pfft. The sheetrock wall exploded where she had been standing.

Rocky reacted with the speed of a combat soldier, pulling his weapon to return fire. But the gunman was ahead of him, firing before Rocky could get his gun up.

The shot missed and Rocky pointed his gun and pulled the trigger at the same time the gunman fired again.

Rocky's gun was not silenced and the noise sounded like a bomb exploding in the narrow hallway. The sleeping baby came awake and screamed at the top of her lungs.

The gunman's shot hit Rocky high on the chest. The shot spun him around and his gun fell and clattered across the floor.

But Rocky's shot found its target too, hitting the shooter in his left arm.

"Son of a bitch," the man growled as he twisted with the impact of the bullet.

Bonnie could see Rocky's pained expression as he bent down and picked up his gun, but as he raised it to shoot again, Bonnie heard another shot from the silenced pistol. Rocky grunted, grabbed his gut, and fell to the floor.

She twisted around and saw the gunman coming at her. His breathing was rapid and shallow. "Where do you think you're going? We told you we'd be watching and I'd kill you if you fucked up."

The fury in his voice told her he intended to carry out his promise. He stopped beside the stroller and glanced at Olivia who was wailing at the top of her lungs. He looked down at Bonnie, who was on her hands and knees, and raised his pistol.

Bonnie's legs felt glued to the floor. At this range he couldn't miss.

"And you fucked up."

But before he could shoot, a cry of terror came from behind him.

The man spun around to see a woman in a blue business suit standing in an open doorway. She had probably stepped out of her office to investigate the noise.

The man turned and pulled off two rapid shots; both hit the woman in the torso. Her scream was cut off as she flew back against the wall and crumpled to the floor. Bonnie stared as a red puddle of blood began spreading around her body.

The shooter's attention remained on the fallen woman. This was Bonnie's only chance. She scooted forward and snagged Rocky's gun.

It was a semi-automatic, similar to a pistol of Luke's she had shot before. Before she could aim the gun, the gunman turned and aimed his gun at her. Without thought she tensed and squinted as he pulled the trigger.

Nothing happened. He jerked on the trigger again and still nothing happened. He turned the gun sideways and checked the chamber. Something was wrong. He tried to pull back the slide mechanism on top of the pistol, but it wouldn't budge.

Bonnie knew what happened: it was jammed. The empty shell casing had not ejected fully and was wedged half in and half out.

She got to her knees and raised Rocky's gun, holding it outstretched in both hands. The thought of shooting someone had never crossed her mind, but now it seemed as natural as slapping a pesky mosquito.

"Drop it or I'll shoot."

He held his hands up, as if surrendering. But then he blurted out, "You won't shoot me."

"The hell I won't," she said through gritted teeth.

Then in one slick move, he yanked Olivia from her stroller and held her in front of him, against his chest. Any shot she had at him was now blocked.

She glared at him and noticed something—a scab on his chin about the size of a dime. She remembered him.

"I know who you are. You're a guard at the border crossing."

For an instant he was taken aback. He swallowed hard. "You don't know shit."

She pointed the gun at his face. "I fell over some chairs and they thought Luke hit me. They yelled and you came in. Y'all scuffled and your chin got scraped."

His hand went to his chin and he eyed her with a smirk. He started to back up.

"I'll go to the police."

"You go to the police and your husband's dead. I'll promise you that."

He took a couple more steps backwards then disappeared around the corner, carrying Olivia.

Bonnie got to her feet and started to follow, but heard Rocky moan. She looked at him and saw blood oozing from the wound. Crouching beside him she said, "Rocky. Can you hear me?"

His eyes fluttered, and then opened. "Yeah."

"Hold on. I'll go for help."

"No time," he said weakly. "Help me to the service elevator."

She dropped the gun and helped him into a sitting

position. Wrapping his bloody arm over her shoulder, she helped him to his feet and they limped around the corner to the elevator. She pressed the up button and pulled the radio from his belt. "Rocky's been shot and needs help. Repeat: Rocky's been shot. He's coming to the first floor in the service elevator."

The elevator door opened and she helped him inside and he leaned against the wall. She pushed the first floor button and stepped out.

Barely conscious, he raised his eyes to hers. "Where are you going?"

"To save my husband. They forced me to do this and they're holding my husband hostage."

"But you were taking Olivia."

"You must believe me. If I go to the police, they'll kill my husband and Olivia."

As the elevator door closed Bonnie backed away, and looked down the hallway. The woman in the puddle of blood, appeared to be dead. Closer to her she saw Dr. Owens's purse and Rocky's pistol and a trail of blood leading to the elevator.

She grabbed the purse and reached for the gun, but her hand stopped short. *I'm in enough trouble already,* she thought.

Her only choice now was to run. She dashed out into the employee parking lot where Lauren's Suburban waited with the back door open. As she dove inside, Lauren's eyes widened at the sight of the blood on Bonnie's blouse and arm.

"What the—" Lauren asked.

"Just get out of here," she said, slamming the car door. "And don't draw any attention. There'll be cops everywhere within a minute."

As they headed toward the highway, Bonnie wiped her bloody hands on her blouse and thought about the gunman. She could identify him and he knew it.

Luke still had a chance. But what about Olivia?

Chapter 39

Lauren pulled out of the parking lot and merged with the eastbound traffic. "Are you hurt?" she asked.

"No."

"Where do you want me to go?"

"I don't care, anywhere I can get this blood off of me," Bonnie exclaimed. Half a mile down the road, three cop cars with sirens blaring passed them heading toward the hospital. Bonnie sunk lower onto the floor of the backseat. The right sleeve of her blouse was covered with dark, sticky blood. It repulsed her to think about what had happened.

"We'll go to the motel. I've got some extra clothes there," Lauren said. "What happened back there?"

"Everything went wrong. A security guard stopped me and knew I wasn't Dr. Owens. He was going to take me in but they must have been watching because this guy with a gun came out of nowhere. He and the guard started shooting at each other. The guard got shot and so did some woman who stepped into the hallway. He tried to shoot me, too, but his gun jammed. Then he grabbed Olivia and hauled ass."

"Thank God you got away."

"I think I recognized him."

"Who is it?"

"He was one of the agents at the border crossing south of Cardston."

"Are you sure?"

"I'm positive. When Luke and I came across the border Tuesday, they took us inside and questioned us. They gave us a bunch of crap and Luke got so pissed off they had to restrain him. In the process there was a scuffle, and one of the agents got his chin scraped. This guy has a scab on his chin in exactly the same place and he looks exactly the same size. It has to be the same person."

"Why don't you call them and tell them you'll go to the police unless they release Luke?" Lauren said.

"Yeah, but they know I won't do that. As long as they have Luke, they know I won't go to the police."

"It's all we have at this point. It will give us the advantage and some time."

Bonnie thought about it for a few seconds then said, "You're right."

She pulled out the phone and pressed the speed-dial button. When no one answered, it went to voice mail. "Okay, I did what you told me and now you have Olivia. So now it's time for you to let my husband go. If you don't I'll go to the police and tell them I know who you are. I remember you from the Chief Mountain border crossing. Your name is Coley. Call me or I'm going to the police."

A few minutes later they pulled into a motel parking lot.

"Pull off your bloody blouse and put on that parka," Lauren said motioning to a blue windbreaker on the backseat.

Bonnie stripped down to her bra and used the clean part of the blouse to wipe away the blood on her arm. She pulled on the parka as Lauren pulled into a parking space. Bonnie followed her into the motel room, hiding the bloody blouse.

Pete Coley sat on the back seat, holding Olivia like a sack of potatoes with his good arm. Ever since they left the hospital, she'd been crying at the top of her lungs.

"This squalling is driving me crazy. How much farther?" Pete asked.

"We're here," Sonny said as he turned into a parking lot. Immediately after Bonnie left for the hospital, they moved the Winnebago to the edge of town where they had found a small unoccupied warehouse that was unoccupied and for sale. Sonny drove around behind the metal building and parked next to the motor home. Beside it sat the black Jeep which Rita had driven back from the hospital.

Just as Sonny parked the van Rita stepped out of the motor home. She took Olivia and Sonny helped Pete out of the van.

There was a lot of blood on the seat where he had been sitting. That concerned Sonny because there were no provisions in the plan for injuries. Everyone had a part and everyone was needed. And Pete knew that.

"How are you doing?" Sonny asked.

"It's not that bad," Pete said, grimacing as he walked past Sonny, into the RV.

Once inside, he sat at the table. Sonny looked toward the back bedroom and saw Rita put Olivia into the playpen. When she came back she opened the refrigerator and pulled out a baby bottle.

"Give this to Olivia and I'll take care of Pete," she said handing it to Sonny.

He took it as if she were handing him a dirty diaper. Sonny didn't like children, especially when they were crying. But Rita was already turning to Pete.

Olivia was sitting in the crib. Her screaming had turned to whimpering and now she clutched a small stuffed bear in one hand and sucked her thumb on the other.

This was the first time Sonny had gotten a good look at her. As soon as her blue eyes connected with him, he winced. The scowl on his face frightened her and her crying returned.

He lowered the bottle in front of her face and wiggled it around.

"Hey. Here's your bottle," Sonny said as if she was ignoring him intentionally.

His harsh tone startled her and she squeezed her eyes closed and wailed even louder.

"Goddamit, here," he said and pushed the nipple into her lips. She turned away and buried her head in her blanket. "For crying out loud, you fucking baby." Sonny dropped the bottle in her bed and stomped off.

Rita gave him a disapproving look when he walked past

her and scowled.

"You do it," he quipped. "I'll help Pete."

Rita rolled her eyes, went back to the bedroom. A minute later the cries subsided and she returned. Sonny brought Rita the first aid kit. Inside were bandages, gauze, bottles of medicine, tweezers, and all kinds of other medical supplies. She pulled out a bottle of alcohol and poured some on a gauze bandage, then began to dab at the wound.

"How bad is it?" Sonny asked.

"Can't tell yet," she told him. She tossed the blood-soaked bandage into a waste basket and grabbed another. He watched until she doused a cotton swab with alcohol and stuck it into the bullet hole in Pete's arm.

Sonny closed his eyes and looked away and said, "I'm going to clean up the van."

He opened the cabinet under the sink and pulled out a bottle of cleanser and roll of paper towels.

"We've got to ditch the van," Pete said. "I heard her tell the security guard we had a white van that said White Swan Paint Company on the side of it."

"Okay, then we'll have to use the Jeep," Sonny said.

Rita glanced at Sonny. "I don't like the idea of using that Jeep. Don't you think the cops will be looking for it?"

"No one other than Bonnie knows about it and she hasn't talked to anyone," Sonny said. Changing the subject, he said, "Have you talked to Rosemary yet?"

"Just before you got here. She said the guard is still in the ER and unconscious, so at this point no one knows anything about the van either."

"What else did she say?"

"She said the cops are questioning everyone. She told them she was scheduled to be off for three days and they said that was no problem. Her shift ended at three, so as soon as the police give her permission, she'll go home."

"Did she say anything about Bonnie?"

"Nothing, other than she got away."

Sonny noticed a red flashing light on Pete's cell phone on the table. Rita followed his stare and said, "We have a voice mail. Bonnie probably called and left a message."

Sonny grabbed the phone. He listened for a few seconds and his eyes went wild.

"Holy crap!" Sonny's expression hardened and he shot Pete a sideways glance. "Bonnie said she recognizes you from the border crossing. You didn't tell me she saw you there?"

Pete took a deep breath "I told you that when they came across the border, Luke caused some kind of problem and Driver called me in there to help out. I was only in there a minute and I didn't know she would remember me."

"We told you they were going to be crossing the border that morning. You should have stayed clear."

"Don't give me that shit. It's my damn job. How was I supposed to avoid it?" he said defensively. "How about you? You got into an argument with her in your store."

"That's different. How in the hell was I supposed to know she was going to come into my store?"

"Hey," Rita screamed. "You guys settle down. There's nothing we can do about it now." She looked as Sonny. "What'd her message say?"

"She said she recognized you because of that scab on your chin. She even knows your name is Coley. What the hell happened?"

He looked from Sonny to Rita. "I was trying to restrain Luke when Sharp ran into me. That's how I scraped my chin. Sharp called me by name several times and I had to take Luke out and put him in another room. I was in the room for less than a minute."

"This really screws things up," Rita said.

"You should have killed her at the hospital when you had the chance." Sonny said.

"I tried, but my gun jammed."

"What else did she say?" Rita asked.

"She said she wants her husband released or she's going to

the police."

"Bullshit," Pete blurted out. "She won't go to the police. Not as long as we have Luke."

"You think that'll stop her?" Rita protested.

"Hell yes. So far she's done everything we told her because she knows we'll kill Luke if she doesn't. She won't go to the police."

Sonny folded his arms and leaned back against the kitchen sink.

Rita turned to him and said, "We can't chance it. Bonnie's bound to be pretty freaked out right now. I don't think she can take it much longer."

Sonny watched her toss the bloody cotton swab into the wastebasket. She pulled out a cotton ball and soaked it in alcohol. "When she goes to the police, and she will, the first thing she'll tell them is Pete's name. They'll go to Cardston and everyone there knows you and Pete are good friends. They'll come looking for you next. And that will lead straight to me. Everyone at the clinic knows I worked at the hospital in Kalispell before I went to Cardston. Over here, everyone knows Rosemary and I were roommates. And everyone at the hospital knows that Dr. Owens and Kim got me fired."

The room fell silent and Rita went back to Pete's wound. Sonny rubbed the stubble on his chin and considered what Rita said. He exchanged glances with Pete. They knew she was right. They couldn't leave Bonnie out there any longer.

"She doesn't trust us, so how are we going to get her to come out of hiding?" Rita asked as she wrapped bandages around Pete's arm.

"With the one thing she wants." He looked from Rita to Pete. "Luke."

Chapter 40

Pete called Bonnie's red cell phone.

"It's about time." Bonnie sounded pissed.

"Okay, we'll let Luke go. Where are you?"

"It doesn't matter where I am. Did you listen to my message?"

"Yeah, we did. We'll meet you at the Park Hill Cemetery? It's just off Highway 2 east of town."

"Are you out of your fricking mind? I'm not meeting you anywhere like that," Bonnie shouted. "You've already tried to kill me once. I'm not going to let you have another shot at me."

"Okay, then where?"

"The mall."

"The mall? Now you're out of *your* fricking mind. Your picture is all over the news. You want to risk being seen in public?"

"Don't worry about me."

"Okay, hold on," Pete said as he pushed the mute button on the phone and looked at Sonny. "Just like you expected, she won't go to the cemetery. She wants us to drop him at the mall."

Sonny considered it and nodded.

Pete said, "Okay. Give me two hours."

"Call me when you get there and I'll tell you where I want you to drop Luke."

"Okay," Pete said. He pressed the end button on the phone and grimaced, gently holding his hand over the wound in his arm. "She'll be there in two hours."

"We'll need your help pulling this off. How's his arm?" Sonny asked.

Rita said, "It was a clean shot. Bullet went through. I'll give him some painkillers and he should be okay."

"I'm fine," Pete said. "A little sore but nothing I can't handle."

"Okay," Rita said, looking at Sonny. "Give me five minutes and I'll turn on the computer."

"Okay." Sonny held up the bottle of ammonia and said, "We'll need to use the van to get to the mall. I'm going to take the magnetic signs off the side and clean up all the blood."

"Will it take all three of us?" Rita asked.

"Definitely," Sonny said.

"Then Rosemary will need to take care of Olivia."

"How far is she from here?"

"About ten minutes. She lives in Heritage Arms Apartments, remember? It's where I lived when we started dating?"

"Of course I do. When we leave we'll take the Winnebago over there and she can watch Olivia."

Rita nodded and Sonny stepped outside. When he opened the side door of the van he saw a pool of blood on the seat where Pete had been sitting and unrolled a wad of paper towels. But the mention of Rita's old apartment sent Sonny's mind back to the day this whole thing got start.

When Rita and Sonny started dating she lived in Kalispell, almost two hundred miles southwest of Cardston. Their relationship moved fast and he tried to convince her to move back to Cardston, but her job at St. Luke's was too good to give up.

She worked as a vocational nurse on the third floor and had plans of becoming a Registered Nurse. If she worked hard, she knew she could pull it off. In the fall Dr. Tammy Owens started bringing Olivia to the hospital for her treatments. To get to the dialysis unit they walked through the area where Rita worked, and before long, Rita and Tammy became friends. On several occasions she even met Olivia's mother, Kim Townsend.

Shortly after the first of the year, Dr. Owens told Rita she needed to hire an assistant, and she should consider applying for the job. The idea of working in Mrs. Townsend's mansion and traveling on her private jet was the dream of a lifetime, she told Sonny. Rita felt she had a lock on the job since Dr. Owens had suggested she apply, and they were friends.

But after a deeper background check, they found that Rita had not been truthful on her job application. She failed to mention she was arrested for cocaine possession in Canada ten years earlier. The case had been thrown out on a technicality, but it was enough for Kim. Rita didn't get the job and Kim insisted she not be in contact with Tammy or Olivia. Soon after, she was fired from the hospital. With that, any hope of going to nursing school also vanished.

Rita was devastated. Embarrassed and humiliated, she left town and moved to Cardston to be with Sonny. She hated Dr. Owens and Kim for giving the information to the hospital and swore that someday she'd get even.

Shortly after she moved to Cardston, Rita went to Austin, Texas to visit her grandparents. When she returned, she told Sonny an amazing story. After spending a couple of days at her grandparents' house, she and a couple of cousins slipped away for some fun. Their foray took them to The Pecan Street Festival, an arts and craft fair in downtown Austin. They found themselves in a booth admiring some beautiful framed photographs of the Texas Hill Country.

Looking up, Rita couldn't believe who she saw: It looked like Dr. Owens standing in front of her. Right there in Austin, Texas. But the nametag revealed the woman's identity to be Bonnie Wakefield, a photographer, and it was her booth they were browsing. The resemblance between Bonnie and Dr. Owens was unbelievable.

She wanted to ask Bonnie if Dr. Owens was her twin sister, but there were too many customers and her impatient cousins pulled her away before she had the chance.

When she got home she told Sonny about Bonnie. After an exhaustive research on the Internet, they found some amazing information about Bonnie Wakefield and Dr. Tammy Owens. Both women shared the same birthday—August 3, 1970.

The deeper they delved, they found more interesting facts. Both women claimed to be only children. According to Bonnie's website, her mother died of breast cancer shortly after she was born, and she was raised by her father. The information they found on Dr. Owens said her father was killed in Vietnam, and she was raised by her mother.

Sonny compared the pictures of Bonnie and Dr. Owens they found on the Internet. In his mind, there was no doubt these two women were twins who were separated by their parents shortly after they were born. They theorized the parents had split up and each took one of the twins. For some reason, the parents came up with this strange story about the other parent being dead.

Sonny and Rita weren't sure why the parents would do this, but they found the information intriguing, and knew there was some way to use it to their advantage.

They spent hours brainstorming, looking for just the right idea to use it for their own revenge—and financial gain. Finally, one night, after a bottle of tequila, they came up with the perfect plan.

The first part of the plan required that they get Bonnie to Montana. That proved easy. Bonnie's website said she was available for speaking engagements. Rita and Sonny were involved in the photography workshop that was being held at Glacier National Park in July. One way or another, they'd have to get Bonnie on the program. To do that, one of the speakers had to cancel or not be available for some reason. They knew neither fate nor luck was on their side so they took matters into their own hands. And, amazingly, a gas leak and a lit cigarette caused an explosion that killed one of the speakers. A few days later, Bonnie was asked to fill in for the dead speaker. Of course, she was excited to be asked, and more than willing to come.

Sonny and Rita planned copiously until every detail was

discussed and every option was outlined. The ransom they would demand would be huge by historical standards, but would be insignificant to a billionaire.

"Sonny," Rita called out from the open door of the Winnebago. The sound of his name brought him back to the present.

"What?"

"I got the computer running. Are you ready to contact Kim?"

Chapter 41

Bonnie felt much better after the hot shower, but the water couldn't wash away the memory of two people being shot. She prayed they would both be okay.

After she toweled herself dry she opened the door and found a shirt that Lauren had left for her hanging on the towel rack. She held it up and saw the logo for The Sportsman's Outfitter above the right breast pocket. After she put it on she stepped over and saw Lauren was flipping through the channels on TV.

"Has there been anything on about the shooting yet?"

Lauren looked over at Bonnie and said, "Just before a commercial they said, 'Shooting at Kalispell Hospital. Details on the five o'clock news.'"

Bonnie pulled a brush out of Lauren's makeup case and started brushing her hair. She walked over and sat on the bed and thought about a comment Lauren had made earlier. "You said you felt guilty about some advice you gave Luke. What was it?"

Lauren explained how she told Luke he could trust a photographer he met.

"Are you serious? Who are you talking about?"

"His name's Sonny Diamond. He's—"

"An asshole. We met him in St. Mary. Does he have a store in Cardston too?"

"Yeah. They aren't his stores. They belong to an old friend and Sonny runs them for him."

"How did Luke figure out he was involved?"

"I don't know, but his girlfriend Rita is the nurse at the clinic."

"She is the one who contacted me to be a speaker at the photography workshop," Bonnie said, her voice trailing off as she thought. She stood up and started to pace. "I gave my talk from twelve to one, and when I finished there was a line of people who wanted to order my book. By the time I finished, lunch was over and the food was gone. But Rita had saved a plate for me. It was some kind of a chicken dish and it was probably tainted with something because a few hours later I was puking my guts up."

"Being a nurse, I'm sure she knew just what to do."

"And isn't it a coincidence," Bonnie said, slapping her forehead. "She told me she worked at the only clinic in the area and gave me her business card, just in case I needed anything. Of course, I did get sick. I went to the clinic the next morning and when I was about to leave she said the doctor wanted to talk to me...again. She took me back to his office and told me to wait for him there. I sat down and she pulled out a needle and said she was supposed to give me a tetanus shot, which she did. A minute later, I remember starting to feel lightheaded, like I was going to faint. Next thing I knew I woke up, locked in a cabin in the middle of nowhere with no memory of how I got there."

"It all makes sense."

"So what are we going to do?"

"I've got an idea, but it's going to put us in a dangerous situation."

"Okay, but we'll need some way to protect ourselves," Bonnie said.

"You mean like a gun?"

"I wish I had taken that one at the hospital, but it's too late now. Can we go buy one?"

"I don't see how. It's against the law for Canadians to walk into a gun shop in Montana and buy a gun. And even if you *were* crazy enough to show your face in public, you wouldn't be able to buy one because you need a driver's license, and the only one you have is Dr. Owens'."

Bonnie sighed, "You're right."

Lauren's eyes lit up. "I might have a way to get one. I just remembered. I have a friend who lives here. Give me my cell phone."

Bonnie pulled the phone out of her jeans and handed it to her. As Lauren scrolled down its internal phone book, she said, "He's a fishing guide on Flathead Lake just south of town."

"What are you going to tell him? You have a friend who just kidnapped Kim Townsend's daughter from the hospital and turned her over to some kidnappers who are holding her husband hostage. And now we're going to have a shootout with them to get him and the kid back?"

Lauren wrinkled her nose and gave a quick shake of her head. "No, that's not believable…I'll just tell him I'm guiding a group in the mountains up by the Canadian border, and I just found out that a grizzly bear has been causing some problems and I hate to go up there without some kind of protection, so I need to borrow a gun."

"Do you do that? I mean, carry a gun with you?"

"Sometimes if we go too far back in the woods I'll take a pistol with me, but I've never had to use it."

"So, you can handle a gun?"

"You bet I can," Lauren said while dialing. "I've been shooting since I was a kid. My dad's a cattle rancher and we had our share of problems with bears and coyotes getting after the calves. And Daddy and I have killed our share of elk and mule deer over the years, too. How about you?"

"I've shot my share of guns since I married Luke, but I'm not a very good shot. And I don't hunt. I tried it but it just wasn't for me."

Lauren looked away from Bonnie and said, "Hey Roger, this is Lauren Gray from Cardston. How are you?" She listened and then said, "I'm fine. Is Beau in?"

She raised her eyebrows. "Married? I didn't even know he was dating anyone."

After listening a minute she said, "I'm guiding a group up on Lake Koocanusa tomorrow and they've had a problem with grizzlies and I wanted to borrow a pistol. I don't like to bring mine across the border."

As she listened a frown crossed her face. "Well, heck. Do you have one I could borrow?"

A few seconds later, she said, "That's okay, I'm sure everything will be okay. Thanks anyway." When she ended the call she turned to Bonnie, a look of surprise on her face. "Now that's a weird one. He married a lawyer. He always hated lawyers. But, anyway, they're backpacking in the Sequoias for the next week and all of his guns are locked up in a gun safe. Roger, a guy who works for him, said he didn't even take a cell phone with him, so he's out of touch for a week. And Roger doesn't own any guns."

The mention of lawyers pricked a memory for Bonnie. "Hey, I just remembered something, while we were staying at the Red Eagle Lodge in St. Mary, there was a guy and his girlfriend in the room next to us. He said he's a lawyer from Kalispell. He tried to sell Luke a gun he'd gotten from a guy who couldn't pay his bill."

"If we could find him, we could tell him Luke changed his mind? Do you remember his name?"

Bonnie tapped her finger on the tip of her nose and said, "I remember his name was Jack, and his girlfriend's name was Christina...but I never heard a last name."

Lauren grabbed the phone book and started flipping through the pages. "This town's not that big. Let me see how many lawyers are named Jack."

"One thing I remember about him was his car. It was a yellow Hummer with a personalized license plate that reads ISUE4U."

Lauren rolled her eyes. "That ought to make it easy to track him down." She ran her finger down one page, then flipped to the next one and repeated the process. "I see two lawyers named Jack, a few more initial J. and more named John. And some firms that don't even list the names of the lawyers."

"In a town this small, I don't think he'll be that hard to

find," Bonnie said.

"Especially one who drives a yellow Hummer," Lauren said. She picked up the phone on the night stand and dialed a number for one of the lawyers named Jack. After two rings someone answered. "Hi. Yesterday afternoon I backed into a yellow Hummer in a parking lot. I left a note under the windshield wiper with my name and cell phone number on it, but I never got a call from anyone. I think the owner is probably a lawyer because the license plate was one of the personalized ones that said—ISUE4U. Would there be someone who works in your office that drives a car like that?" Lauren put her hand over the receiver and said, "She's checking."

Bonnie smiled. "You're good."

"Most fishing guides are good at making up stories," Lauren said. She smiled then returned to the phone. "Great, thank you." She put the phone down and picked up the yellow pages again. "One of the lawyers in her office knows the Hummer—it's owned by Jack Rosenthal, with Rosenthal and Associates. Want to call him?"

Bonnie thought about it for a few seconds, and then took the phone from Lauren. She dialed, and after a short conversation, hung up. "He's been in a meeting for two hours, but she thinks he'll be out in twenty or thirty minutes. The lady who answered the phone said he may have a few minutes before his next appointment."

"That's also good, because if he's been tied up for the two hours, he won't know anything about the kidnapping at the hospital. I think our best chance is to be there waiting for him when he gets out of his meeting."

Chapter 42

The Southside Professional Building was a three-story brown brick complex about a mile south of downtown. The sign out front listed a dozen different tenants including the law firm of Rosenthal and Associates. Lauren parked and as they walked toward the front door they saw a yellow Hummer with the vanity plate: ISUE4U. The space was reserved for Jack Rosenthal.

"That's it," Bonnie said as they walked past it.

Next to it sat a shiny new Mercedes CLS600, still sporting the dealer's tags. It was in a space reserved for Elizabeth Rosenthal.

They exchanged glances. "Didn't you say he had a girlfriend named Christina?" Lauren asked.

"I did, and I surely didn't know they were married. And she was a lot younger than him. I mean *a lot* younger," Bonnie emphasized.

They found the suite for Rosenthal and Associates. A petite blonde in a short skirt stood behind the receptionist's desk at a copy machine with her back to them. The nameplate on the desk identified her as Christina Crier. Bonnie and Lauren exchanged suspicious glances.

After the copy machine pumped out a dozen more pieces of paper, the blonde grabbed them, turned around to her desk. She began separating the copies into three different piles. Still unnoticed, Bonnie cleared her throat. The blonde glanced up briefly and smiled, then went back to her task at hand. Still looking down, she said, "May I help you?"

Bonnie cocked her head to the side and stepped closer. "Christina?"

The blonde's head popped up and without a hint of recognition, smiled at Bonnie. "Yes?"

"I'm Bonnie Wakefield, from Texas. We met last weekend in St. Mary."

Instantly, the blonde's smile vanished and her mouth fell open, but no words came out. Automatically, her head spun to the side, where a door stood open. Then, just as quick, she turned back to Bonnie with an alarmed look. She spoke just above a whisper. "What are you doing here?"

"I came to see Jack." Lowering her voice she said, "I didn't know you two worked together. Who is Elizabeth Rosenthal?"

Christina shot another quick look toward the open door. "What do you want?"

Before Bonnie could speak, a short, plump woman with collar-length, salt-and-pepper hair stepped out of the open door and looked at them. She had reading glasses propped on the tip of her broad nose and held a manila folder. She stopped when all eyes turned on her.

Bonnie and Lauren looked back at Christina who had become noticeably nervous. She stood, walked around the desk and with high heels clicking across the parquet floor, held out the copies she had just made. "Mrs. Rosenthal, would you mind taking these to Mr. Rosenthal? He's waiting for them. I need to take care of these guests."

The woman shot Christina a look of disdain, and narrowed her eyes.

"Never mind. I'll do it," Christina said and immediately marched across the room in the other direction, then stopped when the woman spoke to Bonnie and Lauren.

"I'm Elizabeth Rosenthal. May I help you?"

"I'm Bonnie Wakefield, and we're here to see Jack Rosenthal."

"Do you have an appointment?" she asked, politely.

"No, but it's very important we see him."

"I'm sorry, but Jack's in a meeting right now," she said, looking at a closed door where Christina stood. "Perhaps there's something I could do for you?"

"Are you Jack's wife?"

"Yes, I am," she said, with a forced smile.

"I didn't realize Jack was married," Bonnie said, catching Christina fidgeting with the stack of copies out of the corner of her eye.

"Oh, yes. For twenty-eight blissful years," Elizabeth replied without irony. "So, are you a friend of Jack's?"

Christina blurted out, "Mr. Rosenthal is almost finished with his meeting and I'm sure we can work them in."

Mrs. Rosenthal shot Christina a look that said she really didn't appreciate being interrupted. She continued, "Do you mind if I ask the nature of your business?"

"She said it's private, Mrs. Rosenthal," Christina said. She looked back at Bonnie, but tried to maintain her composed smile.

Bonnie smiled and agreed. "Yes, it is a rather personal matter."

"He doesn't have another appointment for half an hour," Christina said, looking from Mrs. Rosenthal to Bonnie. She then knocked softly on the tall oak door then opened it and walked in.

Inside Bonnie could see a group of men in dark suits seated around a long table. She recognized Jack at the end of the table with several file folders open in front of him. Christina handed him the copies she'd made, turned and walked briskly back to her desk.

Mrs. Rosenthal turned to Bonnie and asked, "So, did I hear you say you know Christina?"

"That's right," Bonnie said. "We met last week."

"Mr. Rosenthal and I were at lunch at the Buffalo Café in Whitefish last week, and Mrs. Wakefield and her friend were there."

"The Buffalo Café?" Elizabeth asked, stunned. "Jack didn't mention that to me."

"Yes, ma'am. While you were at that conference in Washington D. C., Mr. Rosenthal and I went there for lunch one day," she said looking at Bonnie for confirmation.

Bonnie smiled. "That's right, and she said she highly recommended Jack."

Elizabeth watched Christina suspiciously. "Yes, Jack is very good. We all think he's one of the best, don't we, Christina?"

"Yes, ma'am. I said he's very good when he's hard," Christina said, then caught herself. "I mean he's good and works very hard."

The door to the conference room opened and three men stepped out, followed by Jack. Bonnie and Lauren watched as he ushered the men to the front door. They shook hands all around and the men left.

When Jack turned around, he saw Bonnie and Lauren.

"Mr. Rosenthal, this is Bonnie, from Texas," Christina said quickly. "You met her last week at The Buffalo Café that day we went to lunch while Mrs. Rosenthal was in Washington, D. C. I think she was staying over in St. Mary? She needs to talk to you—in private."

Jack looked from Bonnie back to Christina and her eyes bore into his, until he seemed to understand. He nodded slowly, and then smiled at Bonnie and Lauren.

Christina added, "Your next appointment's not until four."

"It won't take long," Bonnie said.

With an uneasy chuckle, he glanced from Christina to Bonnie, avoiding his wife's confused expression. "Well, sure. Let's go down to my office," he said, motioning to a hallway.

As they started down the hall, Bonnie saw Mrs. Rosenthal's smile dissolve as she marched toward Christina.

Jack ushered them into his office. Bonnie and Lauren sat in plush leather chairs as Jack closed the door. Jack went around the huge rosewood desk that had only a yellow legal pad atop a blotter. Jack settled into his chair, crossed his legs, propped his elbows on the armrests, and steepled his fingers in front of him.

Without commenting about the Buffalo Café cover-up, he said, "The last time I spoke with your husband, he was quite concerned about you. He said you had disappeared."

"I did, but everything's okay now," she said smiling.

With an air of caution, he said, "I'm glad to hear it all worked out." His eyes shifted to Lauren. Without standing or extending a hand, he said, "I don't think we've met."

"I'm Lauren." She tilted her head toward Bonnie, "We're cousins."

"I see," he said without interest. He swiveled in his chair to face Bonnie. "It's quite a surprise to see you here. How did you find me?"

"You said you were from Kalispell and yellow Hummers with vanity plates are quite memorable in small towns."

"Yes, I guess they are," the corners of his mouth showing the hint of a grin. "So, what can I do for you?"

Bonnie cleared her throat. "You showed Luke a gun you wanted to sell."

He appeared surprised, but did not let down his guard. "I did. He said it was out of his price range."

"I know, but his birthday is next month, and I know he really liked it. So, I thought, what the heck."

He relaxed a bit and said, "I wish I'd known sooner. I sold it to a judge from Missoula two days ago." He looked at his watch and said, "And he's going to be here in about fifteen minutes to pick it up."

Bonnie's heart sank. "Oh heck, I really wanted to get it for Luke for his birthday. Could I look at it again?"

He stood and walked over to a credenza and pulled out a wooden case. He carried it over and laid it on his desk, unlocked the gold latches, and opened it.

Inside they saw a beautiful pistol with pearly ivory grips.

"It's beautiful," Lauren said leaning over to get a closer look. Her reaction reminded Bonnie of Luke's initial reaction when he saw it.

"It's a Colt .38. They call it a 'Super Match'. It was made in 1935 and has never been fired. Book value is twenty-five thousand, but I sold it for twenty," he said with a look of satisfaction. "It's going to go a long way when I have to be in the judge's court."

"That's a heck of a deal," Lauren said. She looked at Bonnie and said, "You really should get this for Luke."

"I'll give you full price, twenty-five thousand," Bonnie said.

Jack smiled and closed the display case. "I wish I could, but the judge has already wired me the money."

Bonnie opened the case back up. She lifted her head and gave Jack a piercing stare. "Wire it back. I want this gun and I'm not leaving without it."

Jack leaned back in his chair and shrugged. "I'm sorry, but there's nothing I can do. I already have the man's money and if I don't deliver it would be disastrous for my reputation in the legal community."

"Okay. I'll give you thirty," Bonnie said, leaning back. "And, since when did a lawyer worry about his reputation?"

Jack cleared his throat and ignored the insult. "I can't do that."

"Jack, I was hoping it wouldn't come down to this, but it looks like you are going to have to decide which is more important: your reputation or your marriage."

"What do you mean?"

"I have a number of pictures on my camera from the Red Eagle Lodge in St. Mary. Quite a few of them are of you and Christina. In some you're holding hands; in others you're playing kissy-face."

Jack's eyes went to his desk as he gritted his teeth. He knew he was screwed.

"We're not leaving without the gun," Lauren said.

Bonnie saw his face redden as he tugged at his collar, which suddenly appeared to be too tight. His chest swelled as he took in a deep breath. He jutted his chin out and said, "Blackmail is against the law in Montana, just the same as it is in Texas."

"Who said anything about blackmail? I just want to buy that gun and I'm willing to pay market price for it."

"You can't do this to me," he said, an octave higher.

"Yes I can, Jack."

He was silent for a while, and then said, "If I sell you that gun, then what?"

"I'll destroy the pictures and you'll never see us again. You have my word."

"You expect me to take your word?" he sneered. "You won't get the gun unless I get the pictures."

"Get serious," Bonnie scoffed. "Every third-grader in America knows that even if I give you the pictures, I can still have them downloaded on my computer, or to a website on the Internet. So you're going to have to trust me."

"Why should I trust you?"

"Because you don't have any other choice."

He tugged at his collar again and then used the back of his hand to wipe the sweat that had formed on his forehead. "Okay," he scowled, "but I want my fucking money—and I want it now. Thirty thousand."

Bonnie cleared her throat again, "Well, that's another thing. I don't have a check with me, so I want you to just bill me for it."

"The hell you say. No way I'm going to let you walk out of here with that gun unless I get my money."

"I'm afraid you're in no position to make demands. If Elizabeth finds out about the weekend you spent with Christina, thirty grand is going to be chicken feed compared to what your divorce is going to cost you."

"I'm really getting screwed here."

Bonnie shook her head. "No, Jack, that was last weekend."

Chapter 43

Dr. Tammy Owens had been in the conference room on the first floor of the hospital since the kidnapping. She had given the details to the first police officers on the scene and now was repeating the story to the detectives who had shown up forty-five minutes later.

The detective in charge was a black man named Percy Albright. He was big, about fifty, over six feet with wide shoulders and a waist just as big. He tapped his pen on the table as he fired questions. "Do you ordinarily leave the child alone during her treatments?"

"I usually go across the street to the health club while Olivia's in treatment."

The other detective, Marion Pearl, a white woman in her mid-thirties with curly black hair, spoke. "They had your routine down. Did you make any new friends over there?"

"Not really. I know a few people who work there. It's usually pretty dead during the time of day I'm there. It gets busy after people get off work."

Albright turned to the uniformed officers who stood near the door. "O'Dell, you and Eckley go to the health club. Get a list of new members, new employees, guests, and all service companies that have been in the club for the past month. Go."

The two officers left immediately.

"Let's go over it one more time. Start with when you left the health club," Albright said.

"I left the club and came back in the hospital through the employees' entrance in the basement."

"Is that the way you always come back?"

"It's the easiest way, so yes, I always go that way. Anyway, I was almost to the elevator when something hit me. Maybe they used a stun gun or something like that because the next thing I knew I was on the ground unable to move."

"Did you see anyone?"

"No, it all happened real fast. As soon as I hit the ground something was pulled over my head and I couldn't see a thing. A man said not to make any noise or he'd kill me. Then he dragged me somewhere and shocked me again. I couldn't move a muscle and while I was laying there he pulled off my blouse. I just knew I was going to be raped, but then he tied me up and wrapped tape around my mouth so I couldn't make any noise. And, then he took all my jewelry."

"Then what happened?"

"I guess he left because it got real quiet. About fifteen or twenty minutes later, Carlos found me."

"Who's Carlos?"

"He's the custodian."

"Where were you?"

"In the storage closet around the corner from the elevator. Duct tape was wrapped around my mouth and my arms and legs. Carlos helped me get the tape off and found a smock for me to wear." She rubbed her wrists and continued. "I was totally confused. At first I thought it was rape, but when he took my jewelry, I thought it was just a robbery. But, our security guys have always warned us that Olivia was a prime candidate for kidnapping, so that's when I started to worry about Olivia."

"Don't you usually travel with a security detail?"

"Not really, just DeWayne, my driver. He usually stays in the hospital with Olivia when I'm gone. As soon as I come back he goes out and brings the car up to the front entrance. We've never worried about security in the hospital because they always follow procedure to the letter. Even though they know me, they always check my ID bracelet before they release Olivia to me."

"Can you tell us anything about the person who grabbed you?"

"Nothing more than it was a man. And when he spoke it

was a low, gruff voice, and just above a whisper."

"Do you remember seeing anyone in the hall before you got zapped?"

She tried to remember the minutes leading up to the attack, but nothing out of the ordinary came to mind. Her week had been chaotic. The dedication of the Children's Center and the fundraiser were just two of the events this week. Though she was Olivia's doctor, nanny, and babysitter, she had also become Kim's personal secretary, social liaison, and best friend. Anytime Kim needed help or advice or anything for that matter, Tammy got the call. Today when she came back to the hospital, she remembered her mind was on the layout of the emergency room at the children's center. She could have passed someone in the corridor and not even realized it.

"I can't remember seeing anyone."

"Did he say anything before he grabbed you?"

"I can't remember hearing anything."

"Okay, continue."

"I put on the smock and took the elevator to the third floor." Her eyes narrowed and she looked a bit confused. "When I got out of the elevator I started toward the Dialysis Unit, but remember seeing a woman in the other elevator looking back at me. I saw her for just a fraction of a second, but I know she looked familiar. At the time, I was in a panic and it didn't sink in."

"Have you ever seen this woman before?"

"No, never."

"You said she looked familiar."

"Yes, she looked like me."

"Have you ever seen anyone who looks like you before?"

"Never."

"Do you have a sister or a cousin who looks like you?"

"No, I'm an only child. I really don't have any family."

"Okay, continue."

"I ran down the hall to Dialysis and when I saw Rosemary

I asked her where Olivia was. She looked at me like I was crazy and said that she had given her to me a few minutes earlier. I told her I didn't pick up Olivia, but she didn't take me seriously."

Behind Dr. Owens, Kim paced back and forth. Her BlackBerry buzzed, and automatically she pulled it out of her purse and pressed a few buttons. She began reading and within seconds, Dr. Owens heard her breathlessly say, "Lord, have mercy."

Everyone turned and Dr. Owens said, "What is it, Kim?"

Kim's attention remained fixed on the Blackberry. Dr. Owens stood and walked over to her. Kim handed her the device and stood motionless while she and the detective read the message.

Dr. Owens read the subject line of the email. "I HAVE OLIVIA". It was sent by: MS. RICH.

Dr. Owens clicked on it, and the next screen popped up, showing the message:

If you want to see Olivia again, you must do as I say. My demands are very simple. She will need medication and treatment soon, so don't waste time. Comply with my demands and you'll get her back in time to save her life.

First: Get rid of the police.

Second: When the FBI show up, get rid of them.

Third: When this is done, go to Olivia's Blog and post a message and include this line: Olivia is more important than any amount of money.

When I am convinced you have complied with my demands, you'll hear from me.

Back in the motel room, Bonnie perched on the end of the bed and watched as Lauren held the pistol and inserted the clip.

"What's that noise?" Bonnie asked glancing around the

room, trying to find the source of strange buzzing sound. She picked up Dr. Owens's purse and located a pocket on the outside with a zipper. "It's coming from in here."

She unzipped the pocket and pulled out a BlackBerry.

"Look what I found," she said, holding the phone so Lauren could see it. "Do you know how to use one of these?"

"I had one before I got my iPhone. That buzzing probably means she just got an e-mail or text." Lauren took the phone from Bonnie, punched a few buttons and an e-mail with the subject line *I Have Olivia*.

"Oh, shit," they said in unison. Lauren clicked on it so they could read the message.

"Do you know what blog they're referring to?" Lauren asked.

"Yeah, there was something about it in the stuff I had to study. After Olivia's illness was diagnosed and Kim donated all the money to the Kalispell hospital, it caught the media's attention and Olivia gained celebrity status overnight. Phones at the hospital rang constantly with concerned men, women and children offering to help however they could. Kim created 'Olivia's Blog' to keep the public informed and to channel offers of help into financial donations or other contributions toward the children's center.

"Whenever a new entry is made on the blog, an e-mail is sent to all subscribers, giving them an update. At last count, there were over thirty thousand subscribers."

Bonnie stood up and walked over to the window. "This is the cruelest thing anyone could ever do. How in the hell did I get in the middle of this?"

"You did what you had to," Lauren said. "I would have done the same thing."

"What else is in here?" Lauren said opening the purse.

She pulled out an organizer and a plastic pouch full of makeup. Deeper down she found a wallet. She opened it and saw her driver's license behind a little plastic window. She pulled it out and gave it a hard look.

"It's spooky how much you two look alike," Lauren said.

"We're not twins, so don't go there."

"Is your birthday August 3, 1970?"

Bonnie saw Lauren holding up Dr. Owens's driver's license. "Oh my God," she said in a whisper.

Looking up, Lauren said, "I'll take that as a yes."

Chapter 44

"Is there any way you could have been separated at birth?" Lauren asked, handing Dr. Owens's driver's license to Bonnie.

"I don't see how. My father told me I was an only child. He said my mother died from breast cancer." Bonnie took the license and studied Tammy Camille Owens from top to bottom. Dr. Owens's birthday, height, and weight matched her own. The typical imperfect license photo sent a chill down her spine as she looked into the *green* eyes of Tammy Camille Owens.

"Check it out. Her eyes are green—the same as mine. I guess she does wear tinted contacts."

Lauren gave Bonnie a sympathetic look. "I think you need to have a talk with your dad when you get home."

"I wish I could," Bonnie said sadly. "He died last August."

"Then, when this is all over, you and this doctor will need to have a long talk."

"We will if I live through it."

"Give me that," Lauren said, reaching for the BlackBerry. "We'd better turn that thing off. They can determine our location by triangulating cell phone towers."

"Excuse me?" Beyond Photoshop and email, Bonnie was pretty much low-tech.

"It means if we leave this phone on, the police can call or send a text to it and they can tell where we are. Even if it's turned off, the police have the ability to turn the power on and track you. So, the best way to get around that is to remove the battery," Lauren said prying out the blue battery.

"If that's the case, I think we should get the hell out of here as soon as we can."

"I'm with you there," Lauren said as she started stuffing clothes into the duffel. Less than three minutes later, they were in the Suburban and driving toward the exit of the parking lot.

Bonnie liked Lauren's idea of meeting at the mall, but they needed to check it out before they talked to Coley again. It was only a few miles away and when they got there they drove around the perimeter, checking the entrances. They parked and Lauren ran inside for a few minutes to see the layout. It was smaller than any mall either of them had seen, but they thought that would work to their advantage.

Forty minutes later they were in the parking lot of a grocery store when the cell phone rang. It was Coley. "We're about ten minutes from the mall."

Bonnie said, "There's a Radio Shack about in the middle of the mall. Send Luke in and tell him to stand out in front of it."

"Okay. We'll send him in as soon as we get there."

"Don't try to pull anything on me, okay? When I feel it's safe, I'll come get him. And if I feel it's a trap, I'm going to the police. You hear me?"

"Don't you get it? All we want is the ransom. We don't give a shit about you or your husband. You did what we asked you to do and like we told you in the beginning, now you're free to go."

"Good," Bonnie said, ending the call.

As Lauren pulled out of the parking lot she turned on the radio. "Let's see if there's any news."

A deep voice was already into his report. "...by a woman posing as Dr. Tammy Owens. Police are looking for the woman who shot two hospital employees."

"What?" Bonnie screamed. "They think I shot them?"

Lauren turned the volume up. "A female employee of the hospital, whose identity has not been released, was killed, and the security guard, Rocco Giovino, remains in critical condition at this time. The woman escaped with Olivia Townsend, the eighteen-month-old daughter of Kim Townsend, heir to the Townsend fortune. The woman is approximately five-foot-six and weighs about one hundred and twenty pounds. She has shoulder-length red hair and is considered armed and extremely dangerous. We have posted a photo on our website to help you identify her. If you see anyone matching this description, please notify the police immediately."

Bonnie's mouth hung open as she stared at the radio.

"I'm sure your picture's already plastered all over TV, too," Lauren said, "You need to stay completely out of sight."

Lauren moved the car into the outside lane and turned down a side road at the next intersection.

Bonnie's attention was focused on the radio. The reporter continued. "The child does need medication daily, without which, she will die. There are no leads at this time. We go now to Brook Robins, who is with Mrs. Townsend."

A female voice spoke. "Olivia will die if she doesn't receive her medication and dialysis. If you could speak to that woman right now, what would you say?"

An emotional Kim Townsend said, "How can you be so heartless to kidnap a child like this? You can't let her die. I beg of you, she's all the family I have left."

Bonnie squeezed her eyes shut and lowered her head.

Lauren drove several blocks then pulled over on the side of the road.

"I think it will be best if you get in the backseat. Those windows are tinted and no one will be able to see you there," she said, touching Bonnie on the shoulder.

As Bonnie crawled over into the back seat she felt as if every decision she'd made over the past twenty-four hours was wrong. The word "heartless" echoed in her mind.

"Don't be so hard on yourself," Lauren said. "If Kim knew the entire story, she'd know you made the right decision."

Lauren made a U-turn and went back to the highway. Bonnie couldn't get the news report out of her head. She was sure Rocky would set the record straight when he was able, but what if he didn't survive?

Bonnie shrank into the corner of the backseat and buried

her head in her hands. The fact that she was wanted for murder and kidnapping was inconceivable, but there was nothing she could do about it until Luke was safe. When she opened her eyes they came to rest on Dr. Owens's leather purse. The top of the BlackBerry was sticking out of the unzipped pocket.

Bonnie pulled it out and said, "I think you're right. Kim needs to know the entire story."

Lauren spoke but kept her eyes on the highway. "That's fine, but how's she going to find out?"

"I'm going to call her. I'm sure her number is in here."

Lauren gave Bonnie a hard look in the mirror. "Are you sure you want to do that?"

"I have to. What if things go wrong at the mall and Luke and I end up dead? I'll be known forever as a kidnapper and a murderer. I can't let that happen."

"Okay," Lauren said warily. "But, we have to assume they are going to try to triangulate the location of any calls made from Dr. Owens's phone. I don't know how long it takes to do that, so don't stay on it for more than a minute, two at the most."

Lauren turned into a busy shopping center with several fast food restaurants along the highway and a strip of stores in back. She pulled in between the Golden Dragon Chinese Buffet and Taco Hut, drove to the middle of the lot, and parked. Bonnie powered up the phone and found Kim's number in the directory. A few seconds later it was ringing.

"Who is this?" Kim demanded.

"Mrs. Townsend. I need to talk to you."

"You're calling from Tammy's phone. Are you the one who took Olivia? Ms. Rich?"

"Let me explain," Bonnie pleaded.

Kim's tone was on the verge of panic. "Explain what? Is Olivia okay?"

"She's fine, but that's not why I called."

"I got your email telling me what to do. Please don't hurt

my baby."

"Kim, I'm not one of the kidnappers."

"But, you're on Tammy's phone. Didn't you say you're the one who took Olivia?"

"Let me explain. I was forced to do it. They said they'd kill me and Olivia if I didn't do what they said."

"What do you mean? Who are you?"

"I'm not from around here. I was in Montana with my husband on business. We were abducted and held prisoner. The men holding us said they would kill us unless I did what they told me to do. They had an elaborate plan where I had to impersonate Dr. Owens and pick up Olivia at the hospital after her treatment and then turn her over to them."

"But, how—"

"Let me finish, please." Bonnie begged. She knew Kim would have lots of questions, but had to keep the conversation short and on target. She switched the phone to her other ear and continued. "At first I told them I wouldn't do it, but they said if I didn't they'd kill me and my husband, and they'd kill Olivia, too. I felt like I didn't have any choice."

"I can't believe that. Who are you?"

"I can't tell you yet. They're still holding my husband and said that if I tell the police anything before they get the ransom, they'll kill him. And they said they'll kill Olivia, too."

"But you killed a woman and shot the guard."

"It wasn't me who shot them. After I took Olivia from the dialysis unit I went to the basement as I was instructed. The security guard stopped me and was taking Olivia from me. One of the men who abducted me was watching and he shot Rocky and that woman. Then he took Olivia from me and was going to shoot me too, but his gun jammed and I got away."

Kim was silent for a few seconds then said, "Do you have Olivia?"

"No. They have her."

"So, why did you call me?"

"The people who abducted me still have my husband.

They said they'll release him and I'm going to meet them. But I'm afraid it's a trick and they'll kill both of us before this is all over. And I want you to know the truth. I did what I did to save Olivia. You have to believe me," Bonnie pleaded.

"I…I don't know what to say," Kim said. She paused briefly. "Where is Olivia?"

"I don't know, but they said she'd be released as soon as the ransom is paid. Have they contacted you about the ransom?"

"Yes, and that's going to be a problem," Kim said.

Bonnie sat upright, unsure she heard Kim right. "A problem?"

"Yes."

Bonnie felt Lauren's hand grasp her shoulder, then point out the window. A black and white police car was turning into the parking lot at the west end of the parking lot. They looked the other way and saw two black and whites turning into the east end of the parking lot.

Lauren put her finger to her throat and ran it across it repeatedly.

"I've got to go, but I'll call back as soon as I can." Bonnie disconnected and sunk down in the seat.

"Get the battery out of that phone," Lauren said, starting the car. "We got to get out of here. Stay down."

Lauren noticed the cop cars were closing in fast. She backed out of her parking space and started down the row of parked cars, but a minivan was stopped, waiting for a car to pull out of a parking spot. Their only escape was to make it to the highway, half a parking lot ahead of them.

Lauren checked the rearview mirror and saw one of the cop cars turn down her row and start closing in behind her. The other black and white turned several rows over and was driving much faster toward the end of the parking lot.

"Oh shit," Lauren said, her voice frantic. "One's behind us and the other's coming around to cut us off."

"Have they turned on their flashing lights?" Bonnie asked as she tried to remove the battery from the Blackberry.

"Not yet, but I think our only chance is to cut between these parked cars and see if I can make a U-turn."

"We can't outrun them. Our only chance is that they didn't see where we were parked. I'm covered up by the duffel bag and your jacket. The phone's off and I've got the battery out. If they stop you, just try to act normal."

Finally, the car ahead of them pulled into a parking space and Lauren accelerated around them toward the highway. The cop behind her was closing in and the other one had already gotten to the end of his row and turned in her direction. She calculated the distance and realized there was no way to get to the highway before he cut her off. She slowed down and checked her rearview mirror. The distance between her and the other cop was closing fast.

She waited and the cop in front of her pulled forward with his eye on her while speaking into a radio microphone. When he got to her row he slowed to a stop and put down the mic.

Her heart sank as he took off his sunglasses and locked eyes with her. Then with a slight nod and a smile, he motioned for her to go ahead.

She looked in her rearview mirror and saw the cop behind her was taking a drag on a cigarette while looking out his side window, not in the least concerned about her.

With a sigh of relief, Lauren turned back to the officer in front of her and mouthed the words *Thank You*, then smiled widely as she drove past him and stopped at the exit.

"We're okay," Lauren said as she pulled onto the highway. "They weren't after us after all."

As Bonnie sat up, she saw the cops pulling in front of Daylight Donuts.

Lauren pulled onto the highway and asked, "What did Kim say?"

"She said there's a problem with the ransom. That's when you told me to get off the phone."

"Maybe you should call her back and find out what she was talking about."

"First things first," Bonnie said. She felt a tinge of uneasiness as she anticipated their next move. "Let's go get Luke."

Chapter 45

It took less than five minutes to get to the mall and Lauren found a parking space where they had a view of the entrance on the back side. She turned off the engine and glanced at Bonnie in the backseat.

"You sure you want to do it this way," Bonnie said.

"It's the best way. Since they're expecting you our chances of getting Luke out safely are better if I go in. Plus, the chances of you being recognized are pretty good. Best you stay here, out of sight."

"Okay, but if Sonny's in there he might recognize you.

"You're right," Lauren said, grabbing the cap off the back seat.

As she began to stuff her long hair under the cap, Bonnie said, "Call me as soon as you see Luke."

Lauren nodded, put on her sunglasses and got out. She fell in behind a couple of ladies pushing baby strollers and followed them inside the mall. As they walked down the tiled corridor she thought about how Bonnie described Coley, Rita and Rosemary. She expected several of them, and maybe Sonny, to be inside, out of sight but watching for Bonnie.

At the main concourse of the mall, Lauren went left. She walked at a casual pace looking in stores for anyone who looked out of place. At the end of the mall she turned and came down the other side, again seeing nothing out of the ordinary. Ahead, several stores down on the right, she could see the red Radio Shack sign. She looked at her watch; Luke should be there by now. He'd be looking for Bonnie, but he might recognize her if he saw her, and she didn't want that to happen until just the right time.

Down the center of the mall, a series of rectangular brick planters overflowed with greenery. Lauren moved down the mall on the opposite side, peering in windows like every other shopper. When she was a couple of stores away, several tall Ficus trees in the planter blocked her view of Radio Shack, so she wandered toward the middle for a better look.

As she peeked around a branch she saw a guy with brown hair and a white cap sitting on the brick edge of the planter. She made her way closer, trying to see if it was Luke.

When he was just around the corner from her, he stood up and started to turn her way. But, before she saw his face, she spun around and walked into the gift shop across from Radio Shack. She couldn't let him see her yet.

"Can I help you find something special today?" a heavyset gray-haired lady asked from the checkout counter.

"No, just looking," Lauren said as she turned down an aisle with greeting cards.

With her face hidden behind a display of balloons, she took off her sunglasses and peeked out the front door. The man in the cap was still near the planter, but was now talking to a woman holding a baby in her arms.

It wasn't Luke.

Lauren exhaled and let her shoulders sag. Scanning the faces in front of Radio Shack, she didn't see Luke, so she put her sunglasses back on and walked deeper into the store. On the back wall of the store, Lauren saw a partially opened door with a sign above it that said, *Employees Only*. She glanced back and when the sales clerk started checking out a customer, she walked through the door into a storeroom.

Shelves piled high with merchandise lined one wall and stacks of boxes cluttered the floor. On the back wall, a red *Exit* sign glowed above a gray metal door.

A tall guy with long dark hair stepped around a corner holding a box cutter.

Lauren froze. The guy took a step toward her, and said, "You looking for the bathroom?"

Lauren caught her breath and said, "Uh, yes, I am."

"It's right there," he said. He pointed the box cutter to a

door behind him in the corner.

She walked past him and went inside. A minute later when she came out, the guy was pulling a tall lamp out of a box.

"Thanks for letting me use the bathroom," she said, smiling at him.

"Anytime."

Lauren glanced around and pointed at a door. "Does that door go to the parking lot?"

"Uh-huh," he replied.

"I hate to be a pain, but I have a favor to ask. I bought one of those big lava lamps. It's just like that one." She pointed to the one he had just unpacked. "It doesn't work and I need to return it. It's really heavy. I really don't want to carry it all the way down the mall. Do you think I could bring it in this door?"

"We're not supposed to do that, but I guess we could do it this time." He walked over to a keypad and entered a few numbers, then turned the deadbolt and said, "It's unlocked and I also turned off the alarm. Now you can just open the door outside and come in."

"How do I know which door to come to?"

"Our door is number A61. But don't forget your receipt. The manager's pretty anal about that kind of stuff."

"I will. You are so sweet to do this for me," Lauren said. "I'm parked on the other side of the mall. In a few minutes I'll go get my stuff and come back."

"Not a problem," he said.

She went back into the store and worked her way up to the greeting cards aisle. She looked out towards the mall, let her eyes sweep across the passing shoppers, and noticed someone who had not been there earlier. He had dark hair and was wearing brown cargo shorts, a white polo shirt and a white cap. The same clothes he had on the last time she saw him in Cardston. He fidgeted nervously as he checked the crowd, obviously looking for Bonnie.

Lauren dropped her eyes to the rack of cards and swallowed hard. She pulled a sympathy card from the rack and pretended to read while catching her breath.

Though Coley said they'd send him in, she wasn't really convinced it would happen. Her pulse increased as she thought about what she was going to do next.

First, she pulled the cell phone out of her pocket and dialed.

"Hello?"

"I see him." Her voice was shaky.

"Oh my God," Bonnie said anxiously. "Is he okay?"

"He looks fine, just nervous. He's looking everywhere for you."

"Okay. Now what?"

"I know they're probably watching him so once I make contact with him, we need to move as fast as we can. We'll come out the back door of a store across from Radio Shack. It's a gift shop and I've talked to a guy who has unlocked the back door. He said you can identify the door because it has a number on it—A61. Meet us there in five minutes."

"I'll be there," Bonnie said.

Lauren put the phone back in her pocket and started looking for an accomplice.

Just then, two girls turned down the aisle and stopped at the other end of the card rack. They looked like sisters except one was heavier than the other. They looked like they were fifteen, sixteen at the most. Perfect.

Lauren opened her purse and pulled out a pen and piece of paper. Quickly, she wrote a short note and folded it in half, then folded it again.

She watched the girls as they handed each other cards and chuckled.

Lauren gave Bonnie a few more minutes then eased over to them. "Excuse me, I was wondering if you could do me a favor."

They looked at her, then each other, not sure what to say.

"See that guy over there?" Lauren said, pointing at Luke who stood out in front of the store. "I was wondering if you would go over and give him this note."

The girls looked at each other then back at Lauren, waiting for more information.

"I'll give you ten bucks," Lauren added.

"Just to give him that note?" the heavier one wondered.

Lauren rolled her eyes and smiled sheepishly. "Yeah. Just to give him this note."

The girls were hesitant, Lauren could see. For a few seconds they looked around as if they might be on *Boiling Point*, that old show on MTV that gets people in annoying situations and irritates them until they reach their boiling point.

"Okay, here's the deal," Lauren said, acting embarrassed. "I know, at my age, it's kind of silly, but I really want to meet him and I'm too embarrassed to just walk up to him. So, I wrote him a note. Will you do it?"

They turned to each other, and couldn't stifle their giggles, then looked around as if they knew there had to be a hidden camera. Finally, they must have decided Lauren was telling the truth. The short one laughed and said, "That's so cool. We'll do it."

Lauren handed the heavier girl the note and the ten-dollar bill and said, "When you give it to him, tell him a woman in the gift shop sent him the note. Then just walk away, okay?"

"Not a problem."

"Thanks." Lauren said, relieved.

They walked out of the store and over to Luke.

He looked down at them and appeared to be listening for a few seconds. Then all three of them turned and looked directly at her, as the two girls, simultaneously extended their arms and pointed at her. Luke took the note and opened it. The girls, however, didn't walk away like they agreed to do. They stayed, smiling widely, glancing between Luke and Lauren, while he read the note.

Luke looked over and made eye contact with Lauren, then said something to the girls, and started toward the gift shop at a brisk pace.

As he entered the store his eyes found Lauren's. When he recognized her his pace slowed and he stopped about six feet away. For a second he just stared at her, and then said, "What are you doing here? Are you one of them?"

Assuming he meant the kidnappers, Lauren said, "No, like the note said, I'm with Bonnie. She's in the parking lot."

She waved him toward her and started to walk away. He made no attempt to go with her.

She stopped and turned to him. "Luke—this is a trap. They're going to kill you. We have to get out of here." She turned and walked quickly past the gray haired lady at the counter toward the back of the store. As she reached the door to the storeroom she stopped, looked over her shoulder and saw him still standing there. She took a few paces back towards him. "Damn it, Luke. You left me that picture of Bonnie asking me for help. That's why I'm here."

Luke didn't say a word, but started walking quickly to Lauren. Over his shoulder, she saw a man in a black cap and sunglasses enter the gift shop. Even from across the store, Lauren could see there was something on his chin that looked like a Band-Aid.

"They're here. Run," she said pointing at Coley.

Luke glanced over his shoulder just as the man reached into his leather jacket.

Luke disappeared into the storeroom behind Lauren and ran between stacks of boxes to the exit when the stock boy was lifting another lava lamp out of a box.

"Hi. Me again," Lauren said as she ran past him. She opened the door and said, "My ex-husband's stalking us. Don't let him go out this door, okay?"

"Cool," the kid said, as if he heard this same story every day.

Lauren and Luke ran through the gray metal door and slammed it behind them.

They found themselves standing on a loading dock that

was about five feet above ground. It was late in the day and the surrounding docks were empty.

And there was no sign of Bonnie.

Lauren pulled out her cell phone and pressed Bonnie's speed dial number.

Bonnie answered speaking fast. "None of the doors have numbers."

Lauren looked back at the door. Instead of a number on the door, it said, *Horizon Gifts*. Above the name she could see the number, A61, stenciled lightly in pencil. The smell of fresh paint was in the air. She looked at the adjacent doors and noticed none of them had numbers, but every door seemed to have been painted recently.

"We're just east of Penney's, past those bushes by the loading docks."

"I see you," Bonnie said.

As Lauren and Luke ran down to the end of the loading dock the Suburban roared through the parking lot and stop just beyond a hedge of shoulder-high bushes. At the end of the docks they took the steps down to ground level and ran toward her. The driver's door flew open and Bonnie jumped out and ran, diving into Luke's arms.

Through tears, she said, "I was afraid they'd kill you."

They heard a loud ping, then another, and saw dust fly from the trash dumpster beside them.

They looked back at the door to Horizon Gifts and saw the man in the black cap on the loading docks holding a pistol. Two more shots pinged and they dove between two blue dumpsters for cover.

But, then they noticed, the dumpsters were two feet apart and pushed back against the wall. They were trapped.

Looking out they saw Coley come into view, now thirty feet away, his chrome plated pistol pointed at them. They backed up as far as they could while he moved closer and waved the gun from one to the other. Luke stepped in front of Bonnie and Lauren and Coley narrowed his aim to Luke's chest.

"You know it didn't have to end this way," Coley said, looking at Bonnie. "All you had to do was give us Olivia like we told you. But you had to be a hero. Save the kid and all that shit. Now we have no choice."

Luke held his arms out, palms up, and pleaded. "There has to be some way we can—"

"No. Your time is up."

From under Luke's outstretched arm, Bonnie's hand came up holding the Colt revolver. The pistol fired, hitting the gunman in the middle of his chest.

The gunfire was deafening in that confined area. Coley's torso jolted and he staggered back. His gun hand dropped to his side as a red stain blossomed just above his belt. He swayed and tried to lift his gun.

Bonnie fired again.

This time the impact of the bullet hit him like a sledgehammer in the middle of his chest. The impact knocked him back and he landed spread-eagle on his back.

"Holy shit!" Luke said, looking back at Bonnie.

"Come on," Lauren demanded, tugging on Bonnie's outstretched arm that was still aimed at Coley. "We need to get out of here."

Bonnie grabbed Luke's hand and they all ran for the Suburban. Behind them they heard a scream. They looked back and saw a woman in a blue cap on the loading docks.

Lauren jumped in the driver's seat as Bonnie and Luke dove into the back seat. As the Suburban sped away, they saw the woman run up and kneel beside Coley.

No one spoke as Lauren made her way through the parking lot and pulled onto the highway. As they merged with traffic, Luke pulled off his cap and ran his fingers through his hair. In the rearview mirror Lauren could see his nostrils flare as he inhaled deeply. Finally, he looked from Bonnie to Lauren then back at Bonnie.

"Will someone please tell me, what the hell just happened?"

Chapter 46

"Pete's been shot!" Rita screamed into her cell phone.

"What the hell are you talking about?" Sonny said.

"Bonnie had a pistol and shot him. He's in bad shape. We're at the loading docks next to Penny's. Get over here."

Sonny dropped the phone and drove frantically around the mall.

He had told them to keep out of sight. Not to confront Luke or Bonnie inside the mall. All they had to do was let him know when Bonnie showed up. He would take care of them in the parking lot. That's all they had to do.

The loading docks were secluded from the main parking lot by an eight-foot high brick wall on two sides and a hedge of shrubs on the other. When he drove in, he saw Rita kneeling beside Pete's body, which lay in a puddle of dark red blood.

After the van skidded to a stop, Sonny jumped out and knelt down beside him. Rita was trying to stop the flow of blood by pressing each hand in different spots, about a foot apart.

Sonny had never seen that much blood. "What the hell happened?"

"She shot him twice," Rita cried. Her face was locked in fear. "He's lost too much blood."

"Open the back door," Sonny said. Pete's eyes fluttered as he grabbed him under the arms and muscled him inside onto the floor in front of the backseat. Rita knelt beside him and applied pressure to his wounds.

As the van raced toward the closest exit, Sonny tried to think what to do. This had not been a scenario they had considered. Bonnie was not supposed to have a gun.

"Rita, you're a nurse; what do we do now?"

She didn't answer.

"Where do we go?"

As they got closer to the parking lot exit, he looked back at her. She was holding her hand to Pete's neck, feeling for a pulse. Sonny pulled to the side and stopped where other cars could get around him.

Sonny saw her expression turn to sorrow as she squeezed her eyes closed and covered them with the backs of her bloody hands. She began to wail.

Pete was dead.

"Son of a bitch!" Sonny screamed, slamming his open palm onto the steering wheel, and then yelled again. "Son of a bitch! Son of a bitch!"

For half a minute he sat, trying to grasp it all. Nothing like this was supposed to happen. He stared straight ahead and through gritted teeth he asked, "What happened back there?"

"Bonnie shot him," Rita sobbed.

"I fucking know that. Where'd she get a gun?" he screamed.

"I don't know." Rita screamed back.

"Tell me what happened."

Rita told him about the unknown woman that led Luke out the back door of the gift shop and how Bonnie shot Pete. And that Bonnie may have recognized her when she ran off the loading dock.

"Who in the hell is this other woman?"

"I don't know. She had on a cap. All I know is they got into a big white SUV and hauled ass."

Sonny thought about what losing Pete really meant. Pete was his best friend. But, he was also the one who handled all of the technical details. The entire ransom plan was his, setting up fake email accounts for ransom demands, offshore accounts for the fund transfers, securing fake passports and new identities for them to live in Germany or Switzerland or Costa Rica or wherever they wanted to live.

But, there was nothing they could do about it now. As he started driving out of town, he called Rosemary to tell her what had happened. She was inconsolable. They had started sleeping together three months ago and planned to get married.

"We all knew something like this was possible and now we have to move on." He waited for her to say something but all he heard were her choking sobs. He gave her some time then said, "Has Kim updated Olivia's blog?"

Through her sobs she said, "Yes, it says, 'Olivia is more important than any amount of money.'"

"Good. How's Olivia doing?"

"She's okay, she's asleep right now."

"Good. Can you leave her alone for about twenty minutes?"

"I think so."

"Good." A month earlier, Pete and Sonny had driven around town and located a number of unsecured Internet connections. "Go to the Kalispell Koffee and use their Wi-Fi from the parking lot. Use the first Yahoo email account and send Kim the e-mail with our demands."

"Okay," she said, choking back her sobs.

"We'll be back in about an hour." He disconnected and looked back at Rita, who was covering Pete's body up with a painter's drop cloth. "Give me Pete's phone."

She pulled the phone out of his pocket and handed it to Sonny as she moved into the passenger seat up front. Sonny hit the speed dial number to call Bonnie.

"What do you want?" she snapped.

He knew that he had to disguise his voice. Chances were good she'd recognize his voice from the camera shop and he couldn't take that chance. She had already identified Pete, and now possibly Rita.

To disguise his voice he spoke from deep in his throat, just above a whisper. "If you go to the police before we get our ransom, I promise you, I'll kill Olivia."

"You promised you wouldn't hurt her."

"When you killed my friend, you changed everything."

"He was going to kill us. I had no choice."

"And now I have no choice. I will slit her throat and watch her bleed to death, calling for her Mommy. And for the rest of your life you'll have to remember that it was your fault."

"Okay. We won't go to the police, but how do I know you'll let her go?"

"As soon as I have my money, we'll tell Kim where to find her. But, remember: I have friends in the police department. If you interfere in any way or I hear you had any contact with the police, I'll kill her. *Even* if I get my ransom. Do you understand?"

"Yes. We won't do anything."

"Good. And don't try to call me again."

Sonny ended the call and turned off the phone. He had stalled her. At least for now.

They continued to drive west until he came to a gravel road that led into the forested foothills. After a few miles, the gravel road gently gained elevation. He turned down a one-lane road that looked more like a cross-country ski trail and followed it until they crossed a bridge over a shallow creek. He pulled over and stopped.

Together, they dragged Pete's lifeless body across the creek and into the woods. At a narrow crevasse that fed into a deep ravine, he said, "This is good enough."

He removed Pete's wristwatch and wallet and handed them to Rita who was breathing hard.

"Take these and go back to the van. I'll be there in a minute."

When she was out of sight, he pushed the body over the edge. It rolled into the gorge ten feet below him, then tumbled sideways another twenty feet before coming to rest at the bottom. Sonny watched as dirt and rocks trickled down on top of the bloody body of his old friend.

He kicked more rocks, pine needles, leaves and dirt into the ravine. There were some bigger rocks nearby and he rolled them in until Pete was completely covered.

On the way back to the van he came to the creek where Rita was washing the blood off her hands and arms. He looked at the blood on his own hand and scooped up a handful of sand from the bank and mixed it in the cool, clear water and rubbed his hands together. The blood washed away, leaving only the memory of losing his friend.

This would be the last time he would underestimate Bonnie. Nor would he trust her.

When they got back to Rosemary's apartment complex they found her sitting inside the motor home at the table. Her eyes were red, but most of her tears had dried. Rita went to her and they hugged and both started to cry again.

After a minute, Rosemary lifted her chin and said, "I sent the email just like you told me."

"Good. Did you take care of Olivia?"

"About twenty minutes ago I woke her and gave her a double dose of Benadryl. She'll sleep for the several hours. We'll move her to the compartment under the bed just before we cross the border. No one will ever find her unless they tear the bedroom apart."

"Good. It's time to get going, but there's been a small change of plans. There's too much blood in the van, so we need to get rid of it."

"So what do we do?" Rita asked.

"Rita, you drive the Jeep and Rosemary you drive the RV. Leave now and go back to the house in Whitefish. I'll be a few minutes behind you in the van."

When Sonny got to the house an hour later the Jeep and the RV were sitting out front. He parked the van in the garage and went back to the RV where Rosemary and Rita were waiting.

"Did you check with Vic to make sure he's working at the border crossing today?"

"Yes. I sent him a text earlier saying me and Rita were leaving on vacation today and asked if we'd see him when we crossed the border. He said he'd be there until ten tonight."

Rosemary said.

"Good. Text me when you get across the border," Sonny said as he stepped away.

As he watched the Winnebago drive away, he knew what he had to do now.

He went back to the garage and opened the side door of the van. Blood covered the back seat and floor. There was no doubt their fingerprints were in there, too. As an agent for the Canadian government, Pete's were on file. Since Sonny was an ex-con, his were on file, as were Rita's. He wasn't sure about Rosemary's, but in a few minutes, it wouldn't matter anyway.

Cardboard boxes were stacked along one wall of the garage. They were filled with old magazines, newspapers, books, old clothes and other junk not worthy of a thrift store. Along another wall were stacks of old lumber and broken-down furniture.

He emptied several of the boxes of papers and magazines inside the van on top of the drying blood. On a shelf at the back of the garage was an array of chemicals, most probably banned by the EPA decades ago. Pesticides, herbicides, fertilizers, weed killer, bug spray, and a couple of old gas cans. He wasn't sure which of the chemicals would burn, so he piled everything on top of the pile of paper. Then he carried some of the old clothes and magazines inside the house and piled them along the wall under the old tattered curtains. On his way out back to the old house he had stopped and bought a bottle of charcoal starter at a convenience store. He sprayed it all over the curtains then dropped a match.

Back in the garage, he doused the inside of the van and the lumber along the wall with the rest of the fuel. He dropped a match on the lumber and another one inside the van. A yellow flame slowly started to rise, then gradually spread across one magazine toward the others. As the flames grew higher he moved to the side door of the garage. When the entire interior of the van was ablaze he closed it and walked to the Jeep.

As he backed out onto the road he could see the flicker of

flames through the broken window in the front room of the house. Looking over at the garage he now saw smoke billowing out of the front and side doors.

The house and garage were surrounded by trees and bushes, and the surrounding forest was thick with heavy undergrowth. Sonny knew the fire would spread fast. In five minutes, any evidence or DNA would be gone. Within thirty minutes it would be a serious forest fire.

He didn't care. He didn't care if it burned the whole fricking town of Whitefish.

It took about ten minutes to get to the edge of town. Sonny pulled into the parking lot of Le Chateau Apartments. He powered up the laptop and grabbed the first available wi-fi signal.

While he waited for his computer to boot, he thought about Pete, and that's when it dawned on him. His take in the ransom just increased. The ransom was to be divided evenly between all five partners. Now, with Pete dead, there were only four.

But, there was still the issue of Bonnie and Luke. He was sure that they wouldn't go to the police until the ransom was paid because they knew he'd kill Olivia. But once the ransom was paid and Olivia was released, he knew they would, and they'd tell them about Pete. But, they had no proof. No blood, no fingerprints, no photos. Nothing. Perhaps they'd suspect that Pete was in hiding with the ransom. His body wouldn't be found for years, if ever. And, if they did find him, there was no way to connect him to the others. All they had to do now was wait for Kim to wire the money.

When his computer powered up, he noticed he had two new messages in his inbox. The first was from Yahoo welcoming him as a new member, and the other one was from Kim.

Sonny's pulse quickened as he double-clicked on the mouse pad. The message filled the screen.

He read:

> Ms. Rich,
> When my husband and his parents were killed in the airplane crash, the media reported that I inherited over two billion dollars. That's not exactly true. Though I am the heir to the Townsend estate, all of the money will be held in a trust for the next ten years. I am given a very generous amount of money to live on and I can petition the trustees for funds for special reasons, such as the children's center at the hospital. They have never turned down any of my requests, until now.
> There are rules that govern the trust. One of them says no money can be paid for blackmail, extortion, or ransom demands, under any conditions.

Sonny could not believe what he was reading.

> I have begged the trustees to make an exception to save Olivia. But, they said the rules were set up specifically to prevent situations like this. There are no exceptions.
> I don't have $40,000,000 I can give you.

Chapter 47

Sonny thought he was going to throw up. His eyes went to the top of the page and he read it again. When he finished, he leaned back and stared blankly out the windshield at the brick wall of the apartment building.

This can't be happening.

Sonny gritted his teeth and stabbed at the reply icon on the email. *They are not going to screw this up. Not now. Not after all we've done. This was the perfect plan. Pete died for it.*

His breathing increased as he stabbed at the keyboard.

I don't care what the rules are. If you ever want to see your child again, you will wire $40,000,000 as we have instructed or she will die. Olivia's next treatment is less than 37 hours from now. If we do not have the money by then, she will die. If you do not wire the money, the next time you hear from us will be to tell you where you can find her body.

Without another thought, he hit the send button.

"We have to turn ourselves in to the police," Luke said.

"We can't," Bonnie said.

"Why not? You shot that guy in self defense. You were abducted and held hostage for four days. If you had not kidnapped that little girl they would have killed me and her. Isn't that what you told me?"

"Yes, but—"

"Then the best thing we can do is turn ourselves in to the police."

"They said that if we go to the police before they get the ransom, they will kill her after they get the ransom."

"Bonnie, they won't kill her. They want the ransom."

"I won't take that chance. It's because of me they have Olivia."

Luke leaned back and slowly nodded. She knew he understood.

As Lauren drove, she said, "So, where do you want me to go?"

Luke turned and looked behind them as they drove through the middle of town. "I think we need to get this vehicle out of sight as fast as we can. You don't just shoot someone in a parking lot that big and drive away unnoticed. I think we can count on the fact that the cops will be looking for a white Suburban very soon."

"Where do you want to go?" Lauren asked.

"I don't know," Bonnie said. "Somewhere we can lay low for a day or two."

"If you and Luke had passports and driver's licenses we'd go back to Cardston."

Bonnie noticed a green road sign—*Flathead Lake 7 miles.* It gave her an idea. "You said that fishing guide friend of yours is out of town. Maybe we can stay at his place."

Lauren nodded. "That's a good idea. Let me call Roger. He always takes care of Beau's pets when he's not around."

She told Roger that her fishing trip had been delayed and she was low on cash and needed a place to crash for a day or two. "Would it be okay to stay at Beau's place?"

"Sure. Would you mind feeding his cat while you're there? That would save me a trip over there every day."

"Is Gato still alive?"

"Yeah, she's at least fifteen, and still mean as ever. Her food is in the pantry by the washing machine. Remember how to get there?"

"I do if he still lives in that little house down on Big Arm Bay."

"Still does. When you go to the back door, you'll see a little birdhouse in the tree. Inside is a key chain with two keys—one to the back door and one to the garage. Make yourself at home. He won't be back for a week, but let me know when you leave."

Beau's house was about an hour south of Kalispell and by the time they turned in his long driveway, the sun had dipped behind the mountains to the west and his entire yard was in the shade. The small cottage had a low hedge across the front and a detached garage off to the right. Next to it were two empty boat trailers. After they got the garage unlocked, Lauren pulled in and they closed the door.

While Lauren was unlocking the back door, an old Siamese cat came up and brushed against her leg and followed her inside. The house was neat and cozy. In the living room a big flat panel television hung on one wall and several mounted fish adorned the others.

"Pretty nice place for a bachelor," Bonnie said.

"Beau's not a slob like a lot of single men. And he's an excellent cook, too," Lauren said. "Roger said to help ourselves to anything we need."

"I could use a shower and a change of clothes. How big is Beau?" Luke asked as he spied a jar full of what looked like chocolate chip cookies. He lifted the top off and pulled out a couple.

"Beau's about your size, maybe a little shorter, but I bet his clothes will fit. Let's go look."

As they disappeared around the corner, Bonnie rummaged through the cabinets and pulled some pasta and canned goods out of the pantry. By the time Lauren came back to the kitchen, Bonnie had a pot of water heating on the stove and was adding an assortment of ingredients and spices to some tomato sauce.

Lauren said, "Beau's clothes are going to fit Luke fine. He's taking a shower now."

"Good. How does spaghetti sound?" Bonnie asked.

"Sounds great," Lauren said as she opened the refrigerator and pulled out a head of lettuce and two tomatoes.

While Lauren started on a salad Bonnie tried to concentrate on the spaghetti sauce, but her mind kept whirling back to the events earlier in the day. For the second time in four hours, she had narrowly escaped with her life. The first time was at the hospital when Coley's gun misfired. Then again at the mall. This time he hesitated, not realizing she had a gun.

And she had committed murder. Had taken the life of another human being. Never in her wildest dreams did she ever think that could happen. She never thought she'd have to kill to protect herself and the ones she loved. Although it was self-defense, it was hard to believe she had killed a man.

As she tried to get the image of his bloody body out of her mind she thought about seeing Luke for the first time in five days. There were many times she thought she'd never see him again. Now that they were together, she didn't want him out of her sight.

In the refrigerator she spotted a six-pack of beer. Shiner Bock—one of Luke's favorites. She pulled one out and told Lauren, "Keep your eye on the sauce. I'll be back in a minute."

Bonnie opened the bottle and walked through the living room and down the hallway to the master bedroom. There she found the bathroom door closed. She tapped lightly and said, "Luke?"

"Yes?" came a muffled answer.

She pushed the door open and stepped inside.

Dense steam filled the small bathroom and Luke stood on a bathmat beside the tub. He was naked, a white towel hung in front of him while he dried his chest.

He watched as she closed the door and stepped closer.

"I thought you could use one of these," she said, holding the beer out to him.

He took it and set it on the shelf above the toilet.

"You are what I need." He dropped the towel and pulled her closer.

He kissed her softly and their arms wrapped around each

other. They kissed again, this time more passionately. His lips were soft and they covered hers, filling a need she never felt so strongly. His hands pulled her tight against his body. One hand at her waist pulled her close and the other moved up her spine until it stopped at the nape of her neck, where it began to caress handfuls of red hair. Luke had always said her hair was like an aphrodisiac to him. She felt sexy as he played with it.

They kissed and Bonnie felt Luke getting hard as he pressed himself against her. Her hands slowly slipped down his back until they reached the bare cheeks of his butt. With both hands, she pulled him against her body and slowly worked her hips against him. His hand moved to her rear and pulled her hard against him. Slowly, they began to move in rhythm.

He was naked and fully erect now. Her breathing quickened as their hips pushed harder and faster against each other.

This was not the right time or place. The kitchen was on the other side of the bathroom wall. Lauren was not twenty feet away in this quiet little cottage. She would hear them for sure.

"Not now," Bonnie said, breathlessly. "We can't do this here."

But her comment fell on deaf ears as his hand moved from her hair to her breasts. He caressed them and never had his touch aroused her like it did now. His other hand came around and began to fumble with the button of her jeans.

Stopping now was the last thing Bonnie wanted. She needed Luke more than ever. She reached down, undid the button for him, and quickly pushed down her pants and panties, and kicked, until one foot was completely out and free.

Luke reached down and grabbed her by the back of the thighs and lifted her on top of the counter beside the sink. As she spread her legs and lifted her knees, he moved to her. Her heart pounded wildly and she wrapped one arm around his neck and pulled herself closer. The other hand went down and grabbed his erection and guided it between her legs. When her lips were just inches from his, he thrust himself inside her.

She cried out and dug her fingernails in his back. With a grunt, he withdrew and thrust again, and again, and again. Unable to control her emotions, Bonnie cried out each time, each time louder. As the pace quickened, she felt as if every nerve ending in her body was on fire and Luke knew just what to do.

It was hard, raw passion like Bonnie had never experienced. And she didn't want it to end.

But it was over quickly.

They held each other tightly; breathing hard, a feeling of satisfaction, a feeling of love like she'd never felt before. Luke held her close, and gently, she started kissing him on the neck, and ear, and lips, not ever wanting to let him go.

When Bonnie went back into the kitchen she saw three salads on the table. Lauren sat quietly thumbing through an issue of *Field & Stream*. Without looking up, she said, "Everything okay in there?"

"Oh, yeah…everything's great," Bonnie replied, noticing a hint of a smile on Lauren's face as she turned another page.

"Well, dinner's ready if you're still hungry," Lauren said.

Bonnie cleared her throat and said, "Starving."

A few minutes later, as Lauren was putting the spaghetti on the table, Luke strolled into the kitchen wearing a pair of Beau's fishing shorts and a clean T-shirt. His hair was wet but neatly combed and he had shaved off his four-day beard. He slipped up behind Bonnie, who was opening a bottle of wine, and kissed her on the cheek.

"I didn't thank you for bringing me a beer a while ago," he said quietly.

You certainly did thank me, Bonnie thought, but instead said, "My pleasure," while trying to stifle a grin.

This was the first chance they had to sit down together and there was much to talk about. When they started to eat and Luke told Bonnie how after three days the Cardston police department decided he was an abusive husband and they had proof she had taken a bus to the Calgary airport, and from there caught a flight back to Texas. But, he wouldn't give up. He told her about Dr. Duncan's apartment, the blood on the floor, and how it disappeared by the time the police got over there. And why he was now convinced Sonny was behind it all.

"I should have told you not to trust Sonny," Lauren said to Luke.

"But, there was no way you would have known Sonny was involved," Luke said.

"But there's a lot more I should have told you about him."

"Like what?"

"I told you we used to date, but I didn't tell you why we broke up."

"Would it have mattered?"

"Probably. Our senior year, he was sent to prison for murder," Lauren murmured.

"Murder? Who'd he kill?" Luke asked.

"A professor he was having an affair with."

"My God, what happened?"

"I don't really know for sure, but here's what came out during the trial. She was in her thirties and had a thing for football players and—"

"Was Sonny a football player?" Bonnie asked.

"Yes. He went to the University of Wisconsin on scholarship. In high school he was one of the best quarterbacks in Alberta."

"I thought hockey was the big sport in Canada," Luke said.

"It is, but we love our football, too."

"Were you dating him at the time?"

"Yeah, we dated our last few years of high school and I followed him to Wisconsin." She picked up her glass of wine and swirled it for a few seconds, seemingly lost in thought. Without taking a sip she put it down and continued. "Our junior year he had her for Kinesiology. All the jocks tried to get her class because it was an easy A. According to what came out in the trial the professor had had affairs with a number of the football players over the years. Sonny started having sex with her while he was taking her class.

"That summer we got engaged and according to his testimony he went over to tell her it was over and she didn't take it too well. He said she came after him with a butcher knife and he turned it on her, killing her in self-defense. But instead of going to the police, he tried to make it look like she had been killed by a burglar. He might have gotten away with it but he tried to fence some of her jewelry. To make things worse, they had had sex before he killed her. So, they even had his DNA."

"Did he confess to killing her?"

"Not at first. He tried to get me to give him an alibi but there was no way I was going to lie for him. That's why he hates me now. He thinks if I had vouched for him he never would have gone to prison and would be playing football in the NFL."

"So, what happened?"

"When he found out what all they had on him, he took a plea. He went to prison and was paroled after ten years. He got out about five or six years ago. He spent a couple of years in a halfway house in Wisconsin then came back to Cardston a few years ago. An old friend hired him to run his camera shops."

"He had me fooled. I thought he was sincere and really wanted to help," Luke said.

"I know and I'm sorry I didn't tell you this earlier. When you asked me if you could trust him, I said yes, because he *can* be a nice guy," Lauren said, shaking her head. "So, when I found your message telling me you were sure Sonny was behind it all, I almost died. If I had warned you about him maybe you wouldn't be in this mess. But I didn't and that's why I'm here. I'll do whatever it takes to help you get out of this mess."

"It's not your fault. This all would have happened, regardless of what you told me. I'm convinced of that," Luke said.

"And without you, I'm not sure either one of us would be alive right now," Bonnie added.

"I'm so sorry," Lauren said.

"I don't want you to feel obligated in any way. If you want to, you can leave right now and go back to Cardston because you don't owe us a thing. Okay?"

"Absolutely not," she said without hesitating. "I'm not leaving until that asshole is behind bars where he belongs."

Bonnie couldn't help but smile. She knew Lauren wouldn't leave until this was over.

"Okay, so what do we do now?" Luke said, looking from Lauren to Bonnie.

"I think we need to find out if Kim's paid the ransom," Bonnie said.

"How do we do that?" Luke asked.

"Hopefully they'll say something about it on the news."

After they cleaned up the kitchen, they moved to the living room and the news was just starting. The lead story was about the shooting at the hospital.

"At this time, police will not comment on whether Mrs. Townsend has been contacted by the kidnappers and a phone call to the Townsend residence was not returned. A hospital spokesman said security guard Rocco Giovino's condition has been upgraded to serious, but he remains in a coma."

The next story was about the city council debate on zoning. Several more local stories aired, including one about a forest fire near Whitefish that burned over one hundred acres before they got it under control. After a few commercials the weatherman started talking about the seven-day forecast.

"They didn't even mention anything about the shooting at the mall," Bonnie said.

"Maybe the police haven't given them any information on it yet," Luke said.

"You're probably right. Let's see what they say tomorrow," Bonnie got up and turned off the television. "I'm ready for bed.

I have a feeling tomorrow's going to be a long day."

"I think you're right," Lauren said, standing and stretching.

Bonnie walked over and gave Lauren a long hug, and said, "Without you, I don't know what I would have done. We can't thank you enough." Lauren nodded and smiled. Bonnie said, "We'll lock up. You go to bed."

A few minutes later, Bonnie washed her face and thought about how things had changed. Now that Luke was no longer held captive, her greatest fear was gone. And Rocky was improving. As soon as he was able to talk, he would tell police that she did not shoot him, nor did she shoot the woman who was killed. After the ransom was paid, Olivia would be released, and they could turn themselves in and tell their entire story. They'd identify Sonny, Coley, Rosemary and Rita as the true kidnappers.

When she crawled into bed and snuggled up beside Luke, she felt safer than she'd felt in a long time. But, it was far from over. She wanted to believe this nightmare would turn out their way, but deep down, she had a bad feeling. Something wasn't right.

Chapter 48

The next morning Bonnie and Luke wandered into the kitchen just after seven to find Lauren sipping on a cup of coffee while watching the news on a small TV.

"Anything new?" Bonnie asked as she pulled two coffee cups out of the cabinet.

"Nothing new about the kidnapping," Lauren said. "Rocky obviously hasn't spoken to the police, because they are still saying you're the one who shot him and killed that woman."

Bonnie's optimism faded as she filled two cups with coffee.

"How about the shooting at the mall?" Luke asked.

"Still, not a word." She pushed her chair back and turned to face them. "What do you think we should do today?"

"Luke and I talked about it last night. We don't think there's any reason for us to put ourselves in jeopardy. It's probably best if we just stay here."

"Didn't you say that Kim told you there was some kind of problem with the ransom?"

"She did, and even if that's true, I don't think we can do anything about it."

"You're right. Staying out of sight is probably the best thing to do," Lauren said. She flipped through the channels for more news.

Bonnie found a can of biscuits in the fridge and while they were baking she scrambled some eggs. After they ate, Lauren surfed the Internet looking for news about Olivia's kidnapping, the shooting at the mall or news about Kim or the ransom.

By noon, they still knew no more than they did the night before. A raid on Beau's refrigerator resulted in chicken salad sandwiches for Bonnie and Lauren. But, Luke said that after being a captive, even if it was for only a day, it had changed his perspective on happiness and he would not be deprived of the good things in life. He opted for three hot dogs smothered in chili and onions, chased by a Shiner Bock. This lead to a discussion about his opinion of good food. It was the first time in days any of them had laughed. For a brief five minutes they felt their world was normal again.

After lunch, Luke and Lauren went back to their quest for news while Bonnie washed their dirty clothes. While she was at the dryer she heard Lauren yell, "Hey guys, come read this."

With an armload of socks and shirts, Bonnie ran into the breakfast nook and read the Internet story over Lauren's shoulder.

KIM TOWNSEND CAN'T PAY RANSOM

Lauren moved her mouse and the page began to scroll down.

"Oh my God. Look at that," Bonnie exclaimed. She pointed to a small inside headline: *Kidnapper Demands Forty Million Dollars.*

The article said the kidnappers are demanding the same amount Kim donated to build the Children's Center onto the hospital. It also quoted an anonymous source that said when Kim inherited the Townsend estate, all of the money was put into a trust fund as dictated by the Townsends' will. According to the covenants of the trust, no money can be used for blackmail, extortion or ransom.

"I wonder if this is what Kim was talking about yesterday," Lauren said.

The final paragraph of the story said that Kim was told by the kidnapper that regardless of her situation, they would show no mercy.

"If this is true, and Kim doesn't pay, they will let Olivia die," Bonnie said. "We have to find out if this is true. I want to call Kim."

"Okay, but not from here," Lauren warned. "We need to go somewhere else to make the call, and after that, we need to get rid of the BlackBerry. I don't really know if we're safe, even when the battery is out of it. I'm sure the FBI has technology we don't even know about."

"Then we need to do it as soon as possible," Bonnie said.

"Where do you want to go? Back to Kalispell?"

"I think we should avoid going there." Bonnie and Luke watched as Lauren pulled up Flathead Lake on a Google map. "There's a little town about ten miles south of here, Polson. But there are only two roads in and two roads out."

Luke said, "I don't like it."

"Missoula is about an hour further south. It's the biggest town in the area and it's on the interstate. That's probably the safest bet."

Half an hour later, they were on the road, driving south. Luke drove, Lauren was in the passenger seat and Bonnie rode in the backseat, hiding behind the tinted windows. When they got to Missoula they pulled into a shopping center with a huge grocery store about a mile off the interstate. The parking lot was packed and when Luke pulled in, Bonnie put the battery back in the phone and pressed the power button. As soon as she had a signal, she placed the call. The feds knew that Bonnie had Dr. Owens's BlackBerry and they were sure the FBI would be tracking any calls made with it. That meant they had to keep the call short because they had no way of knowing how long it would take for their location to be identified and for the police to close in on them.

"Hello?" Kim sounded anxious.

"Kim, I need to know if the reports on the Internet are true."

"I replied to your ransom demand telling you my situation. You know it's true."

Disappointed, Bonnie remembered their first conversation. Kim sounded like she believed her when she said she was forced to kidnap Olivia. But, now, she didn't.

"Kim, please believe me. I have not sent you any messages. I don't even know what the message says. I'm not one of them."

"You say that, but you've given me no proof. If you are telling me the truth, turn yourself in to the police and help me get Olivia back."

"They said if I go to the police before the ransom is paid, they'll kill Olivia. They said they would know," Bonnie explained.

"You have to turn yourself in."

"But, there's nothing I can do."

"You're the one who took her. You have to know where she is," Kim said firmly.

"I don't. You have to believe me. I didn't have any choice," Bonnie pleaded.

"You had a choice, and you chose to kidnap Olivia and kill those people at the hospital."

"I didn't kill anyone," Bonnie said, frantically. "As soon as Rocky comes out of his coma, he'll tell you. Another man shot him."

Kim paused. "Rocky's dead."

"What?" Bonnie hand came to her mouth.

"He died an hour ago."

"You've got to believe me, I didn't do it."

"I'll believe you if you turn yourself in."

"But they said they'd kill Olivia if I do."

Bonnie glanced at Luke. He held up his one arm and tapped on his wristwatch with the finger on his other hand telling her she'd been on the phone long enough.

"Then I have to believe you are one of them," Kim said.

Bonnie frantically tried to think of what to say, but then she heard a click.

"Kim? Kim?"

Bonnie looked at Luke, tears streaming down her cheeks. "She hung up."

Luke steered the vehicle through the parking lot and sat at

the exit waiting for an eighteen wheeler to pass by before pulling into traffic. As he accelerated, he eyed Bonnie in the rearview mirror.

"What did she say?"

"She can't pay the ransom," she said haltingly. "And Rocky's dead."

Chapter 49

The drive back to Beau's house was as quiet as a limo in a funeral procession. Knowing that Kim couldn't pay was bad, but finding out that Rocky had died tore Bonnie apart. Luke reminded her several times that it wasn't her fault, but she couldn't stop wondering what would have happened if she would have done things differently.

When they got back to Beau's house, Bonnie went straight into the bathroom where she could spend some time alone. Fifteen minutes later she came out into the living room to find Lauren on the sofa with Gato in her lap and Luke in an easy chair with the remote in one hand. They were staring at the muted TV where a weather map tracked a hurricane off the South Carolina coast. Bonnie walked to the front window and looked at the placid waters of the lake across the street. After a silent minute she turned around.

"I don't believe Kim."

Luke said, "What don't you believe?"

"I don't believe she can't pay. The original email Kim got from them said she had to get rid of the cops and the FBI. I don't think she did. When we spoke, she kept saying I needed to turn myself in so we could help *them*. *Them* must be the FBI, and they are probably telling her exactly what to do."

"I've always heard the FBI is against paying any kind of the ransom in kidnappings," Lauren said.

"And because of Olivia's condition, the amount of time they have is limited."

"So, what do we do? Turn ourselves in?" Luke said.

"No. I'm afraid if we do they'll kill Olivia," Bonnie said. She sat on the sofa by Lauren and looked her. "Let's assume Sonny is in charge of this whole thing. You know him, how he thinks. Do you have any ideas where we might start looking for him?"

Lauren slowly shook her head. "I don't know him anymore. We haven't spoken in over fifteen years. But, don't underestimate him; he's smart. The reason he was such a good quarterback was because he always had a plan. He was a master at getting out of trouble. I'm sure he has everything planned down to the last detail. He is not going to risk getting sacked."

Bonnie nodded. "I guess the first place to start is where we know they've been. How about that house where you found me locked in that motor home. But, I don't know if I can find it again. Can you?"

"That's easy. It'll be on the vehicle tracking program," Lauren said.

Bonnie looked up at Luke and said, "And how about that old house where they had me tied up?"

As Lauren stood and started out of the room, she said, "It's on the tracking program, too. We'll be able to see exactly where you drove the Jeep since you left Cardston."

Lauren pulled out her laptop. "The program keeps a detailed log of everywhere the Jeep has been for the last thirty days. It shows the route, the speed at which it travels, how long it's parked. Everything."

Lauren clicked on an icon and they all watched as the tracking program opened. After a few clicks, a map of northern Montana and southern Canada filled the screen. After a few more keystrokes, a yellow line appeared tracing the highways from Cardston, Alberta, down to St. Mary, Montana, through Glacier National Park, then over to Whitefish and down to Kalispell. There it looked like it crisscrossed town a few times then went north, back through Whitefish and into Canada, where it turned back to the east. It finally came to a stop in British Columbia, in the middle of nowhere.

Confused, Bonnie asked, "What are we looking at?"

Lauren's eyes were locked on the screen and her reply was hesitant. "That yellow line shows the route the Jeep has taken.

It shows where it's been and where it is now. According to this, the Jeep is about a hundred and fifty kilometers west of Cardston." She twisted her head around and looked at Bonnie. "Don't you have the keys?"

"No, when I parked it at the hospital, they told me to leave the keys under the floor mat."

"Either someone stole it or the kidnappers have it. Let me check something else."

Lauren moved her mouse to the upper left corner of the screen to a plus sign and clicked on it a couple of times. The map zoomed in more with each click, until the cities of Whitefish and Kalispell filled the screen. The yellow line now went down various streets, from the east side of Whitefish to the west side, then down south of Kalispell, out of town, back to Kalispell, up to Whitefish, then north into Canada.

Lauren studied the map a minute then put her finger on the screen and tracing the yellow line said, "This is the route the Jeep took yesterday."

Lauren pointed to a dot in the middle of the yellow line and looked at Luke. "Does this look like the place where you found Bonnie?"

He leaned forward and focused. "I think so."

"The Jeep was parked there on Friday afternoon from 5:59 to 6:22." Her finger moved down the screen. "Then it was driven here. It shows it was parked there from 7:13 until 1:57 yesterday afternoon. Then it was driven to the hospital."

"That sounds right because I got to the hospital and was supposed to go in at exactly 2:10," Bonnie said.

"Then at 2:14, the Jeep left the hospital and went over here, then back to the house near Whitefish." Lauren leaned back, still looking at the screen. "It has to be them."

"They must have taken it right after I went into the hospital."

"Then it went north, crossed back into British Columbia and over to here," Lauren said pointing at the map. "And it's been there since last night at midnight."

While Bonnie and Lauren continued to study the map, Luke said, "So, according to Kim, they have no leads. And when she says that, we have to assume she's talking about the FBI. So, if Coley said they have contacts with the police, we have to assume that's true. That could be either the Kalispell PD or the FBI. So, if we turn ourselves into the police, Sonny will know. And he said they'll either kill Olivia or let her die from lack of treatment. Right?"

Bonnie nodded.

"So, what are we going to do?"

"I think it's up to us. We're the only ones who can save Olivia," They nodded and Bonnie said, "I think we have only one choice. Follow the Jeep."

It only took them a few minutes to pack, feed the cat, load the Suburban and lock up Beau's house. As they pulled out of the driveway heading north, Lauren said, "I just realized we have a huge problem."

"What's that?" Luke asked.

"We'll all need a driver's license or passport to get across the border."

Luke reached and touched his empty back pocket. "They took my billfold when they tied me up."

Lauren glanced at Bonnie and said, "And every law enforcement agency in the states and Canada is looking for you."

"But your car is from Canada. Will they check it when you are coming back across?"

"Before 9/11, they hardly ever checked private vehicles, but now things are different," Lauren said. "Sometimes they'll check you, sometimes they don't. I think now, with the kidnapping, they'll be checking most vehicles, especially one as big as this."

"Any idea how we can get across?" Bonnie asked.

"No, but we've got about two hours to think of something." Lauren said.

***

An hour later they got to the city limits of Kalispell. Even though they had found no news on the Internet about the mall shooting, Luke still worried they might be looking for a white Suburban. They took back roads and residential streets and fifteen minutes later they made it through town. With a sigh of relief they headed for the Canadian border.

They got to the town of Eureka forty-five minutes later, which meant they were only ten minutes from the Canadian border. Lauren pulled into a convenience store and at the gas pumps parked across from a Ford Expedition with a boat in tow.

"This is as far as we go until we come up with a plan to get across the border," Lauren said as she turned off the ignition.

Luke said, "The only thing I can think to do is to hide under that tarp you have in the back. What are the odds we'll be checked?"

She shook her head. "The odds are probably about two to one we'll get across without a problem, but I'd like something better than that."

Lauren noticed a piece of paper was taped over the credit card slot that said, "Out of Order. Pay inside," so she grabbed her wallet and headed inside.

While she went into the store Luke got into the backseat to talk to Bonnie. Another truck pulling a boat eased up to the pump on the other side of them. The truck was painted red and silver to match the red and silver ski boat it was pulling. The driver got out and tossed an empty beer can into the trash then went over and started pumping gas. On the other side of the truck another guy got out and went to the back of the boat carrying two towels. He was wearing a tank top and flip-flops. He tossed one towel to the driver and they started wiping down the boat. They were both good-looking, thirtyish, with flat bellies and surfer haircuts.

A minute later, Lauren came out of the store and as she walked to the Suburban, Bonnie noticed the tank-top guy motion to his buddy to check her out.

After Lauren started the pump, she sat down in the front seat and dropped her wallet back on the seat. Bonnie asked, "Is there a lake around here?"

"Lake Koocanusa is just west of town. Not thinking of swimming across the border, are you?"

"No, I was just noticing these boats," Bonnie said, looking at the boat in front of them and the other one across the bay.

"Yeah, fishing's not bad. They do some boating over there. I like Flathead Lake down where Beau lives better, but it's further." Lauren glanced at the boats, "These are all from Canada. Most Canadians fill up before going home because gas is cheaper in the U.S."

She got out and pulled a squeegee out of a bucket and started cleaning her windshield. From the backseat through tinted windows Bonnie noticed the guys with the red and silver boat watching Lauren while she cleaned on her windshield.

When Lauren finished, she leaned inside and grabbed her wallet off the front seat. "You guys want me to get you something to drink?"

Bonnie said, "Wait a second. Get in and sit down, but don't look back at us."

Lauren did as instructed.

"I think I know how we can get across the border. Those guys at the pump to the left have been lusting after you ever since they pulled up. I've got an idea."

After a quick discussion of the plan, Lauren got out, replaced the hose into the gas pump, and glanced over toward her admirers.

"That sure is a pretty boat," she said, giving them a big smile as she started for the store.

"Thanks," the shirtless one said. He watched her butt until she disappeared inside.

When Lauren returned a minute later, the top two buttons of her blouse were unbuttoned. The guys were cleaning the back of the boat when she came up and stood beside them.

"I've never seen a boat painted to match the truck. I think it's the prettiest boat I've ever seen," she said, running a finger down the side.

The one in the tank top immediately noticed her breast bulging out the opening in her shirt and when she looked the other way, he mouthed "Oh my God" to his buddy.

The shirtless one moved closer to get a better look and said, "We have a paint and body shop, and a few weeks ago I painted the truck to match the boat."

"You did an awesome job. Could I see the inside of the boat?" she asked.

The boat set high and she couldn't see inside from the ground.

"Sure, step up here," the shirtless guy said. He pointed at the fender over the wheel of the trailer. She held out her hand for help and he took it, helping her up on the fender. While she bent to examine the interior, the guys checked out her well-toned legs.

"It's beautiful," she said.

Shirtless helped her down and she pointed to two colorful boards strapped to the chrome apparatus on the top of the boat and asked, "Have you guys been wakeboarding?"

"That we have. And drinking a few brewskis," said shirtless.

She grinned flirtatiously at him. "Sounds like fun. I'd like to try wakeboarding some time."

"Where're you from?"

"Pincher Creek. How about you?"

"Fernie. You aren't that far from us. Give me your number and I'll call you next time we're going out," the shirtless man said.

"I'm changing cell phone carriers and will be getting a new number next week. Why don't you give me your number and I'll call you."

Shirtless got her a business card from the truck and handed it to her.

"L & R Paint and Body—Lance Wells and Ryan Gillespie,"

she read aloud. "Which one are you?"

"I'm Lance, this is my business partner, Ryan," Shirtless said.

"I dated guys who were partners one time. Now that was interesting," Lauren said laughing while tugging at her shirt. "I'll tell you all about it if you take me wakeboarding."

"Yeah, I can hardly wait to hear that story," Lance said, stepping closer.

"So, what's your name?" Ryan asked.

"I'm Lauren," she said, extending her hand.

"How about next weekend?"

"I'm not sure if I can. Can I get back with you later?"

"Sure," Lance said.

Lauren looked at her watch and acted surprised. Backing toward her Suburban, she said, "Wow, I didn't realize it was so late. I need to be going now, but I'll call you in a few days."

They watched as she hopped in the Suburban and quickly left the station.

Ten minutes later, five miles south of the Canadian border, the Suburban sat on the shoulder of Highway 93. Lauren stood beside it, watching the road back toward Eureka. As soon as she saw the red and silver pickup pulling a red and silver boat come round the bend, she pushed the hood up and started waving her arms frantically. The pick-up coasted up behind the Suburban and slowed to a stop.

Lauren ran to the driver's window and said, "Lance, I'm so glad you're here. I don't know what happened. My car just quit. Could you take a look at it and see if you can tell what happened?"

Lance and Ryan got out and went to the open hood to look for problems.

"What happened?"

"Nothing, I was driving along and all the sudden, it just quit. I didn't know what to do, so I just pulled over. I know I'm not out of gas because I just filled up. I let it sit a minute, then tried to start it. It goes *rrr, rrr, rrr,* but won't start. What do you think is wrong with it?"

"Could be the fuel pump?" Ryan said to Lance.

He shrugged and they looked back at the engine. But Lauren could tell they didn't know the fuel pump from the voltage regulator.

"Do you know a lot about cars?"

"Well, sure," Lance said.

"What do you think is wrong?" She moved up beside Lance and leaned in to look at the engine, mashed her breast against his arm.

"Could be the alternator," Lance said to Ryan, not wanting to move.

She gave them a minute to look around but they didn't seem to know where to start.

"You think one of those wires came loose or something?" Lauren said, pointing to the spark plug wires.

"That might be it." Tentatively, they reached in and started wiggling wires.

Lauren grabbed the hood with one hand and raised a finger, giving a signal to Bonnie.

Bonnie and Luke slipped out of the backseat and ran back to the boat and climb inside.

The guys were still pulling off wires and pushing them back on a minute later when Lauren felt the cell phone in her back pocket vibrate. That told her that Bonnie and Luke were safely hidden in the storage compartments of the boat.

Ryan pushed on a few more wires and said, "Why don't you try it now?"

Lance nodded, and she walked around and sat in the driver's seat. The engine started on the first crank and purred like a kitten.

Lauren got out as Ryan was pushing the hood closed.

"I thought one of those wires I pushed on was kind of loose," Lance said.

"I don't know what I would have done if you guys hadn't stopped." Lauren gave him a full body hug and kissed him on the cheek. "I can't thank you enough."

"Don't worry about it," he said.

With her arms still around Lance's waist, she said, "I've got an idea. There's a little bar about fifteen kilometers across the border just before you get to Elko, The Silver Dollar. Know where it is?"

"Sure. It's got the coldest beer in the Rockies."

"Let's meet there. Drinks are on me," she said and flashed him a devilish grin.

"I thought you were in a hurry."

"Not anymore," she said.

They looked at each other and nodded. "Sounds good."

"Great. Follow me there, okay?"

"We'll be right behind you."

At the border crossing, Lauren fell in line behind a dozen cars, campers and several other pickups pulling boats. When she got to the front of the line, she showed her passport and driver's license to the agent and after a cursory glance in the backseat waved her through. Lance came through after her and the guard passed him and barely noticed the boat he had in tow.

They stayed on Lauren's back bumper until they pulled into the parking lot of The Silver Dollar Bar and Grill twenty minutes later. The parking lot was full so Lauren pulled around to the side and motioned for them to follow. When she got out she left the Suburban unlocked and ran over to where Lance and Ryan were getting out of their truck. She snuggled up between them, locked her arms in theirs, and they walked inside.

"We'll take a pitcher and three glasses," Lauren told the waitress as they settled at a table.

They were halfway through their first beer, when her cell phone rang.

"Hello," she said. She lowered her head and put a finger in

the other ear to block the loud music coming from the jukebox.

"We're out and in the Suburban," Bonnie said.

"Oh…hi," Lauren said. She glanced at Ryan, to see him listening close to what she was saying. She hesitated a few seconds, then rolled her eyes and said, "I'm at The Silver Dollar in Elko, why?"

Another pause, then "I was just going to have a beer or two, then I was coming home."

Ryan looked at Lance and sucked down about half of his beer.

"No, I'm not with a guy," she said, emphatically, speaking a little too loud. "I've had a long day and just wanted to stop and have a beer. Is that okay?"

At that comment, everybody at the surrounding tables was listening.

"Don't be a jerk, okay? I watch the kids all the time. You can do it for once, okay?" Lauren snapped. She turned away from Lance and continued, "Okay…there's no reason to come over here. I'll leave after this beer."

Without another word, she ended the call and put the phone back in her pocket, shaking her head in disgust.

"What's up?" Lance asked.

"Oh, that was my husband," Lauren said as she leaned back and guzzled the beer.

"Husband?"

"Sometimes he can be a real asshole. He's a cop over in Cranbrook and thinks that just because he wears a gun, I should bow down to his every wish."

"You didn't mention—" Lance said in a concerned tone.

"We've got four kids and I take care of them all the time. He never does. Don't you think he should take care of them once in a while and let me have some fun?"

"Sounds only fair to me," Ryan said, smiling at Lance. He was obviously enjoying the predicament Lance was in.

"And something else; he's the jealous type—always thinks

I'm running around on him," she added.

Lance gave Ryan a look that said *I should have known this was too good to be true.*

"I guess I'd better go. If I'm not home pretty quick, he'll come looking for me...and he's not the kind of guy you want to meet when he's mad."

"We still have half a pitcher left," Ryan said holding it up.

"Thanks, but I'd better go. But, I do want to go wakeboarding sometime. Would it be okay if I bring the kids?" she asked.

"Maybe it's not such a good idea...you being married and all," Lance said.

"Oh, come on, Lance," Ryan said. "You love kids."

Lance gave him a, *Go to hell look*, and reiterated, "I don't think it's a good idea."

"I guess I understand," she said, standing up. "But I really do want to thank you. You helped me more than you know."

As Lauren hurried across the parking lot, a pang of guilt tugged at her. They were really nice guys. She planned to keep their card. And maybe after this was all over, she'd contact them and tell them the truth.

When she pulled open the door of the Suburban she saw Luke and Bonnie inside. As she started the car and pulled out, she said, "Welcome to Canada."

Chapter 50

It was past nine by the time they went through Elko. They followed the Jeep's trail on Car-Trecker north into the forested mountains of British Columbia, through the small town of Fernie and on to Sparwood. There, they turned back to the east. After Crowsnest Pass, darkness fell as they descended onto rolling terrain and plowed into farm land, passing few other vehicles on the two-lane road. They traveled in silence, uneasy about what they would find at their next destination.

It was two hours later when Luke reached over the seat and gently squeezed Bonnie on the knee to wake her.

"I think we're getting close to our turn," he said. "Could you check the computer and make sure."

From where she sat in the backseat Bonnie stretched and looked out the front windshield to see a desolate stretch of straight highway with open pastures on both sides of the road. She pulled the laptop off the floorboard and powered it up. Blue light filled the backseat.

A minute later, she said, "It looks like the Jeep hasn't moved. We'll come to our turn in about twenty kilometers. When the highway veers hard to the left, we'll continue straight onto a smaller road. It looks like it might be gravel. The road will take lots of turns going up the mountain, probably about ten or fifteen kilometers. Just before the road end it looks like there's a private road off to the left, and the Jeep is down there about two kilometers."

When they turned off the highway the gravel road passed through open pastures until crossing a cattle guard. There the forest reappeared and the road began to ascend back into the mountains. For half an hour they followed the winding road until it came to a dead end. They backed up until they found an old wooden gate held closed with a chain around a fence post. An old weathered sign said *Private Property* and beyond it a narrow one-lane road disappeared into the darkness.

"Is this it?" Lauren asked Bonnie while the truck sat idling in the middle of the road.

"It has to be. It's the only other road I've noticed. The computer's no help because we lost the Internet connection shortly after we left the pavement."

They looked at the hidden trail with apprehension; it was dark and appeared barely wide enough for a Mini Cooper.

Luke said, "This has to be it. Find somewhere to hide this truck."

Lauren drove to the end of the road and pulled in behind a thicket of tall bushes. As soon as the engine died and the lights went off, everything became deathly quiet, except for an occasional creak from the hot engine.

They sat in silence for almost a minute then Bonnie asked, "So, what are we going to do now? Just go down that road and see if the Jeep's there?"

"That's our only choice. If we can find out, for sure, that Olivia's there, I think it's best we contact the RCMP and let them handle it," Luke said.

To Lauren he said, "But we need to be ready for anything. Where'd you put the pistol?"

She reached up under the dashboard and pulled it out and handed it to him. He retrieved a box of bullets out of the console and stuffed some into the pockets of his cargo shorts.

Quietly they made their way back to the old gate and climbed over, one by one. A foreboding feeling came over Bonnie as they stood staring at the narrow road that disappeared in the blackness of the forest. Luke led the way as they started down the dark, narrow road. After a few minutes occasional patches of light broke through the tree tops giving them enough light to see their surroundings.

After about twenty minutes they came to a fork in the road and they went left, which appeared to be the more traveled route. Half a minute later they came to a clearing that was lit by a full moon and a star-filled sky.

The football-field sized meadow was covered in what looked like dry, knee-high grass. Across it, at the crest of a hillock, a small cabin sat silhouetted on the horizon. Lights glowed from two windows. As they stood staring at the structure, Bonnie's blood ran cold.

"This is it," Bonnie said, hugging herself. "This is where they held me."

"Are you sure?" Luke whispered.

"Positive," she assured him. "That cabin is perched on the edge of a cliff."

"This must be Sonny's famous Cliff House," Lauren said. "Over the last few years, there have been stories about the drugs, gambling, and wild parties that took place out here. I never knew where it was."

"We need to get closer," Luke said. He turned to Bonnie and asked, "What's the layout?"

Bonnie spelled it out. "The window on the left is the bathroom. Two bedrooms run down the left side. The window on the right is the kitchen. There's a dining and living area beyond it. A deck runs across the back and most of it is suspended over the cliff, but it comes back onto solid ground on the right side," she said. "There are three doors to get inside. The front door, another one on the right side and one on the back wall that goes onto the deck. That building off to the right is the garage."

"How big a cliff are we talking about?" Luke asked.

"At least a hundred foot drop."

"How are we going to get up to the cabin? We can't just walk up the road. With the full moon, if someone looks out the front door, we'll stand out like a nun at a pool party in the middle of that dry grass."

"Maybe that other road back where the road forked would be better," Lauren said.

They doubled back and Lauren's hunch was right. The other road took them through the woods and they came out on the side of the cabin by the garage. For the next few minutes they watched from the edge of the forest. When they were sure no one was outside, they ran to the garage and started to make their way down the side. Off to the side they saw a smaller metal building, a prefab structure that looked like a storage shed and beyond it, illuminated by moonlight, sat a motor home.

When they got to the corner of the garage, they stopped and took in their surrounds.

"Does that look like the motor home they had me locked in?" Bonnie asked Lauren.

"I think so. And look." She pointed. "There's the Jeep."

They were still about forty yards away and because of trees, bushes and the angle where they were, the cabin was hard to see.

"We need to get closer," Luke said.

Single file, they crept closer until they got to a waist-high stack of firewood wedged between two trees. They ducked down behind it and looked over the wood and could see the cabin more clearly. The front was visible as well as the right side. In addition to the two windows in front, there were two more windows on the side that were brightly lit. They could hear voices coming from an open kitchen window.

"Get down," Luke said in an urgent, hushed voice as he lowered himself to the ground.

A pair of headlights burst out of the forest and lit up the cabin. The vehicle, which appeared to be a minivan, came up the gravel drive and stopped in front of the garage. Bonnie could hear a low whine coming from the garage and realized it was a garage door opener. The van pulled forward and disappeared inside. Seconds later, they heard a different, much more powerful engine rev up and saw a pickup back out and stop near the front door. The garage door started to close as the driver got out of the truck and hurried inside the cabin.

"Who's that?" Luke asked.

"Too dark, I couldn't see him," Lauren whispered.

From the open window they could hear voices but were too far away to make out what they were saying.

"We need to get closer to hear what they are saying," Luke said.

"My hearing's a lot better than yours and I'm quieter," Bonnie said. "Stay here. I'll creep up by that window."

She dropped to her hands and knees and crawled closer until she was behind the trunk of a tall pine tree ten yards from the cabin. Through an open kitchen window she could see a woman with short blonde hair. It was Rosemary, the nurse at the hospital. It looked like she was washing dishes.

Bonnie could hear the low pitch of a man's voice, but it wasn't loud enough to understand him. A few seconds later Rosemary stepped away from the window and Bonnie ran up to the cabin and positioned herself to the side of the open window.

From there she heard a different woman speak and it was loud and clear.

"Have you found out anything about the trust Kim says her money is in? Is she telling the truth?" It sounded like Rita.

"I can't get any information," a man said.

"What happened to your buddy on the Kalispell police force? You said you could find out what was going on from him?" Bonnie recognized Sonny's voice.

"I called him, but he said when it became a kidnapping the FBI took over. And they won't tell the local cops anything," the unknown man said.

"But, even if it is part of the Townsends' will, you don't think they'll let the kid die, do you?" Sonny said.

"I wouldn't be surprised if they don't pay. Remember, I worked with these types of people in the security business for thirteen ass-sucking years. In Calgary we didn't have any clients who were billionaires, but the millionaires were just as bad. In the media they come across as real do-gooders, but the only thing they care about is their damn money. If she doesn't come up with the ransom, I say we don't back down. Let the kid die before we give in."

"You said you wouldn't do that!" exclaimed Rosemary.

"That's not really what we said," the new guy told her. "We said we would take care of her the best we could. But Kim knows if she doesn't pay, Olivia won't get her treatment. So, it will be Kim's fault if she dies, not ours."

"You're such an asshole." The contempt in Rosemary's voice was clear. "All you can talk about is how much you hate rich people, but you're as bad as they are. You don't have to take it out on Olivia. I was promised nothing would happen to her."

"I'm sure we won't have to worry about that," Rita interjected. "I'm sure she'll pay. I think the FBI is making her hold out as long as possible. I bet we get a wire from the bank early tomorrow telling us she's made the transfer."

"Okay. Let's say she pays, then what?" asked Rosemary.

"We drop off Olivia and catch our charter to the Caymans," said Sonny.

"But where do we drop her off? We can't just leave her at a bus stop. I want to know how it all works and where we are going to leave Olivia."

"Why does it matter?" asked the new guy.

"I know you don't care if Olivia lives or dies. But, I do. No one's told me anything. I've risked as much as everyone else and have a right to know." Rosemary tearfully demanded.

"We weren't hiding anything from you," Sonny assured her. "The only reason we didn't tell you is because you had enough to worry about just getting her out of the hospital. Here's how it works: as soon as the bank notifies us that the money's been transferred, I'll tell you to sedate Olivia. We know where there's a church that we can get in and out of, without being noticed. We'll leave her in a baby crib in the nursery. As soon as we leave we'll contact Kim and let her know where she is. All she has to do is tell the FBI or the police and someone will be there to get her within ten minutes."

"Okay. That sounds good. I just wanted to know because I

don't want anything to happen to Olivia," Rosemary said.

"Good, so how's she doing?" Sonny asked.

"She's okay. Right now, she asleep in the back bedroom, but it's been very hard on her. She's running a fever and she needs more rest. It's not good for her to be on the move all the time."

"We know that Rosemary, but we didn't have any choice," said Sonny as if he had heard her say that a dozen times.

"I need to get back," the unknown man said. "I brought you a minivan like you wanted. It's blue, complete with a car seat and diaper bag. I stole it from the parking lot at the mall."

Bonnie heard chairs scoot across the wood floor and she strained to hear what they were saying as they walked toward the front door.

"Did you get an extra set of license plates like I told you?"

"Yeah, I put them on the workbench in the garage. Have you figured out what we are going to do about Bonnie and Luke?" the man asked.

"I'm working on it," Sonny said.

"When are you coming in?" the man asked.

But, Bonnie was unable to hear anything else and a few seconds later the front door opened. She quietly slithered back to the woodpile where they waited for the man to leave. After the pickup drove off, Bonnie signaled for them to follow her and they all ran back to the forest, where Bonnie filled them in on what she heard.

"We have to assume that they are leaving in the minivan soon. When they do we won't be able to track them anymore since the tracking device is on the Jeep," Lauren said. "Should we try to get back to the Suburban so we can follow them?"

"We might not have time and we didn't see any other vehicles on the mountain coming up here. I'm afraid it'll be too hard to tail them. I think we have two choices. Either get Olivia now, or keep them from leaving. And we don't have a lot of time, so we need to make a decision and do it now."

They came up with a simple and straightforward plan. The

odds of pulling it off without a hitch weren't good, but it was all they could do. They were out of time.

"How long will it take you to go get the Suburban and come back?" Luke asked Lauren.

"Fifteen minutes, twenty at the most," she said.

"Good. We'll wait fifteen minutes before we start."

Chapter 51

While Sonny packed in the bedroom, Rita gathered their gear in the living room. Rosemary was in the kitchen packing an ice chest when she saw something outside the window that scared her. She let out a blood-curdling scream and started backpedaling. Her feet got tangled and she fell back. When Sonny got to the kitchen she was scooting backwards across the floor.

"What's wrong?"

"Something's out there," she cried out, pointing a shaking finger at the window. "It was looking in the window."

Sonny followed her finger to the window but saw nothing but darkness.

"What the hell are you talking about?"

"Something's out there," Rosemary repeated, still scooting away. "I swear."

"Like what?" he said, and saw the fright in her eyes.

"Maybe a bear. Or a man. I don't know. It's too dark and it moved so fast," she said, trying to catch her breath.

Sonny had owned the cabin for several years and bears never came up to the cabin. Bears weren't uncommon, but to be looking in the window it would have been huge, and standing on his back feet.

"Okay, kill all the inside lights, then turn on the lights outside," he commanded as he switched off the light in the kitchen and went toward the front door.

Rita started turning off the lamps while Rosemary got up and ran down the hallway flipping switches. Seconds later, the entire cabin was dark. Sonny retrieved his pistol from the cabinet drawer and came back into the kitchen and waited for Rita to turn on the outside lights.

When they came on Sonny peered out the window but saw

nothing but trees and bushes. Everything looked normal and he could see nothing moving. He stepped out the front door, his pistol at his side. There the lights were brighter and again, everything was just like it was supposed to be. No bears and nothing out of the ordinary. When he turned to go back inside he heard a noise on the other side of the garage.

Clang, clang, clang.

The sound was that of trashcans banging against each other. The sound reminded him of something that happened before he bought bear-proof trashcans. Bears and raccoons were cleaver and could get into them if the iron bar wasn't secure across the top of the can. He thought about the meal they had eaten earlier and tried to remember who had taken out the trash after they ate. But, it didn't matter. Whoever it was, probably didn't close the trashcans right. He looked back and saw Rita and Rosemary huddled together just inside the open front door, watching him.

"It sounds like we might have a bear getting in the trashcan." Sonny knew that most bears ran off when someone yelled and threw rocks at them. "I'm going to lock down the trashcans, but we need to get going as soon as we can, so start getting everything together."

"When you're sure it's safe, let me know and I'll change the license plates on the car," Rita said.

"Good. How long will it take you to get Olivia ready?" he asked Rosemary.

"Just a few minutes," Rosemary said. "I need to gather her meds and clothes. After I wake her up, I'll probably need to change her diaper, but I can be ready in five minutes." She started down the hall toward the back bedroom.

With Rita standing in the front door watching, Sonny went out a little further. He could see the garage, the motor home and Jeep under the bright floodlights, but no bear.

Clang, clang, clang.

Again he heard the trashcan lids, this time in the distance. Now he was positive it was a scavenging bear. He told Rita to wait while he looked on the other side of the garage.

With the gun in one hand, he picked up a rock the size of a tennis ball and started for the other side of the garage, while keeping a safe distance in case something came out of the darkness. The trashcans were on the back side of the garage and the lights didn't illuminate that area. But there was enough moonlight to see they were overturned and the iron bar used to secure the tops was in the open position. Garbage was everywhere and several white plastic bags were scattered halfway to the woods.

"Looks like it's gone. I'll open the garage and you can change the license plates," he said to Rita.

He punched some numbers on a keypad beside the garage door and the door started to open. Rita came up behind him and he pointed to a tool box on the workbench on the side of the garage.

"There's a screwdriver in the top drawer you can use to switch the license plates. After I clean up the trash and lock down the trashcans, I'll come in."

As soon as he got to the other side of the garage he noticed one of the garbage cans was bent, like a bear had stomped on them, and one of the lids was missing. In the forest he heard what sounded like the other aluminum lids being dragged around. He knew the bear was gone for the night as he stuffed the pistol in the waistband of his pants and started picking up trash.

Luke hid behind the storage shed and watched while Sonny picked up garbage. When he got close enough, Luke stepped out of the darkness and hit him with a heavy tree limb, dropping him like a sack of dog food.

Luke grabbed him by the ankles and dragged him back into the storage shed. After he closed the door and latched it he looked back toward the forest. Bonnie, who had been banging the trashcan lid on some rocks, trotted up next to him and stopped.

"Let's go get Olivia," Bonnie said.

They ran around the cabin and slowly opened the front door. All of the lights were still off except one down the hallway. It was probably the bedroom where Olivia was sleeping. When they were halfway down the hall, Rosemary stepped out of the back bedroom carrying Olivia, a pink diaper bag slung over her shoulder.

As soon as she saw them, she screamed and tried to run back to the bedroom, but Luke lunged and grabbed her from behind, wrapping his arm around her neck. He pulled her to him and clamped down on her throat, cutting off her air. When Rosemary started to choke, her mouth opened wide and she gasped for air. At that point Bonnie pulled Olivia from her weakened grasp and ran back down the hall. All of the commotion woke Olivia and she started to scream.

"Rita's in the garage. Go out the back door," Luke shouted.

As Bonnie disappeared around the corner, Luke started to drag Rosemary down the hallway. He had never fought a woman before and couldn't believe her strength. She kicked and twisted and clawed like a wild cat. When they were almost to the back bedroom, she reached between his legs and squeezed so hard he thought his eyeballs were going to pop out. In an automatic reaction, he threw her against the wall like she was a rabid rat.

She started to run, but Luke grabbed her shoulders and again threw her against the sheetrock wall.

"You bastard," she screamed as she leaped at him.

Her arms moved like a windmill; she had all claws out, tearing at his arms. Luke tried to hold her off but she was out of her mind with anger and when she started biting at anything close to her mouth, he doubled up his fist and hit her square in the nose. Her head rocked back like a bobble head doll, and she dropped to the floor, unconscious.

By now he knew Lauren would be waiting by the garage, and within seconds, Bonnie would be there with Olivia. All he had to do now was go to the garage and take care of Rita the same way he did Rosemary. He'd tie her up with whatever he could find, disable the vehicles by firing bullets into the tires, and then they'd get the hell out of here.

He started to run and when he was almost to the front door when he heard Olivia's terrified cry.

His head jerked around and his eyes searched the darkness inside the cabin. He couldn't see anything until movement on the deck caught his eye. He stepped closer and the luminous figures became clear. Bonnie was on the deck holding the crying child.

But they weren't moving. Edging closer he saw why.

Over her shoulder he saw Sonny's face. And a pistol was pointed at Bonnie's head.

WTF? It couldn't be. Sonny was locked in the storage shed.

But this was no apparition. He had Bonnie, Olivia, and a gun.

Luke raced to the back door while pulling out his own gun. As soon as he stepped on the deck, Sonny pulled Bonnie close to him like a human shield. In the bright moonlight, Luke could see blood streaming down the side of Sonny's head where he'd hit him with the limb. Luke breathed hard and tried to steady the gun he aimed at Sonny' head.

Through a murderous grin, Sonny said, "Drop the gun or I'll put a bullet through her head." Luke hesitated and Sonny screamed. "Drop the gun!"

Luke's heart raced. He was a pretty good shot with a pistol, but he had never shot this gun before and his hand was shaking. And the way Sonny was holding Bonnie, only about four inches of his face was exposed. He could easily hit Bonnie.

He had no choice. Slowly, he bent over and laid the gun on the deck.

"Now put your hands on your head and back away."

Luke laced his fingers over his head and started backing up.

"You've been nothing but trouble." Sonny's eyes were wild

with rage.

Luke caught movement in his peripheral vision and saw Rosemary stagger into the living room, then onto the deck. Her hand covered her nose and trails of blood ran down to her chin.

"Rosie, get his gun, then come get this kid," Sonny commanded Rosemary.

She picked up Luke's gun and like a Frisbee tossed it over the wooden railing into the dark abyss below.

She turned to Luke and yelled, "You fucking asshole," then drew back her arm and slugged Luke in the mouth with all her might.

Luke's head rocked back and he fought the urge to pounce on her, but Sonny had the gun. In seconds his mouth was full of blood. All he could do was watch as Rosemary pulled Olivia from Bonnie's arms and ran off the deck.

"This could have been so fucking easy if you would have just done what we told you. But you just couldn't leave well enough alone."

Sonny redirected the gun from Bonnie, to Luke, extended his arm and tightened his finger on the trigger.

Suddenly Bonnie grabbed Sonny's arm and pulled it down hard. The gun fired into the deck beside Luke's feet. Sonny pulled the gun back up, but again Bonnie jerked at his arm and this time the bullet went wide.

Bonnie twisted to the side just as Luke plowed into Sonny, knocking both of them backwards. As the three of them fell, Luke grabbed the pistol and yanked. It came free and clattered across the deck in the opposite direction. They began to wrestle on the wooden decking, with Sonny on the bottom. Luke pushed away and scampered over and grabbed the gun.

Luke could see the desperation in Sonny's face as he got to his feet and eyed the pistol in Luke's hand. Bonnie, breathing hard, got to her feet and just as she stood Sonny grabbed her and pulled her in front of him.

Luke pointed the gun at him from ten feet away.

"It's over, Sonny. Let her go," Luke said as he stepped closer.

Before Luke could react, Sonny lifted Bonnie and slung her over the railing. He held her dangling her over the hundred foot drop.

"If you shoot me, she'll fall to her death," he threatened as Bonnie's screams echoed through the canyon. "Now, drop the gun or I'll let go of her."

"I'll kill you," Luke screamed, jutting the gun at Sonny's face. "Bring her back on this side."

Sonny didn't move. Luke's heart raced, knowing Sonny held Bonnie's life in his hand.

Then Sonny's grip around her waist loosened, and Bonnie dropped a foot lower. She screamed. Now he held her under her arms and she appeared to be slipping more.

Luke wanted to try to grab her but knew if he did, Sonny would let her go.

"I can't hold her much longer," Sonny threatened, his evil eyes widening. Bonnie's breathing was frantic as she reached to the side, trying to grasp the top board of the railing.

"Sonny, please," she begged.

"You've got three seconds," Sonny said, narrowing his eyes at Luke. "Slide that gun over here or I'll let her fall."

"Okay," Luke said, knowing he was taking the word of a man who wanted them both dead. "Just bring her back."

The gun slid over and it stopped a few feet short of Sonny.

"There's the gun. Now bring her back on this side."

"Want her? Come get her."

Sonny let her go.

As she started to fall, one of her arms reached over and hooked over the railing. It stopped her long enough for her to grab hold with the other hand.

Bonnie dangled over the hundred-foot drop. Luke saw the pained grimace on her face and remembered the thumb she'd injured five days ago. *Can she hold on?* But, at this point, Luke didn't have much choice. If Sonny got the gun, they were both dead.

When Sonny bent and reached for the gun, Luke took a quick step and kicked. Just as Sonny grabbed it, Luke's hiking boot connected with his face. Sonny flew back and the gun skittered further away. Luke dove for the gun and pulled it up as Sonny recoiled and took a defensive stance. Luke aimed the gun at him.

"I'm slipping—hurry!" Bonnie screamed to a terrified Luke.

But, if he leaned over the deck to help her, Sonny could easily push him over the railing, killing them both.

There was only one thing to do. He turned the gun toward Sonny and pulled off two quick shots. Sonny dove to the side and landed inside the cabin. The bullets splintered the log on the outside wall where Sonny stood a fraction of a second earlier. Through the dim light of the cabin, Luke could barely make out Sonny's form as he ran. He fired three fast shots through the windows and the glass exploded into a million pieces. Now he could see Sonny's dark form racing toward the front door.

"Luke!" Bonnie shrieked.

Luke dropped the gun and reached over the railing and grabbed Bonnie by the arms. Adrenaline surged through him and with a single jerk he pulled her up and over the railing. He fell back, pulling her on top of him. As they hit the deck, he wrapped his arms around her so tight a herd of horses couldn't separate them. From the front of the cabin Luke heard the engine of the minivan revving as it drove away.

A few seconds later they rolled over and sat up. Luke brushed the hair from Bonnie's face and neither spoke as they tried to catch their breath.

A minute later Lauren called from the darkness. "Luke! Bonnie!"

"We're on the deck," he shouted back.

A few seconds later she came through the cabin and onto the deck. She rushed over and knelt beside them, a look of panic on her face.

"Are you okay?"

Bonnie closed her eyes and nodded her head. "We're okay."

"I heard shots and saw them driving away. What happened?"

Luke looked from Bonnie to Lauren and exhaled loudly.

"They've got Olivia."

Chapter 52

"What now?" Luke asked.

"Should we notify the RCMP? There are only a couple of roads getting down from this mountain. Did you see what kind of minivan they were in?" Bonnie asked Lauren.

"No, where I was parked, I couldn't see anything. When I heard gunfire, I ran to the cabin. But by the time I got here, the car was leaving and all I could see was the taillights in a cloud of dust. Besides, my cell phone hasn't had any service since we left the pavement."

"Let's see if we can find something that might give us a clue to tell us where they went," Bonnie said.

Inside the cabin they turned on the lights and except for the broken glass from the shattered back windows, they found the cabin uncluttered. The tables and countertops were as clean as if maid service had just left and inside the drawers and cabinets they found nothing of interest. Lauren went through the trash baskets and there was not as much as an old envelope or a grocery store receipt.

They moved into the front bedroom, but it looked like no one had been in there for months so they continued down the hallway to the back bedroom. Bonnie stopped at the door, hesitant to enter. Luke came up behind her and put his hands on her shoulders.

"Is this where they kept you?" he asked.

"Yep, this is it," she said as her eyes moved from the bed, to the dresser, to the portable baby crib that now sat against the opposite wall. The window she had broken out was now covered with a piece of cardboard.

She walked over to the crib and bent down to pick up a fluffy white bunny rabbit that lay on top of the pink blanket. For a few seconds she looked at it with interest, and then felt the pure white fabric that almost looked like fur. She pulled on the big floppy ears, then turned it over and almost smiled when she saw the fuzzy button of a tail.

She sighed, dropped it and turned her attention to the window. She grabbed the cardboard by the corner, pulled it off and let it drop to the floor. Sharp edges of broken glass protruded from the corners where the windowpane had been. Careful to avoid them, she stuck her head through the window and stared into the darkness a few seconds.

"You should see it during the daytime. That's one hell of a view," she said without emotion.

Bonnie left the room, and after a brief look inside the dresser and closet, Luke and Lauren followed. When they got to the front door, they saw the interior light of the Jeep was on and Bonnie was seated in the passenger seat.

Luke walked up beside her and saw her going through the glove compartment.

"Find anything?"

"Nothing."

"Let's check the RV," Lauren said.

On the way over to it they came to the shed where Luke had locked up Sonny. He said, "I want to find out how in the hell Sonny got out of here."

The front door was still latched but behind it he saw a small patch of the ground lit up. When he looked closer he was unsure what to say. The side and back wall were separated at the corner, allowing fluorescent light to escape. Luke bent down and grabbed the lightweight aluminum siding and pulled on it with both hands.

"Son of a bitch," was all he could say.

The separation between the side and the back created an opening big enough for a man to crawl through. He hadn't realized how flimsy the portable building was.

He walked around to the front and removed the latch. When he opened the door a light attached to the ceiling revealed what he hadn't seen earlier when he had dragged

Sonny's unconscious body inside the dark shed. On one side sat a partially disassembled snowmobile, and on the other side was a workbench cluttered with engine parts. Lying over by the corner where the siding was separated, he saw the answer to his question.

"Sonny had everything he needed to get out," Luke said looking back at Bonnie and Lauren who were standing at the open door. He picked up a crowbar lying on the floor beside the opening. "The shed was full of tools and all he had to do was turn on the light to find the one he needed to pry off the back wall."

They left the shed and went over to see what they could find in the RV. Bonnie started in the living area and Lauren went to the back bedroom. Luke went forward to the driver's compartment and had barely opened the storage compartment when Bonnie found something.

"Look at this," she said.

He turned around and saw her looking in an opaque plastic box. She put it on the kitchen table and they went over and watched as she pulled out several manila folders bulging with papers. When she opened one of the folders Luke saw a blue print of a building. Across the top in architect's scroll, it said, *St. Luke's Memorial Hospital.* She closed the file and set it aside. The next file she pulled out said *Employees* on the tab.

Luke looked over her shoulder and saw several VCR tapes and more folders. He watched as she pulled out folders and set them on the table. At the bottom of the box lay a chrome-plated pistol. Luke leaned in to get a better look and saw what looked like smears of dried blood on the handle and the trigger guard. Beside it was a black metal tube about six inches long. Bonnie looked back at Luke.

"That looks like the gun Pete had in the hospital," Bonnie said. "I remember it was chrome with a gold trigger and the silencer was black."

"The gun he had at the mall was chrome plated, too," Lauren said.

"I'll bet this is his blood and his fingerprints are on it, too. That will prove I was not the one who did the shooting in the hospital," Bonnie said.

"Is that a laptop computer?" Lauren asked pointing to the shelf behind the table.

She went over and grabbed it and sat down at the table. When she opened it the screen brightened at once.

Lauren clicked on the icon that said My Computer, then My Documents. A dozen folders appeared, among them were Accounts, Addresses, Alex Townsend, Bonnie Wakefield, Dr. Owens, Employees, ISP, Kalispell Hospital, Kim Townsend, and Wifi.

"We may have just hit the jackpot," she said.

She clicked on the one that said 'Alex Townsend' and a long list of document names appeared. Randomly, she clicked on the one titled, "Crash Takes Hedge Fund Billionaire and Family." An article from *The New York Times* came up telling how Kim's husband and her in-laws died in the crash of their private jet. She opened another. It was an article from *Forbes* magazine with details of Mr. Townsend's wealth.

She closed it and went to the folder titled 'Accts.' A box appeared asking for a password.

"I was afraid of that," she said, closing the file.

"I'm sure the cops can hack into them," Luke said.

While Lauren tried to open more files, Bonnie walked over and sat down at the table across from her and next to Luke. He leaned his head forward and rolled it around stretching the muscles in his neck. The adrenaline no longer pulsed through his veins and his body felt weary.

"I was just thinking about the last time I talked to Sonny. He said, if we interfere in any way, he'll kill Olivia, even if he gets the ransom," Bonnie said.

"I know. And now we've interfered."

"So, now what are we going to do?"

"There's not much we can do unless we know where they are going. Are you sure you didn't hear them say anything about where they might leave her?" Luke asked.

Bonnie leaned forward and rested her face in her hands. "They said they were going to leave Olivia at a church where they could get in and out without being noticed, but they didn't say anything about which one or where it was. He said when the ransom was paid they'd call Kim and let her know where she can find Olivia. She can notify the police and they can pick her up within minutes."

Luke said, "Okay. So, that means they aren't going to be in Kalispell or else Kim would be close enough to go get her. So, let's look at it from another direction. Olivia's condition can't be treated by just any doctor's office or hospital, can it?"

"No, Kim had to buy equipment for the hospital in Kalispell, and it's the only hospital in Montana that can treat her condition," Bonnie said. "This type of treatment is available only at the bigger or newest medical facilities, and all of them are in larger cities. That's why this new children's hospital in Kalispell is so important."

"Okay, where's the closest place that might have a medical facility that can treat her, *and* be close enough for them to get to by early morning?" Luke asked Lauren.

"Other than going back to Kalispell, there's only one place," Lauren said. "Calgary. It's probably four hours from here."

"Then, I say we go to Calgary."

By the time the Suburban was loaded, it was 1:26 a.m.—less than eleven hours before the ransom deadline, and less than thirteen hours before Olivia's next needed treatment.

Luke said he'd drive, which was fine with Lauren. She crawled in the backseat and Bonnie got up front with Luke. He turned sideways to face the ladies.

"I've been thinking about it and I think it's time we turn ourselves in. We've done everything we can, but now it looks like we've lost them. If we go to the Calgary police and give them this computer, maybe they can figure something out before it's too late. I'm sure it will help our case later."

Bonnie said, "I guess you're right. The Calgary police might even be able to contact the security businesses there and get a lead on this other guy."

"What are you talking about?" Luke said.

"You know, the other guy said he worked in the security business in Calgary?"

"Which guy?"

"The guy in the minivan."

"No, I don't remember hearing anything about this," Luke said.

"I thought I told you."

"You mentioned that to me," Lauren said.

"That's right. I guess I got mixed up," Bonnie said. "Anyway, he said for the past thirteen years he'd been working in some kind of security job."

Something about *thirteen years* sounded familiar to Luke—something from a recent conversation. He started the engine and tried to remember who said it, but he was exhausted and he couldn't bring it to the forefront of his mind. "What else did he say?"

"Nothing really, other than rich people are assholes who only care about their money instead of people," Bonnie said.

While the truck was idling, Luke searched his memory. Then it hit him like a sucker punch in the solar plexus. A feeling of betrayal ran through his soul. "When he said thirteen years, did he happen to use the phrase, 'ass-sucking years'?"

"That's exactly what he said," Bonnie answered.

"Son of a bitch," Luke exclaimed as he pulled the gearshift down and started down the gravel driveway. "Looks like we're not giving up yet."

"We're not?" Bonnie asked.

"Because I know who that new guy is. First thing we need to do is get down off this mountain because I have a phone call to make."

Two hours later, with the cruise control set on one

hundred fifteen kilometers per hour they were headed for Calgary when Lauren's cell phone rang. Luke answered.

"This is Luke Wakefield."

"I got a call from my office and they said you had something urgent to talk to me about that can't wait." The caller sounded quite irritated after being awakened at two-thirty in the morning.

"I do. Have you been keeping up with the kidnapping of Olivia Townsend?"

"That little girl over in Montana?"

"Yeah, that one."

"Now why in the hell would I be keeping up with that?" he barked. "I'm in charge of the RCMP in Cardston, Alberta, for Christ's sake. That doesn't have a damn thing to do with us here in Canada."

"I hate to tell you this, Ernest, but it has everything to do with you. And Cardston," Luke said.

Luke let a few seconds pass, but Ernest was in no mood to wait.

"Well, are you going to tell me what in the hell you're talking about or do I have to wait for it to come out on the news tonight?" Ernest snapped.

"A lot has happened since I saw you five days ago," Luke said as he straightened up behind the steering wheel and focused down the long straight highway.

For the next hour Luke filled Ernest in as he drove through the darkness.

Chapter 53

Sonny grabbed his watch off the nightstand. It was just past eight, which meant he had slept for almost four hours. The surprise attack at the Cliff House had complicated things, but the plan was still on track. They had come to Calgary, where they had a two-bedroom suite reserved just off the freeway.

Sonny pulled on his pants and walked out into the living room to find Rita at the desk staring at the screen of her laptop.

"Any updates on the blog yet?" he asked, walking up behind her.

"I was about to wake you up. I got an e-mail a few minutes ago saying there was an update. I'm checking it now."

When the website opened, Rita clicked on *Kidnapping Update*. It started with a several paragraphs about the ongoing investigation. Kim had been given instructions how to send them information by hiding coded messages in Olivia's Blog. As Sonny read the message he pointed at the first word of the first paragraph.

"I," he said as he moved his finger to the second word of the second paragraph. "will." His finger went to the third word of the third paragraph. "pay."

"She's going to pay," Rita screamed. She threw her arms around Sonny's neck.

He pushed her aside and took her seat at the desk. He read the rest of the post. The final paragraph said *The search continues but at this time there were no new leads. At ten o'clock we'll post another update.*

He spun the chair around and looked at Rita. "She's going to make the transfer at ten, about two hours from now."

Sonny stood and walked over to the window. This was the

news they'd been waiting for, but he had a knot in his stomach. There was still unfinished business that could derail the entire job. Bonnie and Luke were a problem, because they knew his identity.

His thoughts were interrupted by three soft knocks at the door.

He went over and looked through the peephole.

Paul Simpson, the police officer from Cardston, was standing outside.

Sonny cracked the door three inches and looked at the RCMP officer. He checked from side to side, saw the empty hallway and pulled the door open. "Come in."

"Well?" Paul asked as he walked into the room.

"Kim just posted the message we've been waiting for. The ransom will be wired at ten o'clock."

Chapter 54

"I told you the FBI was calling the shots," Paul said as he poured himself a cup of coffee. "They wanted her to hold out as long as she could. But, in the end, I knew she'd pay. We did it," Paul said, walking over to Sonny and bumping fists.

"It took all of us: you, me, Pete, Rita and Rosemary," Sonny replied.

"You're right," Paul said. He shook his head. "I just can't believe Pete's gone."

"Me too. Have you checked on our charter?" Sonny asked.

"Yeah, they said the jet will be ready at noon. They asked if we needed a limo to the airport and I said no," Paul replied.

Paul's cell phone rang. He looked at the caller ID, but didn't recognize the number. He held a finger to his lips, signaling for Sonny to be quiet.

"Simpson," he said.

"Paul, this is Luke Wakefield," said the voice on the other end of the line.

"Luke Wakefield?" he said, looking at Sonny and raising an eyebrow. "What can I do for you, Luke?"

"I need some help," Luke said. "The last time we talked in Cardston, you said you were closing the missing person's case on my wife because you thought she left me and went back to Texas. I didn't believe that and kept looking for her."

"I thought you might," Paul said in a matter-of-fact tone.

"Well, I finally found her. She was abducted and held hostage for five days."

"What do you mean, she was abducted? We never heard anything about it in our detachment."

"You wouldn't have because I didn't report to the RCMP."

"Why not?"

"It's not that simple."

"What do you mean?" Paul sounded confused.

"Have you heard about the kidnapping of Olivia Townsend? The daughter of that billionaire in Kalispell, Montana?" Luke asked.

"The Olivia Townsend kidnapping? Yeah, we've been getting some information about it over the wire, but I haven't kept up with it."

"It gets complicated, but…Bonnie is the one who kidnapped her."

"What do you mean, she kidnapped her?" Paul asked.

"The day after you and Ernest told me to go back to Texas I found an envelope in my car with Polaroid pictures of Bonnie, tied up and lying on a bed. There was a note enclosed that said she was being held and if I wanted to see her alive again, I had to do what they said. So, that's what I did."

"Why didn't you call me?"

"It said they'd kill her if I contacted the police. I had no choice. All I could do was follow their directions, which took me to an old house in Montana the other side of Glacier, near the town of Whitefish. When I went inside, I found Bonnie tied to a chair. Before I knew it, two guys jumped me from behind. They tied me up and for the next ten minutes they beat me while Bonnie was forced to watch. They told her that if she didn't do exactly as they said, they'd continue to torture me until I was dead. So she said she would."

"What did they want her to do?"

"Kidnap Olivia Townsend."

"You're kidding," he said. "How in the hell was she supposed to do that?"

"They had it all worked out. Bonnie looks exactly like Olivia's doctor, so she posed as her and kidnapped her from the hospital."

"I don't know how she could get away with something like that," Paul snapped. "Hospitals have tight security—unauthorized people can't just come in and take kids."

"One of the nurses at the hospital was in on it."

"One of the nurses was in on it?" Paul repeated, a signal to Sonny.

"Yeah, all Bonnie had to do was go to the third floor where Olivia was having her treatment. The nurse would give her Olivia, and then she'd go down to the basement and out to the parking lot where these people were waiting."

"And she did it?"

"She really didn't have any choice," Luke said, defensively. "They told her if she didn't do what they said, they'd kill Olivia. Then they'd kill me."

"They say she killed a couple of people at the hospital."

"It wasn't her. It was one of the guys who abducted us. They got Olivia from Bonnie and she was able to escape, then she helped me escape."

"How did you do that?"

"A friend from Cardston helped."

"Who are you talking about?"

"The lady who rented me the Jeep, Lauren Gray. She owns The Sportsman's Outfitter. Her shop's there on Main Street in Cardston."

"Yeah, I've seen that place," Paul said, trying to hide his surprise at the identity of this mystery woman. "Is she still with you?"

"Yeah, we're all in her truck right now."

"You were lucky she was willing to help," Paul said.

"You're right. Anyway, we've managed to figure out who the kidnappers are and—"

"You know who the kidnappers are? Who are they?"

"The main guy is Sonny Diamond. He runs a camera shop there in Cardston. Ever heard of him?"

"Yeah, an ex-con. I've heard he's a lowlife piece of shit," he said sardonically, glancing at Sonny who was listening to his half of the conversation. "Can you prove all this?"

"We can. We've got one of their guns, and I'm pretty sure it's the one that was used to kill those people at the hospital. We also have a laptop that's loaded with information they used to plan the kidnapping. There are files on Kim, the Kalispell hospital and even files on Bonnie and me. There are more files that are password-protected, including some with information about foreign banks, account numbers, and wire transfers."

"You're kidding," he said. This really pissed Paul off. They had his computer. He'd backed up all the files from Rita's laptop in case they had a problem with her computer. The day before the kidnapping, he told Rita to put it somewhere where it would be safe. "How'd you get the gun and computer?"

"I don't have time to go into that now, but I'll tell you something else," Luke took a long breath and cleared his throat. "We know they're in Canada. More precisely, Calgary."

"You're sure about that?" Paul asked.

"Positive. And…we've got more information that will help the cops find them."

"What kind of information do you have?" Paul asked.

"Paul, we're running out of time. I'd rather not go into that right now, but here's why I called: When I was in Cardston, Ernest treated me like I was a criminal, but you treated me right and I feel like you're the only one I can trust. We're on our way to Calgary and I need to know where to go and who to talk to."

"I understand and you were wise to call me. If you walked into any of the stations in Calgary with that story, you'd be interrogated for hours and it's doubtful the information would get to the right people in time. But, I can get you where you need to go," Paul said. "How far are you from Calgary?"

"I think we're about two hours south."

"Good. Let me call the Deputy Chief of Major Crimes up there and tell him what you told me. I'll call you back and tell you what to do."

"Sounds good." Just before he hung up, Luke added, "And Paul, you don't know how much I appreciate this."

"Anytime, Luke."

Paul clicked off and looked across the table.

Sonny pulled out a chair and sat down. "Who's a lowlife

piece of shit?" Sonny asked with a smirk.

"You are," Paul said with hint of a grin. Then he became serious. "They're about two hours south of here and have information that will help the cops find us."

"Like what?" Sonny said, sensing trouble.

"He wouldn't say, but he also said they have Pete's pistol and my laptop. If the RCMP gets that we're dead. It's registered in my name and it has all the files. Once they get past the passwords on those files, they'll have everything. The accounts where the ransom will be wired, our new names on our new passports, hotel reservations in the Caymans…everything."

Sonny closed his eyes and cursed silently.

Paul continued, angry now. "Last night you called me after you left and told me they'd found you. I told you to go back. There was too much there to leave behind."

Sonny was defensive. "I didn't even have a gun. How was I supposed to fight this guy?"

"I don't know, but that computer and gun will be our downfall."

Sonny ignored that comment. "What else did he say?"

"He said they're on their way to Calgary and needed to know where to go to turn in this information."

"Oh, bullshit. Any dumbass knows all you have to do is stop at any police station."

"He knows they don't have much time and if he stops at the first substation he sees and starts at the beginning, it's going to take hours before he convinces the detectives he's not a nutcase. When he was in Cardston, he and Ernest didn't get along, but we did. He trusts me. He wants me to run interference for him and get him to the right person before it's too late."

"I don't like it," Sonny said. He shook his head. "They showed up at the Cliff House half an hour after you left. If they saw you, this could be some kind of trick."

"I thought about that, but he doesn't want to see me. He thinks I'm three hours south of here in Cardston. The only reason he called me was to find out where to go and who to talk to."

Sonny nodded as he thought. "So, what do you think?"

"If they go to the police, we're dead," Paul said. "That laptop has all of the account numbers for the Cayman Islands and the other accounts in Switzerland. They've got Pete's gun, which ballistics will match to the murders. Even if we get the ransom, we'll always be wanted. We'll never be free to live in Canada, the U.S. or any other country with an extradition treaty." Paul watched as Sonny thought about it. "But, now we have a chance to stop them."

"Okay. Where are they?"

"He said they're about two hours south of here." He looked at his watch. "If Kim transmits the funds at ten, we should get confirmation of the transfer from the Caymans about the time he gets here. I'll have them come to the church and we take care of them there. It will look like they were double-crossed by a partner who decided not to share the forty million. After we get the computer and the gun, they won't have anything to connect us to the kidnapping."

Sonny nodded then furrowed his brow. "I heard you say something about the woman who was with them. Did he tell you who she is?"

"You're going to love this," Paul said with a devious grin. "It's the woman who sent you to prison for ten years."

Sonny's eyes opened wide. "Lauren?"

"That's right."

"You've got to be kidding me."

"Nope. She rented Luke the Jeep and let him stay in the bunk house on her ranch. We should have connected her before now. This could be your chance to get even."

"Is she the one who was with them at the mall?"

"She has to be. And she's probably the one who got the gun for Bonnie."

"That fucking bitch," Sonny said. He turned away and looked out the window.

As Paul watched Sonny, he thought about the day he and Sonny met. After working in the security business in Calgary for thirteen years, Paul was accused of stealing jewelry from the homes of several wealthy clients. Though he was never charged, Paul reputation was ruined when rumors of the theft spread around town. He decided to leave the security business and Calgary, finally going to work for the RCMP in Cardston.

There was little about small-town life he liked. Other than writing parking tickets and settling domestic disputes, the only thing to do was gamble. Like most of the other Mounties on the force, he didn't consider betting on sporting events a crime. The bets were small, usually a hundred or two, mostly on hockey, boxing, football or horse races. To place their bets, they had to go to Lethbridge, a town about an hour northeast of Cardston. He'd go to The Silver Slipper, a second-rate strip joint on the edge of town. Usually around midnight every Tuesday night, the local bookie would show up. One night while waiting, he met Sonny, who was there for the same reason. Unlikely friends, the cop and the ex-con, soon found they had similar stories. Both claimed they were wrongly accused of a crime that ruined their life.

Paul's gambling was casual until one day when his horse came in—literally. On a longshot, he banked over forty grand and soon his hundred-dollar bets turned into a thousand. His luck continued and the bets went to five thousand, then ten. He was up over a hundred grand when he hit a cold streak. In a matter of months he lost everything and wound up sixty thousand in debt to the wrong people. It didn't take long before they put pressure on him to pay up. With no winners on the horizon, Paul turned to the one friend he knew had the money—Sonny.

Their friendship had grown over the year and it was apparent Sonny had money, but two things he was sure of was—it didn't all come from his job at the camera store or gambling. But he really didn't want to know any more than that.

Sonny was glad to help. Paul turned over the title to his car and promised quick payment, but after nine months he had barely put a dent in his balance. One night Sonny called and said they needed to talk. Over drinks, Paul admitted it was going to take years to pay off the debt. Sonny told him he had an idea that might interest him. Sonny said he had a small business on the side and could use his help. If Paul was willing to come on board, he'd forgive his entire debt. He said Paul's involvement would be peripheral, making it simple for him to participate.

Sonny told him how shortly after he got out of prison, he was talking to the lawyer who represented him in his murder trial. They were discussing his outstanding bill and the lawyer mentioned he was looking for someone he could trust to get him some cocaine. Sonny said he would do it if it would help wipe out his debt. With the contacts he'd made in prison, he started supplying the lawyer with the illegal drug on a regular basis. The lawyer turned him onto other lawyers, then a few stockbrokers, then some businessmen. Before long, Sonny was smuggling a brick of cocaine at a time to supply them and his client list grew to include an elite group of white-collar executives all over southern Alberta. With the RCMP cracking down on illegal drugs, Sonny told Paul he needed someone on the inside to protect him. All he had to do was be his eyes and ears down at the RCMP. Paul accepted.

Paul soon found he wasn't the only partner. Pete Coley, who worked at the border crossing, was the other.

The three men worked well together and after a few months, Sonny told Paul and Pete they could get a bigger cut if they helped him distribute the drugs. They agreed. With Paul's contacts from his years in the security business in Calgary, he brought in more clients to their discreet customer base.

Business was good and profitable, since they were dealing with only white-collar clientele. But none of them liked the drug business and knew it was a matter of time before their luck ran out. What they wanted was one big score so they could get out before that day came.

The idea came when Sonny's girlfriend, Rita, was on vacation in Texas and saw Bonnie Wakefield selling her photographs at an arts and crafts festival. Bonnie looked exactly like a doctor Rita worked with back in Montana. She returned home and they dug into the background of both women. After days of discussion, an elaborate, well-thought-out plan was laid out for the kidnapping of Olivia Townsend.

Sonny glanced at Paul. "Did you bring me a gun?"

Paul opened the canvas bag he was carrying and slid out a black pistol and handed it to Sonny.

"Nice," Sonny said, taking the weapon.

"Nine millimeter Beretta with a fifteen round clip. Loaded."

He palmed it and switched it from one hand to the other.

"And take this, too," Paul said, handing him a silencer."

Sonny took it and pushed it in his back pocket."

"So, how do you want to play this?" Paul asked.

"Call Luke. Tell him the Deputy Chief is anxious to meet with them," Sonny said. He closed one eye as he aimed at an imaginary target across the room. "This is working out better than we could have planned it."

Chapter 55

"When we decided on the church, our plan was to drop off Olivia and get the hell out of there. Now, with Bonnie and Luke coming to Calgary, are you sure this is the best place to do this?" Paul asked Sonny.

"Why not?"

Paul shook his head. "The church is huge. There's bound to be a thousand members of this church. What if someone shows up?"

"They won't."

"How do you know that?"

"When I was looking for a church to use, I called several and told them I was an exterminator and it was time to fumigate their buildings. I told them no one could enter any of the church buildings for twenty-four hours. Most of them said they had things scheduled three to six months in advance. But the secretary of this one, Mrs. Flannigan, said there was nothing on the calendar and she'd make sure there was nothing scheduled. She said the only people who will be there will be her and the preacher, and they'll be in the office, which is in a smaller building behind the church."

"I guess this is as good as anywhere, so where do you want me to tell Luke to go?"

"Tell them to park on the street in front and go into the sanctuary to wait. When this is all over, that's where I want the cops to find their bodies."

Paul pulled out his phone, scrolled down the list of his recent calls, found Luke's number and pressed the redial button.

"The Chief is anxious to meet with you. He's in a meeting with some local church leaders, but will leave as soon as you get there. He's at Trinity Baptist Church on 23rd."

Sonny listened as Paul gave Luke directions. When Paul ended the call, he said, "They're on their way. Just went through Stavely."

Sonny knew the little town of Stavely was about an hour and a half from Calgary. He looked at his watch. "We need to get moving pretty quick. I'll tell Rita and Rosemary."

As Sonny walked to the back bedroom, he felt much better than he had the night before. They finally had a plan to get rid of Bonnie and Luke. Their biggest problem would be solved.

When he opened the bedroom door, Rita and Rosemary were sitting on the floor watching Olivia play with some building blocks.

"We need to leave in twenty minutes. Give Olivia what you need to so she'll go to sleep," Sonny said.

Thirty minutes later Olivia was nodding off in the car seat between Rita and Rosemary as they drove toward downtown. Rosemary reached across the front seat and handed Paul and Sonny a pair of latex gloves.

She looked through the windshield. "Is that the church?"

In the next block, Sonny saw the tall gray steeple of the gothic structure soaring high into the cloudless sky. "That's it," he said.

A row of arched, leaded glass windows came into view down the side of the huge building. They were all dark, showing no color; only the bold lines between the glasswork were apparent. The medieval architecture and mildewed limestone blocks gave it the eerie look of an old English cathedral. As they slowly passed the front of the sanctuary they saw a sign on the front door that said, *Church Closed Today for Fumigation*. Sonny was relieved. Mrs. Flannigan had done what she had promised.

Paul turned at the next corner, drove around to the back of the church and followed an arrow that pointed to the office.

After they parked, Sonny said to Paul, "As soon as you and

Rita get inside the office, I'll take Rosemary and Olivia to the nursery."

Paul nodded and looked over his shoulder at Rita.

"Ready?"

She gave a breathless, "Yes," and grabbed a paper sack off the floor.

They walked up to the building and stopped at the door. Rita pulled two masks out of the bag and handed one to Paul. After they pulled them over their heads, Paul pulled a gun out from under his jacket and held it to his side. He pulled open the door and they stepped inside.

As soon as they were out of sight, Sonny got out and slid open the back door of the minivan. While Rosemary lifted the sleeping child from the car seat, he pulled out a black computer case and slung the strap over his shoulder. Rosemary followed him to a wing that connected to the back of the church and entered through an unlocked door. At the end of a long hallway they entered the nursery where Rosemary found a crib where she laid Olivia.

"How long will she be out?" Sonny asked as he set the laptop on a table near the door.

"The dosage I gave her should make her sleep for at least four hours," Rosemary said. She tucked a blanket around Olivia.

"Good. Get online. Keep an eye on Kim's blog and the e-mail. Text me if anything comes in. We'll call you when we're done."

Sonny went back to the parking lot and got into the driver's seat of the minivan. A few minutes later, the office door opened and Rita came out carrying the paper sack.

As she approached Sonny got out and she took his place.

"How'd it go?" he asked.

"Perfect," Rita said, tossing the sack into the backseat. "When we stepped inside, Mrs. Flannigan saw our masks and thought it was some kind of joke. But when Paul pulled out the gun, she screamed. He tasered her and when she fell, she knocked over a vase of flowers that made a hell of a racket. That brought the preacher and Paul got him as soon as he stepped into the room."

"Where are they?"

"Mrs. Flannigan is tied up on the toilet in the bathroom. The preacher freaked out, but Paul's got him under control now."

Sonny stepped away from the car as it started backing out of the parking space. "Once we're inside the church we won't be able to see anything so if you see anyone in any of the parking lots or going to the front door, call me. Bonnie and Luke are in a white Suburban and are supposed to park out front. Call me as soon as you see them. We'll let you know when we're finished."

"Okay." She gave him a nervous smile and left.

Sonny ran into the office and locked the deadbolt behind him. He saw Paul dragging a heavyset man in gray slacks and a white short-sleeve shirt down the hallway. The man's hands and legs were wrapped with silver duct tape and there was a pillowcase over his head. Duct tape encircling the pillow case about where the man's mouth would be. Paul disappeared through an open door and Sonny ran in behind him.

They were in a large supply closet. The man was tossing his head from side to side and making muffled noises. Paul propped him up against a metal pole in the middle of the room. He grabbed the man's jaw through the pillowcase and squeezed it, pushing his head back against the pole. The man stiffened.

Paul leaned down to his ear and spoke in a voice just above a whisper. "I am not going to hurt you unless you don't settle down." The man became still, his chest heaving as he took in deep breaths. "That's better. We have Mrs. Flannigan tied up, too. She's okay, but if you try to escape, we'll kill her first, then you. Do you understand?"

He gave several exaggerated nods making it clear he would cooperate. Paul grabbed the roll of tape and started to wrap it around the preacher and the metal pole. "Someone will come let you lose in about an hour. Until then, just sit here and be quiet. If you try to escape, I will hurt you, do you understand?"

Again he nodded vigorously.

Sonny grabbed Paul's arm and mouthed the words, "Get his keys."

Paul patted the preacher's pockets and came up with a key ring with about eight keys on it and tossed them to Sonny.

They left the supply room and ran down the hall to the bathroom. Inside Sonny saw a fully clothed woman sitting on the toilet. She had a pillowcase over her head and duct tape encircled her just above the waist and the toilet. Her skin looked soft and wrinkled and her clothes appeared to be that of a woman in her late seventies.

He leaned close to her and spoke softly in her ear. "Are you okay Mrs. Flannigan?"

Startled, she jerked away and her breathing quivered. She nodded with rapid head movements.

"Good. We aren't going to hurt you, okay?" he hissed. Again, she nodded and took rapid breaths. "But, remember—if you try to escape, we'll have to kill Reverend Chenault. You don't want us to do that, do you?"

She shook her head from side to side.

"Good. We don't want anyone to get hurt. Someone will cut you lose in about an hour," Paul said and patted her on the shoulder.

They stepped out and closed the bathroom door. Sonny and Paul left the office and walked through the parking lot to the back door of the church and stepped inside.

They were in a wide hallway that went left and right. Neither had been inside the church so Sonny made a random guess and went to the right. Around the corner, they came to a short flight of stairs. He took them two at a time and at the top they had a choice to go straight or to the left. They went straight and came to a door with a sign that said *Choir Room*. Past it another door said *Choir Loft*. It was probably the way to get inside the sanctuary. But when he tried it, he found it locked. For a second he considered finding the key on the key ring, but decided that's not where they wanted to be. They turned around and went back to the *Choir Room*. It was locked, too.

They retraced their route back to the door where they came in and went the other way. After passing a couple of offices and a storeroom, the hallway turned and they went up another short flight of stairs. They came to a room with a sign over the door identifying it as the *Pastor's Study* and beyond it a closed door. Sonny twisted the knob and this time the door was unlocked. Slowly, he pulled it open and stepped inside. They were now at the back of the massive sanctuary.

It was dimly lit by sunlight coming in through the row of stained glass windows along both sides. A couple of spotlights shone on a cross that hung on the back wall. He couldn't help but look up at the arched ceilings that had to be at least forty feet at the peak.

It was cavernous and creepy. It reminded Sonny of the last time he had been in a church. His mother made him go to his grandfather's funeral when he was about six years old. It was in a huge Catholic church and the memory of seeing a dead person for the first time was something he couldn't get out of his mind for years. During the entire service all they talked about was the Ghost, the Holy Ghost. It gave him nightmares for months. His lasting memory of that day was that ghosts haunted all churches.

Sonny and Paul padded across the altar and down the steps to the center aisle that ran between the rows of polished mahogany pews. Sonny's eyes were drawn to the intricately sculpted stained glass windows that, from inside, glowed brightly with Biblical scenes. In one, Christ's mournful eyes watched him as he walked toward the back door. Chills ran down his spine and he started to run.

When he burst into the foyer he realized he had been holding his breath. He breathed deeply as Paul came up beside him. Sonny found the key to the front doors and unlocked them. They glanced at each other, knowing that now all they had to do was wait.

Sonny went over and stood by tall narrow windows that looked out on the street in front of the church. Traffic was light and in front of the church all of the parking spaces were empty. That was good. It would make it easy to see the Suburban when they arrived.

Sonny reached under his windbreaker and pulled out his handgun. For the second time today he ejected the clip to confirm it was full. He pushed it back into the butt of the gun and chambered a round. From his back pocket he pulled out the silencer. As he started to screw it on the barrel he could feel Paul's eyes watching him. He shot him a sideways glance and for a second they locked eyes.

"Before we do anything to them, we need to make sure we have the laptop and Pete's gun," Paul instructed.

"I know what I'm doing." Sonny didn't like Paul's condescending tone.

"Good, we can't afford another fuckup."

Sonny looked away. Paul had become more difficult to get along with over the last few weeks. Paul was really pissed after Bonnie killed Pete, but Paul hadn't been there. He wasn't the one who had to make split second decisions. Bonnie and Luke had turned out to be much more difficult than anyone expected.

Sonny's phone buzzed. It was Rosemary. She could hardly hold back her excitement. "We just got five e-mails from the bank in the Caymans. They are confirmations of deposits in five different accounts, each in the amount of eight million dollars."

At first Sonny didn't know what to say.

"Sonny? Did you hear me? We got the money."

"Yeah. I heard you. That's…good." He ended the call and looked at Paul. He said, "We got it. Forty million. She transferred it to our accounts."

Slowly, he let a smile creep across his face.

A minute later, Sonny's phone buzzed again. This time it was Rita.

"They're here. The Suburban just drove past me."

Sonny looked out the window and saw it pulling up in front of the church.

Chapter 56

As Lauren drove, Luke rubbed his eyes. He was still tired.

After they left the Cliff House he drove while Bonnie and Lauren tried to sleep. When they got to the outskirts of Calgary they checked into a motel and got a room with two beds. Within minutes they were all asleep on top of the bedspreads. It seemed as if he had just fallen asleep when Bonnie woke him two hours later. That was all the time they had.

After a hot shower and a cup of coffee, he spoke with Paul Simpson, the RCMP officer who had helped him in Cardston. Paul gave him directions to a church just south of downtown and said the Deputy Chief of Major Crimes would meet him there.

Traffic was light as they turned onto Twenty-Third. About a mile down they saw the church. It was huge, reminiscent of some of the old churches in downtown San Antonio, built with huge limestone blocks and stained glass windows.

As Lauren pulled up to the curb, Bonnie said, "I think we should switch laptops. That one's got all the evidence that will prove our innocence. We can't risk losing it."

"Good idea. Take mine instead," Lauren said.

She made the switch and handed the computer case to Bonnie while Luke got the plastic box that contained the files, pictures and VCR tapes out of the back of the Suburban.

They made their way up the steps and when Bonnie pulled open the door, Luke looked back at the Suburban and gave a slight nod and Lauren drove away.

Now inside the church they were standing in a large foyer that stretched across the back of the sanctuary. And as expected, there was no one there. About thirty feet in front of them, they saw a set of double doors. To the left was another set of doors and on the right side another. Each door had a small window about one foot square.

Bonnie stepped over and peered through one of the windows while Luke looked through another to see inside the huge dark sanctuary. Only one light was on, a spot light that illuminated the cross that hung on the wall behind the pulpit.

"Should we go in or wait out here?" Bonnie asked.

"Go in, I guess. That's what he said to do."

Bonnie pulled open the door and held it for Luke, who was holding the plastic box. They stepped inside and the door closed behind them. After their eyes adjusted to the low light, Luke noticed someone sitting near the aisle on the second row.

Luke wondered, *Could it be someone had come in to worship?*

Bonnie put the laptop on the pew beside the box and walked up and stood beside Luke.

"Hello," Luke called out.

It was a few seconds before the person in the second row moved. The man turned and looked over his shoulder. In the dim light Luke could barely make his features, but there was something about him that was familiar.

"Hello, Luke," the man said as he stood.

Bonnie shot a quick glance at Luke, as if to ask, *Who is that?*

Luke stepped forward cautiously. The man stepped into the center aisle and slowly started to walk toward them. As he neared, Luke recognized him—barrel-chested with a full head of hair.

"Paul?" Luke said, surprised. "I thought you were in Cardston."

"Yeah, I'm sorry I couldn't say anything earlier, but I'm on special assignment and no one's supposed to know I'm here." He slowly moved closer to them.

"I'm glad you are here. I'd rather work with you than a bunch of strangers."

As Paul approached he shook his finger at Bonnie and

smiled. "And this must be the elusive Bonnie."

"I am," she said.

"You had the whole town of Cardston worried. I'm glad you're okay." Then he focused his attention on Luke. "Did you bring the evidence you told me about?"

"Right there," Luke said, pointing to the box in the last pew. "Is Chief Ames here? And didn't you say there'd be a team of detectives, too."

"I know that's what I said, but there's been a change of plans," Paul said. He walked over to the box and started sifting through the contents, pulling out several thick files and setting them beside the box. After he pulled out the VCR tapes, the pictures, and the rest of the papers, the box was empty. He gave a frustrated grunt and turned his attention to the computer case. He unzipped it and pulled out Lauren's IBM laptop. He held it at eye level and turned it from side to side. "And *this* is the laptop with all the incriminating files on it?"

"That's it."

"Hmm," Paul said. He jutted his lip out and shook his head. "You said it was a Dell."

Luke stammered, "I...I don't remember saying that. I think I just said it was a laptop."

Paul looked back at the empty box. "You also said you had the gun that was used to kill those people in the hospital. I don't see it here." Paul said.

"Oh, I guess we left it in the Suburban," Luke said and looked at Bonnie.

Paul turned his head toward Luke and tapped his lips. "Where's that other woman? What's her name? Lauren."

"She's out front in the—"

"Suburban? I don't think so," said a booming voice on the other side of the sanctuary. In a dark corner they saw the silhouette of a man. He hadn't been there half a minute ago, Luke was sure of that. The dark figure stepped into the light and Sonny's blond hair shimmered. Luke could see he held a pistol down by his side. The long barrel indicated it was equipped with a sound suppresser. "The Suburban drove off before you came into the church."

"Sonny?" Luke's head jerked toward Paul. "What's he doing here?"

"Like I said, the plan has changed." Paul said.

"What the hell's going on?" Luke asked. He looked from Sonny to Paul.

"I'm sorry to have to tell you this Luke, but—" Paul said before Luke cut him off.

"Is he with you?" Luke asked.

"You might say that," Paul replied. He reached behind his back and pulled a pistol out of his waistband. It too had a silencer attached to the barrel.

"I trusted you. You're a Mountie with the RCMP." Luke scowled as he took a few steps toward Paul with his fist clenched.

Paul pulled up his gun and pointed it at Luke's face whose chest heaved as he breathed deeply.

"Enough of this bullshit," Sonny said. He turned to Paul. "So, what are we missing?"

"The gun and my laptop. They brought this one, but it's not mine," he said as he angrily hurled the IBM laptop toward Luke and Bonnie. They cowered as it landed a few rows short crashing into the polished wood on the back of a pew. Paul raised his gun and moved the safety into the firing position. "I want the gun and my computer, now. Or I'm going to start shooting."

"Okay, okay," Luke said. He put his hands up as if surrendering. "It's all in the Suburban, but let me explain something. The RCMP treated me like a criminal when I was in Cardston and I wasn't going to let that happen again. When we got to Calgary I decided to hold back the gun and the laptop so I could have some leverage."

"What about Lauren? Where is she?"

"She's not far from here, but I wanted to keep her out of it as long as I could."

Sonny stepped a little closer. "Like we said, things have changed. You're not dealing with the RCMP now, and you don't have any leverage. Either you get us the computer and the gun, or we'll end it all right here."

"I was afraid something like this might happen," Luke said. "So, I did what I had to do. And the way I see it is like this: If you kill us, you'll never get those two things. So, we do have a little leverage because right now, Lauren is sitting in front of an RCMP substation. And if she doesn't hear from me in the next—" he looked at his watch, "—two minutes, she'll go in and turn everything over to them, who I'm sure will share it with the FBI. There will be no doubt who the real kidnappers are, and who killed those people at the hospital. You'll be wanted all over North America."

"Bullshit," Sonny blurted out.

"No bullshit. Let me show you something." Luke moved slowly, and with his thumb and forefinger, reached into his shirt pocket and pulled out a cell phone. He held it in front of him. "See this? Before I walked in here, I called Lauren. She answered and I put the phone back in my pocket. We're still connected. She's been recording everything you've said. I'll prove it to you. She's on speaker now."

Luke extended his arm toward them and said, "Lauren, can you hear me?"

"Loud and clear," came a tinny voice from the cell phone. "And I've recorded everything that's been said since you walked into the church."

Paul and Sonny looked at each other, not sure what to say.

"So, now it's time to make a deal," Luke said.

There was no way to hide the shock on Sonny's face. He looked from Luke to Paul in disgust, and said, "Okay. What do you want?"

"It's very simple. Just two things: First we want Olivia."

Sonny said, "Okay, what else?"

"We want half the money. I believe that would be twenty million dollars."

Paul exploded, "You're out of your fucking—"

But Sonny held up a hand, signaling him to hold his comment. Paul paused and Sonny said, "We don't have much choice. So, we'll do it."

Paul looked at Sonny in shock, at first, but then seemed to acquiesce. Luke knew no one in their right mind would give up twenty million this easily, unless they knew they could win in the end. It was exactly what he expected.

"Good, where's Olivia?"

"I can have her in here in two minutes."

"And the money?"

"All I have to do is call my banker and he'll set up an account for you. We can transfer the money, and it will be in your account within a few hours."

"Good. Bring me Olivia and it's a deal."

"What about Lauren and our stuff?"

"Lauren? Did you hear that? We've made a deal. You can come back to the church now."

From the phone, they heard her. "I heard you. I'll be there in a minute."

Paul pulled out his cell phone and placed a call. "Bring Olivia to the sanctuary."

Luke ended his call and put the phone back in his shirt pocket.

Up until now, everything was going as expected, Luke thought. Since the ransom had been paid, they knew the kidnappers wouldn't have any problem giving up Olivia. And, Luke knew Sonny would see a flaw in his plan. Sonny and Paul were holding the guns. As soon as Lauren was here, they'd be able to eliminate the only people who could tie them to the kidnapping. So, of course they'd agree to it.

No one spoke while they waited. In a matter of minutes, the back door of the sanctuary opened and Rosemary stood holding the sleeping Olivia.

"I'll take her," Bonnie said, starting toward her.

"Not until we get our gun and computer," Sonny said. He

stepped between them and held his gun on Bonnie. "Rosie, come over here."

Luke's phone rang. He looked at the screen. "It's Lauren."

"Tell her to get her ass over here," Sonny growled.

Luke pressed the button to answer. He listened a second, then said, "Okay."

He looked at Sonny and said, "It's for you." Luke tossed the phone to him.

Sonny caught it and shot Luke a look of distrust. With the gun aimed at Luke, he put the phone to his ear.

"What?" he said angrily.

After listening a few seconds, Sonny's head jerked toward the choir loft behind the pulpit. Four men wearing black helmets were now visible, crouched behind pews with rifles aimed at them. In the middle of them was a gray-haired man in a flak jacket holding a cell phone to his ear. Everyone but Bonnie recognized him. He was the man in charge of the Cardston detachment of the RCMP, Sergeant Ernest Oliveras.

"Son of a bitch!" Sonny screamed as he turned his pistol toward the choir loft and fired two quick shots.

As Sonny retreated behind the pews, he turned his gun toward Luke and Bonnie. They lunged between the pews as three silenced shots splintered the dark mahogany wood just above their heads. Paul dove to the ground near Sonny.

A thunderous, amplified voice bellowed from the choir loft. "I've got a SWAT team up here and there's no way you can escape. Drop your guns and this will all end right now."

Sonny already had his cell phone up to his ear and spoke in a low growl. "We've been set up. Cops are here. Get back over here as fast as you can."

"What the hell do we do now?" Paul shouted to Sonny.

"I'm sure as hell not giving up forty million dollars, if that's what you mean."

Rosemary stood petrified against the back wall, her expression a mix of confusion and panic.

"Sonny?" she whined.

"Get down here," Sonny screamed.

Her legs buckled and she dropped down to the ground. With wide eyes, she said, "What's happening?"

"It was an ambush. There's a SWAT team up there." Sonny looked around. "I called Rita. She's on her way, probably out front any second now. We've got to get out of here. We'll use Olivia for cover."

"How?" Rosemary asked.

"Hold Olivia in front of you and stand up. We'll hide behind you. All you have to do is back out as fast as you can."

"They'll shoot me," she whimpered.

"Not if you're holding Olivia," Sonny snapped. "Did you see any cops out front?"

"No."

"Good, then let's go," he said.

Terrified, Rosemary couldn't move. Sonny grabbed her around the waist and lifted her up in front of him. Her entire body trembled and her eyes darted around the sanctuary. It was only ten feet back to the door and with Sonny behind her and Paul behind Sonny, they backed out. But as they stepped out into the foyer a demand came from the side.

"Drop your weapons!"

Four men in fatigues and ballistic vests were crouched off to the side with rifles aimed at them.

Paul panicked and in a fatal reaction swung his gun toward them. Before he could pull the trigger, two deafening shots exploded, hitting him in the middle of the chest. He flew back and his lifeless body landed spread-eagle on the tiled floor.

Rosemary screamed and pulled Olivia closer to her face. The loud gunfire had startled the sleeping child and she began to scream.

Sonny, who had started to raise his pistol, froze when the shots tore into Paul. He knew he was trapped, but he had come too far to give up.

Slowly he raised his hands, and as he turned to face them,

gave a look of surrender. But, instead he pulled Rosemary over in front of him. Just a sliver of Sonny's face was visible behind Rosemary as he pulled his gun around and pressed it into Olivia's head.

"I'll kill her," he said and started backing toward the door, pulling Rosemary and Olivia with him.

The gunmen didn't have a clear shot but they held their weapons on them as Sonny backed into the door. As it opened he glanced behind him. Rita was stopped in front of the church with the back door of the minivan open. He tried to push Rosemary to the side, but she grabbed his arm.

"Sonny, wait," Rosemary wailed, pulling him closer. He tried to jerk away, but she held tight, pulling him around. As he backed further, the men in fatigues emerged from the church doors.

Olivia was his only chance.

He grabbed Olivia with one hand and tried to pull her away from Rosemary, but her vise-like grip was too tight. Yanking harder, he saw the determination in Rosemary's eyes. She wasn't going to let go. He turned his gun on her and fired once into the middle of her forehead.

Her head flew back as a red cloud of atomized blood filled the space between them. Sonny grabbed Olivia as Rosemary's arms fell away. As the men raised their rifles toward Sonny, he put his pistol back to Olivia's temple.

"I'll kill her," he promised as he backed toward the open door of the minivan. "Drop your guns."

The SWAT team held their position; no one lowered their weapons. As Sonny fell back inside the open door of the minivan, Rita hit the gas. As the van lurched forward and Sonny saw police cruisers emerging from side streets half a block in front of them. Two units stopped their vehicles blocking the street. He looked out the back window and saw the same thing behind them. From blocks away he saw a dozen more units converging with flashing lights. An army of cops in body armor and with automatic weapons ran in from the side streets.

He and Rita were trapped in the middle of the block.

"What do I do?" Rita screeched as she slammed on the brakes.

Sonny looked around and saw the parking lot behind the church. From it there was another exit there to a side street. It was their only chance.

"That way. Over the curb!"

Rita turned the steering wheel and mashed the gas pedal to the floor. The van bounced over the curb and tore across the lawn. Shots rang out and immediately both tires on the right side of the car went flat.

Rita shot Sonny a panicked look.

"Don't stop," he screamed over Olivia's wailing.

The van continued to roll on flat tires as it reached the asphalt parking lot and passed the preacher's car behind the church. Rita turned toward the exit between two buildings only to find it already blocked by two police cars and a dozen more cops in combat position. She turned and circled around, the rims of her flat tires grinding into the pavement. More shots rang out and the other two tires went flat.

Rita continued on the rims, making a complete circle before more shots were fired into the engine. The motor fell silent and smoke billowed out from under the hood. Now the only sound anyone could hear was Olivia's waling cries from inside the van.

From behind the SWAT team, the squadron commander pulled up a portable microphone. "Throw out your weapons and get out of the vehicle. Lay face down on the pavement, arms away from your body."

Everyone waited but there was no movement from the van.

"Do you have a clear shot?" the commander said to the officer, whose rifle rested on the roof of the police cruiser across the lot.

"Negative, sir," he said, his eye pressed tightly against the scope. "The dark tint of the van's windows makes it impossible to isolate the perp. I see the hostage, but she is in constant motion. I can't get a clear shot."

Seconds ticked by until the silence was broken when the driver's door opened.

"Don't shoot me," Rita yelled as she stepped out, holding her hands high. "Don't shoot me." She lowered herself to the pavement and stretched out her arms.

Everyone waited as Olivia's screams seem to diminish. Then the officer spoke to the commander.

"I have a clear shot. Less than twenty percent risk to hostage."

"Fire when ready," the commander ordered.

As his finger tightened on the trigger, the back door of the van slid open. The commander said, "Wait."

Every police and SWAT officer realigned their aim.

"I'm coming out," Sonny shouted through the open door.

"Fire if he raises his weapon," the commander said.

A second later, Sonny stepped out holding the limp child in front of him, his pistol lowered at his side.

"Drop your weapon," demanded the SWAT commander.

His demand went unanswered as Sonny's eyes drifted around the parking lot, looking at the array of weapons positioned to end his life.

Every officer now had a clear head shot. The SWAT sharpshooter said, "Sir?"

Olivia was obviously exhausted. Her cries had become choking sobs. Sonny could take no more. He bent and lowered Olivia to the ground where she stood unmoving, huge tears streaming down her face.

After lowering his head, Sonny tossed his pistol to the pavement. Slowly he went to his knees, and lowered himself to his belly. As he stretched out his arms half a dozen officers moved in and surrounded him, their guns aimed at his head.

From behind one of the police cruisers, Bonnie broke through the row of police in dark uniforms and ran to the frightened child. When Olivia saw her, she stretched out her arms. Bonnie picked her up, pulling her tear-soaked cheeks tightly against her own.

Chapter 57

The EMT pushed a gurney up beside Bonnie and when she tried to hand Olivia over, Olivia would have no part of it. She held tight and Bonnie didn't want to let her go.

"She's scared to death," Bonnie said taking her back. "Let me go along and I'll hold her."

"I understand but she's required to be on a gurney," the young man said as he opened the back door of the ambulance. Then added, "Aw, what the hell, just hold on to her real tight. It's a short ride."

Less than ten minutes later they were at the Alberta Children's Hospital and Olivia was already drifting off to sleep. The drugs in her system were too much to fight. The back doors of the ambulance opened and Bonnie saw two nurses and a tall, slender man wearing surgical scrubs and a stethoscope around his neck. As the nurses took Olivia, the man went to Bonnie.

"I'm Dr. Montgomery from Nephrology. We've spoken with Mrs. Townsend and she's having all of the records sent over. We'll take Olivia from here."

"Can I go with her?"

"Sure," the doctor said.

As they started inside she heard a voice behind her.

"Excuse me, Mrs. Wakefield." She turned to see two men in dark suits. "We're detectives Jackson and Burnet from Calgary Police Service. We need you to come down to the command center and answer some questions."

"But, I'd really like to stay with Olivia."

"Ma'am, the doctors will take good care of her. Your husband and Miss Gray are downtown answering questions now. As soon as we're finished, you can come back."

***

The officers took Bonnie downtown where she was led into an interrogation room where they were met by another man in a dark suit. He introduced himself as the real Sergeant Ames, Chief of Major Crimes.

"Mrs. Wakefield, you are not under arrest, nor are you charged with any crimes at this time. But, I'd like for you to start at the beginning. Tell us everything you can remember, from the time you got to Montana and all events leading up to the kidnapping and eventual rescue of Olivia Townsend."

Bonnie started with the day she received a phone call asking her to speak at the photography workshop. The detectives fired dozens of questions and had her repeat various parts of her story. But, in the end, were impressed by the courage and ingenuity that they used to help capture the kidnappers while keeping Olivia safe.

"That's enough for today, but I'm sure we'll have many more questions for you later," Detective Burnet said.

She found Luke and Lauren in the waiting area with the short gray-haired man she'd seen in the choir loft earlier at the church. As she approached, they stood up. The man held his gray cowboy hat in one hand and extended the other hand as Luke introduced him.

"Bonnie this is Ernest Oliveras. He's in charge of the RCMP in Cardston."

"I was telling Luke that for the past two hours my office has been looking into your missing persons file. It looks like Paul Simpson, the officer who was in charge of your case kept feeding me bad information. Everything I saw made it look like you had slipped away from Luke and gone back to Texas."

"What do you mean?"

"The first thing he told me was that a bus driver identified you as a passenger on his bus from Cardston to Calgary. We contacted that driver this morning and he said Paul had not contacted him. Paul also said he found charges on your credit card for airline tickets from Calgary to Austin, Texas. And he said the airline showed you as a passenger on that flight. Neither of those is true either."

"I would have never done that," Bonnie said, looking from Luke to Ernest.

"That's what Luke kept saying, but I had to go with the evidence I had. Paul had been an ideal officer before all this happened."

As they moved toward the door Ernest said, "Oh yeah, I've got something for you." Ernest pulled something out of his shirt pocket and held it out for Bonnie. She opened her hand and he dropped two gold earrings into her palm.

"Thank you," she said, but looked at Luke, confused.

Ernest said to Luke, "After you called, I went over and roused Willy Standalone. Following your advice, I asked him about that earring he was wearing. He said he found it on Little John's dresser. We woke up Little John and asked him where he got it. Little John confessed to everything. You know, Sonny Diamond was one of the best quarterbacks to come out of Alberta. Many kids, including Little John Standalone idolized him."

"Little John seems like a good kid. Why would he get mixed up in something like this?" Bonnie asked.

"For about a decade we've had an unsolved murder on the books in Cardston. The rumor around town was that Willy did it. Little John said Sonny told him he had evidence that would convict his father, sending him to prison for life. And he would turn it over to the RCMP unless he helped him. So he did. But, the sad part is that Willy had a solid alibi the night of the murder, and I've always known that. Because at the time he was serving a six month sentence for drunk driving in Missoula. He never told his family and everyone thought he was hiding from the law."

"Will Little John go to prison?" Bonnie asked.

"It's too early to tell. I think all depends on the charges filed against him. But I'm afraid his football scholarship is history."

"I'll do what I can to help Little John. He treated me with respect and I can appreciate the fact that he was doing it for his father," Bonnie said.

Ernest nodded and turned to Luke. "And I want to say I'm sorry for the way I treated you in Cardston."

Humbled, Luke said, "If I'd have been in your shoes, I would have done the same thing."

"Paul kept finding this evidence, and it all pointed to you. Never in a million years would I have suspected him to be on the wrong side of the law."

A question nagged at Bonnie. "We came up here because I was asked to fill in at the photography workshop for a man who was killed in a freak accident. Could they have had anything to do with that?"

"They could have, but from what I understand, the house blew up and everything burned. I don't think there was enough of it left to collect any evidence. Unless Sonny confesses to it, I don't think we'll ever know."

Detective Burnet stepped into the room followed by a stocky man in a black suit. The detective said, "Olivia is doing fine. Mrs. Townsend is at the hospital and would like you to come by when you can."

"We'd like that," Bonnie said.

Luke and Lauren nodded.

"A limo is out front. This is DeWayne, he'll take you over," he said, gesturing to the man in the black suit.

As they rode to the hospital, Bonnie held Luke's hand. She was nervous about meeting Kim. Even though they saved Olivia, it was Bonnie who put her in danger by kidnapping her.

The limo stopped at the entrance to the hospital and DeWayne said, "Olivia is on the third floor, room 3066."

They all went inside and found the elevator across from a waiting room. Bonnie pressed the button and the elevator opened immediately. As they stepped on and turned around they saw a television mounted on the wall where a news program was just beginning. A bespectacled anchor started his lead story. "The kidnapping of Olivia Townsend ended today in a dramatic rescue here in Calgary. The daughter of billionaire Kim Townsend was kidnapped two days ago and—"

The elevator door closed and began its ascent. Bonnie's stomach began to tighten and when the elevator stopped at the third floor, she took a deep breath. The door opened they stepped out and started down the long corridor.

When they came to room 3066, Luke knocked softly and stepped back. The door was opened by Kim and her expression was difficult to read. She looked into the eyes of each of them, one by one, settling on Bonnie. Bonnie tried to smile, but the muscles in her face wouldn't work right. The only thought in her mind was that she kidnapped this woman's child. Her chin began to tremble and though she tried to keep a stiff lip, tears began to flow.

"I'm sorry," was all she could get out as she stood in front of the woman. A warm, sympathetic smile spread across her face and she opened her arms wide. Bonnie went to her and Kim held her in a tight embrace. Through her sobs, Bonnie tried to continue. "I didn't want to but—"

"I know," Kim said, her voice also breaking. "You did what you had to do. It was the right thing. You saved my daughter's life and that's what's important."

Tears streamed down Bonnie's cheeks and she was afraid to let go. Finally, Kim stepped back and Bonnie wiped her cheeks with the back of her hand. She sniffled and said, "This is my husband, Luke."

Luke extended his hand, but Kim ignored it and embraced him warmly, too.

"And you're Lauren," she said and hugged her, too.

Their attention turned to the sleeping child in the hospital bed. She looked so small as she lay sleeping soundly. Her pretty blonde hair now clean and combed, hung perfectly across her shoulders.

"The doctor said the kidnappers gave her a sedative to make her sleep, and with everything that's happened today, she probably won't wake up for a while," Kim told them. "But she's going to be okay."

They heard a knock on the door and Kim stepped over and opened it. Bonnie could see a woman in a dress standing outside. They spoke in whispers and the woman left.

Kim returned and said to Bonnie, "Would you come with me?"

Kim took her hand and they stepped out of the room into the hallway.

"There's someone I want you to meet," Kim said as they walked.

Deep in Bonnie's soul she knew who it was. Her heart started pounding so hard she felt it might burst. When they stopped at the door labeled *Conference Room*, Kim tapped twice before pushing the door open. Inside a woman with shoulder length red hair stood with her back to them. She was talking to someone sitting on the sofa.

"Tammy?" Kim said in a soft voice.

The woman turned to Kim then to Bonnie.

For the next moment neither woman moved. They searched the other's face like it was an old friend they hadn't seen for years. They stepped closer and for Bonnie it seemed like time stood still. She marveled at the same emerald green eyes she had seen in the mirror her entire life. Tammy had the same auburn hair and the same little, turned up nose. And now, seeing her up close, in person, Bonnie knew they were identical twins.

Tammy wiped a tear from her eye, then slowly reached down and took Bonnie's hands in hers. Both women stood in amazement, trying to grasp the reality of the moment.

"Bonnie," Tammy said in a shaky voice. "I'm glad to meet you."

"Me too," was all she could get out as she fought to keep her voice from breaking.

"I want you to meet," Tammy said, as she turned and watched the woman on the sofa stand up, "our mother, Anita

Owens."

She was thin, like them, and beautiful like her father had always said. Her hair was red, flecked with gray and cut just above her collar. Bonnie saw where she and Tammy got their upturned noses. Anita Owens came around the sofa and took Bonnie's hands in hers and stared deeply into her eyes. Her smile was warm but Bonnie could tell she was nervous. For a few seconds, neither of them spoke. Then she dropped one hand and took one of Tammy's. She looked from one to the other before taking a deep breath.

Their mother glanced toward the heavens, then said, "For years I prayed for this day, but I thought it would never come."

Bonnie wanted to say something but wasn't sure what. She waited as this woman, her mother, tried to find her voice.

After a long breath, she spoke with trembling lips. "I know you have a million questions and I'll answer them all. But first I want to tell you a story that will answer a lot of them. Is that okay?"

"Yes," Bonnie said in a small voice. She glanced at Tammy who was also nodding.

She motioned toward the sofa. "Do you want to sit down?"

"No, I'm too nervous to sit."

"Me, too," Tammy said. The twins stood facing their mother as she started to speak.

"In 1970, I was a junior at the University of Georgia and engaged to the most wonderful man in the world. The war in Vietnam was raging and my fiancé, Nathan, unfortunately drew a low number in the military draft." She glanced at Tammy who gave a slight nod. "He loved his country and was honored to serve it, so he left college and joined the Army. They told him after boot camp he would be shipped out to Vietnam. I was devastated. Of course, I didn't want him to go, but he assured me everything would be okay. I told him I didn't know what I would do without him. So, before he left he said his roommate would be there if I needed anything.

"I didn't know his roommate very well, but after Nathan

left, his roommate would call every week or two to check on me, like he promised Nathan he'd do. Sometimes, if I was lonely or worried, we'd go get a burger or go to a movie. I liked him, and before long we became good friends. We began to spend more and more time together. It didn't take long before we were inseparable."

She paused and looked at Bonnie. "I never meant for it to happen, but Kurt and I fell in love."

Bonnie's heart skipped a beat at the name. "My father?"

"Yes," she admitted, nodding her head. She paused and collected her thoughts. "I decided to tell Nathan it was over, that I was in love with Kurt. He came home a week before he left for Vietnam. And it was just like he'd never been gone. Nathan was home for five days and the time we spent together was glorious. I realized I was still deeply in love with him.

"When his leave was over, Nathan went off to Vietnam. I never did tell him about Kurt and me because I was still in love with him. But I was in love with Kurt, too. And he was hurt and confused and couldn't understand. I didn't know what to do because I couldn't choose between them. I told Kurt I needed some time alone to try to figure things out. Six weeks later, I found out I was pregnant.

"When I told Kurt, he was ecstatic and wanted to get married immediately. But the due date was close enough that Nathan could be the father, too. There was no way to be sure.

"When I told Nathan he was on cloud nine. He couldn't wait to come home and get married. But Kurt wasn't about to give up. He begged and pleaded for me to marry him right up to the minute they took me into the delivery room.

"Well, none of us expected twins, but there you were. The most beautiful babies I'd ever seen in my life. Kurt was extremely proud, but he couldn't stand waiting for me to make a decision. I was released from the hospital five days later and Kurt took me home. He told me he wouldn't wait any longer. I had to choose either him or Nathan. I told him I couldn't. He told me he would make the decision for me. He said the only fair way to do it was for him to get one of the twins and Nathan would get the other. And if I wouldn't marry him, he would leave."

"Oh, my," Bonnie said. "So, he took me, and left?"

Anita lowered her head and nodded. "He was convinced it was the right thing to do. I never thought he'd leave and not come back. But he did."

Bonnie tried to imagine what it must have been like, but she couldn't.

"So, what did you tell Nathan?" Bonnie asked.

"Nothing. Nathan never knew I had twins, and it was too much to tell him while he was in Vietnam. I decided, for the moment, all I'd tell him was that he had a beautiful baby girl named Tammy. He came home about six months later and we got married."

"Did you tell him then?"

"He was only here for four days and was so happy. I just couldn't do it. I decided I'd tell him when the time was right."

"But, how did you…I mean, didn't other people know?"

"Not really. We had kept my pregnancy a secret, and it was late summer when you were born. Kurt and I were the only ones who knew. As for family, my parents were divorced and I wasn't close to them. Kurt's family was back in Texas and his father was a preacher in the Church of Christ, so he didn't want to tell him. Nathan's family was from Iowa and all they knew was that he knocked up some girl in college. After we got married, I got to know them, and that's who Tammy knows as grandparents. But no one ever knew Tammy had a twin sister. Not even Tammy."

"What happened then?"

"Nathan went back to Vietnam and was killed four months later. He only got to see Tammy once."

"How sad," Bonnie said, clasping her hands to her mouth. "What did you do? Did you try to find Dad, or Kurt?"

"No. It just wouldn't have been right. Nathan's family was wonderful and they were my family. They've always been there for us."

Anita watched as Bonnie struggled with this information. She had a million things she wanted to know, but there was one question at the top of the list. She looked deep into her mother's eyes and asked, "Did you ever find out who our real father is?"

Anita looked from Bonnie to Tammy and said, "As far as I'm concerned, your father is Kurt and your father is Nathan. That's all we will ever need to know."

"What did you do then?" Tammy asked. The girls watched their mom try to open up the tear-soaked tissue in her hand.

"I couldn't stay there anymore, I needed to get away. I moved to California where I got a job teaching in Santa Barbara. When Tammy was about three I got married again, hoping it would help me move on. But I guess I wasn't ready. We divorced less than a year later.

"All these years I've carried this secret and I've never been able to get over it. Every time I met a man, I just couldn't…you know, tell him. I dated on and off over the years, but I guess I just never gave any other man a chance. I never did get involved with anyone again." Anita raised the tissue and dabbed the corners of her eyes. "I decided that when Tammy was old enough, I'd tell her what really happened. But I kept putting it off, and putting it off…"

Tammy wrapped her arm around her mother's shoulder and looked at Bonnie. "What did your dad tell you about your mother?"

Bonnie closed her eyes tight and tried to find the right words. She looked at Anita, and said, "He told me…you died of breast cancer."

Tammy looked at Bonnie, a hurt expression. "Why would he do that?"

"I'm not sure, but I think he wanted me to love my mother as much as he did." Bonnie noticed their puzzled expressions and said, "I don't know. Maybe if he would have said you were divorced, I would have always wondered why you didn't have custody of me. Was it because you didn't want me or what?"

Tammy and Anita nodded. Each understood what she meant.

"He always talked about how much he loved you. If anything ever came up about my mother, would always say good things. He'd talk about how pretty you were, or how much he missed you. I think he wanted me to feel the same way."

"Do you hate me…for what I did?" her mother asked.

She grabbed her mother by her shoulders and stepped closer. "I've loved you all my life. The only thing I have ever hated was the fact that you weren't here. But now you are and I can start sharing my love with you."

As Anita pulled Bonnie close, she could feel the love she had missed all those years.

Bonnie pulled away when she heard the door behind her open. Luke stood in the doorway and Bonnie motioned him over.

"This is my husband, Luke. And this is my mother, Anita Owens and my sister, Tammy."

"I can't tell you how happy I am to meet you," he said. "This is absolutely amazing."

"Yes it is," Tammy said, looking at Bonnie.

"Bonnie had always said she wished she had known her mother," Luke said. "But I never thought it would happen." They were all silent as they looked from one to the other. "Kim's about to leave and I thought you would like to talk to her before she goes."

Arm in arm they walked out of the conference room and Anita said to Bonnie, "I heard your dad died recently."

"Yes, after a two-year battle with cancer."

"I'm sorry to hear that. I hope he didn't suffer."

"Not really. At the end, the doctors had him on so many drugs, he was out of it most of the time," Bonnie thought about his last week in the hospital, and the last conversation she had with him. Goosebumps rose on her arms as she looked at

Tammy and Anita.

"But something really strange happened the night he died," Bonnie said as Tammy and Anita stopped to watch her recall the memory. "The doctors had him on strong painkillers. The last few days he was in bed and very restless. At times he'd ramble on and on, most of it incomprehensible and sometimes I could tell he was hallucinating. Most of the time, he didn't even know I was in the room. But the last night, just before he died, I had been asleep on the sofa for several hours. I woke up and saw him sitting up in bed. He was watching me. His eyes were focused and for the first time in days his speech was very clear.

"He said, 'Bonnie, you know your mom isn't really dead. She's out there and she's looking for you. I think you should go find her.'

"I wasn't sure what to say, so I said, 'Where will I find her?'"

"He said, 'Might try the west coast somewhere. She told me she loved the beach.'"

"I said, 'But, I don't know what she looks like. I've never even seen a picture of her. How will I know her?'"

Bonnie looked from her mom, to Tammy. "He said, 'You'll know it's her as soon as you see her. She'll be with your sister.'"

* The End *

Mark Bentsen

I grew up in Edcouch, a small town in the Rio Grande Valley of south Texas. Dad was a citrus farmer and mom's primary job other than being city manager was keeping me and my three brothers in line. The summer after each of us turned twelve we went to work for our dad on the farm. It was hot, tedious work and it convinced me that I didn't want to do that the rest of my life. After high school I went to college at Texas Tech University where I got my degree in Range and Wildlife Management. I had dreams of being a wildlife biologist, but unfortunately jobs were scarce, so I followed my horticultural interest and went to work for a large, wholesale nursery. That was in 1975 and I'm still there today. It's been a great career with a wonderful company.

I started writing fiction about six years ago and hope to do it for many more years. My wife, Sharyn, and I live in Austin, Texas, not far from our daughter, son-in-law and three grandsons.

Ten percent of the profits of this novel will be donated to both Dell Children's Medical Center of Central Texas and Meals on Wheels and More.

Made in the USA
San Bernardino, CA
22 January 2014